Dictates of the Servators: Book 2

LEVIGATOR

Kallen Samuels

ISBN: 978-1-7779901-1-4
Imprint: Innov@t Publishing - https://www.innovat.org

DEDICATION

Thank you to my family and friends
for their feedback and support.

CONTENTS

ACKNOWLEDGMENTS

Cover design: Kallen Samuels
Editor: Theresa Rempel

Other books by Kallen Samuels

Leviticus – Dictates of the Servators: Book 1
Leavening – Dictates of the Servators: Book 3

Chapter 1

Leviticus strode atop the rampart surrounding the old quarter of Ebot. He liked to come here to think. He needed time away from the expectant stares that followed him wherever he went. Since his encounter with that mysterious gateway, everyone at the base was acting strangely, fawning in his presence. The ancient buildings of Ebot's old quarter reminded him how insignificant he was, in the grand scheme of things. It grounded him.

Lev held no illusions of privacy. He could count several rangers keeping pace. They maintained a respectful distance while remaining close enough to come running to his aid if necessary. They moved with the practised ease of men familiar with such duty. It was the closest thing to privacy he could hope for.

The rampart widened in spots to create muster points. Over the years these had become food courts or rest areas. The city's architects transformed this particular spot into the famous hanging gardens of Ebot. This was was Lev's destination. As he approached, he veered in the direction of his favourite bench. Lev smiled at the irony. Another bench in a different part of the world had precipitated a dramatic change in his life. Now, he was heading toward his new favourite bench, to reflect on an even bigger life change. *What is it with me and benches anyway?* This particular bench faced an archway of flowering vines. It framed the view of an oasis some distance from the city wall and created the impression of a green path carving through arid dunes. Lev was disappointed to discover that someone had already claimed the bench. As he drew closer, his disappointment turned to surprise. A familiar voice answered his unspoken question.

"Beniti said I might find you here."

"Chief Sentry Vantos! What are you doing here?"

Cello motioned him to join her on the bench. "It's a mesmerizing view, I can see why you like to visit this spot. The whole world seems to fall away."

"It's my little escape," Lev admitted. "It's good to see you, Chief Sentry. Are you here on business?"

"Please, call me Cello."

Lev curled his lip. "You, too?"

Cello Shrugged. "It is the way of things. Actually, I'm here for *you*. Beniti thought you might appreciate a familiar face from home."

Lev wondered if he could call any place home these days. "I'm fine, you really didn't need to travel all this way."

"I wanted to come, Leviticus. Nico and Kayla had hoped to join me, but they have a possible lead on the person responsible for the murder of Nico's parents. They didn't want the trail to get cold."

"That's good." Lev nodded. "Nico needs closure."

"Nico is coming into his own. He's very much like his father." Cello smiled fondly. "He's good for Kayla. I don't think I've ever seen her so happy."

"I could say the same about Kayla's influence," Lev added. "Nico seems whole now, and it's because of her presence in his life. Kayla makes him very happy."

Cello patted Lev's arm. "And they would say you've been a very good friend to them both. It's important to have friends you can rely on."

"I wish I could see them more often, but..." Lev shrugged. "You'll give them my well wishes when you see them again?"

"Of course. They send their greetings as well. I want to assure you that they're doing fine. I hope it will relieve you of any concern for their welfare. You have more than enough on your plate without having to worry about friends or family."

That's an understatement, Lev thought. He had been proclaimed 'Levigator', a title that came with authority he wasn't comfortable wielding. Lev considered the many people he'd already placed in danger. Kayla had lost her career as a result of saving him from a Breacher planned abduction. That action led to the abandonment of the Servator base beneath Denmount.

Tark, a ranger and friend, had been stabbed in the shoulder trying to protect him. Even Kade Brixton, his school nemesis, found himself a captive of the Breachers. Their original plan was to abduct him, but they grabbed Kade as an alternative. *Disaster follows me and still, I'm asked to lead.* Like everything in his life these days, he hadn't been offered a choice in the matter.

"Speaking of family," Cello continued, "your parents are also doing well. I have rangers checking in on them regularly. The agents pose as employees of InnovaMech, the company providing your cover story. A weekly payment is delivered to your parents' home. The company subsidizes families of employees who work abroad. I'm sure your family would appreciate the inclusion of a personal note, on occasion. It helps to keep up appearances. If you have anything you'd like to send home, just bring it to the InnovaMech office here in Ebot. They'll see to its delivery."

"That's very generous. Thank you for keeping an eye on them. I do have a copy of a Kemetican recipe that I think my mother would enjoy. I'll pen a note to include with it and have it delivered to InnovaMech."

"That would be perfect. Your parents will be happy to hear from you." Cello leaned forward tilting her head and looking up into his face. When she caught his attention, she asked, "And how are *you* holding up, Leviticus?"

Lev grunted. "In a few short months, I've discovered that an ancient, clandestine organization lives in an underground base below my home town. I've seen technology that shouldn't exist. I've learned that my abnormal brain is actually a gift more powerful than I could imagine. I've been drafted into the Servator cause and I can't tell anyone from my past or go back to my former existence. My life has been in constant upheaval. I hoped by now I'd have a better grasp of my situation. I thought I could settle into this new life, but I have no idea what I'm doing. In truth, I have even less of an idea now, than when this all began. For a short time, at least, I had instructors teaching me things. People would explain what my role might be, but now...."

"You still have access to those resources, Leviticus."

"Sure, but those relationships have all changed. Now, I'm this so-called *Levigator*, whatever that means. I'm treated like a commander when I don't even know what it means to be a Servator. My instructors, and those of higher rank, tiptoe in my presence. They preface every answer with hesitant caution. My *mentors* worry they'll limit my potential by inserting a personal bias. That, I'm told, might interfere with the will of the Maker. They refuse to help me understand what the Maker's *will* might be. I ask for more guidance and I'm offered less. They give me freedom to do or say *anything*, without the context to make such decisions."

"They don't know what you should, or will do, Leviticus. There hasn't been a Levigator for..."

"Seventeen hundred years, yes I know. Surely someone as familiar with the histories as you, could venture a guess. I have spent less than a year with the Servators, but have been granted keys to the kingdom. If I told rangers to turn themselves over to Breachers, would they do it?"

"They might," Cello admitted.

"That's insane. That's — that's terrifying!"

"Leviticus, I can't begin to guess what you're going through."

"No. Don't do that! It's not helpful. This isn't the same as when someone loses a loved one. There are no feelings to consider here. I need practical knowledge, if I'm to be of any value. I'm not the type of person who can blithely make uninformed decisions. I agonize over detail. It's part of my *gift*, or call it a curse if you prefer."

"Sometimes, you're asked to make a decision that has no obvious solution," Cello noted. "Perhaps it simply requires faith."

"Then I need to know *that*!" Lev insisted. "I need to know what former Levigators have done and what we've learned from those actions. I need to know what events preceded the arrival of previous Levigators. I need to know the outcomes — I need to analyze the..."

Lev stiffened. *The patterns. It's my gift. I need to analyze the patterns.*

"Leviticus? Are you alright?"

"Yes — yes, I think so. Do you mind answering a few questions without worrying about how it may influence me?"

"I'll try."

"What does *Levigator* mean?"

"A Levigator is something or someone that alleviates burden and smooths the way. In your case, someone."

Lev cocked his head. "In order to do that, a Levigator would need to know what the burden is, wouldn't they? Surely pointing me in the general direction of the problem won't create a bias will it?"

Cello smiled. "I suppose not."

"I need you to explain that to Chief Sentry Abrax."

Leviticus was overcome with a wave of relief. He'd felt adrift and didn't know how to express his concern. Cello had helped him to frame his thoughts. Now, he saw a way to get what he needed from his mentors. It was a start.

"Thank you, Chief Sentry Van — I mean, Cello. I'm glad you came. You've already helped more than you know. I hope you can stay a little while longer. I have a few more questions."

Chapter 2

Lev stared at the testing stage. He squinted his eyes and ground his teeth, while clenching his fists in a vain hope that his theatrics would convince the token to form by the power of his will.

"What are you doing?" Akhen was shaking his head in amusement.

Lev threw his arms toward the stage. "Why isn't this working, Akhen? You tell me I'm the most gifted analyst of this generation, yet I can't master what the least gifted novice can do with ease."

"Don't be too hard on yourself, Leviticus, you're excelling in many areas and at a rapid pace."

"How does any of that matter? If I can't form a simple token, I'm useless!"

"It will come in time."

"I've been at it for weeks with nothing to show for my efforts," Lev grumbled.

"Let's take a break for a bit and refocus your mind on something else." Akhen motioned for Lev to follow him to the back corner of the room. They spent so much time here that Akhen had arranged for some furnishings. He'd found a few cots, a table and chairs, and a counter with equipment to brew kofa. Akhen poured two mugs and placed a few pastries onto a plate. He carried it to the table where Lev had already taken a seat. Lev started to rise, but Akhen placed his hand on Lev's shoulder and pressed him back down into his seat. He headed back to the counter and cleaned up the crumbs and carefully oriented the handle of the kofa urn so it was perpendicular to the edge of the counter. He glanced back at Lev and raised an eyebrow in question. Lev sighed and nodded in approval. Everything had a proper place in his orderly universe.

"You have to let such distractions go, Leviticus."

"I know. It just catches me off guard when I'm stressed out."

Akhen nodded once and changed the subject. "Why don't we continue our discussion from yesterday?"

Lev sipped from his mug while he tried to remember where they had left off. He gazed at the well-worn tabletop. Over the weeks a habit had formed and he inevitably found himself tracing the many stains and marks with his finger. He found the exercise soothing. He wondered if perhaps Akhen had chosen the table for that very reason, though the man would never admit it.

"Why is it that the chaos of patterns on this table doesn't trouble me like the disarray of so many other things?"

Akhen considered for a moment before speaking. "I believe it's because the marks don't interfere with the purpose of the surface. I've noticed you become agitated if a pattern fails to match your perception of proper *function*."

Lev furrowed his brow in disagreement. "Then why does the kofa urn trouble me when I notice it turned the wrong way? The urn functions fine, regardless of the handle's orientation."

"Ah, but you can perceive things in two different ways. The way it is, and the way you would like it to be. In the case of the kofa urn, you have developed a habit. You may not have noticed yourself doing it, but you always grab a mug and the urn at the same time. When the handle orientation is different than you expect, it interrupts the flow of your routine. That falls in the category of your *perception* of how you *want* it to be. It's an irritant, but not difficult to ignore. You've just said so yourself. You find it relatively easy to ignore unless you're feeling a bit agitated to begin with.

"You have a particularly keen sense of the patterns around you. You understand how things move within a space or remain rooted. It's the way things are. You see disorder wherever you look, don't you?"

"Yes, but that's part of a much bigger pattern. That chaos exists for a reason."

"That's my point. You can ignore quite a bit of chaos as long as it fits within a pattern you can perceive. You wouldn't be able to function in the world, otherwise. You've shared a bit about how it felt when you first encountered a token. It caught your attention because it was beyond any pattern you've previously encountered."

Lev nodded in affirmation. "It was unsettling — alien. I had no point of reference for its existence in that place."

"But now that you've encountered tokens on numerous occasions, you have a new explanation for such disruptions. They no longer bother you unless they're affecting a larger pattern in some other inexplicable way, yes?"

Lev inclined his head in agreement and motioned for Akhen to continue.

"Physical laws define human interaction within our world. This is the pattern you've come to understand. Now imagine if the laws of physics suddenly no longer applied. Would it trouble you?"

Lev had never considered how such an occurrence might affect him. He didn't want to think about such an utter lack of continuity in his surroundings.

Akhen's lip lifted a tiny bit. It was a look he had when he was about to win at Jumkano. "When a world-encompassing pattern begins to break down, people will notice on some level. They don't need to be as perceptive as you, Leviticus, to feel uneasy. It's why the Servators are willing to follow you. They sense the pattern unravelling and believe you can perceive how to mend it."

Lev had to smile. Leave it to Akhen to bring this conversation back to the point where they had ended their discussion from the previous day.

"I understand that people are placing their hope in me even if I don't yet appreciate their logic. That doesn't explain why every Servator on the planet is treating me like a king."

"Is that what you think, Leviticus? They don't view you as a *king*. The Servators have existed for a very long time. Over the centuries we've amassed a great deal of wealth, power, and numerous followers. Even so, we view our existence as a function, not a kingdom. We aren't a nation or people group. We don't seek to enforce political ideologies or expand borders. Servators exist only to serve the world. When a Levigator arises, it doesn't matter who they are as a person or their qualities as a leader. We follow them because they further our function in a way that we can't. A Levigator has always represented change that benefits the Servator purpose. To a Servator, this is an exciting time filled with potential."

"I feel like the whole world is watching me," Lev sighed.

"It might help if you adjusted your perspective a bit. People know that you possess the potential to effect change. They're watching and waiting to see what that change will be. You happen to be the catalyst so they look in your direction. They're looking less at you than the implied future. Perhaps you imagine they're judging you or second-guessing your actions. That may be the case for some, but for the most part, people have no preconceived notions about your role. They can't imagine the patterns that you see. They don't have a clue how you should or might act. All they know is that something significant will occur when you do act."

Lev leaned his chair onto the back two legs as he propped his feet on the table. "So, what you're telling me is that my vain imagining is nothing but hubris?"

"I always said you were my brightest student." Akhen flicked his foot up under the raised front legs of Lev's chair in an attempt to topple him, but Lev anticipated and was already in a roll, landing in a crouch before the chair hit the floor.

Akhen nodded in approval. "Good, cataloguing potential for pattern disruption is becoming a habit. Your response time is improving and your reactions are more deliberate. It's as I said, you're excelling in many areas. Are you ready to try forming a token again?"

Lev stood and strode to the practice stage. *Maybe this time.* He lifted his arm and danced his fingers across the Q-view on his wrist. He settled on the simplest token he could find — a six-sided die. He knew the pattern by heart. Not that it mattered, all he needed to do was select the token and inform the Quantum Positioning Network of the coordinates where the token should form. The system would take care of the rest. As he selected the coordinates, he realized he could visualize those as well. Like Akhen said, he was getting better at cataloguing his surroundings. Directing his gaze towards the stage, he was looking *precisely* in the spot where it should materialize. He could even imagine the pattern forming, but like every previous attempt, nothing happened.

Akhen saw the frustration written on Lev's face. "Let's call it a day and try again tomorrow. One of the technicians mentioned that the QPN has been acting up at odd times lately. Perhaps the fault isn't with you at all. I'll check in with them later and see if they've discovered the cause." Akhen patted Lev on the shoulder. "I hear Tark and Yori are ready for a warkata rematch."

Lev perked up. "Truly? They've been avoiding me for over a week — some nonsense about strategy sessions."

"I may have given them a few pointers," Akhen admitted.

Lev snorted. "I hope you have some balm ready to spread on their bruises. I suggest the smelly stuff you keep in the cabinet." Lev grinned and rubbed his hands together as he left to search for his truant sparring partners.

Chapter 3

Nico was in a mood. He'd been checking progress on the new Servator air field in the Tellur mountain range south of Denmount when the call came on his tote-comm. It was Tenika Sheriden, former head of Callan International. She required his presence at an *emergency meeting* for the chiefs of staff. Nico sighed. Everything was an emergency as far as the chiefs were concerned. He wondered how his father put up with it while he was still alive. After the tragic death of his parents in a murder made to look like an accident, Tenika had managed the company until Nico was old enough to take over. Sometimes he wasn't sure he'd made the right decision by absorbing so many of Tenika's responsibilities, but he felt he owed it to his family to run the company just as they had intended.

It wasn't all bad. He'd discovered that his parents were secretly Servator rangers. Every facet of the family business was in some way contributing to the Servator cause. The prospect of running an international company became less of a burden and more of an adventure. The Servator side projects he'd initiated made him feel alive. He was making a difference in the world. It also made him feel connected to his parents, something that had eluded him for most of his life. Unfortunately, the adventure portion of his day was about to end. He put on the mask of businessman once more, preparing to feign interest in the boring minutiae of ledgers and staffing.

The ground transport pulled up to the Callan building and Nico stepped out. He watched the driver pull away with a little twinge of jealousy.

The big sign above the front entrance always made him feel insignificant. *Callan International* — the little fishing and delivery service his grandfather started had become a globe-spanning transportation and logistics behemoth in the hands of his father. Now he was supposed to fill those shoes, somehow. At times it was overwhelming, but then some innate talent, a gift of genetics, would kick in and everything seemed to work out. It didn't hurt that Seri was at his side. As his assistant, she'd become proficient in the daily requirements of helping him run a multinational organization. As his girlfriend, she was so much more. It didn't hurt that she was secretly Kayla Vantos, daughter to the Chief Sentry of the Caralithican Host. It was yet another tie to the Servators that made his life exciting. Her skills as an analyst and the backing of the Servators were powerful resources bringing him closer to discovering who had killed his parents. The Servators had determined the plot had come from within the corporation. Seri had since discovered signs of someone covering their tracks and planting evidence to frame him. Someone was targeting his family. It strengthened his resolve. He wouldn't allow the destruction of everything his family had built.

The ever-vigilant doorman greeted him as he crossed the threshold.

"Good afternoon, Mr. Callan, do you require anything?"

"No, thank you, Arlen.

"The staff chiefs are waiting for you in the boardroom."

"Actually, Arlen, could you have some bread, cheese, and water sent to the boardroom? I'm famished."

"Tenika has already ordered food for the meeting, sir."

"Of course." *They have no problem spending my money on their appetites but penny pinch when I ask for more from their projects.* "Thank you, Arlen. Tell them I'll be there shortly — I just need to clean up a bit."

It wasn't really the money that bothered him. It was just that his parents raised him with a strong work ethic — they were always ready to roll up their sleeves and help the workers. The entitled attitude of these staff chiefs galled him. Here he was washing away dust from a morning of getting his hands dirty and now he would have to apologize to a pampered bunch whom he'd kept waiting. *Wouldn't want to keep them from an afternoon of sitting on their backsides.* Nico gave his head a shake as he strode to the boardroom. Thoughts like that weren't going to put him in the frame of mind necessary to get through the day.

The boardroom table held the crumbs and half-empty mugs of a long-finished repast. Nico ignored the impatient looks and grabbed a plate of food and some water for himself before sitting at the head of the table. He nodded to Tenika on his immediate left to begin the meeting.

"We're all glad you could make time to join us for this emergency meeting, Mr. Callan."

Nico mentally rolled his eyes at the dig. *Patience Nico.* He put a slice of cheese on some bread and took a bite.

"Our security staff has brought to my attention the substantial withdrawal of funds from company reserves. This was carried out without prior authorization." Tenika paused until the murmurs around the table died down.

"We've gathered here to discuss the seriousness of this matter and to take steps to prevent further abuse of authority."

The murmurs grew in volume as the chiefs realized she was accusing one of them.

"Perhaps it's an innocent mistake. Before this becomes something bigger than it needs to be, I'm providing an opportunity for the responsible person to speak up and offer an explanation."

It's constant drama with this bunch. Nico took another bite. Someone was always skimming off the top. It was upsetting but nothing new. Why was Tenika dragging this out?

Tenika glared at him and let out a theatrical sigh. "I had hoped that the information would be volunteered. I suppose I have no choice but to be more direct. The financial records show that withdrawals took place on four separate occasions. The funds removed totalled one hundred thousand gold standard."

Gasps erupted from around the table at mention of the amount. It was equivalent to a year's wages for ten of their highest-paid employees.

"The authorizing signature belongs to Nico Callan."

All eyes turned to Nico. He stopped chewing and looked around the table. Someone had released the ledger Seri discovered. He knew it would come out sooner or later, but they weren't ready with a response. He swallowed and turned red with anger, despite himself.

"What a preposterous accusation. This is my company. How can I steal from myself? Who's making this claim?"

The staff chiefs looked uncertain as they considered his logic.

"Mr. Callan, you know as well as anyone that an organization as large as this has many partners and contractual obligations. The missing funds were allocated to a partner project, not the company proper. The partner is threatening legal action to reclaim their losses."

"Fine! Pay them from my personal funds."

"Is that an admission of guilt?" Tenika pushed.

"Of course not! I'm just suggesting we smooth partner relations until we can figure out what's going on. You still haven't told me who's making this accusation."

"I'm not at liberty to name the source of this information before the claim has been verified. An investigation is pending. Nevertheless, the contractual obligations of this company are clear on the matter. Individuals under investigation for possible criminal activity can't hold an executive post. Not until the matter is settled."

Nico looked around the table. "You can't possibly believe someone with my resources would need to resort to theft. Besides..." Nico bit his tongue. He had been about to say *'Besides those withdrawals took place when I was just a child.'* That would have proven he knew about the misappropriated funds. "This is ridiculous, you can't keep me from running my own company."

"With all due respect, Mr. Callan, unless you can give us proof, here and now, of your innocence in the matter, we'll have no choice but to suspend your vote. You'll be prohibited from taking part in any decision-making, pending conclusion of an investigation."

Nico could have sworn he saw a glimmer of triumph in Tenika's eyes — just for a moment. It brought out a pettiness he hadn't known was in him.

"*With all due respect,* Ms. Sheridan, when I had a lawvocate look through my original signing contract, he noted that it was written in such a way as to deny me my birthright and give you ultimate authority."

All eyes at the table turned to Tenika and it was her turn to blush. She started to protest, but he held up a hand and opened the door to speak to the message boy waiting on the other side. "Go and fetch my assistant, Seri Quin. Tell her I need her in the boardroom immediately and that she's to bring my lawvocate, Enis Kirrvon. She'll know what to do." He pressed a silver in the boy's hand. "Quickly now, this is an emergency." The boy sprinted away and Nico returned to the boardroom table.

"You'll forgive me Tenika, if I wish to have my assistant and my lawvocate present to make sure we're all correctly interpreting the contractual obligations you spoke of."

Oh, she didn't like that at all.

"Of course. We will abide by the legal interpretation." She pulled out her tote-comm and spoke loudly enough for everyone to hear. "Halen please come to the boardroom." She hung up and raised an eyebrow. "I know you prefer to have outside counsel for some reason, but it seems to me the *company* lawvocate should be present."

Nico nodded in assent. *Sure, go ahead and heighten the suspicion, Tenika.* He didn't trust Halen Tu, but Tenika's argument was difficult to dismiss. They all watched each other in tense silence while waiting for legal counsel to arrive. Seri and the two lawvocates arrived at the same time, breathing heavily. *They must have run.* Their struggle to be the first through the boardroom door would have been comical under different circumstances.

Both lawvocates produced a copy of the contract. Tenika waved them off and explained the situation. Halen was first to talk. It sounded like a rehearsed speech.

"Tenika is correct — the contract states that anyone who is under suspicion of a criminal offence must step down from a position of authority. The suspension remains in place for the duration of any investigation. As the person who previously managed Callan International, it falls to Ms. Sheridan to continue in that capacity until the investigation reaches a satisfactory conclusion."

There it was again. Nico was certain this time. Tenika was gloating.

Enis held up a finger for silence and furiously paged through the contract. When he spoke it was to Nico. "Halen is correct. The contract states you must temporarily step down for the duration of an investigation."

Halen was nodding sagely.

"However, I want to assure you, Nico, that whoever is in charge can only make decisions about the use of funds allocated for day-to-day operations and partner projects. Your personal funds are yours to manage and you can choose whether or not to release them for company use. I can only make a guess, but since Callan International is a wholly owned company under your name, that would mean at least eighty percent of all available funds remain under your control."

Enis turned to Tenika and Halen before continuing. "Mr. Callan can use those funds at his discretion for any projects not directly allocated for the day-to-day operations of Callan International."

Tenika was clearly fuming at the way her hands were tied, but Enis wasn't finished. "As for the assumption that Tenika will manage Callan International during the investigation — the contract leaves that to the discretion of Mr. Callan. He's allowed to choose his replacement as long as that individual isn't a suspect of the investigation. Mr. Callan, do you wish for Ms. Sheridan to manage the company in your absence?"

Nico didn't hesitate. "I'm placing Seri Quin in charge of Callan International, effective immediately. I hereby voluntarily relinquish control until I can prove my innocence."

The chins of both Seri and Tenika dropped at the same time.

Tenika sputtered, "That's unacceptable! She's his assistant."

"Seri Quin has only been with this organization for a short time," Enis countered, "do you have evidence that she was in the employ of Mr. Callan when this offence occurred?"

Tenika held her tongue. *Interesting*, Nico thought. *Why is she holding back now?*

Enis stood. "Well then, I guess this meeting is adjourned."

Chapter 4

Kade wrinkled his nose as he sidestepped some scat. Decar didn't seem to notice. A side effect of growing up in this heat oppressed place, Kade imagined. Sumakad had its charms, but Kade missed the cool sea breezes of Denmount in Caralithica. *Stop torturing yourself man, you can never go back.* Kade glanced at Decar to see if it was safe to talk yet, but he ignored Kade and continued to look straight ahead.

This was a new thing — going for a walk with Decar, unescorted by his watchers. Since Second Anarch Trantor had taken over, the restrictions had been loosened considerably. He'd never understood Third Anarch Villecrest's need to monitor his every move. It wasn't as if he could walk past the heavily guarded entrance to the compound. Actually, he had been away from the compound a few times with Decar, but he supposed Decar had served as guard on those occasions. Maybe this was no different after all. *That's not true,* Kade corrected himself, *everything is different. Toller Villecrest is dead and Breachers no longer stand guard outside my living quarters. I'm no longer followed in the halls.* Maybe he had a lot more freedom than he realized. He silently chastised himself for not testing his newfound freedom. He'd try leaving on his own tomorrow. Just a quick walk to a food vendor in the bazaar to see what happened. Surely that wasn't pushing things. Villecrest had allowed the development of an area inside the compound to serve as a marketplace. The Breacher compound operated under the guise of a diplomatic embassy and vendors were eager to display their wares to potential foreign investors. It was also popular with the townsfolk because Villecrest's guards provided security for the vendors. It was Villecrest's way of keeping his human assets under a watchful eye while bringing some normalcy to life in captivity.

Walking the bazaar flanked by guards had robbed him of that mental escape, but now, without his brutish shadows, he could almost imagine holding Selica's hand and walking away from all of this. Would it be possible during this transition of power? Maybe everyone would be too busy figuring out their new roles to notice a few missing bodies. It was a pleasant daydream but a pointless one. Trantor had identified him the moment they met and ordered Kade to teach his engineers everything they needed to know about the facial recognition algorithm.

It would be impossible for Kade to slip away — though Selica might have a chance. It was possible she'd already left. He hadn't seen or heard from her in the two weeks since the Second Anarch arrived on the scene. No one commented on Selica's absence. Kade wasn't sure what to think about her absence. He hoped with all of his heart that she had indeed left. She'd been a slave since childhood. The man who owned Selica had brutally murdered her mother in front of her. She deserved her freedom. He clung to that hope as a way to smother the growing dread that something far worse had happened to her. He wasn't sure what that might be. Their new anarch clearly handled his affairs differently than Villecrest. It was why Kade had asked to speak privately with Decar — the reason for this walk. He needed to understand their new taskmaster and Decar knew who they were dealing with.

The two of them were nearing the bazaar. Midday heat and exotic spices mingled with the bubbling of voices. Colourful booths vied for attention as hawkers tried to lure customers with promises of the finest merchandise or the most delicious pastries. His mouth watered as they passed some cinnamon rolls. *When was the last time I was here?* The past several months had been a whirlwind of deadlines and death threats with no time for relaxation. He hoarded the sights and sounds like a starving man at a banquet.

Caught up in his pleasant distraction, Kade found himself lagging several steps behind when Decar suddenly broke into a trot. Kade scrambled to keep pace as they wove through the crowd. Somehow Decar managed to slide through the crowd like a skiff through reeds. Kade was more like a clumsy barge plowing through the sea of humanity, leaving a wake of irate voices.

Decar veered behind some booths and eventually stopped beside a midden heap. He scanned the area to see if anyone had followed. "Okay, now we can talk."

"Talk?" Kade gagged, "I can barely breathe! Why did you stop here?"

"You left me few options with the way you stumble around like a drunken camel. The worst scout in the land could have followed the trail of cursing patrons shaking their fists at your backside."

"You could have warned me before you picked up speed."

"Pah! Caralithicans — always blaming others for their shortcomings. I might have chosen this spot regardless. No one comes back here unless they have to. Those who do, never stay long. We'll notice if someone comes through the clearing between the heap and the booths. I assume you wish to discuss the Second Anarch?"

Kade swiped at his watering eyes and tried to speak without breathing through his nose. "You assume correctly."

"This is the only time I will speak on the subject. It's far too dangerous and will become more so as Kenric familiarizes himself with the people under him. Use the time wisely — we can't stay here for long."

Like anyone would want to stay here long. Kade decided to keep his comments to himself. Decar was right though, he wouldn't have a lot of time for questions no matter where they stopped.

"Tell me about the Second Anarch's personality. How does he compare to Villecrest?"

"The Third Anarch had a temper and zero patience, as you well know. Toller Villecrest was a brutal man. He enjoyed menacing his victims. Kenric Trantor is almost a polar opposite. He's meticulous and his plans are methodical. When he loses his temper, it's a subtle thing. Many fail to notice his ire before it's too late. When he does decide to act on his anger, he never dirties his hands. He employs only those Sicari known for their cunning and stealth. When someone dies at the Second Anarch's command, the evidence always suggests an accidental death. When Kenric strode into the compound and informed us of Toller's tragic death, it appeared to be exactly that. The investigators declared it an unfortunate accident — a tragedy. Even if it were true that Trantor played a part in ordering the assassination, he would insinuate otherwise, increasing his terrifying mystique. It's part of his power. No one ever knows for certain the method of death or Kenric's involvement.

Even so, everyone here understands that Kenric had Toller assassinated. Villecrest had been pushing his luck for far too long. It was only a matter of time, he was too ambitious."

It was much as Kade suspected. He thought carefully before asking his next question. "I've noticed that the Second Anarch has relaxed security somewhat. I haven't had guards shadowing my every move. You've said he's the opposite of Villecrest. Am I to understand he's more patient and forgiving? Easier to work for?"

"Don't believe that for a moment. When you think of the Second Anarch, don't mistake his patience and restraint for kindness. He's a man in control of himself but also everything and everyone around him. Villecrest raged, threatened, and bullied — Trantor forms alliances and quietly eliminates his competition. The Third Anarch's disappearance is evidence of Kenric's more dangerous methods. Villecrest was a fool to believe that any of the Sicari worked for him. They're all in league with Kenric. He doesn't try to control them, he works alongside them. They have a mutually beneficial relationship."

Decar looked past Kade's shoulder and then glanced over his own before continuing. "As for the loosening of restrictions, that is equally a mirage. Kenric has spent decades developing a network of spies and informants. They're everywhere. Villecrest's quiet disappearance suggests Kenric infiltrated Villecrest's inner circle long ago, possibly shortly after the Third Anarch took power. Kenric Trantor thinks far in advance. For all you know, as Villecrest's second-in-command, I might be one of Trantor's plants."

Kade paled and looked Decar in the eyes.

"Ha! The look on your face! Calm yourself Brixton, I have no previous affiliation with the Second Anarch. I told you the truth about how Villecrest was threatening my family. While Trantor isn't quite the monster Toller was, I know that my family will be in danger the minute I displease him. I want to be very clear — I won't risk my family.

"We worked together when it served to save both of our lives. It was possible to manipulate Villecrest, but that tactic is no longer feasible. Trantor hears everything and won't be easily fooled. In the future, I will be a model employee of his regime. I won't attempt subterfuge in any way — it wouldn't work. Don't approach me with ideas to misdirect our superiors like you've done in the past. I have been tasked with ensuring you train Trantor's engineers. I intend to fulfill that duty to the best of my ability. I won't give our new taskmaster a reason to become suspicious of me. If I feel you're in any way interfering in that process or even if it appears that way because of incompetence, I won't protect or defend you. Your actions or failures will be entirely your own."

Kade stared, dumbstruck by the pronouncement. Decar was exceedingly talented at deception. If he was unwilling to consider using his skills while under Trantor's command, then the Second Anarch was far more terrifying than Kade imagined. At one point Kade had wondered if Decar and his family might join in the attempt to escape. That clearly wasn't going to happen. All things considered, he was relieved that he hadn't extended an invitation. He and Selica would be dead now if they had taken Decar into their confidence.

"Perhaps you think I'm ungrateful," Decar continued. He placed a hand on his forehead and then drew it down his face with a heavy sigh. "I'm telling you this now as a courtesy. I don't want harm to come to you, but this is our new reality. I implore you to be cautious from now on. Don't believe anyone is your friend, they're all potential betrayers. Trantor will learn what he wishes to learn either by threat or reward. No one is immune. From this point on, you must do what you're asked to do without delay, without excuse, and without cause for suspicion."

Kade's voice was flat when he responded. "Since you've already told me that you'll be monitoring my training of Trantor's engineers and reporting back to him, might I ask what you expect of me?"

"When we were bringing the facial recognition algorithm online, I watched as you led untrained technicians through the necessary steps. You're a capable instructor when motivated. This time you'll be working with computational engineers who are already well educated. The process should be faster."

"Handing a technician some instructions to follow is a lot different than helping someone understand theory."

"Then I apologize, Kade, but I have already given The Second Anarch an estimate. He'll expect you to meet it. I won't be the one held accountable if you fail."

"What did you tell him, Decar?"

"Two weeks to cover the theory and another two weeks of working with the engineers to gain proficiency and answer questions that arise."

"Four weeks total?" Kade whispered. He had to sit down. The fact that he sat in a midden was far from his mind. He couldn't stop shaking his head in denial. "You've killed me, Decar."

"You underestimate yourself. I'm confident you can accomplish this. Do you have any further questions?"

Kade was still shaking his head.

"Good, then I suggest you set your mind to the content of your lectures. You begin tomorrow morning. I'll take this opportunity to bid you farewell since we won't likely speak casually with each other again. Good luck, Brixton. If you succeed, you'll gain favour and a future with the Second Anarch."

Kade wasn't sure how long he sat after Decar left. Judging by the smell that permeated his clothing, it was probably an hour or more. He found his way back to his suite in a daze and stripped the offensive clothes from his body, leaving them to air out on the windowsill. His mind bounced between planning and panic as soap and water scrubbed away the stench. He had to come up with something for his first lecture — tomorrow. It was going to be a long night.

Chapter 5

"Watch carefully. First I enter the QPN coordinates for the mark on the testing stage." Akhen held up his wrist Q-view for Leviticus to see.

Leviticus rolled his eyes and sighed. "Yes, I know."

"Then, choose a token from the list of options on your Q-view. I'm selecting a simple cube."

"You've shown me a hundred times, Akhen!"

"You must be missing something because you continue to get it wrong. Watch! Now, I activate the sequence."

A cube appeared on the testing stage.

"There, you see? Simple."

"Do you think I haven't been paying attention? You know I can't forget something once I've seen it. Here, you watch me. Look — I'm entering the coordinates." Leviticus held up his Q-view. "Do you confirm that these are the correct coordinates?"

Akhen nodded. "Yes, those are the correct coordinates."

"Good. Watch me carefully as I select a simple cube. Did I do anything wrong? Anything out of sequence?"

"No — you've done it exactly in the same way I would have."

"Fine. I activate the sequence by tapping here, correct?" Leviticus held his finger above the activation icon and waited for Akhen to nod before pressing it. They both looked toward the stage. The air shimmered as if trying to coalesce and then quickly dispersed.

"You see? It works for you, but not me!"

Akhen shook his head. "I've tried your Q-view myself and it works fine, so we know it's not the device. You must be doing something subtly different."

"You observed me performing every step."

"Did your finger slip when you activated the sequence?"

"No! I've used more caution than should be necessary. It's maddening. I've watched the particle clusters forming when you do it and I can see the same process begin when I try, but then it suddenly falls apart."

"What did you just say?" Akhen stared at him with his mouth hanging open.

"I said, I've been meticulous in following the procedures..."

Akhen cut him off. "Not that part. Did you say you can see the clusters forming? No one can see a particle without a device to detect the radiation emitted."

"Not in the traditional sense, but when I perceive the shifts in the pattern, I know the coordinates of the particles as they form. I guess it would be more accurate to say I can tell when each coordinate point forms. I know you understand what I mean. You can see the patterns."

"Not to that degree or with such precision. I can sense where a fully formed token has materialized in a darkened room, but it never occurred to me that it might be possible to see a token form particle by particle. I'm not sure I could hold that much detail in my mind let alone at that speed." Akhen had an excited look on his face. "Have you memorized the entire pattern for this cube?"

"Of course. You've formed it in front of me often enough, how could I not?"

"Give me your arm!" Akhen Grabbed Lev's wrist and began entering coordinates into the Q-view. "I've set the coordinates and the template for the same simple cube. When I give you the order, I want you to look at the coordinates on the stage where the cube should materialize while I start the activation sequence."

"Um... Okay?"

Akhen tapped Lev's wrist Q-view and said, "Now."

The air shimmered on the stage and a cube formed. A second cube formed right next to it a few seconds later.

Leviticus twisted his head to peer at Akhen who began laughing hysterically.

"What's going on? Why did two cubes appear on the stage?"

Akhen wiped his eyes as he collected himself. "I changed the coordinates."

"Pardon me?"

"When I entered coordinates for the cube, I didn't use the default settings for the stage marking. I set the cube to materialize a few inches to the left, and a few seconds later."

"Then, where did the first cube come from?"

"That's the one you formed. I've been a fool! Why didn't I think of this before?"

Lev frowned. "Perhaps you could explain so I can share your amusement."

"It's not possible for more than one token to share the same space at the same time. There are safety protocols put in place to prevent the reaction that would occur. It's one of the first things we teach a novice. That's why you've been unable to form a token."

"Wait — slow down. You used my Q-view to form a second token, but I didn't enter anything into the Q-view for the first one."

"Exactly. You were looking at the marker where you expected the cube to appear, and you watched it form in the pattern, correct?"

"Yes. It formed in the same way as when I've watched you create it on numerous occasions. How is that possible?"

"It's your mind, Leviticus. That fabulous, beautiful mind which absorbs everything it sees in the pattern and keeps a permanent record. You, my boy, are your own Quantum Positioning Network."

"But — I didn't push an activation button!"

"You knew the coordinates — you knew the pattern — you expected it to form. It did so, while you observed. The activation sequence on a Q-view is just another type of observation to start the process."

"Then why do we need the Q-view at all?"

"Technically, it's not necessary for activating a sequence. Our problem is that no human mind can hold the detailed coordinates for each particle of a template. We need to access the QPN archive for that. We need the Q-view to connect with the QPN and initiate templates."

"So, you're saying I'm the only one who doesn't need a Q-view?"

"Apparently you don't have the same limitations. Have you memorized all the patterns in the library?"

"I have, but they don't feel the same as the ones I've watched form. Tokens I've observed in the process of materializing feel…" Lev struggled for a description and failed. "They just feel right."

Akhen was running his fingers through his hair as he paced the training room. "That makes sense. The QPN uses its permanent location as the originating point for all other coordinates. If you're your own QPN, it stands to reason that the same would hold true. When you view a token materializing, you see coordinates in relation to your own position. Your mind has been mapping the travel of your body through the patterns that surround you for your entire life. It has become second nature to calculate the position of objects within your range of perception. Fascinating. Astonishing! This answers so many questions."

"What questions?"

Akhen waved him off. "Another time. We have so much catching up to do."

Leviticus was satisfied holding on to his questions for the moment. He was finally making progress and wanted to see where that led as much as Akhen did.

Without waiting for instruction and without his wrist Q-view, Lev materialized a sphere, a pyramid, and an eagle figurine. "Yes!" Lev pumped the air with his fist. "Finally."

Akhen smiled. "What's the most complicated thing you've watched me materialize?"

"You formed a view token once." Akhen gestured for Lev to make the attempt and he turned to the stage to comply. It took longer, but the view token materialized right where it should.

"Now try connecting to it with your Q-view."

Lev made several attempts, but nothing happened.

"Lev, form a mallet for me."

Lev did as he was asked. Akhen picked up the mallet and shattered the view token. Using the handle, he spread the pieces out. "This view token is malformed. Components are missing. See the hollow space in the centre?"

Lev thought about it. "While the token was forming, it felt like I was only seeing key positions and letting my subconscious fill in the missing details. Is it possible I never completely captured the coordinates due to the complexity of the device?"

"We have a sure way to find out." Akhen used his Q-view to form another token and Lev allowed himself to fall into pattern sight. He watched carefully as the view token formed. Then Lev tried to form one of his own. Akhen smashed that one too. It was better formed, but still not complete. After the fifth attempt, they were able to connect to a fully functioning view token.

"So," Akhen summarized, "the more complex an object is, the longer it will take for you to absorb the pattern. No less significant is the fact that you can materialize simple objects by identifying key coordinates. It appears that, at a certain point, enough coordinates are present for the logical pattern match to fill in the blanks. I can tell you right now that the analysts will be very interested to learn about this discovery. If they can activate a pattern using a smaller coordinate set, it will dramatically reduce the load on the QPN."

Lev rolled his eyes.

"Do you have a problem with that?"

"With the analysts? Yes! You treat me like you always have, but with others it's Levigator this and Levigator that," Lev sighed. "I suppose this development is a good thing. Everyone is watching to see what changes the Levigator will bring. It's time I brought something to the table. Maybe this is a good start."

"Working with the analysts will use up a substantial proportion of your time. They'll need you to identify the key coordinates to enter into the system for each template. I suspect you would benefit from that exercise as much as they would, but we can't afford to be distracted now. I'll talk with them and set up a reasonable schedule."

Lev nodded his acceptance. "Now that we have a solution, what's the plan?"

"Starting tomorrow, we begin the tedious process of materializing every token in the QPN library until you've catalogued them all. I'll make a list of the most practical items and we'll tackle those first."

Lev's cheeks puffed out and he exhaled loudly, considering the work ahead. After the fruitless effort of the past few months, he was excited to make up for lost time. *I'm not a failure after all.*

He grinned as he materialized a pyramid with a sphere balanced perfectly on the point. This was going to be fun.

Chapter 6

The door to his office had barely closed before Seri started in on him.

"Nico! What were you thinking?" Seri had a hand on either side of her head clutching her hair. "I can't run your family's business!"

"Seri, calm down — of course you can. You've been with me from the start. You know everything I know."

"That's beside the point. Everyone knows you're heir to the Callan family business. They have no choice but to accept you. It's different for me. I'm nobody. I was hired as your assistant. They're not going to listen to me."

"They had better or they won't remain in my employ. You now have the authority to hire and fire people as you see fit and I'll back your decisions. In fact, fire the first person who gives you trouble and the rest will fall in line."

"I can't do this, Nico. What if I make a mistake that costs you thousands of silvers? What if I cause irreparable damage to your family name? What if I...."

Nico wrapped her in his arms, pressing her face into his chest — muffling her words. Seri laughed. "I can still talk. You're not shutting me up that easily."

"Seri, do you really think I care about losing a few silvers? And what were you imagining you could do to ruin the reputation of a business that has been around for three generations? You'll just continue doing what you've been doing these past several months. Nothing has changed. You heard Enis, no funds are available for new projects without my approval and I'm not going anywhere. You can contact me on my tote-comm, day or night, to talk about anything that makes you uncomfortable."

Seri lifted her chin to look up at him. "What if I don't want to?"

"Please, Seri, I need you to do this. You're the only person here I completely trust. You saw how Tenika was acting in that meeting. She must have set this up. I can't let her take control of the company again. Now that Tenika's made her intentions clear, she won't waste time. She'll be reinforcing her position. Who knows what kind of damage she might cause?"

A knock sounded at the door and Seri pulled away. It was important to keep up appearances, especially now. Nico took a seat at his desk. "Enter."

The door opened and Cello Vantos strode through. Seri closed the door behind her.

"I came as soon as I heard."

Nico wore a disgruntled expression. "News travels fast."

Cello waved away his concern. "Enis called me right after the meeting. He is my lawvocate after all, and I have a vested interest in Callan International, as you well know."

Nico sighed. "It's fine. I was planning on calling you shortly anyway. I may be needing your help navigating these waters. It seems Tenika has shown her true colours."

"If you recall, I told you early on that she was untrustworthy. Tenika Sheridan puts her interests before all others."

"Actually, I'm not all that surprised. She hasn't made any effort to help me settle in. Still, she hasn't been outright hostile before. This felt different — as if she was coming after me. Something about that meeting troubles me. Tenika said security staff, who were conducting an investigation, brought this to her attention. She gave the impression that she knew very few details other than possibly the name of the person who provided the evidence. Later, Tenika implied that Seri was suspect since she's my assistant. Yet, she held back When Enis asked if these alleged criminal activities occurred while Seri was working for Callan International. Tenika clearly doesn't want Seri around.

"Enis's comment spoke directly to the question of Seri's potential guilt or innocence. If Tenika didn't know details and wanted Seri gone, you'd think she would want Seri investigated. Why did Tenika suddenly hold her tongue? It felt like she knew more than she was letting on. The only reason for her silence I can think of is that she didn't want anyone looking at the timeframe for the withdrawals. If she knew that the evidence pointed to a date before I took over, it would explain why she didn't want to share that information yet. That suggests two things to me. One, she has seen the doctored ledgers, and two, she's biding her time for some reason. If that's the case, then Tenika must be involved somehow. It seems we have a few more avenues to investigate."

"So what do we do?" Seri asked.

"Both Tenika and Halen Tu would have had access to those doctored ledgers. We need to keep an eye on them. Until we learn more, I don't think we can afford any more surprises. We need to get ahead of this."

Cello had a predatory gleam in her eyes. "After all these years, we might finally see some justice. At least things didn't go quite as Tenika planned. That may have gained us some time to prepare a defence. Naming Kayla as your replacement was quick thinking."

"Mother! It's *Seri*, now."

"That's right, I'm sorry. It's not so easy for me to set aside your birth name. It's ingrained after all these years."

"It's for my safety. You need to try harder."

Cello nodded once in acceptance A Servator accepting a professional duty.

Seri shook her head. "I'm not convinced I should be playing this role."

"Whatever do you mean? You've trained for just this type of infiltration for years."

Seri cast her eyes to the floor. "The last time I tried to play at being a Token Ward, it was a disaster. The entire Servator base had to be evacuated because of my actions. I can't be responsible for that happening a second time. I don't want harm to come to Nico's business too."

Cello's face softened. "K... Seri, you're not that person anymore. The impulsive child with something to prove no longer exists. The young woman standing before me now has passed through a crucible and learned from her mistakes. That previous girl was headstrong and overconfident. Your hesitance proves how much you've grown. All Servators are tested by loss. Those who learn from their mistakes and push ahead become our best agents. I have no doubt that you'll be among them."

"Thank you, that means a lot, but I still don't know how I'm going to manage this."

"I'll gather a list of all Callan employees — those who are friends of the

Servators. That way you'll have trustworthy people to contact for help. No doubt Tenika will be trying to sabotage your efforts. Don't trust the advice of anyone until you receive that list."

"I'd like a copy as well, if you don't mind." Nico interjected.

"Of course, I'll have it compiled and Enis can deliver it tomorrow morning. I've asked that he make himself available to you for the foreseeable future. Enis is one of our best lawvocates. You'll be in good hands. Can you find an office space for him?"

"I guess if I'm doing this, I'll be using Nico's office, so Enis can have my desk. It's in the records room, so that will give him easy access if he wants to do some digging."

"That would be perfect."

"You'll do it then?" Nico asked. "You'll accept the role as acting head of Callan International?"

"I don't see that I have much choice." Seri turned to look at Cello. "My mother's right. I need to get back on the horse and see what I'm capable of when I'm not acting impulsively."

Nico breathed a sigh of relief. "Thank you. Now, we just need to figure out what Tenika and Halen have been up to."

"Actually, I have a thought about that. Mother, do you think you could arrange to have Both Tenika and Halen leave the premises for a few hours tomorrow?"

"I'm sure I could manufacture a publicity concern that requires some senior intervention and legal counsel. Why? What are you thinking?"

"We need to set up some spy tokens."

"I could arrange to have some rangers take care of that. It will be tricky. Tenika is sure to be on guard."

"I agree, we don't want to raise suspicion. I was thinking it wouldn't seem out of place for me to drop some paperwork off on their desks. I do that regularly. I wouldn't have enough time to place any spy tokens, but I could use my Q-view to map coordinates for several suitable hiding spots."

"Yes, I see, then you could send me the coordinates to enter into the QPN. We can initiate the tokens to materialize during the night when the offices are empty."

"Exactly. This way we won't need to put rangers at risk of discovery by night staff. No one will be the wiser."

"It's a practical solution. As soon as I receive the coordinates from you, I can dedicate some analysts to materialize the tokens and monitor them around the clock. Now, about that distraction." A wicked little grin formed on Cello's lips. "Perhaps a potentially expensive product recall. Yes, that will do nicely. It will bring them running. I'll contact you when they arrive at the site of our manufactured disaster."

Nico's head had been bobbing back and forth between mother and daughter as they fleshed out their plans. They were different in so many ways, but sometimes he felt like he was caught between mirror images. They turned their heads in unison as if they could read his mind. Nico cleared his throat under their scrutiny "I'm glad you two are on my side."

Chapter 7

The man was precisely on time, not too early or too late. *Good.* Kenric liked punctuality. These preliminary meetings were tedious, but necessary for long-term effectiveness.

"You called for me, Second Anarch?"

"Yes, Decar, please have a seat." Kenric waved toward a pair of comfortable chairs near the window. One was larger and slightly more comfortable. It was one of many little tests he used to determine deference or ambition. It wasn't a pass or fail type of test, but it did give him a better idea of how to employ someone as a resource. The ambitious ones received the dangerous work, of course — at least until they proved their loyalty.

Decar hesitated.

"Go on," Kenric offered him a friendly smile. "Make yourself comfortable. Can I offer you some wine?"

"No — thank you, Second Anarch, it's not my place. If you'd like, I will happily pour the wine for you."

"Don't be bashful. I offered and was just about to refill my mug. Give this wine a try, I insist. I had it brought from Jaihuwan. That nation isn't known for its grapes, but this one particular vintage has surprisingly pleasant notes. Please do take a seat. I will bring a mug for us both."

Decar wavered, then sat in the lesser chair.

Ah, this one is both wary and deferential. He doesn't seem to be afraid so much as unsure of my intentions. Kenric handed a mug to Decar and took a sip first, as custom demanded. Decar held the mug in both hands but made no move to drink.

"Relax, my friend. I'd like to get to know you better."

Decar seemed to settle a little.

"I would like to discuss your future."

Decar stiffened again.

Kenric chuckled. "I understand — you've been working for Toller Villecrest a long time. The man was brutish and had a taste for blood. You'll find me far more enlightened. Toller suffered cruelty as a child, so inflicting punishment came naturally to him. I prefer to use reward as an incentive. Everyone makes mistakes, after all, and constantly hounding people is more work than most problems are worth. You seem uncertain."

"I'm not sure what you would have me say, sir. It's true that Villecrest was a violent man, but on the few occasions I received a blow, I deserved it."

"Nonsense! Crippling your workers is shortsighted. Toller was always a fool. Well, we need not worry about him any longer, hmmm? I suppose he used non-physical threats as well. I understand you have a family."

Kenric watched carefully as Decar's face became a shade lighter and he began to tremble. The poor fellow slumped into his seat as though resigned to a conversation he knew was inevitable. His research on the man was accurate. Decar was a loyal man. Currently, that loyalty was strictly to his family, but that was about to change. "Tell me about them."

"Sir?"

"Your family — tell me about them. You have two children if I'm not mistaken."

Clearly, talking about his family was the last thing Decar wanted to do, but it was a necessary part of the process. Kenric waited patiently.

"My youngest, Bella, is six years old. Portia is turning ten in three weeks."

Only daughters then, unfortunate. "And your wife?"

"She's well, sir. She works the loom at the textile mill."

"Her name is Dhian, is it not?"

Decar had been fidgeting, but stilled at the mention of his wife. Perfect. *That's correct, Decar, I have been investigating.*

"I can see that you love your family very much. Let me put your mind at ease. As I've already mentioned, I'm nothing like Villecrest. I believe that family is important. In fact, I like to think of those who work for me as one big family. I can see that Toller has done you a great injustice. I would like to correct that mistake. If you're willing to serve me faithfully, I give you my word that no harm will come to your family for as long as you're in my employ. Further, if any harm should befall *you*, I promise to care for your family as though they were my own."

Dread must have been holding Decar erect because he suddenly fell back into his chair as relief washed over his face. A minute later he was out of his chair and kneeling before the Second Anarch.

"I ... Sir, I don't know what to say except that my life is yours to command."

Kenric would keep his word. For as long as Decar was in his employ, no harm would come to his family. Granted, that employment could terminate at any moment. If Decar knew how Kenric treated his own family, he wouldn't want Kenric caring for them. Emotional manipulation was so easy. People heard what they wanted to hear. A mule never responded so well to a stick as to a carrot. *Loyalty is purchased with the thing that holds most value to a person.* "Are you with me then?"

Decar stood with a new resolve. "Whatever you need, my lord."

"Excellent! I have a few tasks in mind. You've worked closely with the computational engineers on the facial recognition software and network. Is that accurate?"

"Not as an engineer or technician sir, but as the project manager. I oversaw procurement of staff and other resources as well as the distribution of funds."

"Yes, I heard you were the Third Anarch's right-hand man on many of his projects. Considering his temper and the fact that you're still alive, you must be extraordinarily proficient. I'd like you to continue in that role at this base. I have other staff who function in similar roles, but my interests are widely scattered and I'm not of the mind to interrupt any of my projects to bring someone here. This will be a rare chance for you to climb swiftly in my organization, if things work out."

"I will do my best, Anarch!"

"I'm sure you will. So then, let's get straight to it. I'd like you to begin two projects immediately. One of my tech companies has designed wireless miniature viewcorders with a 180-degree view. They're far more economical than the motorized versions used in Toller's replacement strategy. I'd like you to relocate and evenly disperse the existing motorized viewcorders along major streets where they'll remain highly visible to the public. I want the public to believe the motorized viewcorders are the only viewcorders. Then, I'd like the less noticeable miniature versions to saturate all other areas. See to it that we have blanket coverage of the city. The smaller devices look nothing like a viewcorder, so if anyone asks, including the installers, they're to be told that the devices are signal boosters for the tote-comm network. They do indeed serve that purpose as well. It's how they function in a wireless capacity."

"The costs will be prohibitive, Anarch."

Kenric waved off the objection. The cost is of no concern. I've been preparing for many years. The facial recognition algorithm was a project I initiated. Villecrest interfered with my objectives when he abducted Kade Brixton and has forced me to advance my plans. We must move swiftly now. I will put you in contact with the facility responsible for manufacturing the new viewcorders. They have thousands ready to ship and can produce as many as you need. Once the streets are accounted for, we will meet again to discuss the possibility of hiding viewcorders within public buildings.

"That brings us to the second assignment. I have agents operating within all levels of governance and key businesses. They have been tasked with identifying suspected Servators in all walks of life. We will need to speed up the process and I believe the facial recognition software can help.

"Kade is to train my engineers as quickly as possible. I want the whole team, Brixton included, to weave some new writs. My agents will provide names and photos of those they currently suspect to be, or have, Servator contacts. I want the facial recognition algorithm to catalogue and identify every person who comes into contact with those suspects. I need those same agents to have access to the results so that they can focus their efforts."

Decar looked thoughtful for several minutes before he spoke. Kenric waited patiently.

"I will need discretionary funds to build the cover story necessary to hire enough technicians to install hardware on such a scale. I'll also need to convince the public that improving network speed will solve many problems — ones they don't yet know they have. Do you know of a communications company that would provide a viable front?"

Kenric smiled, admiring the man's mind at work. "As a matter of fact, I own the largest communications company in Sumakad. I will have the corporate head contact you. He'll be instructed to give you his full cooperation."

Decar nodded and paced the room as he continued. "Many of the staff we hired previously would be eager to return for another project. Yes, this could work."

"I can see that I've chosen the right man for the job. I'll leave you to it." Kenric exited the room while Decar droned on. He could still hear the fellow all the way to the end of the hall. The Second Anarch chuckled, *He didn't even notice me leave*. Things were meshing nicely.

Kenric was still displeased with Villecrest's interference, but if he played this right, he might actually find himself ahead of schedule. It would gall him to admit he owed Villecrest any gratitude, but if things worked, out he would begrudgingly raise a glass in his memory.

Chapter 8

Kade's mind wandered as his feet did the same in the busy marketplace. He was exhausted. Why couldn't he be allowed a good night's sleep for once? This new life of his was one deadline after another — if you could call this living. After a sleepless night of preparation, he had managed to cobble together enough material for his first lecture. He'd almost bolted when he set eyes on his would-be students. Everyone was several years his senior, tested by industry. What could he possibly hope to teach any of them? Then he reminded himself they were seeing the algorithm for the first time. Regardless of the knowledge they possessed, they didn't know what he knew about facial recognition writs.

He had decided in that moment not to pretend. He acknowledged their seniority and assured them he only intended to provide the missing pieces of information necessary to bring them up to speed. Then, in a moment of inspiration, he told them that he didn't want to insult their intelligence or waste anyone's time. Instead, he asked them each to share their areas of specialization so he could better gauge what areas to focus on. The tension in the room had relaxed visibly. Everyone was allowed some time to share the depth of their knowledge and boast a little about achievements. It levelled the playing field and turned the exercise into an interesting collaboration instead of a burden. *It's what I would have wanted if the roles had been reversed*, Kade realized. These people weren't the enemy. They were writ weavers like himself. Accepting that reality wouldn't prevent the confrontation that was heading his way, but it provided an opportunity to delay the inevitable. If he could develop a rapport with these men, perhaps they would be inclined to give him the benefit of the doubt when his suspicious code inevitably surfaced. Maybe he could pass it off as the bad weaving of a rookie and ask for advice on preventing such mistakes. It might work, he thought, but he'd have to be careful to lay the proper groundwork.

Kade chuckled to himself as he dodged a woman carrying a basket laden with vegetables. In the past, he wouldn't have been able to swallow his pride long enough to convince anyone that he was a novice seeking help from someone wiser. A lot had changed. The colourful tents of the busy bazaar within the compound walls punctuated that observation. Back in Caralithica, marketplaces were orderly. Booths stood in rows and people strolled through wide lanes with purpose. Here, everything was a riot of noise and jostling bodies.

His mind returned to the morning lecture. He had been expecting competent computational engineers, but the group he was supposed to teach were far more. Each was highly educated and experienced. Truth be told, any one of them could teach *him* a great deal. All he had to offer were some specifics about the algorithm itself, they had no need to be educated in any type of theory. He noted immediately that several people in the room were already working with logic models that would mesh well with the facial recognition algorithm. Others nodded in appreciation as they absorbed the implications and potential applications. It surprised Kade that none of them had considered the facial recognition angle on their own. It relieved him somewhat to know that he could easily accomplish the task given him by the imposed deadline. Unfortunately, that also meant he had even less time to find a way out of his predicament before his attempts to sabotage the algorithm were discovered.

People might believe the cover story that his team had created a contagion writ to use for testing network security — Villecrest had given them the go-ahead. He could show the isolated test server and explain its purpose, but depending on whom people talked to, it would become apparent that Kade was the one who made the suggestion to Villecrest. If Kenric Trantor had intelligence gathering resources to the degree Decar suggested, what hope did Kade have of remaining above suspicion?

A flicker of an idea blossomed. What if, after he laid out the basics to the class, he leveraged their combined wisdom to point out weaknesses?

Perhaps he could voice his inexperience in such matters. If he explained his attempt to create something to test his fears — maybe he could get them all involved in modifying the contagion writ as a system hardening tool on the isolated server. If it became a team project, it would gain credibility. As it evolved, the newly added weaving might dilute his efforts enough to hide his original intent. *Yes, this could work.* In fact, he should come clean immediately and use the isolated memory stash for practical experimentation. It would make sense not to risk compromising the working archive and network while they gained familiarity with the system.

So then, what should he teach first? He supposed he should acknowledge the similarities he'd identified in the various projects his students were already involved in, then... "Urk!" Someone yanked Kade out of his planning with a hand clamped around his wrist. *What on earth?* A blanket was quickly draped over his head and wrapped around his body. A sash found its way around Kade's waist, tying the blanket in place like a robe. It happened quickly and the sudden ministrations disoriented him. "What's happening?"

"Shush."

"Did you just shush me? What kind of bandit shushes their victim?"

Kade felt the hand on his wrist again. The fingers tapped a code — be still. *Selica!* He glanced to her face, but her head was hooded. She pulled back the cloth enough for him to see her face as she whispered, "quickly! Follow me. Stay close."

She was still alive! The relief he felt made his legs weak, but he wasn't about to lose her in the crowd having just found her. He did his best to stay in her wake and was more successful than his last attempt at following Decar. No one was shaking a fist at him this time. After several twists and turns, they entered a bake tent and stopped in front of a long table where several people were busy forming loaves. Selica began kneading dough and elbowed Kade in the ribs when he just stood there.

"Act busy," she whispered.

"Selica, what's going on? Where have you been?"

"Keep your voice down and act like you belong here."

Kade tentatively picked up some dough and began to mimic what others were doing.

"Someone may have followed you. It's the reason for the blanket you're currently wrapped in. Hopefully by covering your clothing we were able to escape watchful eyes."

"What do we do now?"

"Now, we wait to see if anyone searches this tent. If no one followed you, then we can talk."

They worked side-by-side in silence, kneading the dough and forming loaves. Kade pictured himself working alongside Selica in a home of their own, far away from danger. He longed to give her a peaceful life.

When Selica decided enough time had passed, she spoke. "I'm sorry I left so abruptly without talking to you first."

"I'm just happy to know you're alive. What happened?"

"When Trantor walked into our workspace and announced that he was taking over, I had to leave immediately."

"I don't understand. I thought you'd be relieved that Villecrest was finally out of your life for good. I've even wondered if it might mean we had a real chance to escape together."

"Villecrest was a monster, but I'll say this for him, he recognized that women could be just as useful as men. Kenric Trantor isn't known for his love of women. He's of the mind that they're only good for rearing and, well, making children. He would never have allowed me to learn writ weaving as a child. He certainly wouldn't have sent me on that mission to Denmount as Villecrest did. If I had remained, Trantor would have wondered what I was doing there. As it stands, he'll think I was running an errand for one of the technicians. If I had stayed, and he discovered I was weaving writs, he would have immediately sent me to the brothel."

Kade felt ill. Selica was facing the threats of her past all over again. It was unfair and he didn't know how to protect her. "What will you do? You can't wander the bazaar forever."

She gave him a look that suggested she was questioning his intelligence. "You think I was wandering around the bazaar for the last ten days?" She snorted and shook her head. "Of the limited options currently open to me, I chose to raise babies rather than make them with strangers.

"After I left, I went to the children's slave quarters. I still have a good relationship with the housemother there — Momma Renna. She's getting on in years and has been asking for an assistant to train as a replacement. Her financial allowance for running the house isn't enough to cover the expense of hiring additional staff and Villecrest always turned a deaf ear to her petitions. Renna readily agreed to take me on when I offered to work in exchange for food and shelter. She understands my predicament. Since we last spoke, I've been working at the children's quarters and letting everyone I meet know about my new role. With the change in leadership, no one is surprised at the shuffle of people and responsibilities. I needed to establish my position before Kenric develops an extensive informant network."

"I glad you've found a safe place, Selica, but time is running out for me. We can't stay here."

"I know, it's time to take a chance. I'm working on something, but I need a little more time to figure out the details."

"How will we stay in touch?"

"I come to the bazaar every morning to purchase food for the children. The owner of this tent donates day old baking in exchange for a few hours of my help. I come here at around the same time each day. You can find me here when you need me. Create a routine where you stop here each day for kofa and a pastry or something."

"I'll try, but Selica, I'm testing my limited freedom for the first time today. I don't know if I'll be allowed to wander around the compound unescorted. It was never permitted under Villecrest's reign."

"You haven't given Kenric any reason to follow you yet, have you?"

"I don't think so. I just finished leading my first training session before I came to the bazaar. That was my only task for the day. Decar is still managing projects. He and I went for a walk the other day without interference — perhaps it's okay."

"Good! make it a routine to leave at this time every day if possible." Selica led him to the end of the table, packaged a bag of pastries, and handed him a mug of kofa. "Here. Bring these back with you and give some to Decar. Offer to pick something up for him whenever you're about to leave. Use the same route each time. Let the merchants notice you. Stop and look at their wares on occasion — perhaps purchase a trinket or two. Establish a pattern."

"I should start back." Kade admitted, though it was the last thing he wanted to do. He had grown to rely on Selica and the idea of an ongoing separation felt wrong — like leaving part of himself behind.

Selica removed his sash and folded up the blanket she'd used for his disguise.

"You won't need these anymore. If someone followed you and is waiting outside, they'll see you carrying your pastries and sipping a kofa as you return to the compound. Everything should be fine." Selica led him out of the tent after a quick embrace and sent him on his way.

Chapter 9

Seri was only one hour into her first day as head of Callan International and she'd already called Nico three times. *Why did I agree to this?* Thirty-seven messages waited for her when she arrived and she was still making her way through the list. Nico had assured her it wasn't that bad every day, but she felt like he was understating things to ease her alarm. That was the right call because she was on the edge of panic.

Seri sat back in her chair and took a few deep breaths. Thinking about it, she realized that she had a ready response to most of the requests. Nico had been right about that, she did know almost as much as Nico about the day-to-day workings of the company. She'd been knee-deep in it as his assistant since Nico took over his family's empire. Now, she would be alone at the helm. The idea was unnerving.

Her thoughts were interrupted as the office door flew open and Tenika Sheridan came striding in. A tall stack of parchment was dropped unceremoniously on the corner of Seri's desk.

"What's this?" Seri glanced from the pile to Tenika.

"You need to read through these documents and sign each of them."

Seri frowned. "I don't suppose you can tell me what they're for?"

"Oh, project proposals and requisitions I imagine. These things come across my desk pretty regularly, but since I no longer have signing authority..." Tenika shrugged, looking a little too pleased with herself.

"They need to be signed before the end of the day. I have to leave to meet the company lawvocate at one of our facilities. Apparently, a manufacturing flaw was discovered and threats of a lawsuit followed." Tenika put on a concerned expression as if something had just occurred to her. "Unless, of course, you wanted to handle it personally. I didn't mean to overstep." Tenika's voice was devoid of contrition.

"No, by all means, I trust you to handle the situation." *Especially since I know my mother fabricated the entire emergency.*

"Very well," Tenika replied.

Seri rolled her eyes as Tenika bowed her head. *As if you had any intention of letting me handle a legal matter.*

Tenika studied her wrist chrono. "I'm running late. If you can have those signed before I return, I'll see that they find their way to the proper people."

Seri had difficultly keeping the sarcasm out of her voice. "You're too kind."

Tenika tapped the pile of documents with her finger. "My pleasure."

A sadistic pleasure. Seri thought.

"I'll see you later."

"Close the door..." Tenika was already out of earshot — or ignoring her. The woman was infuriating.

Seri rose to shut the door herself. She turned to stare at the pile of paperwork and sighed. *I suppose it will give me the excuse I need to enter her office while she's away.* Her mother had come through with the promised distraction. It sounded like both Tenika and Halen would be away for a few hours, at least. She needed to complete the paperwork quickly.

Seri smiled to herself. "Tenika — did you really think this little display would intimidate me? You're dealing with a trained analyst. We go through piles of parchment four times this size before lunch." Servator analysts had training in speed-reading and memory retention techniques and she called on those skills now. She needed to be ready to deliver these documents when her mother called to inform her of Tenika and Halen's arrival at the site.

Within thirty minutes she had skimmed everything in a first pass. Most of them were simple low-risk requests. She signed those quickly and set them to the side. One of them involved a new partnership contract. She attached a note with a few questions asking Halen for legal clarification. It would give her an excuse to visit his office as well. *This is working out nicely.*

Seri's wrist Q-view vibrated. She activated it and watched as the skin-like camouflage gave way to reveal the communications device hidden there. A message scrolled across the screen.

-Halen-and-Tenika-are-here-will-keep-them-as-long-as-I-can-

Seri sent an acknowledgement and assessed her progress. She still had four documents left. She quickly signed those and appended notes saying she had a few questions and not to proceed before speaking with her. She captured images of the remaining documents with her Q-view to review later. That done, she deactivated the device, returning it to its dormant camouflaged state.

Come on Seri, you're losing precious time. She made a hasty pile and placed the document for Halen on the top. Picking up the stack, she raced out of her office and down the hall. Halen worked on a lower level. She'd visit his office first.

When she arrived, she was relieved to see that Halen's assistant wasn't at his desk. "Is it lunch hour already?" Her stomach growled in confirmation.

Seri slipped into Halen's office and closed the door with her foot as she balanced the pile of documents she was carrying. Setting the cumbersome weight on the desk was a relief. Grabbing the top document, she rounded the desk and sat in Halen's chair, setting the document on the desk where he would be sure to see it. Then she surveyed the room looking for potential spots to place a few spy tokens.

Seri activated her Q-view and pulled her sleeve down to help conceal it in case someone suddenly entered. She only needed to expose it for a few seconds at a time as she mapped QPN coordinates. *Where can I hide these tokens?* Halen's office was utilitarian. Personal effects, paintings or sculptures were absent. Seri couldn't see any obvious places to conceal a token. That left the desk itself and the bookshelves filled with legal documents.

Dropping to her knees, she took a snapshot of coordinates for the underside of the desk. That would serve for a sound token. The bookshelves were the only other option. Removing a volume from the top shelf, she mapped the vacated space and entered those coordinates for a sight and sound token. She placed the volume she'd removed into the lower cabinet. Hopefully Halen wouldn't notice something was missing before a book shaped token materialized later that night.

It wasn't ideal. She would have preferred a sight token above his desk to capture anything he might be writing. Unfortunately, Halen's office had plenty of natural light from the windows so he didn't have any desk or floor lamps. *I guess he never works late — maybe I should have become a lawvocate.* Seri stared at the ceiling above the desk. *Hmmmm, I wonder what the ceiling tiles are made of.* She jogged to the door and opened it a crack. Halen's assistant hadn't returned yet. Closing the door, she ran back and climbed onto the desk. Grabbing a pin from her hair, she worked a small hole through the tile and confirmed an empty space beyond. She took several still-views of her handiwork so the analysts would have an idea of what she was attempting. Then she carefully aligned her Q-view to the small hole and recorded the coordinates, including the estimated thickness of the ceiling tile.

Jumping to the floor, she hastily swept dust and fallen crumbs of material from the ceiling tile off the desk and into her palm. She was about to dump it into a waste basket beside the desk, but thought better of it and placed it into her tunic pocket instead. Sitting behind the desk once more, she leaned back in the chair and looked upward. The hole was visible, but not so obvious that someone would notice unless they were looking right at it. When people regularly prop their feet up, it leaves scuff marks. Halen's desk was unmarred, so Seri didn't think he spent much time leaning back in his chair gazing skyward. It would have to do.

Seri glanced at the wall chrono above the door. She'd spent too much time here, but decided the wall chrono would be a good spot to place one more sight token. It would allow them to see Halen's facial expressions while seated at his desk, talking on his tote-comm. She dragged a chair to the door and stood on it as she recorded still-views, dimensions, and QPN coordinates. The analysts could create a thicker, false bezel around the chrono to hide a sight token. They would figure something out. She glanced at the chrono once more. Definitely time to move on. Seri grabbed her pile of documents and opened the office door to discover Halen's assistant had returned. "There you are," she bluffed. "I have a document for Halen to look over. No one was here so I left it on his desk. When Halen does return, can you let him know that Tenika was hoping to have it sent to her by the end of the day?"

"Yes, Ma'am."

At least someone was showing respect. Seri walked calmly into the hall. Once out of view, she pulled off her sandals and ran silently to the stairwell and back up to Tenika's office where Tenika's assistant was eating at her desk.

"Hi, Seri, don't you stop for lunch?"

Seri liked Marret. They had crossed paths often in their assistant roles. She lifted the pile of documents for emphasis. "No rest for the servants."

Marret laughed. "You're not an assistant any longer. Don't you have someone to help you with that?"

"Are you volunteering?"

"I don't think you'd want my help with those. It would take me all day to get through a pile like that."

"Do you mean to tell me that Tenika reads through all of these herself?"

"Dear me, no. The department heads bring their proposals when they meet with her each morning. They explain the request and walk her through the details. She just signs the approvals and they take it with them when they leave."

"Oh, they do, do they?" Seri was seething, but clamped down on her anger. "Well, I'll just set these on Tenika's desk. I need to organize them so I may be a few minutes."

Marret nodded absently. Her attention was already back on the gossip sheet she was reading, her apple forgotten halfway to her mouth.

Seri entered Tenika's office and quietly closed the door. Setting the pile of documents on the desk, she divided them up in order of importance for the sake of appearances. Then she sat behind the desk to consider her surroundings, as she'd done in Halen's office.

Tenika's tastes were a stark contrast to Halen's austere sensibilities. A subtle opulence suffused the room. Statuary, plants and paintings proliferated. "I never thought I'd be pleased to see so much clutter, she muttered under her breath." It would prove much easier to hide tokens here.

Two arching lamps stood on either side of the desk. Having learned from her experience in Halen's office, setting a sight token above Tenika's desk was the first priority. She took QPN coordinates for sight and sound tokens at each lamp. A carved bust on the corner of the desk would provide a good view of Tenika's face. After a quick circuit of the room, she had taken readings for a few potted plants and locations among the knick-knacks on the bookshelf.

Sitting back at the desk, she considered her handiwork. Ten minutes — not too bad. Marret wouldn't be wondering yet. Seri was about to rise, but curiosity got the better of her. She opened one of the desk drawers to peek inside and discovered the expected instruments for daily work, among other things. A bottle of perfume, makeup and a small mirror sat in one corner beside a bag of dried dates. Seri shook her head, annoyed with herself. *What did you expect to find? A bloody knife and keys to the dungeon? Wait...* Seri saw something peeking out from underneath the dried dates. She grinned as she moved the bag to the side. *Maybe not keys to the dungeon, but keys to a ground transport are even better.* If she could set a tracker token, she might be able to follow Tenika. If this key started Tenika's transport, it wouldn't remain in the desk overnight when the analysts were scheduled to place the rest of the tokens. She'd have to place this one herself. Activating her Q-view, she mapped the key fob where it sat in the desk. It was a carving of a serpent. *How appropriate.* Tracking tokens were tiny devices, it would be easily hidden in the eye of the carving. After setting the coordinates, she carefully closed the desk drawer and scrolled through the token options on her Q-view. She selected the size and colour, superimposing it on the images she had recorded of the key fob until she was satisfied with the result. Now all she had to do was materialize the token and activate it.

Voices carried from beyond the door. "Good Afternoon, Ms. Sheridan. How did your meeting go?"

Seri panicked. What was Tenika doing back so soon? Why hadn't her mother warned her?

"It was a complete waste of my time. Halen is perfectly capable of handling something like this on his own. Now I'm running behind schedule. Cancel my afternoon meetings and make sure I'm undisturbed for the remainder of the day."

"Yes, Ms. Sheridan."

The door opened and Tenika froze, seeing Seri sitting in her chair. "What are you doing in my office?"

Seri steeled herself. *You can do this. It's just like your Token Ward training. You're playing a part.* She remembered something an instructor told her once. "If you want to gain the upper hand, you must maintain eye contact until you notice your opponent drop their gaze first."

Seri relaxed her features and raised her eyes to focus through Tenika's as she spoke. "I've brought the signed documents you dropped off this morning."

She noticed Tenika averting her gaze. Her nostrils flared. Clearly, she didn't like someone standing up to her.

"So, you thought you would reward yourself by lounging at my desk?"

As if it were a reward to be in her office! Seri didn't need TokenWard training for the glare she was directing at Tenika now. "I was sorting them in order of importance and was about to leave. Besides, if I'm not mistaken, this

office and desk are the property of Callan International. I don't believe I need your permission to sit at company property. Pull up a chair and have a seat." Seri almost laughed. *If looks could kill, I'd be on a spit over a fire.*

Tenika clenched her teeth and looked at the chair in front of her desk. She looked like she'd swallowed something distasteful as she slowly sat.

"Tenika..."

"That's, Ms. Sheridan."

Seri ignored her. "Tenika — I realized this morning that I need an assistant to help me with the workload. I wasted a good part of the morning going through the paperwork you left on my desk. I'm behind schedule as a result. I'm sure you know what that's like."

The woman was bristling with barely concealed rage.

"Unfortunately, it takes time to find qualified staff. It occurred to me that since I now have the only signing authority, your workload has been dramatically reduced. You have less need of an assistant these days, so I've decided that Marret will spend half of her time assisting me. I value your experience and Marret is familiar with your routine. By sharing an assistant, it will be easier for us to coordinate as you mentor me in this new role."

All pretense now gone, Tenika was exuding hatred. Her voice was level and cold. "You don't want to make an enemy of me."

"Enemy! Tenika, dear, whatever are you talking about? Didn't I just tell you how much I value you as a mentor?" Seri lifted her voice so it carried beyond the office door. "Marret, could you come in here please?"

"Can I get you something? Ms. Quin? Ms. Sheridan?"

Seri was pushing matters, but she couldn't help herself. "No need to be so formal — Seri and Tenika will be fine."

Tenika was almost vibrating in her seat.

"Marret, starting tomorrow you'll be assisting me in the morning and Tenika in the afternoon."

Marret looked uncertain as she glanced between Seri and Tenika, but then she remembered who paid for her bread and butter. "As you wish — Seri."

"Please schedule morning meetings for me with any department heads who have proposals or requisitions that need signing."

Tenika grew still. Seri raised an eyebrow and looked straight at her. *That's right — I know what you did.*

Seri offered Marret a smile. "Thank you, Marret. You can continue to work from your current desk, but if you wouldn't mind, I'd like you to meet me in my office at the start of each day."

"It would be my pleasure. I'll see you first thing in the morning." Marret smiled back and returned to her desk.

While Tenika was glaring at Marret's retreat, Seri darted a look at her Q-view out of sight below the desk. She activated the tracking token in Tenika's keys and deactivated her Q-view.

"Well, I don't want to take up any more of your time, Tenika. I look forward to learning from you."

Seri stood up in the strained silence, tapped her finger on one of the documents and walked out.

Chapter 10

Life had become very busy. Lev spent each morning training with Akhen, while two hours of every afternoon was reserved for the analysts. Akhen had been correct. They were very excited about the possibility of using reduced coordinate sets for tokens. The benefits quickly became apparent with simple objects, but the analysts were positively ecstatic when they discussed the potential for complex objects. Lev didn't understand at first. To hear them discuss the matter, it sounded to him like complex objects remained complex regardless of this potential advancement. When he had expressed his skepticism, they'd been all too eager to provide him with a very detailed explanation on the process for creating a token pattern.

Over the centuries, Servators had created a memory stash of data containing the molecular breakdown of all known substances. It was relatively simple to create a hollow or solid sphere made of steel, for example. All you needed was the particle structure of the desired substance and coordinates to form it in a specific size. Things became dramatically more complicated when an item consisted of more than one material or part. A view token, for example, contained glass lenses, copper wire coated with insulators, layers of carbon substrate etched with silver circuits and many other components. Each was its own template joined together to form a much larger template. It could take years to develop a complex token template. It amazed Lev to think of how much work had gone into creating something that could now materialize in a few moments. The thing that had the analysts excited was the potential for a compounded reduction in complexity. They needed Lev to identify the key coordinates for each sub-component. It was a huge undertaking, but in the end it was possible to render a very complex token with a much smaller instruction set.

The analysts also seemed to think that it would allow them to create highly structured amalgams by providing key coordinates of dissimilar materials and allowing the molecular scaffolding to form on its own. It was something that hadn't been easy to do before.

Lev didn't understand the details well enough to judge the veracity of such a claim, but was pleased to see the analysts herald it as a revolutionary advancement. Unfortunately, they now looked at him with even more awe than they had before. He didn't feel worthy of their respect. It's not as if he had done anything particularly difficult. His input was limited to looking at patterns and pointing out a few coordinates. It was second nature for Lev to view the world in that way — it felt akin to receiving praise for naming colours in a child's painting. Nevertheless, the analysts saw things differently. At least he was doing something to live up to the Levigator moniker thrust upon him.

Is this what past Levigators felt like? Lev wondered. *Obliged to lead because they could do something that others couldn't?*

He needed to stop feeling sorry for himself. These people saved his life and strove to do the same for others. He would do the best he could to help.

Mornings melded into afternoons. He'd been moving about in a tired haze for days. A loud bang startled him.

"Leviticus!"

Lev shook his head, remembering where he was. *Right, mornings with Akhen.* His instructor currently wore a scowl as he eyed the dent in the wall beside his head. The steel sphere that produced it lay on the floor at his feet.

"Sorry, Akhen. I'm pretty tired today."

It seemed as though Akhen developed a new experiment for Lev's abilities every other day. Lev knew the man well enough to expect a test of every premise. Akhen had been toying with the notion that Lev knew how his body moved through the pattern, adjusting the coordinates of his surroundings instantly. Today he had decided that meant Lev should be able to form a token as it moved along a calculated trajectory. Doing so would impart velocity depending on how quickly he could do it. It worked, but it wasn't easy to control. Especially when he wasn't focused. Hence the dent in the wall.

"I'll keep working on it, but it raises a question. You have me throwing objects at targets, but what if someone is throwing an object at me? Is it possible for field agents to defend themselves with some kind of armour token?"

Akhen rubbed his chin in thought. "Hmmm... We have archaic templates for shields, chainmail, and the like, but no one has ever been able to materialize such a thing over their body without standing very, very, still. Normally they would create it and then put it on. You might be the one person able to accomplish the feat of forming a token over your body while moving, but those old templates would be of little value against modern projectile weapons. I once formed a wall to hide behind in an alley, but I was far enough ahead of my pursuers that I had time to find a template and enter the coordinates on my Q-view. You could accomplish something like that a lot quicker than I could and it would provide a screen at least. The problem is that doing such a thing with an audience would draw far too much attention to the Servators."

"What about laminated glass?"

"What are you thinking?"

"We use laminated glass in ground transports and other vehicles, right? Do we have a pattern for that material?"

Akhen searched his Q-view. "You won't find specific templates, but you already knew that — having memorized the catalogue. The analysts do have specifications for the raw materials used to form something very basic. What did you have in mind?"

"Can you form a standing sheet about my width and height and the thickness of my thumb? Add a ninety-degree bend at the bottom to form a base."

Akhen made calculations for the dimensions and activated the pattern while Lev watched. A crystal-clear sheet formed between the two of them.

Lev memorized the formation of the pattern and realized he had another question. "I've seen it done, but I've never asked before — how do you deactivate a token?"

"Our Q-views have a sequence for that, but from your perspective it's just a process of disassembly. The sequence is ordered in the reverse of the template used to form something. Watch as I disassemble this clear pane."

Lev observed using pattern-sight and it was just as Akhen had said.

"Could you do that for me a few more times? Form the pane, then disassemble and repeat?"

Akhen complied, with a questioning look in his eye.

"Okay I've got it, let me try." Lev disassembled Akhen's work and then reformed it. He began walking backwards forming consecutive panes a handbreadth apart as he went. Once he had three panes between Akhen and himself, he deactivated the first one. The farthest panes fell like disintegrating dominoes. As Lev backpedalled, he continued to add new ones with each step. To an untrained eye, it almost looked like they were following him rather than appearing and disappearing. Akhen shook his head in amazement and then began nodding in appreciation. He quickly formed several fist sized spheres and began hurling them at Lev. With each strike, a shield disintegrated, replaced by another. Akhen's missiles lay impotent on the floor as successive barriers reduced their kinetic energy to zero. Lev stopped as he came up against a wall at the back of the training space.

"This is incredible, Lev! The shields are visible if you know what to look for, but from a distance.... If you can increase the speed at which they disintegrate, the casual observer might think any artifacts were just their eyes playing tricks. I'd also suggest adding an anti-reflective coating. I'll have the analysts calculate the optimum thickness and distance to stop ammunition from ballistic weapons. Perhaps we can leverage this concept for Q-view activation. The QPN could calculate an offset from a user's location and set a series of five panels between a field agent and a pursuer. We could set them to deactivate after several seconds. It would be a one-off proposition because the QPN can't continuously update with enough speed to do what you just did. Still, it might be enough to make a difference in an emergency."

Lev hoped so. Breachers didn't hold back when it came to Servators. They needed every defensive advantage they could get.

Akhen was looking at him through narrowed eyes. That particular gaze always made him feel like an experiment. It meant that his mentor was hatching an idea of his own.

"Remember when I was training you to use your observational abilities to supplement your warkata skills?"

"How could I forget? Throwing Tark and Yori to the mat was a glorious moment, considering all the bruises they've given me in the past."

"Yes, well, you know I had given them some tips so they wouldn't telegraph their intentions to someone with your observational abilities. They tell me those techniques don't work anymore. Why is that?"

"It worked for a while, so I changed my strategy."

"What did you do?"

"I stopped looking for physical tells. Now I remain in pattern-sight while I'm fighting. It doesn't matter what they try to conceal. I can always tell the start of any motion by the pattern shift. I've sparred often enough to understand the range and limitations of the human body. I suppose it's a little like seeing the key points in a template. Once established, the direction of travel is a foregone conclusion. I have plenty of time to react."

Akhen was nodding like he suspected as much. "So when I was throwing spheres at your shields, you could sense the movement of those projectiles in the pattern, correct?"

"Yes, so?"

"So, if you can react that quickly to a pattern change while sparring, why didn't you just place an appropriately sized shield directly in the path of the projectile instead of spacing out body sized partitions? A much smaller shield would be far less conspicuous."

"I guess I just didn't think of it."

"Also, if you could materialize a small shield directly in front of a projectile, and then disintegrate it immediately after impact, no one would even realize what had happened. You wouldn't need to worry about transparency, you could use a small steel block."

"Do you think I would be fast enough?"

"I'm not sure, but I know what we're going to work on next!"

"It figures." Lev affected the manner of a tormented student, but he was eager to push himself. A lot of people were counting on him and he didn't want to let anyone down.

Chapter 11

Selica brushed away a loose strand of hair that had fallen across her face as she washed the floor. One final corner and the chore would be complete. No one had asked her to spend the day on her hands and knees scrubbing away years of grime, but the children were too young to do a proper job and Momma Renna was too old. Selica supposed Renna's eyesight was aging like the rest of her body. She probably didn't even notice the greasy film forming on every surface. She decided to make up a list of chores for the children, to keep things from getting this filthy in the future.

This last room at the end of the hall on the third floor was the one she had shared with four other girls as a child. Her mind sorted through memories as she scoured. She paused when she came across some letters carved in a floorboard. They were her mother's initials, a memorial. She had carved them there during her first week, with a promise that she would never forget. When Toller Villecrest murdered her mother in front of her, she had screamed for hours. Guards dragged her to this place and dumped her unceremoniously onto the floor, closed the door and locked her in. This room had been a self-imposed prison to her for many weeks. She remained in the room long after the door had been unlocked. She refused to participate in life, wishing she had died with her mother. It seemed wrong to continue without her. Momma Renna had slowly broken past her defences and helped her to see that giving up was letting Villecrest win. It was during one of those talks that Selica realized she wanted revenge. In her mind, ending Toller was winning. Renna hadn't meant it that way, but it did fuel a thirst to survive. Selica decided she would overcome, if for no other reason than to spite the man who had taken away her mother.

It had been years since Selica entertained such thoughts and now that Toller Villecrest was dead — she wasn't sure how she felt. Relief was part of it, but also disappointment that she hadn't been the one to bring him down. It felt as if she had failed her mother somehow. Selica grimaced, squeezing out the unwanted thoughts. *Don't be ridiculous, Mom died trying to protect you. She would have wanted you away from this place, not risking your life by playing avenger.*

Selica never heard what happened to her mother's body. As far as she knew, no ceremony was held to celebrate her life. No gravestone marked the place where her body was interred. Years later she had tried to find the burial site, but too much time had passed and no one had any useful information or even a memory of her mother's passing. It was a testament to how little value life had under a Breacher regime. Selica kissed her fingertips and pressed them into the carved grooves as she had done so many times in the past. "I'm back, Mom," she whispered, "but I can't stay for long. This time I'll find the escape that eluded us both." A tear slipped free and joined the puddle of soapy water on the floor. She swiped at her eyes, finished the last spot, and tossed her brush into the pail.

Enough with the self-pity. Selica arched her back and kneaded the stiff muscles at the base of her spine. She had a lot of planning to do and judging by Kade's reports on his own situation, not a lot of time. She decided to head to the roof. It had been her secret place when she needed to get away. It was a good spot to be alone with her thoughts.

A closet stood at the end of the hall beside her childhood room. It had a maintenance hatch to the roof accessible by an iron rung ladder attached to the wall. The hatch was unlocked, but the children had been warned by the Breachers not to venture onto the roof under threat of a beating. Selica glanced down the hall before she opened the door to slip inside. She chuckled at the cautious habit. She wasn't a child anymore, she was the assistant housemother. No one would question her. Besides, the children were all outside helping in the garden under Renna's supervision.

The closet was so much smaller than she remembered and she banged her elbows on the side walls as she climbed. The latch was stiff and the hinges squealed as she flipped open the hatch. She'd need to oil those if she planned on sneaking up here while others were around. She didn't want to give the children any ideas. The opening was smaller than she remembered as well, but that only made things easier as she placed her hands on either side of the enclosure and levered herself onto the flat roof.

A parapet surrounded the roof, five hand spans in height. Selica walked to the parapet and looked over the edge. When she was a child, the parapet had been just below her waist. Now, it was about mid-thigh and didn't provide the same sense of security. The Children's quarters backed up against the compound wall. The roof rose a full story higher than the wall surrounding the compound. The wall itself stood four cubits away. As a child roaming the grounds, it had seemed a great distance from the building, but an adult with outstretched arms could almost touch both. Selica experienced a wave of vertigo looking down the three-story drop as she imagined attempting a leap to somehow land on the narrow top of the wall. No child would try to clear such a distance and risk falling three stories. Her young mind hadn't considered it as an avenue for escape. Now, she wondered — an adult, with the aid of a rope, might be able to traverse the gap.

She stood on her toes trying to get a better view of the alley beyond. It was narrow and bounded by the backside of local businesses for its full length. One end was gated and the other fed onto the street running past the main entrance to the compound. Sunlight didn't penetrate very far into the dimly lit alley. Shadows draped the buildings on either side. That was a plus for someone scaling the wall, but offered little hope of exiting the alley onto the main street unnoticed. Perhaps at night? Attempting such acrobatics in the dark would be dangerous. A full moon or some other light source would be necessary. *Am I really contemplating this?* She had come up to the roof to think. It hadn't occurred to her that she might find a potential avenue for escape.

Plans started to form. They could secure a rope ladder to the iron rungs in the closet to provide a margin of safety while attempting to reach the wall. It would need to be long enough to reach the ground in the alley. The route was dangerous, but the possibilities were intriguing. No one would question her presence in this building. No one would be on the rooftops to observe them and it was unlikely anyone would see them descend into the alley if they had the cover of night. The primary hurdles would be sneaking Kade into the Children's quarters and finding a way to exit the alley without drawing attention.

Selica walked the perimeter of the roof, surveying the compound. She stopped at the back side of the building as she was making her second circuit. Something about the sheepfold against the neighbouring building created an itch in her mind. Why was the fenced area so small? It would only hold a few animals. Why was it attached to a building *inside* the compound? A pasture separated the back wall of the compound from the river. That was the reason for a gate at the same end of the alley. It kept the flocks from wandering into the streets. From this vantage point, she wondered how she had never noticed the sheepfold on the other side of the hedge surrounding the children's yard. Her smaller stature again, no doubt. Now that she thought about it, she did recall hearing the occasional animal. She remembered thinking it strange because she only noticed it during festivals. Wait — festivals? Of course!

The pieces came together as bits of information from years of living in the compound floated to the surface. The neighbouring building housed the kitchens. They were part of the administration facilities. Her mental map of the compound included the location of the administration building, but she'd never considered how the various entrances might lead to different services within. She'd only been allowed inside the building on a few occasions and didn't know the layout very well. She knew the kitchens were at the back and accessible from the interior, but the possibility of a separate entrance to the kitchens from the building's exterior hadn't occurred to her. The kitchens held animals for slaughter in the small enclosure when they were preparing a large feast for a celebration — a celebration like the upcoming gathering of the anarchs.

While Toller Villecrest was alive, he had arranged to host the annual gathering. It was part of his plan to curry favour toward his eventual attempt to overthrow Kenric Trantor and take his position as Second Anarch. The annual gathering was a prestigious event. A Second Anarch usually hosted and they vied for the opportunity. Selica still didn't understand how Toller had managed to claim that coveted honour. The favours, bribes, or threats, must have been substantial. Ironically, hosting would now fall to Kenric Trantor, the very man Villecrest was hoping to overthrow. Perhaps it was more inevitable than ironic if the rumours about Kenric's intelligence gathering were true. Regardless, Kenric certainly wouldn't pass up the opportunity conveniently dropped into his lap. The gathering would continue as planned.

Selica's mind was racing. For years, she'd been seeking a chance to escape. She had played out endless scenarios, but always hit a roadblock. The points of egress were well guarded thanks to Villecrest's paranoia, and the compound of a Third Anarch was relatively small. The possibilities for distraction were few and far between. This was an unprecedented opportunity. The compound had never hosted a gala and the many distractions it would offer. Second Anarchs would arrive from all over the world, each with a large retinue. Entertainers and servants would be running to and fro, each playing their part. Unfamiliar faces would fill the compound. Security would be on heightened alert, with resources stretched thin. Their focus would be on the main entrance dealing with drunken guests and external threats, not vetted staff who were already within the walls. Adding to the chaos, vendors would line the streets in front of the compound hoping to sell their wares to visitors before they entered the bazaar within the walls. Voices would fill the lantern-lit night. No one would notice a few people coming out of the alley.

The ramifications hit home. On that one night, she and Kade would be insignificant — not enough that they could walk through the front gates, but enough that They could move about with relative freedom within the compound. They could blend in with the busyness of the event. They only needed to make it from the kitchens to the alley. A stone's throw away from freedom.

The festival was in twelve days — just enough time if they moved quickly. During such events, the kitchens always recruited volunteers to help with food preparations. The sign-up sheets should be posted in the next day or so. Kade needed to get his name on that list. It would give him access without raising suspicion. At an opportune moment, he could slip out of the building into the animal pen. A quick climb over the hedge into the playground behind the children's quarters would bring him to the back door where Selica would be waiting to let him in. From there she could sneak him up to the roof. If they timed it right, the children and Momma Renna would be asleep. Once over the wall and into the crowded street, it was less than a quarter league to the Aiguptos River. Her eyes returned to the gate at the other end of the alley. It led to the pasture directly adjacent the river. She didn't know if the banks were traversable, but it was an alternative to keep in mind. If Kade could get word to the Servators, and have them waiting with a boat, they could put enough distance between themselves and the compound to ensure their escape.

There were loose ends to weave into place, but they might never get another chance like this one. Kenric was still getting a feel for the day-to-day running of this compound. That, combined with the chaos of a celebration seemed almost too good to be true. Perhaps the Maker was finally answering her prayers.

Chapter 12

Leviticus stood in the centre of the sparring mat. He had been practising his newfound skills all week and Akhen felt it was time to test him in a less predictable setting. Tark and Yori slowly circled him. They had refused the exercise at first, finally agreeing when Akhen assured them that Lev would be blindfolded.

None of the rangers had been able to best Lev for some time. Tark and Yori were some of the Servator's best fighters, but even they grew tired of the one-sided sparring matches. Lev smiled to himself. *They weren't fond of the bruises either.*

"What are you grinning about, Radix?" Tark twirled a staff barely holding back a smile of his own.

"I believe he's happy because someone is finally going to lay hands on him," Yori quipped. "It's traumatizing to be untouchable when the child inside longs to be cuddled. Come, let me rock you to sleep." Yori made chopping motions with his two wooden practice swords.

Lev continued to smile, making no effort to move. At some point during his sessions with Akhen, he had come to understand that he didn't need his eyes to sense changes in the pattern. In fact, his reliance on physical sight had been slowing him down. His eyes were limited. During their sessions, Akhen had Lev materialize shields to block items thrown at him from all directions. Akhen had asked him how he knew where to place shields when blocking items coming from behind. They both began to realize that Lev knew his position in the pattern without thinking. It was similar to walking. A person didn't have to look at their feet to take a step.

Once Lev stopped trying to force the pattern to fit his visual expectations, he found he could see the world in pattern-sight with greater acuity. It was disorienting at first. It didn't feel natural to visualize three hundred and sixty degrees of the world at once — especially when one's eyes were closed. He had to unlearn a lifetime of relying on binocular vision. And yet, it didn't take another lifetime to learn this new way of seeing. Soon enough, it became second nature and he found that he was relying on his pattern-sight more than his regular vision. It seemed supernatural and for the first time Lev began to wonder if the Maker truly had chosen him to be the Levigator. How else could he explain these abilities?

"Look at him, Yori — he can barely contain his excitement. I don't think we should keep him waiting any longer."

Lev broke his silence. "Enjoy yourselves, my friends. You best try to get your licks in while you can."

"Oooo, did you hear that Tark? Our golden boy has decided to decline our offer to teach him some humility."

Brave taunts, but Lev noticed neither of them had come any closer. Tark and Yori were two of his closest friends among the Servators and among the few who didn't insist on calling him Levigator. For that, he was truly grateful. "I've decided not to inflict any bruises today. You're welcome." That drew a laugh from Yori.

Lev saw them nod to each other in preparation for a two-pronged attack. They weren't taking any chances. In his pattern-sight, they appeared as loose knit masses of particles. He knew the loose structure represented key points. If he focused, he could pick out greater detail, more akin to looking at densely packed grains of sand. That took more effort and slowed him down. Maybe it would come with time and experience, or maybe it wasn't necessary.

Tark directed a thrust of his staff toward Lev's chest. Lev held a palm out and created a wedge with matching velocity. It appeared and disappeared in the blink of an eye. The staff was redirected past Lev's rib cage into Yori's shoulder stopping his advance from behind.

"Hey!" Yori yelped in pain. "Whose side are you on?"

"I don't know what happened. I was aiming for his sternum."

"Remind me to stand behind you during target practice."

The two began circling again. Yori nodded to Tark, a signal for something they had discussed beforehand.

Lev watched, curious. Tark crept stealthily to join Yori behind Lev. As one, they threw their weapons to either side of Lev for a distraction and prepared to tackle him from behind, one high and one low.

They crouched and Lev formed bands around their ankles just as they were about to spring. They ended up face first on the mat in a pile.

"Get off me, Yori, you oaf! What's the big idea tripping me like that?"

Yori picked himself off the floor and gave Tark a shove with his foot. "I didn't trip you. You tripped me!"

Akhen was laughing from the sidelines. Tark and Yori looked from Akhen to Lev, suspicion clear on their faces. "You're cheating! I don't know how, but you are."

They shook their heads in disbelief when Akhen explained. It wasn't until Lev offered to take a blow to the face from each of them that the truth finally sunk in. He blocked each swing within inches of his face without lifting a finger. They didn't ask to try again as they rubbed sore knuckles. *I probably should have chosen something other than steel as a blocking medium.*

They stared at him with awe. "Come on, you guys, not you too. Please, I need you to keep treating me as you've always done."

Yori shrugged. "Sorry, Lev, you caught us off guard. Those were some serious Levigator worthy moves."

"Yeah, I've never seen anything like that. It's incredible!"

"Thank you, gentlemen. I believe our little experiment was successful." Akhen lifted a finger in admonition. "As Lev's security detail, I trust you to keep this to yourselves."

"Of course, but does he even need security anymore?"

"You know I need you for more than security. I don't have your experience. I still have a lot to learn," Lev assured them.

Yori nodded. "This new development has some serious tactical implications. Tark and I will give some thought to how we can harness these abilities in practical ways during an engagement. Honestly, Lev, we were beginning to worry that we wouldn't be able to protect you once the Breachers discover who you are. This could make all the difference. We may have some questions after we've had some time to talk strategy."

Akhen stepped in. "That's fine, gentlemen, but right now I need some time with Leviticus to discuss what we've learned today."

"Sure thing. Come on, Tark, I need to ice my knuckles."

Akhen turned to Lev. "I think that's enough training for today. Walk with me?"

"What's up?" Lev asked as he matched pace with his mentor.

"You're progressing very quickly now. I suspect we'll uncover new surprises every day. Events surrounding a Levigator tend to accelerate toward a goal only the Maker understands. I want to make sure all of your questions are answered before that happens."

"*All* of my questions? You've been hesitant to discuss certain matters."

"I know, Leviticus. It's not because I wished to withhold information. It's that I wasn't sure where, or how to begin. You've had some incredible experiences lately. I suspect not much would shock you at this point."

Lev snorted. "You mean like being able to spar blindfolded, learning I'm a nearly mythical Levigator, or seeing a rift to another world?"

Akhen smiled. "Yes, just like that. Actually, that may be a good place to start. You once asked me how I knew that the flood prophecy was real."

Lev gave him a sideways glance. "Are you truly ready to share that *classified* bit of information?"

Akhen nodded. "Having worked with you, I've come to understand something about the Levigators — something poorly understood previously. I now believe all Levigators shared your abilities. The analysts of the past just didn't have words to describe it.

"What we do know is that they possessed the ability to sense a thin space between worlds."

"Like the rift in the lower levels?"

"More like the potential for a rift. When a Levigator comes across a thin place, he or she can cause a rift to form between two worlds."

"Levigators made the rifts?" The thought stopped Lev in his tracks.

Akhen paused and waited for Lev to catch up. "Not made so much as enabled by their presence. Anyway, wherever a rift was formed, the Servators built a base to surround it. We have been both the protectors and beneficiaries of those rifts.

"I must deviate somewhat to help provide context. Over the years there have been many debates about free will in light of the Maker's omniscience. Questions about why and when the Maker decides to intervene. The existence of the rifts has shaped some of those discussions."

"What does free will have to do with anything?"

"It has everything to do with our current circumstances, if free will is leading to our demise."

"I don't understand."

Akhen chuckled. "Do any of us really? Think of it this way. If the Maker knows all things, then He knows what we will do before we do it. However, if we can freely choose our path then how can the Maker foreknow what we will do? How and why does he offer help in advance? These are foolish speculations. We know that we can choose our own path by the very fact that many reject the Maker and His ways. Why would the Maker allow such a thing, unless it were very important that we choose? The fact that the Maker intervenes through seers and by Levigators suggests a concern for us. Otherwise, why warn us of the perils of our ways and impending doom? These debates have grown into a theory. Keep in mind that this is merely conjecture."

"Unproven — I understand. What's this theory?"

Akhen hesitated. "First, let me ask you a question. What did you think of the kin world you saw in the garden?"

Lev's face screwed up in confusion. "It's difficult to describe. It seemed both familiar and alien at the same time. Other than the vegetation, I didn't notice any other signs of life. What sort of creatures live there, do you suppose?"

"You and I."

"I'm sorry, I don't think I heard that correctly. Are you saying that humans populated the world I saw?"

"Not just any humans — you, Tark, Yori, myself. Or, in the case of the particular world you witnessed, our ancestors."

"You're not making any sense, Akhen."

Akhen stopped and turned to look Lev in the eyes. "Leviticus, what you saw wasn't a different world. It was a parallel world."

"How can you know that?"

"Every rift on every base once gave us a view of humanity on the other side.

Servators on the kin worlds keep track of thin spaces in much the same way we do. It's a slow process, but we're able to share information through those rifts. Some worlds are more advanced than others. It's how we've gained the technological advantages we enjoy. What we've learned in those exchanges is that while histories may vary, too many things remain the same to be coincidence. We've seen records of the same people, places, and major events. On a few somewhat upsetting occasions, Servators have seen their counterparts."

At first Lev thought Akhen must be joking, but the earnestness in his eyes said otherwise.

"How can this be?"

"All I can offer you is a theory. Some of us believe that every time we're confronted by a life-altering decision, our choice gives birth to a parallel world. All possible choices continue, on other worlds — in a different timeline."

Lev shook his head in confusion. "That would mean billions of parallel worlds."

"More like an infinite number." Akhen corrected. "Every major decision we make affects other people. Decision points cascade across humanity."

"You're saying there's another me on a kin world somewhere making bad choices?"

Akhen laughed. "This is all speculation from a very *Servator* perspective. We like to imagine that the Maker is the ultimate analyst, compiling trends from a pristine data set. It helps us to grasp the concept of free will. All of our decisions or potential decisions are playing out as we speak, and the Maker is watching."

"That's quite a leap."

"I admit that this particular free will supposition has little to support it. The ancient texts are silent about such things. Who can truly know the mind of the Maker?"

Lev wasn't willing to let it go so easily. "If so many parallel worlds exist, why do we have so few rifts?"

"Ah! Now that's the proper question. Whatever speculation we may have about free will and parallel worlds, we can't ignore the rifts or the worlds they reveal. We suspect that kin worlds are those in which a large enough portion of society forms a corrupt consensus."

Lev frowned skeptically. "How did you come to that conclusion?"

"A Levigator arises when the world has great need, and those same

Levigators will ultimately discover thin spaces and form rifts. That connection exists for a reason. We have been working on the assumption that the Maker wants us to learn from those worlds — to change our path and avoid similar consequences. So, in answer to your question, we only find kin worlds that were — or are — on a similar path to our own."

"That doesn't prove a parallel world theory. Rifts could be an illusion, or maybe some kind of mirror." Lev argued.

Akhen nodded in agreement. "You may be right. Regardless, whatever the rifts are, we need to learn from them before it's too late."

"Too late? Too late for what?"

"Now that we have some context, we can directly address your question about the flood prophecy. On all of the kin worlds, one thing is consistent. The prophecy of the flood. Through the rift, you saw only vegetation. For a time, all anyone could see through that rift was water."

Lev was stunned. "A flood?"

"You asked me why I believed in the prophecy of the flood. I believe it because it's already happened. Many times. All of the kin worlds are silent now. There are no new technological wonders to learn. Our advantage against the Breachers is dwindling. A new rift hasn't opened in centuries."

Lev's eyebrows rose in surprise. "You hope I'll find new thin spaces." Lev suddenly understood why everyone was looking to him with anticipation.

Catching a glimpse of Akhen, Lev noticed his countenance fall.

"There's something else," Lev realized. "The secret that Chief Sentry Abrax wouldn't share. The thing you've been holding back. What is it?"

Akhen sighed. "Leviticus, few people know this among the Servators. It's not something we share. We don't want people to lose hope. I'll tell you, but you must repeat it to no one else. You're the Levigator — you need to know. Do I have your word?"

"You have my word. I won't repeat what you tell me."

"One other consistency appears among kin worlds. Just before the flood waters come, a new technology emerges. It gives the Breachers an advantage that leads to the destruction of the Servators. Once the Servators are removed, nothing remains to counter the influence of the Breachers. The fulfillment of prophecy occurs at that point."

"What could the Breachers possess that would lead to the destruction of the Servators?"

Akhen shifted uncomfortably and cleared his throat. "Facial recognition technology."

It took a moment for the words to sink in. Lev turned white and fell to his knees. "I helped design that algorithm!" He raked his hands through his hair. "I'm the herald of death," he whispered, "the world-ender."

"No, Leviticus, you're not. This is why I hesitated to tell you. You're not responsible for the choices of an entire world, nor how evil men use technology. You're the Levigator. The Maker chose you, because you're at the centre of this. You *will* fix this. You're here in this moment to discover a way out. You'll find it. I know you will."

Chapter 13

"This cannot stand! Bad enough the young Callan has bitten off more than he can chew, but now I have to deal with this Seri person. I can't believe Nico left his *assistant* in charge. Children are making decisions for an international empire!"

Halen lifted placating hands. "It was his legal right to choose a replacement."

Tenika's eyes bored into Halen. "Have you forgotten I was standing in the same room when Nico's lawvocate pointed that out? I'm not hard of hearing. Why didn't you raise an objection?"

"That's not the way these things work. I need time to search for legal precedent before I can launch a plausible challenge."

"And what have you found?" Tenika demanded.

Halen hung his head. "Nothing. The contract is very concise. It's free of any ambiguous language I might exploit."

"Then, what good are you?"

Halen glowered indignantly. "Nico's choice of replacement is for the duration of the investigation. Nico will retain ownership if convicted, but he'll be stripped of authority. Retroactive decisions will be invalidated. At that point, the board members will decide who runs the company."

Tenika threw her hands out in frustration and continued pacing. "Do you have any idea how much business we could lose by then? Without signing authority, I can't properly run this company. What have you learned about Ms. Quin?"

Sorting through his leather bag, Halen found the sheets of parchment he was seeking. "I've been conducting some research in that regard. Her references were impeccable, but I can't find any history for Seri Quin prior to her coming to work here. That may mean nothing if she grew up in another country."

"She's hiding something. If you'd seen how she took control of our conversation yesterday — how she manipulated the situation — those aren't traits typical of an assistant. Her confrontational agility and fearlessness reeks of street smarts. Keep digging. If we can provide the investigators with evidence that she has an unscrupulous past, perhaps we can get things back on track before Callan International crumbles under Nico's ineptitude."

"I will continue with my investigation."

"We need results, Halen."

"Legally speaking, our hands are tied."

"Then maybe it's time I called Garushe."

"Who is Garushe?"

"An old friend. Never mind, go find some answers. Leave me alone to think."

Tenika felt like striking the man as he slowly organized his files before returning them to his bag. Halen knew how to get under her skin. He also knew that she needed him. If it had been anyone else.... She hated needing people. *Come on, come on, leave already!* It took what seemed like another ten minutes for Halen to gather his things and slip out the door before Tenika was finally alone.

She moved to her favourite chair in front of the floor-to-ceiling glass that formed the two exterior walls of her corner office. It provided a spectacular view of the sea that she usually found soothing. A headache had been building behind her eyes and she rubbed her temples, trying to massage it away.

How had this happened? Twelve years of careful planning was beginning to unravel. She couldn't afford to be reckless now. She knew Halen was right, but it went against her nature. She longed for the day when she could be her true self again. That's what this was really about.

When Seri stood up to her, Tenika had almost lost control. She recognized the challenge in Seri's actions and a darkness in Tenika screamed for her to retaliate. When she said Seri had street smarts, that wasn't precisely what she had meant. It was more like she recognized herself in Seri's rash confidence.

Memories of a different place and time flooded her. She had grown up on the streets of Jaihuwan. It was a brutal existence, but she had learned how to survive. No one living on the streets is strong enough on their own — least of all a young girl. She eventually joined up with one of the local gangs and started to make a name for herself. At first, it was picking pockets. Later, she began running cons.

Tenika learned early on that her view of the world was skewed. She didn't have compassion for others and every thought was calculated to achieve a goal. Others thought her cruel, but she was just being efficient. It served her well. As the intrigues increased in complexity, the payouts grew larger. The gang leader, Tibor, provided people and resources. In the beginning he was heavily involved in the planning. Over time, he couldn't keep up with the intricacies of Tenika's schemes and so he left her to run the show on her own. As long as she brought results, he left her alone. The power was intoxicating.

Tibor was a soft fleshy man with bad teeth and foul breath. He'd made romantic overtures at times, but Tenika always responded coldly. She found him revolting. To be fair, she wasn't interested in a relationship with anyone. She didn't understand the concept of love — it made no sense to her.

Eventually Tibor realized that she wasn't playing hard-to-get and he took offence. It hardly mattered to Tenika what he thought, but apparently it mattered a lot to Tibor. He chose to retaliate with petty vindictiveness by interfering with one of her operations and she lost her temper. That was an understatement. She vented her rage with fists and knives until he stopped moving. It was the first life she had taken, but not the last. Tibor's second-in-command came across the scene while Tenika stood over the body.

She had only ever called him Tibor. She didn't even know he had a last name. Tenika remembered the shock when she learned he was the son of Laki Shung. Laki was Chief of the largest criminal organization in Jaihuwan. Tibor was a disappointment to the family and his father held no love for him, but one did not murder a member of the Shung family without consequence. Tenika had avoided the kill squads for several weeks, but she couldn't avoid them indefinitely. She had to flee Jaihuwan. Life on the run weighed on her and Laki's reach was long. After two years, she contacted him by tote-comm in the hope of settling their differences. Laki named an outrageous sum of money and granted her fifteen years to accumulate it. She wasn't allowed within the borders of Jaihuwan for the duration. If she couldn't deliver the sum by the fifteenth year on the anniversary of Tibor's death, Laki would hunt her down to avenge his son's death. She had wondered about the proposition, but learned that Laki had many illegitimate children. Tibor had been an embarrassment and no tears were shed for the loss. However, others would expect Laki to retaliate. So he did it in a way that would give time for people to forget about Tibor while he gained a huge payout. She suspected Laki was as indifferent as she was. It was how she knew he would honour his deal.

She had accepted the agreement. Really, she had no choice and was tired of looking over her shoulder all the time. Tenika had gathered a substantial amount of money from her Jaihuwan operations and pilfered Tibor's accounts before she left. With that seed money, she planned to accumulate the price of her freedom. She bought passage on a large seagoing vessel to the furthest destination she could find. It was sailing under the flag of Callan International, destination Denmount, Caralithica. The journey was long. She had ample time to discover the extent of Callan International's ventures. The wheels of her mind turning throughout the voyage.

Much had changed since then and she was close to achieving her freedom. In three more years, she could begin to live without a target on her back, barring further interference. History was repeating itself. Over a decade ago, Nico's father had come close to interrupting her well-laid plans. Now, the son was threatening to do so again. What was with the Callan family? They didn't seem to know when to leave well enough alone. Her anger spiked again, shooting a stabbing pain behind her eyes. *Stop it, Tenika.* Bottling her rage was an ongoing battle. For someone who prized calculated risk, losing control - like she had with Tibor - was terrifying. *I won't risk everything in a moment of rage. I will not!* Tenika took some calming breaths and turned her thoughts to things she could do something about. If she couldn't regain signing authority for the company, she would have to find a way to influence decisions about who won lucrative Callan International contracts.

Tenika had built up an enviable enterprise maintaining the vast Callan transportation fleet. Shortly after she arrived in Denmount, she had used her seed money to finance a number of repair shops under a pseudonym. She'd grown those businesses to the point where they could maintain and repair any vessel, whether land, air, or seafaring. Tenika made sure that Callan International contracts were awarded to her own facilities under predefined criteria. When a vessel came in for maintenance, her people would strip it of valuable parts and replace them with inferior copies. It meant that the vessels often came back for repairs, but Tenika's shops had a generous warranty that made it appear as though they stood behind their work. Even if they replaced a cheap part more than once, they still made money on the higher quality originals. Tenika kept a close eye on the fleet maintenance records. She made sure that once a vessel had passed through her facilities, it continued on to more reputable depots for future repairs. Eventually that vessel would have enough newer parts to warrant another visit to her own facilities. Callan International had thousands of transport vehicles, enough to continue bringing in profits for decades. She'd move on long before that well dried up. Of course, that all depended on her ability to manipulate the repair orders.

Maintenance contracts weren't Tenika's only income stream. The founder, Nes Callan, had been an innovator who continually diversified the company's holdings. Nes had invested heavily into research and development, resulting in some incredible advancements. Tenika's inside information had allowed her to invest her profits into several ventures that had proven very successful.

When all was said and done, she could live her life in comfort as a legitimate businesswoman. It was a pleasant dream, but before that could happen, she had to pay the price required by Laki. She had three years left to achieve that goal. It was just enough time — barely. If she didn't regain signing authority soon, it would set her back months.

She needed to get Nico out of the way. The original plan had been to generate just enough suspicion to drag out an investigation for a few years. It would allow Tenika to continue in her role as Nico's proxy until she had earned enough to pay Laki. She would happily step down as head of the company at that point. It should have worked, but neither she nor Halen had anticipated Nico would name someone else as his proxy. She had to find a way to add fuel to the fire of Nico's investigation.

It seemed unlikely Halen would find a solution, so it was time to consider other methods — which meant contacting Bode Garushe. He was actually Laki's man, sent to keep an eye on Tenika. Laki wanted Tenika to know that he could find her anywhere. It was also a way for him to make sure she was generating the agreed upon sum. Tenika met with Garushe on occasion to report on her holdings. Playing games with her executioner was pointless, so she chose to be transparent in her dealings with him. She had even employed his services on occasion. Garushe was happy for the extra source of revenue and assured her that Laki had given him permission to assist her in efforts that would ensure she accumulated her life price. This situation certainly qualified. She just needed to figure out how best to use his talents.

Her headache eased somewhat. Having a singular focus was a relief from the juggling of her normal routine. *Let's see what Garushe can do. If it doesn't work — well, it wouldn't be the first time I had to get my own hands dirty.*

Chapter 14

"Mother, what happened yesterday? I was still in Tenika's office and she walked right in on me while I was sitting in her chair!"

"I'm sorry, Kayla.."

"It's Seri!"

"I'm not even in the same room with you and we're talking over a secure Q-view connection. No one can hear us."

"That's not the point and you know it." Seri heard a distinctly irritated sigh at the other end of the connection.

"I'm truly sorry about failing to warn you, Seri. Halen was sharing his professional opinion when Tenika leaned over and whispered something into his ear. He nodded and Tenika asked to be excused for a moment. Halen wanted to see some purchase orders and the records of complaint, so we went to the office. I assumed Tenika had gone to relieve herself. It was almost an hour before I realized Tenika still hadn't returned. I thought perhaps she had gone to inspect the assembly line where the fault took place, or to talk to the crew lead. Halen and Tenika arrived together — how was I to know she would abandon him to find his own way back? He didn't seem concerned when she whispered in his ear. It wasn't until he asked for a ride that I realized what had occurred, and by that time it was far too late to do anything about it. Besides, you've been trained to handle unforeseen circumstances. What happened?"

"Actually, I was able to gain the upper-hand on her little attempt at subversion earlier in the day. It felt good." Seri relished the memory.

"I knew you would be fine. You were never in any danger. The analysts were successful at implementing the tokens you requested. They complimented your mapping technique. All but one of your plots were usable without correcting for interference."

Seri was surprised. She was sure that in her haste, she had messed up more than one. "Which one was a problem?"

"The ceiling tile location above Halen's desk. That was quick thinking, by the way. Eventually they were able to make it work. I've dedicated analysts to monitor in real-time around the clock, but it's standard practice to record the sessions. I'm sending the command codes so you have access to review them at your leisure. Tenika has already incriminated herself, by the way. Not for a specific act, but she mentioned an associate by the name of Garushe. I had the analysts check on that name. We don't yet know if this is the same person, but a few years after the death of Nes Callan, a person of interest arrived in Denmount and never left. He works for Laki Shung, chief of the largest criminal organization in Jaihuwan. Laki Shung has strong ties to the Breachers. We've been keeping an eye on Bode Garushe, but so far we haven't discovered any direct involvement with the Breachers here in Caralithica.

"Seri, if this is the same Garushe, we need to tread carefully. He's a very dangerous man and if Tenika knows him, we have to reconsider everything we thought we knew about her. We already knew that Qas Drugarish...."

Seri heard her mother choke on that hated name. Qas was the Sicari assassin who had murdered her father. Blind fury erupted in Seri's mind every time the name was uttered.

Her mother regained composure and continued. "We knew someone within Callan International contracted a Sicari assassin to murder Nico's parents. It had to be someone high in the chain of command. If Tenika is working with Garushe, who has ties with the Breachers, we may have found the missing piece of the puzzle. We need to keep a close eye on this development. Ideally, we'd like solid proof that Tenika was involved in the doctored ledger as well as evidence she's plotting with a known Breacher associate."

"Thank you, Mother, I wouldn't be at all surprised. Tenika has been actively trying to prevent Nico from controlling his birthright. When I put her in her place the other day, you should have seen the fury in her eyes. I almost jumped into a warkata stance. A darkness was simmering just below the surface."

"Be careful around her. I don't like this. If she's somehow involved with Qas Drugarish...."

Seri wished her mother had given this update in person. She wanted to give her a hug. "I'll be careful. We may finally have a lead on that murderer. He needs to be brought to justice and we need closure. I'll go through the recordings and see if anything jumps out at me."

"You do that. I'll call you tomorrow."

As soon as her mother disconnected, Seri used the command codes to gain access to the spy tokens she'd placed. She would review the recordings later. Right now she wanted to check on the coverage of the locations she'd mapped.

She checked Halen's office first, curious about the ceiling tile token. She selected it and was rewarded with a clear view of Halen's desktop. He wasn't in the office, but a piece of paper lay on his desktop. She zoomed in to read it. It was just a draft of a liability clause he was working on. Disappointed, she switched to the other tokens. They did a reasonable job of covering the room. She could hear Halen's assistant talking to someone in the outer office. Everything seemed to be in order and nothing interesting was happening, so she moved on to check the tokens in Tenika's office.

She tried the view token hidden in the clock above the door. Seri could see Tenika's face clearly. She was talking on her tote-comm and she looked nervous. Seri quickly turned on the sound tokens.

"No ... this isn't like the last time. I need a different kind of help. No, Bode, we can't talk about this over the phone, we need to meet in person."

Tenika sounds frustrated, and she said Bode! It was definitely Bode Garushe. "Gotcha." Seri whispered. She turned up the volume, but could only make out one side of the conversation.

"I've already told you.... Look, are you willing to help me or not? I'll make it worth your while — how much? That's insane! Alright, alright Where do you want to meet?" Tenika pulled out a piece of parchment and a writing instrument. Seri quickly enabled the overhead view tokens hidden in the lamps and zoomed in on the parchment as Tenika wrote — 157 Dockside Road, Berth eleven. Then she wrote — tomorrow, third watch. Tenika disconnected, folded up the note and placed it in her hand bag.

"Early evening. That doesn't give us much time," Seri muttered. "Mother will need to send some rangers to place tokens and scout the area."

She was about to contact Cello, but Tenika picked up her tote-comm to make another call.

"Halen? I need you to bring the ledger to my office — now please..." Tenika rolled her eyes. "I'm well aware of the risk. I have a more secure location in mind... Enough! I'm not asking you, I'm telling you. Have it here within the next ten minutes... Well, drop what you're doing and go get it. I have to take care of this within the hour. Forget my office then, bring it to my parking space as quickly as you can. I'll be waiting in my ground transport." Tenika disconnected and leaned back in her chair. She took a few deep breaths, then leaned forward, opened the desk drawer, and snatched up her keys.

"The ledger," Seri gasped. It was here in the building all along, but now it was about to be moved.

Tenika had grabbed her cloak and her hand bag and was already heading out her office door before Seri remembered the tracker token she'd placed on Tenika's keys. *I can follow her.* Seri paused, recalling how her impulsiveness had cost her in the past. Seri shook her head. This was different — she had nothing to prove. This time it was a matter of limited resources and opportunity. This time no one else would suffer the consequences of any mistakes she might make.

Seri activated her wrist Q-view and contacted her mother directly. "Mother, I don't have time to explain in detail. You were right, Tenika *is* dealing with Bode Garushe. They've arranged to meet tomorrow evening. I need you to send some rangers to place spy tokens. Tenika also asked Halen to bring her the ledger. They're all working together. She's planning to move the ledger to a secure location, right now. I have to follow her... We're out of time and you don't have enough people with you here in Denmount... You have to trust me. I forgot to mention that I placed a tracker token on her ground transport keys when I was in her office... I know, I'm sorry, but I'm sending it now. My wrist Q-view will provide our location if something goes wrong... Don't worry, I'll just follow at a safe distance and report in... Okay, I've got to go. Talk soon."

Seri grabbed her bag. "Marret, I need to leave for a few hours. If something comes up you can reach me on my tote-comm. Don't call unless it's urgent. I'll let you know when I'm on my way back."

Seri thanked the Maker that she was able to work from Nico's office. He had a private exit to a personal garage where a ground transport was reserved for his use. It allowed him to come and go with some privacy. She needed that secrecy now. Grabbing her own keys, she rushed to the exit. *I have you now Tenika.*

Chapter 15

Selica had arrived early for the second day in a row. She wanted to complete her chores for the bake tent before Kade arrived so they could slip away somewhere more private to talk. *Where is he? I've been kneading dough for longer than normal. People are going to start wondering why I'm still here.* She was nervous. Kade didn't show up yesterday and he was late again today. At least she hoped it was just that he was late. They didn't have a lot of time left to make her escape plan work. She needed to talk to him soon.

The tent flap rustled and Selica glanced up for the hundredth time. It was only Pol, one of the regular customers. He was a giant of a man, who greeted everyone with a hearty laugh and sometimes an uncomfortable bear hug. Pol immediately headed for the pastry display, a testament to the quality of the baked goods. The owners treated Pol like royalty, always adding a little something extra to his order for free. The man was hard to miss and the owners had made him into a walking advertisement, providing him with free tunics bearing the bakery name. Selica thought it shameful the way they took advantage of him, but Pol didn't seem to mind.

Selica sighed and turned her attention back to the dough she was braiding. In her distraction, it had become a malformed lump. Now she had to start over. *Kade where are —* "Ah!" She nearly leaped out of her skin as a hand settled on her shoulder.

"Woah — a little jumpy today?"

"Kade! don't sneak up on me like that."

"I wasn't sneaking."

"Then how did you get in here without me noticing?"

"I entered behind that friendly mountain over there. You probably couldn't see me in his shadow." Kade was smiling.

Selica swatted his hands away as he tried to pull her into a hug and then, a moment later, wrapped her arms around him anyway. "Where were you?" She whispered in his ear. "I was worried sick."

"I'm sorry, they rearranged the training schedule yesterday. I came straight here after we finished, but you'd already left."

"So, why were you late today?" Selica's brows knitted in frustration.

"That's actually your fault."

"My fault? How is it my fault?"

"Your suggestion that I offer to pick something up for Decar whenever I come here worked a little too well. Do you remember those sweet rolls you sent back with me? Decar was going on about how they were just like ones his grandmother used to make. He kept offering bites for people to try — sharing a bit of his culture, I suppose."

"So? I'll bag up some more, what does that have to do with your tardiness?" Selica was losing patience. They didn't have time for this.

"Well, when I offered to pick something up for Decar today, I found myself surrounded by co-workers with requests of their own. It took a while."

"Kade, you're supposed to be keeping a low profile," she hissed.

"What was I supposed to do? Wouldn't it seem more suspicious if I refused?"

Selica rolled her eyes.

"Um, here's a list." Kade sheepishly handed her a slip of parchment with the requested items.

She snatched it from his hand with a glare and stomped over to the pastry counter. "Tanis, can you bag these up for me? I'll be back in a bit to pick them up along with the usual order of bread."

Tanis smiled. "A treat for the children?"

Selica glanced back at Kade. "Yes, the children."

She knew she wasn't being fair. She was only lashing out because of her worry for Kade and the anxiousness she was feeling about her plans. She quickly made her way back, grabbing Kade's hand to lead him out into the bazaar.

"Where are we going?"

Selica spun in a circle looking for a suitable spot. "I'm not sure. We need to find a place where we won't be disturbed."

Kade grimaced as if he'd just swallowed something distasteful. "I can't believe I'm saying this, but I think I know the perfect spot."

"Judging by the look on your face, I'm not sure if *perfect* is the word you're looking for. Forget it, we don't have time, lead on."

Kade wove his way through the crowd with Selica in tow, heading to the edge of the bazaar. She looked over her shoulder, repeatedly checking to see if anyone was following. With all of the twists and turns Kade was making, she became less concerned.

"Almost there," Kade announced.

"What's that smell?" She needn't have asked. The stench of the midden hit her like a team of oxen as they rounded the last corner and she saw for herself.

Her eyes started watering and she coughed twice before she could speak. "Please, tell me you didn't have romance in mind when you brought me here."

Now it was Kade's turn to roll his eyes. "Decar brought me here once when he needed to speak to me in private. He said no one came here unless they absolutely had to."

Selica snorted. She couldn't deny the logic in that, but how was she going to explain returning from the bakery smelling like a decomposing carcass? She gave her head a shake. They had their moment of privacy and they needed to talk this though.

"What did Decar need to talk to you about?"

"He was giving me fair warning that he would be kissing up to the new boss. He made it clear that he wouldn't be covering for me or keeping any secrets from the Second Anarch. He won't be joining us in any future plotting. He seemed terrified of Trantor."

"Okay, so we steer clear of Decar from now on. I don't blame him though, Kenric has a well-earned reputation and Decar has his family to worry about. We don't need his help anyway."

Kade lowered his voice. "So, you have a plan?"

"I do, it's risky, but we may never get a better chance."

"Selica, I know you've been looking for a way out for years. You've shot down every suggestion I've ever made on the topic, having already considered and discarded it previously. If you think we have a real opportunity after all this time — count me in. Just tell me what to do."

"You might not be so eager when you hear what's involved."

"Anything is better than death. I'm running out of time and my life will be forfeited once Kenric's computational engineers are up to speed."

Selica hesitated, knowing how Kade would react. "It involves heights."

Kade paled.

"We'll have ropes for safety," she added hastily.

Selica explained about the need to cross from the roof to the top of the compound wall and then descend into the alley.

"Selica, I can't make a jump like that! It will be hard enough looking down."

"We won't be jumping. I tied a rock to a ball of twine and lowered it over the edge of the roof to the ground. I measured that length and accounted for the distance to the wall plus a little extra. Using those measurements, I've been able to manufacture a rope ladder that's long enough to reach from the rooftop across to the wall and down to the ground on the other side. All you need to worry about is getting over the parapet on the roof to start down the ladder."

"How does that get us over the wall?"

"That's the part I'm not sure of. We'll have to descend from the roof to a point lower than the top of the adjacent compound wall for a start. Then, with a free arm and leg, push off of the building and grab the top of the wall as we swing towards it. I've made us some belts that we can clip to the ladder. We'll need free hands to pull ourselves to the top of the wall. We don't want to lose the ladder in the process."

"What if we can't reach the wall, or slip while trying?"

"That's what the belt is for. As long as we're attached to the ropes, the worst we should have to deal with is a bruise from swinging back against the building. As for the distance, it's only four cubits. You're probably tall enough that if you just leaned over, you could touch the wall."

Kade looked dubious. "That's fine for me, but what about you?"

Selica shrugged. "I'll go first. If I can make it, then it will be no problem for you."

"What if you can't?"

"If I need help, you can join me on the ladder and we'll make it work together. Assuming I'm able to make it on my own, I'll straddle the wall, pull

the ladder up and throw it into the alley. I'll give the rope a few tugs to let you know when I'm safely down the other side. After that, you'll have to pull it back up and repeat the process for yourself."

"I don't know how to feel about this, Selica. It's not like you to consider something so dangerous and now you seem to be in a hurry. I hope you're not rushing things just because I'm running out of time. You're not in the spotlight anymore. Villecrest is dead and Kenric doesn't seem to know you exist. For the first time in your life, you have a real chance at freedom. I don't want you risking that for me."

The desperation in his eyes almost broke her resolve. She hated herself for it, but that same thought had briefly crossed her mind. Just as quickly, she realized that she didn't want to be alone anymore. What was the point of freedom at the cost of love? Seeing the concern on his face made her love him all the more. "Listen, Kade, if I've seemed overly cautious in the past, it's because the risks always heavily outweighed the chance of success. This time it's different."

Kade nodded for her to continue.

"The festival."

Kade lifted his palms face up and shrugged.

"The festival, you know, the gathering of the anarchs."

"Oh! I just assumed that wasn't going to happen now that Villecrest is dead."

"It's definitely happening — that means a compound filled with entitled anarchs, their servants, and their bodyguards. Security personnel will be bickering over jurisdiction and servants will be rushing around trying to please several masters. Entertainment will be sprouting up in inconvenient locations. The townsfolk will fill the street in front of the compound gates, hoping selling their wares..."

Kade was nodding now as he took up the refrain. "...add some drunken revelry and we have more distraction than we could ever have hoped for. Selica, this is it!"

"Exactly. An event like this will never occur here again in our lifetime. I honestly don't know how Villecrest managed it. A lowly Third Anarch should never have been allowed to host the gathering in the first place. Regardless, I'm not about to look a gift horse in the mouth. We have no choice. We have to take this chance — the timing couldn't be better."

"I agree. When does the festival take place?"

"We have nine days left to plan. The first thing you need to know is that festivals require lots of food. When a large meal is prepared, the kitchens always ask for volunteers. You should find a sign-up sheet on the posting board near the kitchens. You need to get your name on that list. Pray that they're still looking for help. I had hoped to tell you sooner, but...."

Kade dropped his head. "I'm so sorry, Selica, I didn't realize."

"As you've said, you couldn't do a lot about it." Selica considered the roles Kade might volunteer for. "Do you know how to butcher an animal?"

"Our family had some pretty lean years. Sometimes hunting was our only source of food. I wouldn't pass as a butcher, but I can field dress an animal."

"That should be enough. If you're offered a choice, see if you can get on the list for meat preparation. That would be ideal, because you'll need access to the animal pens at the back of the kitchens for this plan to work. Failing that, any other food preparation should put you in the vicinity. If you have to settle for serving, hopefully you can find an excuse to enter the kitchens."

Selica paused and smiled. Kade was smiling too. They had talked about this moment for so long and now it was finally going to happen. They both stepped into an embrace at the same time.

Selica could feel his grin against her cheek before he spoke. "I knew this was a romantic spot."

She burst out in laughter, then began coughing as she was overcome by the fumes once again. "If this works out, I may let you take me to the fishmonger on our next date." She gave him one more squeeze before filling him in on the rest of her plan.

Chapter 16

Lev stared through the rift to the kin world beyond. This was his first return to the place that marked him as a Levigator. As he stood there, the rift called to him in some strange fashion. It felt both familiar and alien.

He had come seeking answers. Akhen thought he might find them here. "No one knows more about the histories than Hemish Zo." Akhen had said. So here he stood, next to the man who served as both rift keeper and historian, unsure what questions to ask.

"I'm so pleased you've come to visit, Levigator. How may I help you?" The old man's spine curved with age. A cataract clouded his left eye which seemed to gaze into the distance. His good eye was locked onto Leviticus.

"I have questions about thin spaces and Levigators. Akhen tells me you're the best source of information on those topics."

Hemish beamed at the praise. "Yes, yes, I have spent my whole life studying the histories. It's the dream of every historian to one day share those records with a Levigator. I can hardly believe the honour has fallen to me. Why, the world hasn't seen a Levigator..."

"...for over seventeen hundred years. Yes, I know."

Hemish reddened. "Apologies, Levigator."

Lev didn't bother trying to dissuade use of the title any longer. He was the Levigator. Too much had happened to deny it any longer. He needed to get used to the idea, uncomfortable though it may be. "Tell me about the previous

Levigator."

"Ah! That would be Rushoen Nu Lon. Born in Arapanus, he spent most of his final days roaming the earth. He was obsessed with his search for thin spaces."

"Akhen mentioned that Levigators are responsible for the rifts."

"Indeed, but only those of sufficient ability. Rushoen was particularly gifted. The highest ranked of all previous Levigators — at least since we started standardized testing. Levigators may have been stronger prior to those records, but we have no way of knowing."

"What were his test scores?"

"Rushoen could locate twenty tokens in ten seconds. Our own Akhen Hor has half that score, but he's not a Levigator. I believe you recently surpassed him. May I ask what your score is now?"

"When Akhen tested me last week, I scored twenty-four in ten seconds. I suspect that number has increased."

Hemish gasped and his eyes grew large as a smile spread across his face. "Then, I must tell you everything I know about the thin spaces. You most certainly have the ability within you to find and open them."

Lev shrugged. "I understand new rifts may provide answers and technology."

"That is correct, Levigator. You must also know that we're losing our advantage to the Breachers and if we don't turn the tide soon…"

"…that tide will wash right over us." Lev finished.

Hemish grimaced and slapped his hands against his thighs. "It's not too late."

Lev held his hand palm up, gesturing for Hemish to continue.

"Rushoen found more thin spaces than anyone in history. The knowledge we gained allowed us to restrict the Breachers for many years. It ushered in a golden era for the Servators. Sad to say, all of the worlds Rushoen located are silent now. Curiously, the least technologically advanced worlds lasted the longest.

"If we're to have any hope of regaining an advantage, you must find many more thin spaces. Only a few will have new technology to share. However, even the less advanced worlds will have histories that may provide useful clues about preventing disaster. It takes time to initiate contact and find people on those worlds who could help."

Lev rubbed the back of his neck as he considered the monumental task before him. "How are these rifts formed? I thought a Levigator created them, but a high-tech archway is surrounding this rift."

Hemish shook his head. "Levigators don't actually create rifts. It's more accurate to say that they find thin spaces. In the past it was only providence that allowed a rift to form. When powerful Levigators from each world felt drawn to the thin space, their close proximity and simultaneous observance of the space allowed the worlds to bleed into each other. We don't know why. One of those chance meetings found the people who gave us the quantum technology that we use on a daily basis.

"Eventually we realized that when any two highly rated analysts are observing the same space at the same time from either side of a thin space, a rift can form. An analyst isn't powerful enough to find a thin space, but they can tell when someone of equal ability is in the vicinity of a known thin space. To increase the odds of opening a rift, we began leaving highly rated analysts at each location discovered by the Levigator. Constant observance creates a sort of translucence from once side — a further thinning. If someone of sufficient ability from the other side happens by, the probability increases that they'll notice the thin space without requiring the presence of a Levigator. The potential for a rift to form multiplies under those circumstances. We've made some advances since those days. Take this arch for instance. It provides a mechanical means to observe the thin space from our world. It allows us to maintain that translucence without the presence of powerful analysts or a Levigator. It allows the rift to open automatically when someone with sufficient ability draws near from the other side . This is a much more efficient process and allowed Rushoen to move on as soon as he marked a thin space. It's one of the reasons for the volume of his success.

"Unfortunately, we never found a way to use the technology to locate thin spaces in the first place. For that we still require a Levigator. I can provide you with a template for creating an arch so you can produce one whenever you find a thin space. We send rangers to secure any arch placed at a thin space. Where possible, we build a bunker around it and cover it with earth to create an artificial hill.

"When a rift finally forms, we're able to gather coordinates and send a token to the other side. We usually choose something to attract attention and mark the spot. This particular arch used a bright red flower."

"The one I picked." Lev guessed.

"Yes. We haven't bothered replacing the token since that kin world has been silent for hundreds of years. We keep it open on our side to monitor, just in case, but we hold little hope that anything will change. If nothing else, it's a reminder of what we stand to lose."

"Okay, so how do I locate a rift?"

"I have a few thoughts on that, but for now, why don't you tell me what you sense about the rift in front of you?"

Lev fell into pattern sight and focused on the rift. "The particles surrounding the rift appear to be paired off. For each particle from this world, another particle from the kin world remains in close proximity." Lev cocked his head and turned his ear toward the rift as if to listen. "The particles from this world seem to be oscillating at a different frequency than those from the kin world. It's creating a discordance. Strange...."

"What is it?"

"I can't hear anything with my ears, but to my mind, that discordance is creating the equivalent of a low throbbing rumble. I wonder how I didn't notice it before. It's quite loud."

Lev turned around to look in the opposite direction from the rift. "Particles from the kin world dissipate as they exit into our space. From here it looks as though they travel for miles. I'll be right back." Lev walked out of the room and jogged to the end of the hall and back. "I can still hear the dispersed particles as I move away from the rift. The throbbing tapers to a steady whine as they spread apart, but the feel of those foreign particles remains. It's unmistakable."

Hemish was nodding vigorously. "It's as I suspected. Someone like yourself with sufficient ability can sense a thin space from a distance. The particles shouldn't be flowing freely, but I suspect some would still bleed through. According to the histories, Levigators feel drawn in various ways to locations where thin spaces exist. Your description is the first to identify a sound. The experience may be different for each Levigator. On the other hand, you now score higher than any Levigator since testing began, so perhaps their perceptions weren't refined enough to see what you see — or hear."

Lev considered What Hemish was saying. "I'll test your theory when I leave.

It would be good to have an idea how close I actually need to be before I notice one of these things."

"Rushoen Nu Lon claimed he could sense a thin space within ten leagues. I know that he became more sensitive over time. If you're unable to achieve the same immediately, you should notice improvement eventually."

Leviticus gestured to the world around them. "If ten leagues is the best I can hope for, locating new thin spaces will be like finding needles in haystacks! I don't have time to walk across the land in a ten-league grid pattern trusting to chance. Do the histories reveal any other clues that would help refine the search?"

Hemish was grinning ear to ear. "I told you I had a few thoughts on the matter. Follow me." Hemish led Leviticus to the corner of the room where a globe sat on a pedestal. "I've spent a number of years cataloguing the rifts and looking for patterns. After decades of dead ends, I found something."

Hemish stared expectantly, but Lev just shrugged, not knowing what to look for.

"If you examine this globe, you'll see that I've inscribed evenly spaced lines from pole to pole around the globe. A second set of evenly spaced rings begins with the circumference of the world at the equator. Subsequent rings get smaller as they move toward each pole. You will think these to be the typical navigational lines common to globes everywhere, but they're not"

Lev wished the man would get to the point. "So what's different about these lines?"

"It's a grid divisible by twelve. We've discovered twenty-seven rifts so far, each near an intersection on this grid."

Lev raised an eyebrow in doubt.

Hemish reddened and hastened to add, "I know the sample size is too small to reach a definitive conclusion. We've never been able to test it before, but now...."

Lev nodded. "At least it gives me a place to start. It won't take long to test. Do you have the coordinates for these intersections?"

"I can send them to your Q-view along with a template for an arch."

"Actually, I would prefer if you materialize one for me a few times, so I can observe."

"Right! Akhen mentioned this ability. Fascinating! When would you like to do this?

"Do you have time right now?"

"Certainly, Levigator." Hemish fiddled with his Q-view for a few moments and then looked up at Leviticus. "Are you ready, Levigator?"

"Yes, please proceed."

The arch was complex and it took Lev fifteen builds before he had it memorized.

"I think I have it now." Lev disassembled the arch that Hemish had initiated and then rematerialized it himself. "Do you have a way to test if an arch is functioning correctly?"

Hemish moved to the side of the arch and pressed a button. A viewscreen embedded into the face of the arch illuminated and began running through a diagnostic checklist.

"It appears to be functioning correctly. The arch is detecting particles from the rift behind us." Hemish shook his head, mouth hanging open in astonishment. "You memorized that entire template and initiated it without the QPN? Astonishing! If you create these arches on your own, you'll need to send the coordinates to us here, since the QPN won't have a record." Hemish tapped on a module at the top of the arch. "Use your Q-view to map coordinates to this receiver module. Then we should be able to connect." Hemish tapped a few more commands into his wrist Q-view. "I've sent you the grid coordinates."

"I'm not sure when I'll be able to begin the search. I have a few things to take care of first. Am I correct in assuming that if I locate a thin space, I can send the coordinates to you to handle the details?"

"Yes, Levigator! We have been preparing for such an opportunity for centuries. I can gather the appropriate teams. We will be ready."

"One more thing, Hemish... Did Rushoen by any chance keep a journal? If so, I would very much like to read it."

"As a matter of fact, he left several. I can compile the more interesting entries if you wish."

"That would be very helpful, thank you."

"Could I ask one favour in return, Levigator?"

"What can I do for you, Hemish?"

"The passages I have in mind are ones with obscure meaning that continue to elude us. If you have any insight, it would do an old man good to have a few more mysteries answered before leaving this life."

Leviticus smiled, "You have my word."

94

Chapter 17

Halen dropped into his office chair as he tried to catch his breath. He hadn't been running, but walking at a fast clip made him feel as though he had. He was out of shape. *I should cut back on the sweet rolls.*

He set the ledger on his desk and stared at it with a grimace. He should never have let Tenika talk him into helping her all of these years, but he was a greedy man and she understood his weaknesses. The pay was very good and she had kept her word to bring him along as she rose through the ranks. That didn't mean he trusted her. The irony that she held her position largely because of his legal manipulations galled him at times. Yet he had to admit that he didn't have the creativity to come up with the audacious schemes that got them both where they were.

He needed her more than she needed him and he wasn't so foolish to believe she would stand up for him if push came to shove. Tenika was cold and calculating. She would give him up in a heartbeat if it served her purposes. He had agreed to help doctor this ledger because it was in both of their interests, but had insisted that he be the keeper. It gave him some leverage. Since Nico had taken his place at the head of Callan International, Tenika had grown increasingly irrational. This latest demand was a perfect example. He had been off-site at a meeting to finalize a new sea-transport maintenance contract between Callan International and one of Tenika's repair companies. It was a major income stream for her and she'd put it at risk when she demanded he drop everything and attend her. These kinds of contract renewals didn't happen very often. It was almost as if she'd forgotten all about it. It was very unlike her.

Adding insult to injury, she had commanded him like a dog and he responded like one. He wasn't sure who he was angrier at, Tenika or himself.

Since he kept the ledger at a different location, he'd had to make a detour before returning to Callan headquarters. It had taken longer than expected and she was probably fuming as she waited, but he couldn't bring it directly to her. If she was going to take away his leverage, he needed an insurance policy.

For over a decade, Halen carefully recorded everything he had done at Tenika's command. Every legal manipulation, every falsified record, every self-serving contract and shady deal was penned in tiny script on a single sheet of parchment. If anyone in authority set eyes on it, both he and Tenika would be locked away for a very long time. He never intended for it to see the light of day, but if Tenika ever threw him to the lions, he intended to drag her down with him.

Unfortunately, this latest development caught him off guard. He hadn't expected her to take the ledger from him. Why would she do that? She said she was taking it to a secure place, but she knew he already had it in a safe place. If Tenika didn't trust him anymore, then he was in a precarious position. Halen found it difficult to imagine what would prompt Tenika to break faith, but it couldn't be good. Worse than that, she was keeping him in the dark about the reasons for her actions. It unsettled him more than he would have believed.

Opening his desk drawer, he removed a false bottom and took out one of three copies he'd made containing incriminating evidence. He folded the parchment and set it on his desktop where he stared at it with dread. It would destroy Tenika, but it was also an admission of his own guilt. If he did this, he couldn't take it back, but what else could he do? Tenika was clever. If she decided to craft a narrative framing him for doctoring the ledger, it would be convincing. His only recourse would be to have some proof hidden within the ledger itself so the incriminating evidence would be there when he needed to defend himself. If the evidence remained with the ledger, then no one could claim it was planted after the fact. It wouldn't sound like he was making desperate claims if the evidence was a pre-existing part of the ledger.

He had originally planned to conceal the evidence by gluing it between the last page of the ledger and the leather cover. Or, perhaps he would split the leather cover itself and glue it between the two halves. As time went on and he added more misdeeds to the document, he'd never gotten around to concealing it. Now he was out of time. He inspected the ledger looking for options, but they eluded him. He tried placing the folded sheet of parchment between pages, then grabbed the cover and opened it slightly to see if the parchment would fall out. It did. Maybe he could attach it to a page with an adhesive strip to hold it in place. He laid the ledger open and turned to a section of empty pages to do just that. The thought of placing it into Tenika's hands and trusting fate made him queasy. She probably wouldn't open the ledger. If she did, it would be to check the doctored entry. Surely she wouldn't turn through the empty pages, would she? If she did, and found the parchment, he was a dead man.

Filled with apprehension, Halen frowned as he leaned back into his chair. How had it come to this? Tenika's actions could be nothing more than paranoia. He may be risking his future by considering this course of action. If only he had more time to properly conceal the document. From his reclined position, he saw something he'd never noticed before. When the ledger lay open, the curve of the stitched spine formed a space between it and the leather that covered the spine.

Halen unfolded the parchment and rolled it into a narrow tube. By flattening it slightly with his hand, he found he could slide it into the cavity. It expanded slightly once inside and remained there when he shook the ledger. The ledger was longer than the parchment tube. He was able to push it deeper so it wasn't easily visible. As a test, he opened and closed it several times. A slight bulge was visible in the spine, but hardly noticeable unless you knew to look for it. Halen felt like kicking himself. Why hadn't he thought of this in the first place? He could have kept the document hidden there this whole time, pulling it out to add details as needed. He mentally pushed self-recrimination aside. He had a workable solution and no more time for delay. Tenika would be livid by now.

Halen steeled himself. He was literally about to place his future into Tenika's hands and she could be an enemy as easily as an ally. He trembled as he picked up the ledger, a result of the flight response he was feeling. Against every instinct, he stood and began the longest walk of his life. A five-minute journey to Tenika's parking spot.

Chapter 18

After his meeting with Selica the previous day, Kade had headed straight for the kitchen bulletin boards. It was a good thing too, as there were only a few slots still available on the volunteer list for kitchen duty. As luck would have it, animal preparation was one of the options. Or maybe luck had nothing to do with it. Apparently preparing animal carcasses wasn't a popular chore. Kade didn't mind. It wouldn't be the first time he'd had to get his hands dirty both literally and figuratively. He was just relieved to get on the list. That it happened to be in the optimal volunteer role for their plans was a bonus. It would grant him easy access to the animal pens.

Kade still needed to contact Leviticus to arrange a time and location for extraction. He arrived early to the training room for that purpose. It gave him a few minutes alone to access the network. If anyone entered, they would think he was preparing for the training session, at least that's what he hoped. If any of his students decided to show up early, they would likely walk right up and look over his shoulder. They didn't seem to respect any boundaries where writ weaving was concerned and they were an intensely inquisitive bunch. He had already composed the bulk of his message the previous night, so he only needed a few minutes to enter the details.

He somehow had to inform Leviticus of his need for extraction. Leviticus would need to know the date, time and location. The message had proven difficult to craft. It needed to be obscure enough that his keepers wouldn't recognize it as the cry for help that it was. At the same time, it had to be explicit enough to avoid confusion for his rescuers. He was relying heavily on Leviticus to decipher the exact time and location or this would all be for nothing. As far as Kade knew, Leviticus remained unaware of his current location. However, thanks to his Servator friends, Leviticus would know to look for cities that maintained a Breacher presence. That narrowed the range of possibilities, but not by much. Hopefully, it would help in deciphering his message.

After a great deal of thought, he chose three writ weave terms to designate the location — sum, anchor and bridge. *Sum* would represent the nation of Sumakad. *Anchor* would represent the city of Ankhora and *bridge* would, of course, represent the bridge which crosses the Aiguptos river running through Ankhora. The name of the river itself posed a problem. In the end he decided to convert it into a string of numbers using the simple cipher he had employed in the first missive sent to Leviticus. It would have to do. Noting the date and time was easier to accomplish. The time of entry would automatically be recorded when he saved the writ modifications to the memory stash. All he needed to provide was the number of days following the recorded date of entry, plus the hours to the time of pickup.

No doubt Leviticus would have set up an active search routine to look for all instances of characters between a set of opening and closing tags. Based on that assumption, he used the abbreviated terms of address they had employed in previous messages. It would begin with *-sp-*, short for Sage's pet, Kade's derogatory nickname for Leviticus. The closing tag would be *-br-*, short for his own last name, Brixton.

Kade powered up his workstation, then rose from his seat and walked to the door. He peered up and down the hall to make sure it was still empty and then silently closed and locked the door. If someone tried to open the door, it might arouse suspicion, but it would be easier to explain than his writ weaving.

The workstation was active when he sat back down. His fingers danced as he found his way to the spot in the weaving where he had placed his previous message. He deleted that one and took a deep breath as he prepared to post the message that could mean freedom or death. He wrung his shaking hands to stop the sudden onset of tremors. His next actions would commit him to this path. He'd faced the prospect of death enough by now to accept it as a possibility, but Selica.... How could he let her take this risk? They had to try, he decided. If something went wrong, he'd make sure her involvement looked coerced. In the event of a physical altercation, he'd buy her time to escape at the cost of his life, if necessary. Kade nodded. With that settled in his mind, he continued his task.

-Sp exit... *Make sure you get this right Kade.* Eight days from the current time would place them at the morning of the festival. He glanced at the wall chrono. It was seven in the morning. Selica had planned to wait for dark when everyone was well into their cups. She had chosen midnight, so...

-sp-exit-24x8+17x1=sum-anchor-1-9-7-21-16-20-15-19-bridge-br-

He read it three more times looking for errors. Satisfied, he saved the writ, turned off the workstation and rose to unlock the door. As he swung it open, he heard voices approaching from down the hall. *That was close.* Kade grabbed his notes and spread them out so it looked like he had simply been preparing for class. His students filed in, none the wiser.

Everyone took their seats and powered up their workstations. During their first sessions, Kade had sketched out the architecture of the facial recognition algorithm. Considering the wealth of experience in the room, he had suggested that he would prefer not to insult their intelligence by assuming he had much to teach them. Instead, they had settled into a comfortable routine where they would study the writ weaves for the first part of the class and then discuss observations and ask clarifying questions as a group. Kade's role in this was to choose segments that were unique for each session and direct discussion.

It had served the class well, soothing egos and allowing them to gel as a team while they discovered one another's unique talents. Under different circumstances Kade would have enjoyed working with this group. All of them, that is, except for Tridor Flint. He was an arrogant and strident man, clearly not cut from the same cloth as the rest of the engineers. Tridor was competent enough, but he had a way of casting aspersions that made others uncomfortable. He seemed more suited to intelligence gathering than writ weaving and Kade suspected the Second Anarch had him included to keep an eye on the others.

As if he was waiting for that very moment, Tridor broke with routine, interrupting the silence of the other engineers who were busy studying writs. "What is this?" Tridor demanded.

Kade looked up from his workstation. "Did you have a question, Engineer Flint?"

"Can't this wait until discussion time?" Engineer Kith complained.

"We have ten minutes left and I'm almost to the end of this section."

Tridor ignored the man, focusing on Kade with his accusing eyes. "This series of directives and numer strings... they look like gibberish. What is its purpose?"

Kade hesitated. Could his message have been discovered? No, he decided, that was impossible. He'd been careful not to assign that section of the weave for analysis. The plan was to avoid it for as long as possible. "Can you show me?" Kade asked, as he walked over to Tridor's station.

Tridor rose from his seat and offered it to Kade who chose to remain standing. Tridor pointed to a segment on his viewscreen.

Kade panicked when he saw what Tridor was pointing at. His worst nightmare was staring him in the face. Had he run out of time so soon? *Calm yourself, Kade. You planned for this. Don't get all nervous and make him suspicious.* "This isn't the writ that was assigned for today."

"I've been reading ahead, your method is taking too much time."

"We agreed as a group that this would be the most productive use of our time," Kade replied. "It ensures that we maintain parity in our understanding of the concepts. It's a prudent course, considering our diverse areas of expertise. Decar has set a tight time frame and we all need to be fully competent by that deadline. Group learning will help us achieve that goal efficiently without leaving anyone behind."

Kith interrupted. "Sit down, Flint. Your impatience is wasting other people's time."

That earned Kith a glare from Tridor. Kade was glad for the support, but if Kith wasn't careful, he could find himself in serious trouble if Tridor was indeed an informant.

Tridor was undeterred. "Our instructor is avoiding the question."

Kade sighed dramatically and made a show of taking a second look. He used the time to run through his options. Why did it have to be Flint who discovered this? Kade had hoped to avoid the writ contagion issue for a bit longer, but Tridor wasn't likely to accept a casual dismissal. "This looks like an artifact from the contagion script." Kade stated matter-of-factly.

The expression on Tridor's face was that of someone who had just heard a man admit high treason.

"A writ contagion!" Flint's face purpled in anger. "Explain yourself."

Kade schooled his features as if nothing was amiss and gestured for Tridor to return to his seat as he walked back to the front of the class. "Yes, a ontagion script." Kade continued. He had everyone's attention. "I had planned to leave this to the end of our sessions as a practical exercise, but perhaps that's unnecessary. You've all proven to be quick learners. Maybe we should delve into practical applications sooner. I know I tend to learn better that way."

Several heads bobbed in agreement.

"Third Anarch Villecrest wanted to harden our network against compromise. To that end he created an isolated network in a separate building to serve as a testing platform. We loaded a copy of the facial recognition algorithm and created a writ contagion. We were tasked with finding ways to counter any such attempt at corruption."

Kade noticed that the anger in Engineer Flint's face had subsided. It was replaced with interest.

"We designed countermeasures to convert foreign directives into harmless gibberish like this snippet you've just discovered. When a strategy proved successful, we would add those countermeasures to the primary network." Kade put on a facade of embarrassment. "In light of the experience present in this room, I'm ashamed to admit that some of the weaving may have found its way back to the primary network. My efforts weren't as clean as I would have liked. Tridor has found just such an example. In my defence, I was doing much of this on my own. With all of the late nights and stress, well, I'm sure you know how it is."

Tridor nodded at the explanation. "The Third Anarch was wise. Writ contagions can be incredibly destructive and often go unnoticed until it's too late. I'm surprised you were able to accomplish what you did on your own."

Kade took a risk. "Are you familiar with writ contagions, Engineer Flint?"

Tridor looked uncomfortable, but then nodded. "Yes, in my previous employment I was tasked with something similar. We developed several successful countermeasures."

Kade made a show of looking slowly around the room. "I can't tell you how much I would have appreciated having the expertise of the people in this room at hand while we were implementing the algorithm. We could have avoided so many mistakes and delays. If everyone is in agreement, I would like to propose that we move our sessions to the test network building and start playing with the weaves directly. It will provide a safe environment to experiment without fear of disrupting the primary network. Perhaps together we can uncover inefficiencies and learn at the same time."

Sounds of agreement filtered through the room.

"Writ contagions aren't my area of expertise. I would guess that the countermeasures I concocted wouldn't last long against a determined adversary. Engineer Flint, considering your background, would you be willing to develop a strategy to improve both the contagion writ and countermeasures? I would be grateful for your advice on how you would address the shortcomings of my own attempts."

Tridor was sitting straighter. He looked like a hound eager to sniff out his prey, but his reply was all business. "Show me the writ contagion and your countermeasures. I can bring them up to industry standard."

Kade mentally rolled his eyes. The mix of arrogance and superiority was irritating, but it might prove beneficial. If Kade could use Tridor's pride to *fix* his inexperienced writ weaving, he would kill two birds with one stone. A potential informant would become a defender of the algorithm while erasing any evidence of Kade's past duplicity. It might give him the time he needed. It also meant the message he sent to Leviticus would be his last. All he could do now was pray that Leviticus would receive the message in time, successfully decipher it, and understand that he shouldn't try to respond.

Kade brought his hands together in a clap. "This is exciting. I'll be eager to see what we can accomplish together once we start modifying the writ weaves. Why don't you all meet me here tomorrow morning and we can walk over to the test building together." Kade had to wrap this up. The stress of pretending was going to erode his credibility. "I think we can call it a day."

Chapter 19

Seri waited in her ground transport, staring at her Q-view. The tracking token remained stationary at the coordinates she assumed were Tenika's parking space. Halen must be taking his time delivering the ledger. Unless something was wrong with the token. *Did I forget a step when I placed it? Maybe Tenika found the token, left her keys in the ground transport as a decoy, and used a different mode of travel.* Seri shook away the thought. The token was tiny. Even if she noticed it, Tenika would have no idea what it was. The public remained unaware of Servator technology.

The tracker started moving, putting her imagined fears to rest. "Okay, here we go." Seri waited until the tracker moved past her location before easing out of Nico's private garage to follow at a discreet distance. She wasn't worried about losing sight of her quarry since the tracker would provide coordinates, but Seri was worried Tenika would leave her keys in the ground transport once she arrived at her destination. If it proved necessary to follow on foot, she needed to arrive in time to park her own transport out of sight and get close enough to observe Tenika leaving her vehicle.

After ten minutes, Tenika's token signalled a direction change. She was now moving toward the warehouse district by the docks. Interesting. She was scheduled to meet Garushe at berth eleven the next day. Was she planning on giving him the ledger? If so, they needed to gain possession of it before the meeting took place.

The token changed direction several more times before coming to a stop. Seri hid her transport in an alley and jogged to the corner of a warehouse near Tenika's stop. She peered around the corner just in time to see Tenika exit her transport and walk toward a vacant building. The sign above the front entry was sun-bleached, but it was still possible to read the name — Callan Netting. Tenika looked both ways before unlocking the door and slipping inside.

Seri ran across the street and placed her ear against the door. She could hear Tenika's footsteps growing quieter. Seri risked opening the door a crack and watched as Tenika turned right at the end of a hall running the building's length. Seri was about to enter, but hesitated. She'd have no place to hide. Remembering her mother's caution, and past mistakes, she closed the door and raced around the building looking for other options. It was important for Tenika to remain unaware that she was under suspicion. Tipping her off might cause her to cancel the meeting with Garushe.

Scanning the exterior wall for windows, she guessed at a destination based on Tenika's direction of travel. The windows were too high for her to reach, but a nearby barrel offered her a boost. Carefully, she lifted her head to look over the sill. Soot covered the windows and she licked her thumb to clear a peep hole. The room was empty. Hopping off the barrel, she quietly rolled it to the next window and repeated the process. The second window revealed an office that looked as though it hadn't been visited in years. Dust coated everything and Tenika was sweeping the floor. *What's she doing?* After Tenika finished sweeping the floor, she carefully poured the dust into a waste basket and carried it with her to a bookshelf. Old ledgers filled one of the shelves. Reaching into her bag, Tenika pulled out a ledger of her own that she'd been carrying and carefully inserted it between several others. Then she gathered a handful of dust from the waste basket and sprinkled it over the new addition to make it look as if it had been there as long as the others. When she was satisfied with the results, she began blowing handfuls of dust around the room as she backed her way toward the door. When she reached it, she stopped to survey her results. She nodded once and continued to do the same as she retraced her steps down the hall. Having erased the evidence of her recent passage, Tenika locked the front door, got into her transport, and drove away.

Seri sat on the barrel and monitored her Q-view until the tracking token showed Tenika well on her way back to her office. She sat for an additional five minutes trying to make sense of what she had just witnessed. She had imagined Tenika locking the ledger out of their reach, within a vault in a guarded facility. Yet here she sat, the only thing standing between her and the ledger was a pane of glass. It made no sense. Was it a trap? What was she missing?

Something niggled at the fringes of her mind. It had to do with the faded sign at the front of the warehouse. Other than the Callan name, the business wasn't familiar. Callan Netting? She knew Nico's family business had its roots in the fishing trade, but this building had been vacant for years, if not decades. The faded sign attested to a forgotten past. She'd seen the maintenance records for active Callan facilities. Upkeep was important to the brand image and Callan International was meticulous in the care of their properties. They would never allow a functioning facility to reach this level of decay. Seri had poured over old company records at Nico's request, looking for evidence that would help find his parent's murderers. In her analysis of past transactions, she'd noticed that the company tended to sell off unused facilities, redirecting the capital to other ventures. Stagnation seemed to go against corporate culture, yet here stood a relic, abandoned — defying both company practice and time.

What was so special about this building and why would Tenika choose it? Her analytic training took over. Old items that retained their value usually held sentimental or historical significance. Then it hit her. Nico had shared a story about how his father had once given him a fishing net for his birthday. The gift turned out to be more than a single net. Apparently, the Senior Callan was so impressed by the quality of the nets that he purchased the company. Nes had thought the gift would be a good way for Nico to learn a little about the business world. This building must have been the home of that business — Callan Netting. She would confirm with Nico later, but it made sense. It would explain why Callan International never sold it. They didn't own it, Nico did.

The rest came together quickly and Seri's blood began to boil. Tenika wasn't trying to hide the ledger. She wanted the incriminating ledger found in Nico's warehouse sitting under layers of dust. It was fabricated evidence to a crime he never committed, the murder of his own parents. She could imagine the scenario. Eventually, a corrupt magistrate would receive anonymous information about the location of this *evidence*. Seri couldn't allow that to happen. Nico had one copy of the ledger. By obtaining this second copy, they could end this particular threat. Seri looked around. She was still alone. Her Q-view showed

Tenika back at the office. Seri didn't think Nico would mind as she used her elbow to shatter the window. Reaching in, she unlocked the sash, opened the window and pulled herself up and through. It was a matter of moments before the ledger was in hand, she paged through it to confirm the doctored entry. There it was. This was definitely the duplicate ledger. She shoved it into her tunic and prepared to leave, but hesitated. Her first thought was to ignore the footprints she'd left in the dust. No one would find the evidence now, so what difference did it make? *No. Learn from your past impulsiveness. Think.* If a corrupt magistrate didn't discover what they were expecting, they would consider the tracks suspicious and find some way to pin it on Nico. Seri spotted the broom Tenika had used, leaning against the wall. With a sigh, she duplicated Tenika's efforts, sweeping up dust, then redistributing it as she backed toward the window. Once outside, she found a fist-sized rock and tossed it through the hole in the glass to explain the shattered pane — the handiwork of some bored youth, nothing more.

Back in her ground transport, Seri used her Q-view to check on Tenika by employing the spy tokens she'd placed earlier. Tenika had cleaned up. She looked no worse for wear from her clandestine efforts. It was business as usual. Switching to Halen's office was no more exciting. He was reading through some contracts. A blinking light at the top right of her viewscreen indicated that Cello's analysts had flagged something significant in the viewcordings. She played the identified segment. It showed Halen slipping a rolled parchment into the spine of a ledger. Seri felt a flush of adrenaline as she picked up the ledger from the passenger seat and opened it. As the covers separated, a gap formed in the part of the spine covering the stitching. She gingerly poked her finger into the gap and met some resistance. Gentle pressure forced a piece of parchment out the other end of the spine. With shaking fingers, she unrolled the parchment and began reading.

Seri's Q-view buzzed, startling her. It was her mother, checking in on her. "Mother, how did it go?"

"Thank the Maker you're okay! Tenika's tracker left your location some time ago, but your Q-view remained. I was worried something had happened to you."

"I'm fine. How did things go on your end?"

"Excellent. The rangers have surveyed the site. They've determined that the meeting will take place on a pleasure craft located in berth eleven. Security is lax in the evenings and they're confident that they can place spy tokens by nightfall. How about you?"

"Things went very well at this end. Tenika never suspected a thing. I watched her hide the ledger and I now have it in hand."

"Seri, you were supposed to wait until the rangers arrived to assist.

"I was careful. I waited until Tenika's tracking token showed she had returned to the office. It's the reason for my delay. Don't worry, this area is deserted. I was never in danger. I'll explain my actions later, but right now I need you to send some rangers for the ledger. I'll wait here. I want to explain events and have them check my efforts at concealment before we leave the site. Mother — there's something else, but you need to see it. Can you meet me after we're finished here?

"I'll be waiting at your office."

"Good. I'll see you soon."

Seri deactivated her Q-view and settled in to wait. A smile spread across her face. "We have you now, Tenika."

Chapter 20

Training was on hold for the next few days. Preparations were ramping up for the celebration of the gathering of the anarchs. Everyone was tasked with other duties or just given the day off so they wouldn't be underfoot as staff rushed about attending to their chores. Since his revelation about the writ contagion, Kade hadn't needed to do much teaching lately. Given the opportunity to work directly with the writs, the engineers were now nearly as fluent as he was. Placing Tridor in charge of hardening the system against writ-contagions had proven to be the right course of action. He took to the task with relish, modifying both contagion script and counter-measures until the weaves had changed so dramatically that it was no longer evident that Kade had ever contributed to their design. Having direct access to the full weaving seemed to remove all suspicion from Kade. As he had hoped, Tridor became an advocate for the project and Kade was given grudging respect for what he had accomplished given his *lack of experience*. Apparently, his efforts were noted in a positive report to the Second Anarch. That was a double-edged sword. The immediate threat of being discovered as a traitor was gone. Unfortunately, the huge strides made by the engineers towards improving the algorithm advanced the day he became irrelevant. It shouldn't have mattered now that the celebration was upon them. Soon, he and Selica would make their escape. Unfortunately, Kenric had decided to parade him in front of the other anarchs. He was expected to provide a demonstration of the technology. It was surprising to Kade that Kenric was willing to show the algorithm to other high-level Breachers. Kade had thought anarchs were secretive and territorial. Regardless of the reasons, it put a dangerous kink in their escape plans. Kade wasn't given a specific time when the demonstration was to take place. All he knew was that he was to be prepared for when he received a summons.

The administrative building of the compound had the largest gathering spaces and included the kitchens. It was the logical venue for a gathering. The main hall was a hive of activity. The walls were decorated by men on ladders. A stage was being hastily constructed. Porters hauled in lumber, their long loads narrowly missing the heads of those who were setting up tables. It was a surprise no one had been injured in the melee.

Kade hopped out of the way as a cart piled with produce rumbled toward the kitchen. He was headed there himself, carrying a bundle of freshly honed carving knives from the stroppers. He'd already butchered several animals and the blades were dulling.

Selica had everything ready for her part of the plan. It was up to him to slip out through the animal pens when the opportunity presented itself. They had agreed to make attempts at the top of each hour, following sunset. Selica would wait at the rear entrance of the children's quarters for five minutes at the designated times before returning to her duties. If he missed a five-minute slot, he would have to wait and try again. It was a given that their chances would improve as the evening progressed. People would spend less time eating and more time drinking, dulling their wits. It also meant that his reasons for visiting the animal pens would diminish as the request for food slowed. The optimum moment would arrive unannounced and he feared it would happen while he was busy giving a demonstration to the anarchs. *As if plotting an escape wasn't stressful enough!* "There you are," the head cook admonished. "Put those in the knife block and head to the paddock. We need another goat prepared. Try to get a little closer to the bone this time. You left a lot of good meat behind on your last attempt."

Kade tried to apologize, but the cook waved it off. "No time for talk, we can use those meaty bones for broth later, but no one is interested in soup right now."

So it went, hour after hour, switching from meat preparation to stirring pots or cleaning utensils as directed. Occasionally he would be asked to carry a trencher of meat or a flagon of wine to the food table, when servers were overwhelmed. Each visit to the main hall was a reminder of diminishing opportunity.

With his first delivery of food, he was amazed at how the hall had been transformed. Flags from the various nations in attendance adorned the walls. The lights had been rigged to display intricate patterns on the arched ceiling, and musicians played on the stage while exotic dancers twirled about a central area cleared for that purpose.

The anarchs sat at surrounding tables gorging themselves while their retinues alternately loomed protectively or hassled the servers for not attending quickly enough. From what Kade could tell, most of those retainers were simply looking for a reason to surreptitiously sample the fare at the food table. More than a few quickly threw back a mug of wine when they thought no one was looking. *Drink up my friends. All the better if your eyes are glazed when the time comes.* After that, he made sure to bring an extra flagon of wine each time he came out, placing them at one end of the food table near a potted plant. It didn't take long for the retainers to notice the discreet opportunity.

During his second trip to the room, the mood had changed. People were leaning back in their chairs with sated looks on their faces. The smoke from numerous pipes filled the air with a light haze and a pungent scent. Jugglers and acrobats were now entertaining the crowd where the dancers had been performing. Kade caught his breath as the acrobats executed a particularly daring manoeuvre. One of them back-flipped his way toward a large circular target. His partner threw knives, missing the moving man by a hair as each blade reached its destination. The tumbler ended spread-eagle against the target standing on two blades and holding onto two more on either side of his head. The final knife embedded itself into the target between the tumbler's legs. The audience gasped and cringed at the display. *How do you even practice such a thing?* Kade wondered.

He heard the clatter of plates and redirected his attention. The tables were being cleared. He was running out of time. There would be dessert followed by more drinks, but his legitimate reasons to go into the animal pen would soon disappear. If he wasn't called to do his presentation soon, he didn't know what excuses he could give.

Chairs scraped the floor as the anarchs rose to head into private chambers. The time to conduct business was at hand. The guards remained outside as the doors were closed and there was an amusing tussle as the protectors of each anarch vied for positions closest to the doors. Kenric's men won out. Being the hosts, they had greater numbers. Tempers flared and hands rested on sword pommels, but they fell into an uneasy truce.

Another half hour passed in the kitchen before Kade was summoned. Finally, he sighed. *There's still a chance. Hopefully Kenric won't keep me long.* He was checked for weapons, not once, but by a representative of each anarch. When everyone was satisfied, he was granted entry into the chamber of the anarchs. If the dining area was festive, this room was lavish in comparison. An abundance of cushions covered the floor and the anarch's reclined on them. Incense scented the air.

"Ah, here he is." Kenric waved Kade into the room. "I know you've all been patiently waiting for me to get on with our agenda, but before we begin, I wanted to give you a demonstration. It is pertinent to Breacher business."

The other anarchs shifted in their seats, murmuring.

"Kade will be showing you an innovative new technology. Its potential should be obvious."

"Get on with it, Trantor. You've already hijacked this gathering. I for one would like to know the reason why."

Kenric ignored the slight of his fellow anarch and nodded to Kade who made his way to a workstation sitting next to a large viewscreen.

The demonstration was similar to one he had given the Third Anarch before his mysterious death. Except this time there was no need to game the results. The algorithm was working very efficiently now, a fact that filled Kade with both pride and shame. Targets would be entered into the system and everyone would watch as those targets were identified and located in real-time.

"For this demonstration," Kenric began, "I'd ask you each to provide the name of one of your hidden operatives here in Sumakad."

"You can't be serious, Trantor! Even if we were to admit that we had operatives here, no one would reveal who they are."

"Come, come, my friends. We all have our spies. No one here is naive enough to believe otherwise. I am not asking for the names of your high-level agents, merely a low-level informant known only to you. Any operatives you have here would have been keeping an eye on Toller Villecrest who is no longer with us. There is no need to fear retaliation from a dead man. Like many of you, I was curious how a Third Anarch managed to gain the privilege of hosting this gathering. I freely admit that I had agents here seeking an answer. I'm convinced the rest of you did as well. Keeping apprised of Breacher politics is only prudent. As a show of good faith, I will be the first to provide a name."

Kenric passed a slip of parchment to Kade, who dutifully entered the name into the system. It was no longer necessary to enter a still-view image. The network in Ankhor had long since identified each citizen. Unknowns were flagged and quickly identified by agents who filled in the blanks.

"Each of you was handed a blank piece of parchment when you entered. Write a name and Kade will collect them. No one will know which informant belongs to whom. Choose a low value individual and you risk very little, but believe me when I tell you that you'll want to verify the results of this demonstration. This is how you'll do so."

Kade watched as the other anarchs considered Kenric's words, then nodded their heads as curiosity got the better of them. When it seemed everyone had written something, Kade collected them all and entered the names he had been given. The results quickly appeared, and within five minutes the faces of each of the named targets were displayed on the large viewscreen alongside their names and locations. There were gasps as the anarchs recognized the faces of their informants. Tote-comms came out and orders were barked to subordinates as each dealt with their compromised assets.

When things settled down, the murderous glares of four of the world's five anarchs were fixed on Kenric.

"What is the meaning of this, Trantor?"

"Your questions will be answered, my friends." Kenric turned to Kade. "Thank you, Mr. Brixton, That will be all."

Kade glanced at his wrist chrono. It was quarter to the hour. *There's still time.* He walked briskly from the room, barely keeping himself from breaking into a run.

Just before he reached the door, he heard Kenric's voice. "With this technology we can locate all of our enemies and attack them simultaneously. We can finally rid the world of the Servators in a single coordinated action. They'll never know what hit them."

Chapter 21

Tenika paused at the end of the dock leading to berth eleven. A salty tang wafted from the sea, granting a brief reprieve from the stink of the fishmonger stalls. She glanced at her wrist chrono. *Right on time.* She wanted to get this over with as quickly as possible. Cutthroats roamed the docks at night. It was unwise to come here alone in the evening, but this was something she needed to handle on her own. Surely Garushe had arranged safe passage for their meeting. Tenika scanned the area, letting her eyes roam over the buildings running parallel with the docks. Half constructed sea transports, stacks of crates or barrels, and various stalls, provided too many places for a cutthroat to hide. Her peripheral vision caught movement in the shadows near the warehouses. That was probably one of Bode's men, but she picked up her pace just the same.

Slowing at berth eleven, she checked to see if anyone had followed her. She was alone with the gentle thumping of sea craft bumping against each other and the docks. She took a few steps along the dock and noticed berths ten and twelve were empty. A twenty-cubit pleasure craft floated in berth eleven. The craft was whitewashed and featured a polished teak deck. A moniker was painted on the side. It read, *The Bode Well*. Tenika rolled her eyes. Nothing about this bodes well. Apparently, discretion wasn't high on Garushe's list of priorities.

"Ms. Sheridan, how do you like my fine vessel?"

Tenika jerked her eyes from the name on the craft to the man himself, standing on the deck. His sudden appearance startled her. How hadn't she seen him approaching? "Quiet," She hissed. "Don't use my name!"

"Tenika, my dear, you worry too much."

Tenika scowled.

"I assure you, my men have the area secured. No one within a furlong of here is unknown to me. No one can see or hear us."

"Regardless, I'd prefer you not use my name out in the open."

"Very well, hop on board and we'll leave."

Tenika tensed. "What do you mean leave?"

"That's why we're here. We'll head out to sea where no one will bear witness to our conversation."

"I wasn't prepared to travel. I'm not comfortable with this arrangement."

"Yet, as you've said, we need privacy to discuss matters. No place is safer than out in open water far from eavesdroppers and interlopers."

Tenika wasn't so sure about that. She surreptitiously felt under her cloak for her dagger. What choice did she have? Bode was very good at what he did and she needed his help.

"Will anyone else be joining us?"

"Just you and I, my dear." Bode wiggled his eyebrows and Tenika felt sick to her stomach. He must have noticed because he barked out a laugh.

"Relax, Sheridan — you're not my type and you're far too old for me. It will be strictly business. Now, come aboard, you've already put us off schedule."

Old indeed! Men half Bode's age propositioned her on a semi-regular basis. Indignant and without options, she nimbly leaped from the dock to the bow and settled onto one of the nearby seats. Bode pushed off immediately. He powered up the sea transport, turning towards open water. Tenika soothed her frayed nerves by reminding herself she had taken lives before. She wasn't a helpless victim. She had a dagger and her ring concealed a sharp pin dipped in a powerful paralyzing toxin. All she needed was to prick the man if he tried anything threatening. The sea was calm and soon enough her worries settled, lulled by the motion of their passage.

After twenty minutes of cruising, Bode cut the throttle and let the craft coast to a stop. They had made their way around the curving shoreline until the lights of the city were no longer visible. Bode left the wheelhouse and disappeared below deck. She shivered, not sure if it was the night air or the thought of being alone with a dangerous individual. He could toss her overboard and leave her to drown. No one would be the wiser. *Stop it, Tenika. He's here to make sure his master's investment pays off. He's not going to harm you.* Even so, her hand clutched the dagger beneath her cloak as she saw Bode's dark shape rise from below deck with something in his hand. As he came closer, she realized it was only a bottle of wine and two mugs. He poured a glass and handed it to her. When she only stared at it, he laughed, took a sip to show it was safe and handed the mug back.

Bode shook his head. "You'd fit right in with the Breachers." Bode filled his own mug and sat down. "So, here we are. Nice and private. I'm listening. What couldn't you say over the tote-comm?"

"I have a problem that needs to go away."

"You certainly do. I'm aware of your current difficulties. Not good for the bottom line. I have concerns about certain timelines."

"You needn't be concerned. I have contingencies, but your help would certainly expedite matters."

Bode took a sip from his mug. He noticed her hand in her cloak and grinned. Tenika withdrew her hand, embarrassed to have forgotten it there.

"All these years have passed since I solved your first problem and now you find yourself dealing with a... related problem." Bode chuckled at his own joke while Tenika glowered. "I can call our mutual friend Qas. He'd be happy to pick up where he left off. The man is quite fond of irony."

"No! I told you that wasn't an appropriate solution."

"It's the most expedient."

"I already have something else in play. Your suggestion would shift the focus of a current investigation. It would slow things down."

"So, let me see if I understand. You've begun an investigation into your problem and you would like criminal activity exposed so that the investigation will end swiftly and conclusively."

Tenika nodded. "Yes, that is an accurate summary."

Bode shook his head "You truly could be a Breacher, you're alike in how you pursue your interests with single-minded focus."

"That's the second time you've commented on these Breachers," Tenika sneered. "Are you a recruiter now?"

Bode chuckled. "Nothing like that, though I do work with them from time to time. As it happens, your friend Qas also works with the Breachers. Didn't you know?"

"He's *not* my friend."

"Oh, I beg to differ. Only the best of friends share secrets as deep as the one held between you and Qas. Come to think of it, that makes me your friend, too. You really should treat your friends better. You may need their help one day. Actually, you need Qas's help right now."

"I already told you...."

Bode held up his hand to cut her off. "Qas is a man of many talents. In this case you need him because he has *friends* among the sentinels and within the judicial system who are experts at exposing the most heinous of crimes. With a reputation for the speedy execution of justice, they have a one hundred percent conviction rate. Their captives never see the light of day to do further harm. Of course, some of that may be due to unfortunate accidents that occur when so many unsavoury men are confined in the same place, but that is the fate of the guilty."

Bode's grasp of the situation surprised Tenika and she was pleased with his solution. She'd clearly underestimated the man. She knew he was dangerous, but now doubly so. "That sounds — exactly like the proper course of action. We definitely need to right the wrongs and set things back into proper order. Do you think these special investigators will have time to help?"

"Their primary objective is seeing justice served. However, such an endeavour comes with certain expenses, as you can imagine."

"I assure you the fees won't be a problem. Callan International will be happy to support any effort to see a speedy resolution. I can have the company lawvocate make any necessary arrangements."

"Then I'm confident Qas can resolve this in short order. He will have the keeper of records for the City Sentinels contact your lawvocate to work out the details." Bode raised his mug. "To helpful friends."

Tenika smiled and joined him in the toast. It was a good plan. She had already planted seeds of doubt about Nico's character. If the City magistrates brought their own unrelated charges, it would settle the matter in the minds of the board members. She wouldn't need to risk exposing herself by releasing the ledger. Even if Nico could prove his innocence regarding the misuse of company funds, it would become irrelevant. As a convicted felon, it would be impossible for him to regain control of the company. Tenika would automatically regain her authority. Permanently this time — unfortunate accidents occurred in prison all the time.

Bode powered up the craft and headed back to the docks. Tenika grabbed the bottle of wine and indulged in a celebratory refill. Finally, she would get rid of the Callan thorn in her side forever.

Chapter 22

Cello and Seri sat silently at the table in Nico's kitchen, sipping kofa. An hour had passed and Seri was on her second mug. She was furious with Tenika and had spent much of the last hour plotting ways to make her life miserable. Maybe Enis could find a legal way to fire her. Nico was listening to the viewcording of the meeting between Tenika and Bode Garushe. The rangers had done an excellent job of concealing spy tokens. No one had to guess at the words spoken. The captured viewcordings were crisp and clear. Nico took his time, listening to the full exchange several times and then replaying specific segments. His expression changed at various times from indignation, to astonishment, to outrage. He sat back in his chair and looked first at Cello and then Seri. "I'm at a loss for words. Or maybe I have too many to put into coherent sentences."

Cello spoke first. "The evidence provided by the viewcording would prove circumstantial to a magistrate. No crime was discussed, only a problem in need of a solution. Tenika, Qas and the Breachers were all mentioned, but it hardly matters. If there remains any local authorities who are not corrupt, they would have no frame of reference for the criminal nature of Breacher activity. Those who are complicit will make certain that any Breacher influence remains hidden. The language used during the conversation gives the impression that both Tenika and Callan International are seeking an end to criminal activity. Bode is suggesting that Tenika should go through proper channels by enlisting the help of the City Sentinels. Bode was confident no one was listening, even so, he was very careful in how he directed the conversation. He mentioned Tenika's full name, and only the first name of the Sicari, Qas. His own name wasn't part of the conversation. He never allowed an opportunity for Tenika to use it. This is a habit of someone well versed in concealment."

Nico pounded his thigh in frustration. "So, we have nothing?"

"I didn't say that, Nico. I said we can't trust the Caralithican system. You'll find no legal recourse there. The system is corrupt. You wouldn't want to place yourself in their hands, even if we had something to give them. Qas is making his move. Even as we speak, he's likely disseminating fabricated evidence to frame you for a high crime. It's only a matter of time. Bode Garushe suggested it could happen quickly. That was last night. You need to go into hiding as soon as we finish here."

"You want me to hide while my family's legacy is stolen from me?" Nico stood and began pacing the room. "If I run, then it will look like I'm guilty. I'll never be able to prove my innocence!"

Cello responded in her maddeningly logical way. "If you don't go into hiding, you'll be dead and then you'll lose everything anyway."

Seri stood and moved to Nico's side, grasping his hand. "We still have Halen's confession. It incriminates Tenika, but we need time to connect her to Bode Garushe and Qas Drugarish. Before we can make any headway, we'll have to root out the City Sentinels and magistrates working for the Breachers. Revealing corrupt activity within the system will be slow process, but we'll clear your name eventually."

Nico looked about ready to scream, but dropped his head in defeat with a heavy sigh. "Great, and in the meantime, everyone will believe horrible lies about me."

"I'm so sorry, Nico, but I see no other way." Seri gave his hand a squeeze of understanding. "First thing tomorrow morning, Enis and I will begin setting up accounts that guarantee your access to your personal wealth. It will prevent the misappropriation of company funds by board initiatives without your knowledge. Enis assures me that he can arrange to have himself established as the company lawvocate, enforcing a predetermined decision-making process. It will effectively limit the powers of the board. Enis will remain in covert contact with you, acting as your voice in the company. He's confident everything can be in place well before the board makes any decisions resulting in my removal as current head of Callan International."

Nico began pacing again, lifting his arms in a half shrug. "Where am I supposed to go?"

"I was thinking you could stay at the base," Seri offered.

Cello interrupted. "Absolutely not."

"Mother, it's the perfect place. It's currently deserted and has supplies to feed and house an occupant for years. No one knows it's there and it would allow Nico to remain close if he needs to talk to Enis. Besides, it will give him something to do as he continues to oversee the repairs to the tunnels surrounding the base." Seri glanced at Nico and saw his grateful expression. A lot more than maintenance was occurring in those tunnels and he wanted to see that project through to completion.

On her first assignment as a conditional Token Ward, Seri had unintentionally exposed the Servator presence in Denmount. Several rangers died as a result. Breachers had been monitoring the town ever since. So far they only suspected the location to be a safe house, but it was no longer possible to operate as a fully functioning base. With the increased scrutiny, it would be difficult to hide their activities. Her mother, the Chief Sentry, decided to abandon the base and temporarily relocate. No one could guess when it might be safe to return.

Seri's actions had cost lives and forced families to uproot and start over. To make amends, she had hatched an audacious plan to develop several remote means to access the base, facilitating a safe return. The only people who knew, other than herself, were Leviticus, Nico, and a few of his loyal Servator staff who managed the projects. As a cover, Nico had offered the services of Callan International to perform much needed maintenance on the tunnels surrounding the base. Since the base was currently vacant, it was logical to perform the work at a time when it wouldn't interfere with Servator business. It was the sort of thing his father would have offered and Cello, as Chief Sentry, had readily agreed.

Cello remained unaware of those additional efforts, but Nico spent nearly every day working on new air and sea ports along with other security efforts to improve access to the base. It would kill him to be dragged away from the work. Living at the base would allow him to continue uninterrupted.

Cello vigorously shook her head. "Servator law forbids it. Only vested Servators or novices are permitted on a Servator base. We established those laws for good reason."

"It's an abandoned base, Mother…"

Cello cut her off. "A base filled with Servator technology and ancient archives among other things, or have you forgotten?"

Nico wondered what those secretive other things might be, but now wasn't the time to ask. "So make me a novice."

Cello frowned. "Excuse me?"

"When my parents' lives were at risk, you allowed them to train as Servators so they could defend themselves. You said yourself that they became two of your best rangers. I'm asking for that same opportunity."

Cello looked uncomfortable with the reminder. "My decision resulted in the loss of their lives. It cost me two dear friends."

Nico shook his head in disagreement. "It was their choice to make. I understand that decision now more than ever. They wouldn't sit idle waiting to be a victim. Neither can I."

"Nico, this isn't a decision to make lightly. It's not a choice you can turn back from. Once a Servator always a Servator. "

Nico grew angry. "Are you suggesting I'm not fully invested already? Do you think I ever had a choice? I was groomed to take over my parents' roles, including their ties to the Servator cause. I never truly had the option of walking away. My life is irrevocably intertwined with the Servators, and I'm fully committed to it. Do you question my loyalty?" Nico stared at her in disbelief.

Cello reddened. "Of course not. I — it's just that I promised your parents I would keep you safe." Cello straightened, collecting herself. In one heartbeat she transformed from a family friend into the Chief Servator of the Caralithican Host. "Nico Callan, is it your wish to join yourself to the Servator cause, giving your life in service to the Maker's Way?"

Nico drew himself up. "It is."

"Will you obey the dictates of the Servators even to death, placing the lives of others before your own?"

"I will."

"Then, by my authority, you are now one with the Servators." Cello stepped forward and kissed him on both cheeks. "Welcome to the cause."

"I'll train and study hard. You won't regret this decision. When I reclaim control of Callan International, this will facilitate my role as a benefactor. As a Servator, I'll be allowed direct contact with those in authority at bases around the globe. It will ease your burden as my go-between."

"Yes, your parents operated in much the same way in the past. The arrangement was beneficial to all, but first you have to make it through training. I can arrange for an accelerated curriculum. Instructors can take shifts on base, but we'll need to find a way to get them onsite without the Breachers noticing."

"That's easily accommodated. I'm going to need someone to keep an eye on the house in my absence. Perhaps a few could pose as maintenance staff. The property is well out of town and away from prying eyes. It could serve as a staging area, providing a useful alibi for trips into town. You already know about the secret entrance to the tunnels from my father's office. Instructors could arrive here and use the tunnels to travel to and from the base on tri-wheels."

Cello looked thoughtful as she considered the logistics. "Yes, that could work, but an accelerated curriculum requires a steady rotation of Servator staff. I don't like the idea of the increased overland traffic. Even though your property is outside of the city proper, it's still close enough that someone might notice."

"I may have a way around that." Nico hesitated. He hadn't yet told Seri about his recent discovery and he would rather she heard about it first.

Seri had an eyebrow raised and a question on her lips, but before she could ask, a pounding began at the door.

"Open up! This is the Captain of the Watch for the City Sentinels."

Cello frowned. "I have rangers posted outside. They should have warned us."

Seri began pushing Nico toward the office. "Quick, Mother, you and Nico need to escape through the tunnels."

"I'm not leaving you here to face them alone," Nico insisted.

"They're not looking for me, they're looking for you. I'll tell them you've taken an extended vacation and I'm watching the house in your absence. It's a plausible explanation. I'm your assistant, after all."

"What if they arrest you?"

"Then I'll contact Enis and he'll have me released, don't worry. They don't have anything against me. Tenika can take her place as head of Callan International as soon as you're convicted. She doesn't need to have charges brought against me."

"How can you be certain?"

"Trust me." Seri smiled wryly. "Tenika will want to make my life miserable.

To do that, she needs me to continue working at the office. Now go! I'll contact you as soon as they leave. If you don't hear from me in two hours, let Enis know."

Cello caught Nico's eye and nodded. They ran to the secret exit and safety, while Seri went to open the front door before the Sentinels knocked it down.

Chapter 23

Nico listened through the hidden panel separating the tunnels from his home office. The City Sentinels were searching his house and none too gently from the sound of it. He gritted his teeth knowing these were really just thugs hired by the Breachers. More than ever, he was convinced that he needed training and access to Servator technology.

Cello touched his elbow and nodded, urging him to move deeper into the tunnels. She was right. If the sentinels stumbled across the hidden panel, they needed to be far away. The tunnels were a bit of a maze and they had a good chance of evading any pursuers, but they needed to avoid a direct line of sight. The Callan property overlooked the sea atop high cliffs riddled with tunnels and caves. They headed down the tunnel leading to the catacombs. From there they could take another tunnel leading to the Servator base. Cello suggested they surface at the crypt exit and use her view scope to see what was happening at the house. It would also give them some breathing space. If the sentinels found the tunnels, they wouldn't know how to open the false wall of the crypt. It would look like a dead end and they would continue on.

Safely at the crypt, Cello handed Nico her view scope and suggested he take a look. Meanwhile she would try to find out what had happened to her rangers. Nico headed to the crypt exit. One of the tunnels led to a staircase carved into the side of the cliff. He sat at the bottom step, taking in the sea air. The view from the cliffs was a constant in his life and it centred him. He was furious at Tenika's attempts to steal his family's business, but looking out over the water, he remembered a previous declaration that he had no desire to run a company. He was happy with the life he'd been living — attending school, hanging out with Leviticus. How quickly things had changed. Now they had evidence that Tenika was involved in the murder of his parents. He felt rage rising to the surface once more. He took a calming breath. *As much as I'd like revenge, I just took a vow to value the lives of others over my own.* He'd have to find justice another way.

Nico played with the scope, getting a feel for the various adjustments. Once he understood the mechanics, he climbed the steps until he could rest his elbows on the cliff edge. raising the scope to his eye, he brought the house into focus. The estate was a bustle of activity with no less than five ground transports and twice that many sentinels scouring the property. It looked like things were winding down. A few boxes of his belongings were carted to one of the vehicles before it drove off. He felt a moment of panic wondering what they had found, but couldn't think of anything incriminating that he would keep at the house. He shook his head. *Get a grip man, you're not a criminal.* Another ten minutes passed before the last of the transports left. A moment later, Seri exited the house and sat down on the back porch. Nico sighed in relief as he watched her fiddling with the Q-view on her wrist. He pushed down the urge to run to the house and returned to the crypt instead.

Cello looked up at his return. "I just heard from Seri."

Nico handed the view scope back to Cello. "Yes, I just saw her talking into her Q-view. What did she have to say?"

"They asked a lot of questions, but seemed to accept her explanation. It was lucky she hadn't found time to change her work identification. It still listed her as your assistant. They searched the whole house, trashing much of it in the process. Your father's office suffered the worst of it."

Nico felt a lump in his throat. That office didn't just hold memories of his parents. It held memories of his grandfather as well. Tenika was robbing him of his past as well as his future.

Cello seemed to sense his grief and placed a hand on his shoulder. "I spent many happy days in that office making plans with your parents."

Nico nodded. "What else did Seri say?"

"They've brought charges against you for the murder of a high-ranking city magistrate. Most likely one of the few incorruptible men left in the system."

"Murder." Nico whispered. He knew it would be something bad. After all, Tenika seemed willing to frame him for the assassination of his own parents. Now it was real. The public would consider him a murderer and a fugitive. Worse, it made him look like an enemy of the justice system. Every news agency would cover the story for months to come. A massive manhunt would ensue and even those sentinels who weren't on Breacher payroll would be seeking justice for one of their own. The ramifications almost drove him to his knees. The Callan family name stood for honesty and goodness and now it would be dragged through the mud. Vultures would circle Callan International like a corpse, waiting for their chance to nibble at the bones. It seemed appropriate that he was standing in the crypt that held the remains of his family. He was now as dead to the world as they were.

Cello spoke into his grief. "Nico, I know things seem hopeless at the moment, but even if we can't expect justice from the city legal system, we still have other avenues of recourse. The evidence we've gathered won't convince a city magistrate, but don't let that worry you. Servators seldom rely on local enforcement alone when it comes to Breacher activity. Servators are the only ones equipped to police and judge Breacher crime. We'll take care of this.

"We have enough evidence to prove Tenika Sheridan contacted Bode Garushe to hire Qas Drugarish as the assassin who murdered at least two Servator rangers — your parents. They *will* face justice for their actions.

"While you were checking the house, I sent orders to have Tenika and Halen brought in. As we speak, Enis is preparing documents of resignation for them both. Tenika will be in no position to take anything from you ever again."

Nico almost wept in relief. "Thank you."

"Don't thank me yet. We have a long way to go before this wraps up and you'll remain a fugitive for some time after that."

"Even so, it will be easier to stomach knowing that Tenika won't get her way ... justice still exists in the world."

"We have her in custody," Cello agreed. "She'll have to account for her crimes."

"What will happen to them?" Nico asked.

"Halen will be questioned thoroughly and then we'll confront Tenika with the evidence. Hopefully, she'll confess to the murder of your parents and her association with Qas Drugarish. She may know something that can help us find him. We have been tracking Qas for a very long time. Seri may have told you that Qas is responsible for the assassination of her father along with many other rangers."

"She did mention that, yes. I'm sorry for your loss."

Cello looked away. The loss still stung years later. "Yes, well... I've had rangers following Bode Garushe since he returned to the docks with Tenika after their meeting. We're monitoring his activities and those of his contacts in the hope that he'll lead us to Qas. As for Tenika and Halen? They'll be imprisoned on one of our rehabilitation islands. Halen will receive a second chance, an opportunity to return to society after a time. Tenika, as we now know, is a repeat offender. She'll live out the remainder of her life on the island where she can do no further harm. Once Bode's usefulness in tracking Qas is exhausted, he'll join her."

Nico sighed. "At least with Tenika out of the picture, I won't have to worry about what might be coming next."

"It will take time to clear your name Nico, but we'll get there. I'm hoping both Tenika and Bode will confess to having a hand in framing you. Bode may know who the real killer is. He may also be helpful in exposing the corrupt officials embedded within Denmount's legal system. Bode may not be willing to reveal much, but we have analysts who can tell when someone is lying. It's surprising how much information you can glean with leading questions in the hands of a skilled interrogator. Simply placing a still-view image of a potentially corrupt sentinel in front of Bode and watching his reaction will be very educational. Bode will reveal far more than he intends."

"That's fascinating. I have so much to look forward to in my training."

"Speaking of which — did you mention a possible alternative route for instructors to reach your home?"

Nico hoped he would have a little more time to prepare before revealing that nugget of information.

Cello noticed his hesitation. "Let me be your first instructor, novice. Lesson number one — never withhold information from a superior. It could mean life or death for someone under her command."

"Yes, Ma'am. Follow me."

When Nico, Leviticus and Seri had made plans to create other means for Servators to reach the Denmount base, they had scouted out potential locations for new ports of entry. Tunnels had been drilled from the Servator base to two remote locations. One was in a nearby mountain range. It was a port for lighter-than-air craft. The other was a sub-aqua transport station in one of the submerged tunnels below the catacombs where they now stood. Sub-aqua craft had explored several of the undersea tunnels, but ceased that exploration when they discovered a large cavern with a natural beach. It was a perfect location, naturally vented by a vertical shaft. Recently, while excavating a side tunnel, the workers had broken through into a parallel tunnel. Nico had immediately been contacted when they discovered that the tunnel led to a manufactured dock where a small sub-aqua transport was parked. The craft was a very old model in excellent condition. Nico had asked one of the sub-transport pilots to take it for a test run. When he reported back, he declared the craft seaworthy with surprisingly simple controls, not typical for that particular model. He had shown Nico how to operate the vessel and Nico had already taken it out on his own.

On further investigation, Nico discovered that his father had acquired the craft. Company ledgers noted the purchase, but no record of the craft existed beyond that. Maintenance records were absent. Nico suspected that it had been purchased as an emergency escape option for the family. Based on that assumption, he had explored more of the tunnel. If his father had placed the craft here, that necessitated a way to access it. Eventually he found what he was looking for — a small north star engraved in the rock of the tunnel ceiling. It matched the one from the cornice moulding in his bedroom. Triggering the token rewarded Nico with entry to a vertical shaft outfitted with an elevator. The elevator terminated in a chamber beside the crypt where the ossuaries of his parents were interred.

Nico ordered workers to fill in the hole they had made, leaving his father's escape route intact. The trouble was, he didn't know if they had completed that task. Now he was about to show Cello their other option for travel. If the hole remained open, they might arrive just as workers were engaged in a noisy effort. The cat would be out of the bag. Seri's efforts at redemption would be exposed prematurely. It would be impossible to explain that massive undertaking with anything but the truth. Another thought occurred to him then. *I'm a novice now. I have to follow Cello's orders.* He wouldn't be able to continue the development of the new ports as a private project if she deemed it Servator business and ordered it shut down. Seri would never forgive him! He prayed that the workers had completed their task.

They were standing at the back of cave nine near the hidden entrance to the tunnels. Nico led Cello toward the front of the tunnel where it opened to the sea. When he stopped, it was apparent from her expression that she recognized where they were, having paid her respects in the past. Her eyebrows rose when he triggered the token to reveal an elevator. Cello said nothing as they descended. They exited the elevator in silence and Cello waited as Nico triggered the entrance to the tunnel housing his father's sub-aqua transport. It was a tense first few steps for Nico and he breathed a sigh of relief when he noticed the expertly sealed hole. Without knowing what to look for, a person might not even notice. Cello looked at him sideways.

Nico ignored it and picked up his pace. When they reached the dock, Cello took in the cave and laid a hand on the vessel. "So, that's what he was up to. We once completed a mission with this very craft. Your father never told me where it came from or how he managed to obtain it on such short notice. I assumed it was part of the Callan fleet. Now that I think about it, I should have asked him where he learned to pilot the thing." Cello shook her head with a twinkle in her eye. "Leave it to Nes to plan for every contingency. He still surprises me after all these years."

Nico interrupted her reverie. "It's still seaworthy. If the instructors travel by sea transport to a location within sight of the cliffs, I can pick them up and bring them here. They can make their way unobserved through the tunnels from here to my house, or the base."

Cello smiled broadly. "This will do nicely. You're going to make a fine novice, Mr. Callan. I'll see to the details, but for now we need to get you settled in at the base. I'll need to set up your security credentials in the base network and find you some quarters. You'll need at least a rudimentary tour before I leave you for the night. We best get moving."

"Lead on, Chief Sentry."

Chapter 24

"With this technology we can locate all of our enemies and attack them simultaneously. We can finally rid the world of the Servators in a single coordinated action. They'll never know what hit them." Kenric smiled at the angry faces arrayed before him.

"How long have you been spying on us with this technology?" Samitar Patix raged. The Second Anarch of Arapanus, known for his quick temper, was true to form.

"The network here in Sumakad has only recently achieved reliability. It hasn't been deployed in any of your regions. That is what we're here to discuss." Kenric soothed.

Kivar Bantoo of Kemetica was quick to respond. "Why would we believe the man responsible for killing Toller and stealing this venue for his own agenda?"

"Toller didn't die by my hand." Kenric stated honestly. "The fool demanded an audience with the wastrel overlords."

A sharp intake of breath came from several in the room. Heads were shaking in disbelief. Every Second Anarch understood the danger. The overlords were insane. No one willingly requested an audience.

"How can we be sure that is true?" Loo Vishar asked.

"I will personally open the Sumakad gate for any who wish to enter and inspect the body."

The Second Anarch of Jaihuwan paled and vigorously shook his head. "That won't be necessary."

Kenric expected Vishar's response. The man was a coward. How he ever attained the second seat was a mystery. That fearfulness had worked to Kenric's advantage on several occasions and he knew it would work in his favour now as well.

"Toller Villecrest only held the third seat. He wouldn't have known what to expect from the overlords and he overextended in an attempt to take my place. He demanded his right to seek an audience and I was duty-bound to comply. Did it work to my advantage? Yes, but not as a result of any plotting on my part. I kept an eye on Villecrest, but he represented no real threat to me. He was ambitious, but also clumsy and obvious. Almost as obvious as Bantoo."

Kivar sputtered in outrage and Kenric rolled his eyes. "Spare me the theatrics, Kivar. Everyone in this room knows that you orchestrated events to allow Toller the privilege of hosting the gathering this year." Heads nodded about the room in acknowledgment. "How did Villecrest sway you? Did he promise to marry that spoiled daughter of yours?" Barely suppressed snickers could be heard in the background. "Seriously, Kivar, stick with what you know. Spycraft is *not* one of your skills."

The Second Anarch of Kemetica glared, but said nothing more, caught as he was in his own plotting. Kenric would smooth the ruffled feathers later, but right now he needed Kivar to keep his comments to himself.

"We're wasting time." Isau Jax spoke into the lull. "I wish to hear more about this technology and your inevitable *proposal*." That last comment had a sardonic drawl hinting at derision, but Kenric knew it was an act. The Second Anarch of Caralithica was an ally. They had worked together secretly for years. He could count on Isau when it was time to vote. As for the others, Loo would support him out of fear and Kenric was confident that Kivar and Samitar would fall in line out of self-interest.

"Thank you. As I've said, all of your questions will be answered. I know it's not easy for us to trust one another, but the Servators are a common enemy, a constant thorn in our sides. All of us benefit if they're removed from the Jumkano board. Imagine a world where we can operate without their moral codes and interfering rangers. Think of how quickly each of you could expand your influence and increase your profits."

He had them now, the greed shone in their eyes.

"Each of us has employed a great many resources tracking down our enemies. I have agents following suspected Servators in the hope that they'll lead to other Servators. It's an incredibly slow process, but acting too soon would cause them to scurry to their holes, forcing us to start the long process all over again." It was a pattern familiar to each of them and he had their attention.

"I have blanketed Sumakad with viewcorders. The public believes this is an effort to reduce crime." Kenric smiled and several anarchs chuckled. Kivar looked confused so Kenric explained for his benefit — now wasn't the time to antagonize the man further. "Of course the security forces are my own people and the petty criminals are irritants nibbling away at Breacher profits. The public lauds our efforts while paying us to eliminate our competition." Kivar's eyes lit in understanding and Kenric moved on.

"The facial recognition algorithm creates a database of every person in the city. Suspected or known Servators are entered into the system which automatically flags everyone they contact. Now instead of following pointless leads, my people can target only those who have been flagged. They can very quickly recognize casual contacts versus questionable ones. By entering refined contact lists, the system begins to identify patterns. Covert meeting spots and repeated contact between suspected Servators will ultimately identify them. They're unable to hide."

"Surely they notice the viewcorders and avoid them?"

"That's a good observation, Samitar. I started this project several years ago. Somehow Villecrest discovered the facial recognition work for himself, not realizing it was my project. I'll credit him for recognizing its value, but he started deploying it before I was ready to do so. You know how bloodthirsty the man was. He dramatically expanded the deployment of viewcorders and began killing Servators as soon as the network discovered them. The Servators became suspicious as you would expect and began avoiding the viewcorders. They even tampered with a few.

"If Toller had thought to consult with me, I would have shown him this." Kenric held up a transparent device the size of his thumbnail.

"What is it?" Kivar asked.

"This, my friends, is a tiny viewcorder developed by my engineers. It runs on the wireless tote-comm network and has three tiny lenses providing a one hundred and eighty degree view. It's virtually invisible, allowing placement almost anywhere. It will be difficult for Servators to hide from something they can't see."

Samitar stepped up to take a closer look. "Incredible. May I?"

"Of course." Kenric handed the device to Samitar and flipped a switch at the workstation. An image from the tiny viewcorder filled the large screen providing an example of its capabilities. Kenric waited while the device was handed around. Face making and crude gestures paraded across the viewscreen as the anarchs played with it. When they'd each had a turn, he retrieved it and continued.

"Villecrest's inept efforts could have ruined this for all of us by sending the Servators into hiding. Instead, we will turn his mistake into an advantage. The Servators know nothing about these smaller devices. It will be much easier to secrete them around the city. We can place them inside buildings as well as out. The Servators will be so busy avoiding the obvious viewcorders placed by Toller that they won't think to look for these new ones.

"We won't make Toller's mistake. We'll let them become complacent and wait until we have identified all of the Servators. Then, when we're ready, we will act as one. That's where you come in. For this to work, we need viewcorder coverage of the world's cities. We can't risk missing hidden pockets of Servators or they'll just rebuild."

"You want us to allow you to place hidden viewcorders within our territories allowing you to monitor us? Are you mad?"

Kenric held up his hands and shouted over the cacophony of protests. "You misunderstand... Listen!"

The others fell silent.

"I intend to give you the algorithm to set up your own memory stash archives. You will control all data and monitoring for your regions. I have no intention of entering your districts to place viewcorders. That will be your responsibility. I ask only that we agree to make no moves against the Servators until we're confident — as a group — that we've identified a sufficient number of them. We need to make the decision to move against them in a single concerted effort or this won't work."

It was Isau who asked the obvious question. "And what do you get out of this?"

"Like all of you, I will benefit from a world free of Servator interference. However, I'm also willing to sell these tiny viewcorders so you can quickly build your networks."

"Aha!" Kivar shouted. "This is about you filling your coffers while draining ours."

"You've all seen what this technology can do. I've spent decades developing it. I've already offered to give you the algorithm for free. You can hardly fault me for trying to regain some of my development costs. I'm only asking for a few silvers per viewcorder. It took me years to develop these devices and I'm ready to ramp up production — today. If you would rather spend the time and money to develop your own, then be my guest. For those of you who would like to place orders, I can deliver them within weeks. You'll reap the benefits of city-wide monitoring as quickly as you can install your networks. Long before the elimination of the Servators, you'll be able to plan around their movements. Those who don't want my help can take their time and miss out on years of additional revenue."

Everything was out in the open now. It was an obvious choice to invest in automated monitoring over manpower. The technology was a game changer and nobody could afford to fall behind. Even Kivar realized it.

Kenric sensed it was time to put it to a vote. "Each of you will leave this gathering with a copy of the algorithm. You can take it back to your engineers to inspect and modify as you see fit. I ask that you share any improvements with the rest of us. In the coming weeks, you may contact me with your orders or express your plans to develop your own viewcorders. I leave it to you to decide. You can all see the benefits of owning your own networks whether we use it to attack the Servators or not. However, if we wish to eliminate the Servators, we need to agree to set petty differences aside and work together. We must all develop our own networks and orchestrate our efforts or we won't succeed. So that is what we must put to a vote. Do we all agree to develop our own networks and work together to destroy our common enemy once and for all? By a show of hands, who is in favour?"

All hands rose as one. Kenric smiled.

"Then we're agreed. We can move on to discuss the reporting structure for network progress as well as regular business. I'll have the servers bring desserts and more wine."

Kenric moved toward the door to assure the guards that all was well and to place orders for pastries and drinks. All his years of planning were coming to fruition. When all was said and done, he would no longer be referred to as the man who made a small splash with the Trantor uprising. The world would finally recognize his patience and his genius. When the servers returned, he kept a flagon of wine for himself. It was a good day and he planned to celebrate.

Chapter 25

Tenika sat at a table in a small windowless room. The door was locked. She knew it would be, but tried it anyway. The room had remained brightly lit throughout the night. At least as far as she could tell. It was difficult to determine the passage of time.

Two men had grabbed her as she headed for her parking stall at Callan International. They bound her and tossed her unceremoniously into a ground transport that smelled like a fishmonger's delivery vehicle. Tenika wrinkled her nose at the memory. The stink lingered on her clothes. It had happened quickly — the men were clearly professionals.

She'd been granted an opportunity to relieve herself, but not to bathe. Her stomach growled, reminding her that she hadn't eaten since her abduction. A flagon of water and a mug sat on the table. At least she could slake her thirst.

Tenika didn't have a clue who these people were. *Is Bode double-crossing me?* She couldn't think of any reason why he would. Halen had already made arrangements with the keeper of records for payment to the City Sentinels. The price had been exorbitant, but she wasn't paying for it out of her own pocket. Callan International could easily afford it and Bode would earn a princely sum for his involvement. It made no sense for him to stab her in the back. *It can't be Bode. If he threatened his master's eventual payout, he'd have a target on his back.* So who were these people? Were these the Breachers Bode mentioned? That still didn't add up. The Breachers were working with Bode... The sound of locks disengaging from the door interrupted Her thoughts. *Finally.*

A regal-looking woman wearing a uniform of a style she didn't recognize strode into the room. The man following her seemed both hyper-alert and calm at the same time. The door was locked behind them. A quick assessment of their fluid motion and muscle tone warned her that these weren't feeble administrators. *A mercenary group perhaps?* The woman spoke first. "My name is Cello Vantos. I'm Chief Sentry for the Caralithican Host of Servators."

Well, that was unexpected. "Servators? What's a Servator?"

The woman ignored her. "This is Akhen Hor. He just arrived from Kemetica. It's the reason for the delay in our conversation."

Tenika made a mental note. To have arrived so quickly, he must have taken a private LTA flight. This organization had resources.

"Why have you abducted me? Do you know who I am? My work colleagues will notice my absence and I have friends among the City Sentinels."

"We're well aware of your associates, Ms. Sheridan. You needn't worry about them missing you, lawvocates at Callan International have already accepted your resignation."

"What?" Tenika erupted from her seat. "You have no right or authority to do such a thing! I'll have you arrested. You can't hold me here. Release me at once!"

Neither the Chief Sentry nor her companion flinched at her sudden outburst.

The Chief Sentry merely smiled and shrugged. "You won't be going anywhere, Ms. Sheridan. You're charged with the murder of two Servator rangers and the attempted murder of a Servator novice."

"This is madness! I've never even heard of the Servators before this moment. How could I possibly have killed one?"

"Two, actually, and you knew them well — Nes and Tawni Callan, whom you had assassinated long ago. As for the attempted murder charge, that is for framing Nico Callan so that he could be dispatched in prison. You're also indirectly responsible for the murder of a magistrate who died to facilitate your plot. However, that falls under City jurisdiction."

Tenika paled. *How could they know about any of this?* "Lies! I demand to speak with my lawvocate."

The Chief Sentry shook her head. "Perhaps I haven't made myself clear.

You're responsible for the death of two rangers. You'll have no contact with the Caralithican legal system or any other system for that matter. The Servators are a global organization that stands apart from all existing governance. Our primary domain of influence pertains to the Servators and the Breachers. Your crimes fall under Servator jurisdiction. More specifically, you're under my authority as the Chief Sentry of Caralithica. I'm both your advocate and the one who decides your sentence."

Tenika's mind was racing. Breachers — that word again. *Bode, what have you gotten me into?* Obviously, the Breachers were some kind of criminal organization, but Bode had made them sound untouchable. He never mentioned Servators. "This is unacceptable. How can you be my advocate if you're also my executioner?"

"I've said nothing about execution. That isn't our way. You'll spend the rest of your life at a rehabilitation facility on a remote island."

"You've already sentenced me and you call yourself an advocate?"

"I assure you that the Servators do not pass sentence without irrefutable evidence. If there were any doubt, you would remain as my guest and I would have advocated for you until the matter reached a satisfactory conclusion. However, in your case the evidence is irrefutable. Your guilt is clear."

"I demand to see this so-called evidence."

"That is your right." The Chief Servator knocked at the door and spoke to the guard who answered. Moments later, a viewscreen was rolled into the room on a cart. The guard placed it in front of Tenika and started playback of a recording. She watched in shock as her meeting on Bode's pleasure craft played out in crystal clarity. "How did you get this?"

"That's irrelevant. Do you deny having met with Bode Garushe?"

"It proves nothing. Nico is never mentioned nor a plot to frame anyone. It's only a request for help dealing with an investigation through proper channels."

The Chief Sentry smiled indulgently. "Breachers are hardly *proper channels*. You recruited Bode Garushe, a member of the top criminal organization in Jaihuwan. In this viewcording he encouraged you to accept the help of your *friend* Qas Drugarish, a known Sicari assassin, to arrange for a charade of justice through corrupt entities. Thank you, by the way, for acknowledging that the conversation was about Nico."

Tenika silently berated herself for the slip-up. "Is Nico dead?"

"No, he's quite safe."

"Then, no crime was committed against Nico Callan and the evidence regarding his parents is circumstantial at best."

"We both know that's not the case, but we also have this." Cello slid a piece of parchment across the table.

"More fabricated *evidence*?"

"It's the confession of Halen Tu, along with a record of your illegal activities over the years. Halen is in another room confessing your exploits in great detail. He's really not a very brave man. He seems eager to make sure he doesn't take the fall for your crimes. Halen was very meticulous in compiling solid evidence. I suppose one would expect that from a lawvocate. We also have the ledger that you doctored to hide the fact that you hired Qas Drugarish to assassinate the senior Callans. We have viewcorder evidence of Qas picking up his payments."

"Halen!" Tenika pounded her fists against the table. "I'll kill him!"

"I think not."

Tenika glared at her captors. How could this be happening? She couldn't spend the rest of her life in a prison somewhere. She couldn't even spare a year. If she didn't get Laki Shung his payment, her life was forfeited. Now that she knew he had ties to this Breacher organization, she was certain there was nowhere to flee and her demise would be swift.

"I see you understand. You'll be off on a sea voyage very soon to the place where you will serve out your sentence, but not before you've told us everything you know about Qas Drugarish. We've been searching for him for some time. You're going to help us find him."

"What makes you think I'd help you with anything?" Tenika spat. "You've stolen everything from me!"

"You can hardly claim ownership of property which you yourself have stolen from the Callan family. Yes, we know about your various enterprises. Our analysts have been very thorough. We're in the process of selling off your assets. Callan International will be reimbursed with the proceeds."

"No...." Tenika trembled. *I'm dead. Laki will find out.*

"I'll be taking my leave now. A ranger will accept my place as witness. Akhen will carry out the interview. I warn you, his training allows him to detect a lie."

The man stared into her eyes and she believed it. His gaze was unnerving. "What if I refuse?"

The Chief Sentry looked at Akhen and then back to Tenika. "I wouldn't advise it. Akhen is a very talented individual. He has a way of ... getting into your mind. He has certain other abilities that might make you uncomfortable."

The woman nodded to Akhen as though giving him permission. Akhen waved his hand over the table and Tenika was horrified as she watched the air shimmer and materialize into a monstrous device filled with wires and tubes. Tenika backed away, abruptly meeting the wall. "What is that thing? What kind of sorcery is this? Who are you people?"

Akhen waved his hand again and the construct disappeared.

"Tell Akhen everything you know, Ms. Sheridan. I'm sure you'll be fine."

Dread filled Tenika. *No — nothing will ever be fine again.*

Chapter 26

It had been two weeks since Lev responded to Kade's message hidden in the writ weaves of the Breacher viewcorder network. He had to assume that Kade received the message he'd sent in reply, but Kade had been silent ever since. He began to wonder if something bad had happened. Lev wasn't sure how he felt about that. Kade had been a major pain in his neck for years. Lev mentally chastised himself. *Knock it off Lev, you don't want to see Kade get hurt — even if he's the most annoying person on the planet.*

Lev had set up a search algorithm to watch for changes in the writ weaves of the Breacher network. Any string of characters that started with 'sp' and ended with 'br' would trigger an alert on his wrist Q-view. The 'sp' stood for sage's pet, an obnoxious nickname Kade used when referring to him and 'br' stood for 'Brixton.' So much had happened lately that he was embarrassed to admit that he'd forgotten about Kade and Selica. He was reminded by an alert from his Q-view the previous night. Kade had finally responded. His message was cryptic.

-sp-exit-24x8+17x1=sum-anchor-1-9-7-21-16-20-15-19-bridge-br-.

The first part was obvious enough. Kade was requesting an exit. The equation that followed was confusing. 24x8+17x1=sum. That sum would be 192, but that made no sense. He understood Kade's need to obfuscate the message in order to remain undetected, but he didn't think Kade would risk making the message incomprehensible. Thinking about it, Lev realized that the message would need to contain basic information like the date, time, and place.

The code was date stamped, but that date had already passed. Eventually he determined that the number 24 represented hours in a day. So, 24 multiplied by 8 meant eight days. If the first number represented hours, then in the second part 17 multiplied by one meant 17 hours. Eight days and seventeen hours past the time stamp was midnight three days from now.

Lev didn't understand what 'sum' and 'anchor' meant, other than their use as commands in a writ. The numbers that followed, he assumed to be the simple alphanumeric cipher they had used in previous messages. When he translated it, the word 'aiguptos' was revealed. Finding himself at an impasse, he brought the message to some analysts and explained what he thought he knew. He asked them how the words anchor, sum, aiguptos, and bridge might be connected. They surprised him with a quick response. Apparently, everyone knew that the City of Ankhora in Sumakad was a hotbed of Breacher activity, and that Aiguptos was the name of the river that ran through it. Exactly one bridge crossed the Aiguptos River. He supposed it was no surprise that support staff for rangers in the field would instantly recognize Breacher locations. Lev made a mental note to learn more about Breacher strongholds.

Assuming they hadn't misinterpreted Kade's message, they had a date, a time, and a place. It was time to call a proper meeting to discuss what he'd found.

***

Sitting around the table were Tark, Yori, and Chief Sentry Beniti Abrax. It had been Beniti who insisted that Kade needed help and would be an important source of information regarding Breacher implementation of the facial recognition algorithm. Lev understood his perspective much better now. They didn't have the luxury of time, and all leads were important leads. If Kade was deceiving them, Akhen would be able to tell, once they were face-to-face.

"Our sources tell us that a gathering of the anarchs is taking place in Ankhora at that time." Beniti said. "That can't be a coincidence."

"The place is going to be swarming with Breachers. Every anarch will have a full complement of security. Those operatives will be on high alert throughout the city." Yori added. "Every street corner will be watched."

"Do you think Kade is leading us into a trap?" Lev asked.

"I don't believe so," Beniti answered. "I'm still convinced it was a genuine cry for help."

"I'm inclined to agree," Tark added. "The anarchs attend for selfish reasons. They don't play well together. It's highly unlikely they would all agree to work together and no single anarch would risk running a solitary operation while surrounded by their suspicious peers."

"Besides, what would they hope to gain by luring a few rangers to Ankhora on that night of all nights?" Beniti asked. "It makes more sense that Mr. Brixton would take advantage of the uneasy Breacher truce for a risky escape attempt. That he's willing to take such a desperate gamble adds to the credibility of his story."

Lev caught Beniti's eye. "I think we can agree that the risk is necessary. This rescue needs to happen."

Yori stood and began pacing. "Three days isn't a lot of time to prepare for this type of operation. The number of Breachers present will be a problem."

"So, we send a large contingent," Tark offered.

Beniti drummed his fingers on the table. "That will only draw more attention. We can't bring a large enough contingent to counter a Breacher threat of that size without starting a war. We certainly don't want to create a situation that rallies the anarchs under a common banner."

Lev agreed. "It has to be a small force. A stealthy operation. What would be the minimum number of rangers necessary, assuming we remain undetected?"

Yori rubbed his chin, making some mental calculations. "Ideally, we need two people to scout the area looking for threats, one to extract Kade and two more to monitor the point of extraction while providing cover. We'd need an additional person to pilot an escape vehicle. That's six, but any group larger than four would draw attention. We can't have that many walking openly in the street."

"We won't need that many in the street."

"Why, Lev? What are you thinking?"

"The extraction point is the bridge crossing the Aiguptos River. We can have a scout in the streets on either side of the river. The rest of us can travel the river by sea craft and avoid the streets altogether."

"Assuming the scouts give an all clear, that could work, but if things go bad, we'll be sitting ducks out on the water if this turns out to be a trap..." Tark paused as he considered options. "The water would give us a buffer from close quarters fighting, but we'd be vulnerable to ballistic weapons. We could counter that with an armoured vessel, but I'm not sure we could find something on such short notice."

Lev interrupted Tark's musings. "Even if this is a trap, the Breachers won't know if we're coming by land or water. Beniti has already reasoned that it would be difficult for a single anarch to plan something large during the gathering without raising suspicion among the other anarchs. If this is a trap, it will tax their resources."

"You're probably right, but it still makes me uncomfortable."

"What if we could remain unseen until we arrive at the bridge?"

"How do you propose to do that?"

"Knowing we would need to arrange transportation on short notice, I contacted Nico Callan. He's reserved a high-speed private air transport for us to a small town on the river just outside of Ankhora."

"That's great Lev, but it doesn't solve the problem of getting to the bridge unseen unless he's providing an invisible sea-transport."

Lev grinned. "In a way, he's doing just that."

Beniti grew impatient. "I would appreciate a little less grinning and a little more information."

Lev raised his palms in submission. "As it happens, Nico owns a personal sub-aqua transport. The Aiguptos River is deep enough to accommodate his smaller craft, we already checked. Nico's father used that same vessel in past Servator missions. It's reliable and stealthy. We can slip in unseen and surface when we get an all clear from our scouts."

"That *would* give us an advantage," Yori conceded, "but I don't personally know any rangers who can pilot a sub. I don't see how we can find a pilot from another base on such short notice."

"We don't have to," Lev replied. "Nico knows how to operate the sub and he's already on his way. He'll be waiting for us when we arrive."

"What?" Both Tark and Yori exclaimed at the same time. "Absolutely not!" Yori insisted. "Only Servators are permitted on operations like this."

"Then you're in luck since Nico is a Servator novice."

Yori raised an eyebrow and Tark's chin dropped. "Since when? I thought Nico was busy running the family business. Novice training isn't a part-time affair."

"I just found out myself. A lot has happened recently. This needs to remain between us, but the Breachers have framed Nico for the murder of a prominent magistrate. He's hiding at the Servator base in Denmount where he's receiving training in an accelerated program. He was very eager to take a trip. I don't know all of the details, but he informs me that Callan International is in competent hands under the administration of a Servator lawvocate. Meanwhile, his training has been going well." Lev paused to look first at Tark and then Yori. "Nico tells me he's looking forward to sparring with you two."

Tark looked at Yori and smirked. "It appears our little Nico is a glutton for punishment."

Yori chuckled, but then grew serious. "It seems you have this all planned out, Lev. Why pretend you need our input?"

"Are you joking, Yori? I only arranged the transportation. I need your input for the details — you know that. You're in charge of the operation and I know you can work with whatever you're given. Did I choose poorly?"

"No." Yori admitted. "You've chosen useful options considering the timeline and circumstances. I can work with this. How many can fit into Nico's sub?"

"Six people total, including Nico."

"We need to reserve space for Kade and some gear, so that only allows for three others. That's two short of what I suggested for a minimum force."

"That's true." Lev said, "but the two scouts don't need to be with us. They can enter the city by ground transport and proceed on foot. As long as we limit their involvement to information gathering, they should remain safe. They can leave the way they arrived. That leaves room for Yori, Tark and myself."

Beniti burst to his feet, "Young man, this is a poor way of convincing me you don't have a death wish. The Levigator can't be a part of this. We can't risk your safety."

"It's the best option. Kade knows me — he'll immediately recognize us as friendly forces. That alone should help things to go more smoothly. Besides that, I'm better equipped to protect others and myself than anyone at this table. I can make up for the missing forces. Yori, you wanted an armoured vessel? Well, I'm that armour."

Beniti seemed stunned by the proclamation and looked to Tark who nodded and shared their recent sparring experience with Lev.

"Well then, it seems you're now Levigator in deed as well as name. I have little choice but to trust in your judgment, but if anything goes wrong..." The Chief Sentry looked at Tark and Yori. "...you know what you must do." Both nodded once with determination in their eyes. Lev didn't want to know what that meant. He had the weight of too many lives on his shoulders as it was.

Chapter 27

It had been three days since her interrogation. Tenika shuddered thinking of those penetrating eyes. She'd decided that Akhen Hor wasn't human. She had tested him with false information, but somehow he always knew she was lying. How was that possible? At first she thought he could read her mind, but then realized he wouldn't be asking questions if that were the case.

When he pushed her for information about Qas, she pushed back. She already had Laki's death threats to worry about, she certainly didn't need a Sicari assassin seeking retribution. Not that she had much to say about the man other than what they already knew. She had hired him — twice now, although she had only met him face-to-face the first time.

When she continued in her stubborn silence, Akhen waved his hand again and a bust of Qas's head materialized on the table in front of her. It was a perfect replica of the assassin's face. Tenika's insides turned to jelly. "Is this the man you hired?" Akhen asked. It was all she could do to nod in the affirmative. His abilities were terrifying. Could he unmake her as easily as that hideous replica of Qas's head? She tried to watch closely — to see if she could discern the mechanics. Watching the head collapse into constituent molecules and vanish only made her queasy — and no better informed. When the interview finally ended, she spent a restless night dreaming she was trapped in a fighting arena. In the dream, she was fleeing from two assassins and a giant who would grind her to powder if she stopped running. The following night was no better.

***

That Vantos woman had told her she would be leaving this evening for the rehabilitation facility. *Rehabilitation* — she hated that word. The thought of someone trying to change her — endless indoctrination day after day for the rest of her life — it was unbearable. She had to escape somehow. They'd removed her dagger during her capture, but they let her keep her ring. That was careless. The hidden pin had enough toxin to paralyze a single large man. Unfortunately, a minimum of two guards would be present during her transfer. At least, that seemed to be their standard practice — one to drive the ground transport and one to keep an eye on her. *I just need a moment alone with one of them and I might have a chance.* It wasn't much of a hope, but she clung to it.

Tenika had given some thought to what she might do if she escaped. Her options were limited. The Servators claimed they had dissolved her financial assets. She didn't think they could have found all of her cache, spread out as it was. It hardly mattered, she wouldn't have enough to pay Laki Shung. Laki didn't show mercy, which meant a lifetime on the run. Now that she knew he worked with this global organization called the Breachers, she had given up on the idea that she could hide if she got far enough away. In the past, Tenika had lived on the streets working with criminal organizations. She was meticulous in her research when planning an operation. How had she been part of the criminal underworld yet never heard of the Breachers? They seemed to be of interest to these Servators, yet not controlled by them. That meant the Breachers had resources capable of keeping the Servators at bay. If Breachers could resist the Servators and their strange abilities, then they could stand against Laki as well. Bode had mentioned she would fit in with the Breachers. At the time she didn't know what he was talking about. He made it sound like a legitimate option — like they would be interested in what she had to offer. Tenika wasn't afraid to start over. She knew she could prove her worth quickly, but she needed time for that. Time that Laki wasn't about to give her. Maybe she had enough silvers hidden away to purchase Breacher protection. It really was her only option at this point. She needed to escape both the Servators and Laki. To do that, she needed a powerful ally.

Tenika was still trying to figure out how she might contact the Breachers when her captors came for her. A ranger shackled her wrist to his own and proceeded to wrap a blindfold over her eyes. *Not good. I can't escape if I'm blind.* She stumbled along as they led her by her elbow to a waiting ground transport. Strong hands lifted her to a bench seat and she felt the weight of a heavy body settle beside her. The two guards bantered a bit before the engine started and then the transport lurched into motion. The blindfold left her unprepared and her head bounced off a hard surface at the abruptness of their departure. She cursed under her breath when it happened a second time. Then an idea formed. Whenever the vehicle made an abrupt change in direction, she allowed her head to strike harder than necessary until she could feel a trickle of blood on her cheek. After half an hour had passed, she turned toward her minder. "I realize this blindfold is to keep me from seeing where we came from, but we must be far enough away by now that it no longer matters." She turned her head so he could see the blood from her head wound. "It's hard to anticipate the bumps in the road with my eyes covered."

The ranger remained silent for a moment and then she heard a grunt of acceptance as he removed the blindfold.

"Thank you."

Tenika took in her surroundings. They were on the outskirts of Denmount heading towards the sea. Two rangers were in the vehicle with her, the driver and the guard shackled to her wrist. It was as she imagined it would be. Five minutes passed and they entered a forested area. That could work to her advantage. It had to be now.

"I need to relieve myself."

The ranger rolled his eyes. "Hold it in. You can take care of business when we've boarded the sea transport."

That wasn't good. Once at sea, she'd have no other opportunities to escape.

"I can't. No one let me go before you came to my cell. I've already been holding it in for hours. I can't wait any longer."

The ranger glowered at her.

"Look," Tenika nodded out the window. "I see some trees right over there. It will only take a minute," she whined. "If you don't stop, I'm going to make a mess of these nice leather seats."

She received a growl in reply.

"Please — what possible harm could it do to stop for a moment?"

She lifted her wrists. "I'm chained to you! It's not like I can run away."

The ranger sighed. "Stop the transport, Oren."

"You sure?"

"Leave the engine running, we'll be right back."

They pulled to the edge of the road and came to a stop. Tenika's heart pounded as she waited to see whether the second ranger would join them. He remained seated.

"Come on then." She felt a tug at her wrists as the ranger headed to the treeline.

Squatting in the tall grass, she thumbed the cover off her ring, exposing the sharp pin hidden within. "Can you whistle a tune or something?"

"What on earth for?"

"So you can't hear me."

"I'm not going to whistle for you. Just hurry up."

"Well, can you at least turn around then?"

"Oh for — I'm not looking."

"It'll be harder for you to sneak a peek if you're not directly facing me."

The guard looked at her suspiciously and turned his body slightly to the side but no further. "Fine. Is this better?"

"Yes."

"Good, hurry — yowp! What did — you — just — do?"

The ranger's voice trailed off as he slumped to the ground. Tenika quickly fished through his pockets and breathed a sigh of relief as she found the key to her shackles. It took a bit of doing to get the key in her mouth and figure out how to turn it. A satisfying click reached her ears and she shook off her bindings. She quickly ducked behind a tree before standing to peer around it. The driver was no longer in the transport. Her eyes darted back and forth in the twilight. Had he come to check on them? She spotted a figure further away at the treeline. He had decided to relieve himself while he waited. Tenika chuckled as she quietly moved deeper into the treeline. When she felt confident her footfalls were beyond hearing range, she broke into a jog. It was going to be a long night, but the fresh air tasted like freedom and she would savour it until dawn. After that she'd see about finding a Breacher.

Chapter 28

It had taken Tenika most of the night to get back to Denmount. She couldn't return to her home or office, so she spent the night at Callan Netting — the abandoned warehouse where she'd hidden the ledger. She gambled that no one would think to look for her there. Since the Servators now had the ledger in their possession, she hoped they'd think she had no reason to return. In the morning she stole a hooded cloak from a clothes line in the residential section and made her way to the neighbourhood of her former residence. Her house was likely being watched, but there was a park, a short jog from her home, that she'd scoped out for just this type of emergency. It was heavily treed and easy to access without being spotted. She made her way to a copse of trees where she had buried a small stash of silvers. *You can't take the street out of the girl*, Tenika mused. She had similar caches secured all over the city. Those habits were paying off now. She spent a few of the silvers at a food vendor and eagerly filled the hungry void in her stomach.

As she sat in a quiet alley to consider her options, she decided to risk contacting Garushe and have him arrange for her to meet with Qas. She needed to learn more about what it meant to join the Breachers. Stepping back out into the street, she searched for a kind looking stranger.

A mother was walking nearby, towing a small child by the hand. The boy was clearly too young to speak and clutched a toy in his free arm. *Perfect*. Tenika checked to make certain no one was watching, then crept up behind the pair and deftly snatched the toy from the boy's hand. She quickly took several steps backward. The child immediately began to wail.

"Miss? Excuse me, miss?" Tenika trotted up to the mother who was trying to understand what had upset the boy.

"I believe your son dropped this." Tenika crouched beside the child. "Here you are, little man." The boy stared at her suspiciously before accepting the toy from her hand. *Take it, you little brat.*

"Oh! Thank you so much." The mother enthused. "I didn't notice he'd dropped it. It's his favourite toy. He wouldn't have fallen asleep tonight without it. How can I thank you?"

"Not at all, glad to help." Tenika turned to leave and then paused. "Actually, I'm waiting for a friend who seems to be running late. Would you happen to have a tote-comm I could borrow to check in on him?"

"Of course! It's the least I can do. Here — take your time."

Tenika wandered a few steps away, made the call, and returned the tote-comm. "Thank you, my friend said he'll be here shortly."

"It was my pleasure, have a nice day." As the woman walked off, the boy looked over his shoulder and gave Tenika a frown. She scowled back at him, turned and started the long walk back to the warehouse.

***

Another day had passed. Tenika stood near the docks between the designated stacks of crates. As she waited for Qas to appear, the smell of fish on a hot afternoon assailed her nostrils. *How do I keep ending up at the docks?* A hooded figure was moving in her direction. Tenika drew deeper into her hiding place. As the figure passed, she heard the unmistakable gravelly voice of Qas. "Follow at ten paces." Tenika pulled up her own hood and looked in both directions before slipping into the chaos of dock hands, vendors and customers. She dutifully remained ten paces behind until she saw where Qas was heading. *Another sea transport? Men have no imagination.* She hesitated only for a moment. Qas was already untying the vessel. He clearly had no intention of waiting. Tenika quickened her pace and hopped aboard just as Qas pulled away from the dock. She lost her footing and rolled to the stern as the prow lifted out of the water to speed away. Rubbing a bruise on her elbow, she lifted herself into a sitting position and spread her arms to either side to steady herself. Qas made his way to the southern docks on the far side of Denmount and tied off the craft. He jumped to the dock without a word and jogged towards a waiting ground transport. Tenika hurried to catch up and made her way to the vehicle door that had been left open for her.

Qas gazed at her steadily. "Nico Callan has proven difficult to track. He doesn't appear to be in Denmount at the moment. It's a temporary setback, I assure you."

Qas started the transport and began driving.

Is Qas apologizing for failing to complete his contract? The bewilderment must have shown on Tenika's face, because he continued. "I take my contracts very seriously. My reputation has remained untarnished to this point. I will complete this task, but it may take more time."

Tenika shook her head. "It hardly matters now. I release you from your contract."

"Thank you, but my code requires that I see this to completion."

It was a twisted ethic, but Tenika understood the need to maintain a fear-based reputation when dealing with the criminal element. "You can repay me by getting me a meeting with a high-level Breacher."

Qas nodded. "As I've said, I will complete my task. As a token of my word, I've used up one of my favours with Isau Jax to grant you an audience. I've given you a positive recommendation."

"Thank you — how does this work?"

"You must not use Isau's name. You'll address him only as Second Anarch. When you're ushered into his presence, you must kneel and wait for him to grant permission to speak. Never initiate conversation, only answer his questions. Caralithica's Second Anarch is more reasonable than some, but don't test him. He'll have two Sicari with him at all times. Either of them is capable of cutting you down before you recognize the threat."

"I understand."

"We'll arrive at the meeting place shortly. You'll be on your own from there. Give the front entrance three quick knocks, then pause and knock two more times. Someone will usher you in." Qas barely had time to conclude his instructions before they pulled to a stop in front of a dilapidated building. A sign in the window advertised the space for rent. Tenika sounded the prescribed sequence of knocks and the door opened immediately. Clearly, someone had been watching her approach. A burly fellow dressed in black stood before her. He was as wide as he was tall. *This must be another of the mysterious Sicari.* He closed and bolted the door. Gesturing that she should follow, the man spun on his heel and walked briskly down the corridor. Tenika reminded herself not to judge by appearances. Despite his muscle mass, the man moved with the fluid grace of someone confident in his abilities. One of the doors along the corridor was open — the opposite wall awash in sunlight from a window within the room. Her guide waved her in and took up a position beside the door.

The room was empty apart from a table pushed against one wall. A layer of dust covered everything. Motes sparkled in the sunlight, disturbed by Tenika's passage. This obviously wasn't the seat of Breacher power. She was meeting with a cautious man. Isau Jax stood leaning against the table. He scanned her from head to toe before locking onto her eyes. Tenika was startled. He was a handsome man with a dark complexion. His hard eyes were calculating rather than cruel and he appeared almost as fit as the Sicari who protected him — without the bulk. He wasn't at all what she expected. Her experience with crime lords in Jaihuwan had convinced her that such men tended to overindulge in the vices they peddled, leaving them soft and cruel.

One side of Isau Jax's mouth formed a subtle quirk as if he was familiar with the reaction. Tenika quickly averted her eyes and took a knee. She waited silently, head bowed.

"I've offered Qas favours on numerous occasions. This is the first time he has ever made a request. It was painful for him, if I'm any judge of character. The man doesn't like being indebted to anyone — which suggests that the discomfort he felt in asking a favour of me was less awkward than an indebtedness he feels toward you. Not only did he request that I give you an audience, but he gave his recommendation that I accept you into the Breachers. I admit that piqued my curiosity. I would like to hear your request for myself."

Silence dragged on and Tenika tested a submissive query. "May I speak?"

"Please do."

"I wish to join the Breachers."

"Qas suggested as much, but I would like to know why."

Eyes still downcast, Tenika stated, "I have no place else to turn."

"Look at me when you speak."

Tenika lifted her head and met his inquisitive gaze.

"Repeat that, please."

"I have no place else to turn."

Isau nodded as if settling something for himself.

"And what do you have to offer the Breachers? What do you bring to the table that I don't already possess?"

Tenika thought quickly. "You're a man of authority. As you expand your reach, I imagine you're always looking for skilled administrators to execute your plans."

Isau raised an eyebrow. "Administrator? You have yet to be invited and you see yourself in a position of authority? Individuals who have spent decades in the ranks vie for those stations. I would have laughed had the recommendation not come from Qas himself."

"You asked what I bring to the table and these are the skills I'm best known for. Whether my role carries any authority is up to you."

The Second Anarch smiled. "Humble words, but you're a woman used to giving orders — not taking them. My curiosity prompted me to dig a little into your past, Ms. Sheridan. I have spoken with Bode Garushe. He filled me in on your rise to power within Callan International. Your exploits are impressive, but saving your neck after killing a son of Laki Shung — that suggests some unique talents."

Tenika jerked her head, startled by Isau's words.

"Oh yes, I spoke with Laki, I know him well."

Tenika felt a chill run down her spine. Was she about to be handed over to Laki?

"Laki isn't one to waste resources. That he considered you more valuable than his son speaks volumes. He informed me of your current circumstances. You are indeed between a rock and a hard place, but for some inexplicable reason Laki seems to think you could still come through. First Qas, then Bode, and now Laki. Three endorsements that are difficult to ignore. I can only conclude that someone as resourceful as you would find a solution, if I were to turn you away. So I ask you again, why do you wish to join the Breachers?"

Tenika suddenly realized her request was more personal than she had admitted to herself. She straightened and gritted her teeth as anger bubbled to the surface. "Until a few days ago, I had never heard of Breachers or Servators. Now I know that there exists a world of power far beyond my comparatively small ambitions. These Servators..." Tenika spat out the name. "They took away my life's work in a moment. Because of them, my future lies in the hands of others. They hold themselves above the law of the land, like criminals, yet consider themselves righteous. They believe themselves superior, but they're not. If they were, the Breachers would no longer remain a threat to them. I want the Servators to pay for what they've done to me. To exact that price, I need to side with those who can stand against them."

Isau appraised her. "Yes, that is the truth. We have a common enemy, but without the Breachers, you'll either die at the hands of Laki Shung or find yourself recaptured by the Servators. Your conclusion is accurate. Clever as you may be, you don't have the resources on your own to fight on a level playing field. You want to make the Servators pay and I respect that. What if I were to tell you that I've paid your debt to Laki?"

"What do you mean?"

"I mean that I paid Laki's price. You now owe your debt to me."

"Why would you do that?"

"I'm not one to waste resources either. Laki's price was a trifle. He was wasting your potential."

"How much time do I have to repay the debt and what is the cost of failure?

"As I already made clear, money means little to me. I have one task in mind. Complete that task and I'll consider your debt paid. You may then continue on with your life without fear of retribution from Laki. I can't say the same about the Servators, but you stand a much better chance against one enemy than two. You'll have to set aside your wish for revenge, I'm afraid."

"Do you really think I could hide from the Servators?"

"For a while, perhaps."

"Then I'm no better off and I still wish to join the Breachers. I wouldn't be satisfied with my old life knowing what I know now."

"I will extend the offer to you, Tenika, and you'll get your revenge, but know this — if you join the Breachers, you become my property. You'll do whatever I ask, or forfeit your life."

Tenika narrowed her eyes with suspicion. "What kind of things would you be asking me to do?"

"I assure you, Ms. Sheridan, I'm only interested in your mind and your contacts."

"Which contacts?"

"Your contacts within Callan International, of course. The company has locations around the world and we have big plans."

"I'm no longer employed by Callan International. The Servators saw to my *resignation*."

"I'm aware, but that information won't have filtered its way down to every enterprise under the Callan banner. You're a recognizable authority figure. Surely you retain enough contacts that you could still gain access to many buildings. I need you to place some devices during your visits. Do this and your debt is repaid."

Tenika nodded as she considered the possibilities. "Yes, I could agree to that arrangement."

"So, then — do you still wish to become a Breacher?"

"I do."

The Second Anarch looked past her and nodded.

Before she realized what was happening, two Sicari had her gagged and one arm pinned to the table. One of them pulled out a baton-shaped device and pressed it against the crook of her arm. She screamed into her gag, almost passing out from the pain of the searing heat. Just as quickly, they removed the gag and released her arm.

Tenika swayed on her feet, aghast at the angry red welt left by the brand. She looked askance at Anarch Jax.

He shrugged. "It's always best to get it over with quickly. The anticipation can be worse than the reality. Congratulations, you're now a Breacher." Isau held out his own arm for her to see. "This mark will grant you access to Breacher facilities and resources. You'll need to *earn* marks of authority if you wish to rise in the ranks." He pointed to the additional scars around the perimeter of his brand.

"A ground transport is waiting outside to escort you to the Breacher compound. Ask for Nash — he's aware of your situation. He will familiarize you with Breacher protocol and arrange for your quarters. A pair of guards will be assigned to protect you from Servators while outside of the compound. That is all. Nash will fill you in on your assignment."

With that pronouncement, her audience with the Anarch ended. Tenika clutched her arm as Breachers rushed her to the car. What had she had gotten herself into?

Chapter 29

Selica checked the back door of the children's quarters. Still no sign of Kade. *What could be keeping him?* They had agreed that they would try to meet at the top of the hour. Kade would make his earliest attempt at dusk. If he missed an opportunity, she would check again an hour later. She had waited with the back door opened a crack for fifteen minutes at a time instead of the five minutes they had agreed upon. Selica wasn't sure why she had made that suggestion in the first place. It seemed prudent to allow time for her to deal with surprises, like a child refusing to go to bed. Now that the children were all fast asleep, it seemed unnecessary. Even old Momma Renna had gone to bed early complaining about her aching joints. With her poor hearing, she wouldn't be stirring until morning. That was a good thing, she thought, as the floorboards creaked beneath her feet.

With the doors barred and the lights dimmed for the night, Selica felt a pang of loneliness. It wasn't from a lack of people so much as the path that she had chosen. Everything had gone according to plan, but she and Kade would be striking out alone without any support to fall back on. It was a one-way trip with no guaranteed outcome. She hadn't counted on the nervous energy. The stress of waiting, with nothing else to occupy her mind, had her on edge.

Selica busied herself with preparations. She'd made three trips to the roof already. The first had been to carry up the rope ladder and harnesses she had hidden in the roof access closet. Tying the rope ladder to the steel rungs in the closet had taken a good half hour as she double-checked her knots. She rolled out the rest of the rope ladder ensuring there were no tangles that might slow them down later. She'd set the harnesses against the parapet, ready for use.

Selica made a circuit of the rooftop, viewing the festivities in the street below. Maybe one day she could feel safe enough to enjoy life like that. First she needed her freedom. Selica wondered again what she would do if Kade didn't make it. He'd made her promise to leave without him. Could she really do that? She would likely never get another opportunity like tonight. Her former master, Toller Villecrest, was dead. The new anarch didn't yet know she existed. The entire base was filled with unknown faces of raucous visitors — she'd be just another nameless face. It had to be tonight or never.

She wasn't sure if she could bear to leave without Kade. Staying might not be so bad — she could make a new life as a house mother to replace Momma Renna when the time came. It would keep her out of the brothels and give her more freedom than she'd had up to this point in her life. She could maintain some semblance of a relationship with Kade within the confines of these walls. It's not like she ever really knew anything different. Then she remembered her youthful dreams of people walking beyond these walls carrying on a life she could only imagine. She longed for more. If Kade couldn't get away, she'd have to make a decision. If she stayed only to learn of Kade's capture or death, she would have neither Kade nor freedom. That would be unbearable. She wouldn't even have a way to know what had foiled their plans until the opportunity to leave was lost. She shouldn't take that risk, but if she continued without him, she would go through life wondering what she had left behind. *Don't make me choose, Kade... please. You have to make it.*

Selica checked the back door twice more and made a trip to the roof after each missed opportunity. She carried up some food and water on the second trip and cloaks to disguise themselves on the third. Each time, she made a circuit of the rooftop, getting a feel for the atmosphere in the street. She prayed to the Maker for Kade's safety. They were running out of time — it was almost the eleventh hour. Kade needed to show soon, or they had no guarantee of making their scheduled rendezvous with the Servators. Kade didn't know if they would wait around if he and Selica were late. Truthfully, they didn't know if the Servators were coming at all or if they had even received Kade's message. If the Servators weren't there, they would flee on foot and try to put as much distance as possible between themselves and the Breacher compound before dawn. If they could make it to one of the small outlying towns, they might find another way to contact the Servators.

Selica made her way to the back door once more. It was five minutes to the hour. This was their last chance to keep to a schedule. She opened the door a crack and peered toward the hedge dividing the kitchen yard from the playground behind the children's residence. She knew a fence stood on the other side of the hedge. It was the animal paddock for the kitchen. That was where Kade would climb. A rustling of the hedge caught her attention and Selica held her breath. A dark form half leaped, half fell over the hedge, landing in a grunt. It was too dark to see who it was. She stood ready to close the door if necessary.

A whispered voice carried to her ears. "Selica?"

She let out her breath and flung the door open. The dim light from the hall fixture behind her spilled out into the yard. "Kade? Hurry!" She beckoned him with her arms, urging him to get up off the ground before he was spotted. He limped through the door. Selica turned off the light and returned to the door, scanning the yard carefully to see if anyone had witnessed his ingress. It was too dark to see and only silence greeted her ears. After a full minute, she satisfied herself that no one had noticed. She quietly closed and bolted the door. Kade was in her arms a moment later. She clung to him, weeping silently. She was relieved beyond words that she didn't have to make a decision to leave him behind. He was here now. The plan could still fall apart, but at least they would be together.

Chapter 30

The transition of power wasn't easy for Decar. He had been the right-hand man to the Third Anarch, Toller Villecrest. Before anyone could wonder at Villecrest's sudden disappearance, the Second Anarch appeared, informing them of Toller's death. The silent consensus was that Second Anarch, Kenric Trantor, had removed Toller from the Jumkano board... permanently. Usually when a coup of this nature took place, all of the former leader's trusted men were eliminated as well. Decar wasn't sure why he was still alive. He'd met with the Second Anarch, who had assured him that he had a place in the new hierarchy. Kenric had even given him a high-profile task — presumably to test his loyalties.

Decar didn't believe for one minute that his new master trusted him. Kenric had dropped a not-so-subtle bribe wrapped in a threat regarding his family. Perhaps the man believed it enough of an incentive to keep him in line and spare his life. If so, the Second Anarch guessed correctly. Decar felt no allegiance to the Third Anarch. He only served diligently because of Toller's far more overt threats to his family. Decar would do anything to protect them. Kenric seemed to understand how Toller treated his employees, so maybe his promises were genuine. Decar wouldn't hold his breath waiting to see if it was true. Kenric Trantor's reputation as a schemer preceded him. Decar was obviously just another pawn. Still, he needed to ingratiate himself to the Second Anarch. The task of keeping his family alive had become more nuanced. He needed to tread carefully.

As for the tasks given to Decar — they were proceeding nicely. He had orchestrated the roll-out of new viewcorders throughout the city and everything was ahead of schedule. He had been a little concerned about the second task. Ensuring that Kenric's engineers were up to speed on the facial recognition algorithm was daunting. They were an arrogant bunch. Decar had to keep Kade on a short leash since he was the only person capable of instructing them. Selica could have helped, but everyone knew Kenric Trantor's views on women in such positions. Selica had stopped coming to the labs on the very day that Trantor took power. Decar already knew she was smart — her decision only confirmed it. He had checked up on her and learned that she had taken on a role as an assistant house mother for the children's quarters. He was glad that she had avoided the brothels. That would have been a terrible waste of an agile mind.

As it turned out, Kade had proven more compliant than Decar would have imagined. Decar found that he liked Kade, but the man was foolhardy. He didn't seem to understand how dangerous his keepers were. The two of them had worked together to survive under Villecrest's demands, but Kenric Trantor was a different beast. It was critical to remain above suspicion under a Trantor regime. The Anarch had spies everywhere. Decar had warned Kade of this in the one and only meeting he was willing to risk. He owed him that much, since Kade had helped to keep him alive. It seemed to have worked. Kade was performing the duties required of him and didn't appear to be plotting. It probably helped that Kade was alone with his thoughts now. Decar had made his allegiances clear and Selica wasn't part of the program any longer.

Decar should have taken comfort in his success so far, but he didn't feel safe. It didn't help that he now found himself on the roof of the administration building. The Second Anarch had assigned him here for the duration of the gathering. Kenric told Decar that he needed someone untainted by the inter-anarch intrigues to keep an eye out for anything suspicious. Despite those assurances, Decar knew what it really meant — this was an important gathering and Kenric didn't trust Decar to be part of it. It made him desperate to find a way to prove himself, so he set to his current task with determination. If anything suspicious arose, he would investigate. He would gain Kenric's trust and with it the safety of his family.

From his vantage point on the roof, Decar could observe the festivities taking place through the skylights of the administration building. He also had a

clear view of the surrounding streets. He moved between the rooftop shadows —
unseen, but seeing. It had been fairly boring for the most part, a few brawls when
the guards of one anarch clashed with those of another. Those squabbles quickly
resolved on their own. No one was willing to attract the ire of their masters.

Over the course of the evening he noticed something odd. He was making a
circuit around the perimeter of the rooftop when he spotted someone else doing
the same on the rooftop across from him. Decar darted behind a large ventilation
pipe. At first he thought Kenric sent someone to spy on him — to make sure he
was following orders. His opinion changed when he spotted feminine curves.
Kenric wouldn't have sent a woman for that task. Then he realized that the
neighbouring rooftop belonged to the children's quarters and he suddenly
recognized the form. It was Selica. She seemed to be enjoying the night air while
taking in the sights and sounds of the celebration. That in itself wasn't
suspicious, but then she ducked behind the parapet working at some unseen task.
Her head bobbed into sight on occasion, appearing again some twenty minutes
later. He couldn't tell what she was doing. Shortly after, she disappeared from the
rooftop. Selica appeared twice more, always just after the hour. It was the same
each time, a circuit around the rooftop and then some unseen activity before
heading back inside. She seemed to be expecting something. Decar racked his
brains trying to imagine what it could be.

When Selica emerged the fourth time, she wasn't alone. A man had joined
her on the rooftop. Alarms went off in his head. Men weren't allowed in the
children's quarters at night. Perhaps she had invited someone to join her on the
rooftop to view the fireworks. *Are fireworks even part of tonight's entertainment?*
Decar wondered. Even so, Selica would only invite one man to join her this late
— Kade!

They thought they had cleverly hidden their interest in each other, but he
knew they were more than just co-workers. Decar was a married man and he
recognized the kind of familiarity Kade and Selica had together. Right now they
were having an animated discussion. He could only hear snippets of the whispers
that carried on the breeze, but Kade seemed unhappy. The two of them kept
looking over the parapet into the lane behind the building — a place where there
were no festivities at all. What were those two up to? He should have known
better than to think Kade could avoid plotting something foolish.

Decar knew he shouldn't leave the roof, but he had to know what they were looking at. Kade answered directly to Decar and if something bad happened, accountability would fall directly on his shoulders. He might be chasing after shadows, but he wouldn't risk his family with carelessness.

Fuming, yet determined to get to the truth of the matter, Decar arrived in the space between the children's quarters and the compound wall. He looked down the narrow lane trying to understand what might have attracted Kade and Selica's interest. He saw nothing unusual, just some crates and scurrying rats. The rats were startled by a noise from above and Decar looked up to see Selica sitting on the compound wall. A rope ladder spanned the gap from the rooftop to the compound wall and carried over to the alley beyond.

Decar was stunned. Surely they weren't foolish enough to try to escape with so many Breacher guards attending the gathering. Another thought struck him. What if they were providing a way for someone else to *enter* the compound? He wasn't sure which was worse, the lead engineer of Kenric's facial recognition project disappearing, or an unknown enemy in their midst. What he did know for certain was that he would suffer the consequences either way. He was supposed to be watching for just this sort of thing. It would make matters worse if Kenric learned that it was someone under Decar's command who was creating problems.

He had to stop this. It would be a disaster for him if he failed. On the other hand, if he succeeded, Kenric just might afford him the trust he needed to keep his family safe. Decar wanted more information before he alerted anyone. A false alarm at the height of the gathering would be just as bad as doing nothing at all. He needed to see what was in that alley outside the compound wall. It would take fifteen minutes for him to wade through crowds to the front gate and find his way to the alley. Decar ran.

Chapter 31

Tenika checked the time on her wrist chrono. She had parked her ground transport across the street from Callan Biologics. It was a lesser-known research facility under the umbrella of Callan International. Nes Callan had a fondness for technology and this was one of his early pet projects for the development of innovative agricultural harvesting equipment.

It was a quarter past the noon hour. According to Tenika's surveillance, the company manager typically left for his midday meal at this time. She wasn't concerned about running into the man, but it would be easier to plant a micro-corder in his office while he was absent. The staff here knew her well and no one would deny her access to his office, or think it peculiar seeing her there. Or rather, they wouldn't if they were in the dark about her forced retirement. It didn't matter — every Callan owned building she entered was a gamble these days. It was unlikely that the junior staff would know anything about managerial business. It was the main reason for her decision to wait for moments when higher-level staff weren't around. Once the devices were planted, she would be able to monitor reactions to her appearance and learn more about her standing in the various Callan enterprises.

Nash had been very specific about her task. He had provided a list of priority targets for micro-corder placement. Her new handler had done a reasonable job of identifying high-profile members of industry that were likely to have diverse contacts. It increased their chances of discovering Servator connections. Servators strove to develop networks among the powerful just as Breachers did. It was necessary for any organization that chose to operate while remaining hidden.

Tenika had used her knowledge of Callan activities to convince Nash that it would be better to re-prioritize the targets. She didn't want anyone from Callan headquarters to take notice of her visits too soon. It was better to visit as many locations as possible before taking the risk of approaching larger administrative buildings. Nash had argued that the main headquarters held those who were most influential, but Tenika had persuaded him otherwise. Smaller innovative companies actually had a broader audience. Other industry heads came to them in search of new ways to improve their productivity. *Men are fascinated with new toys*, Tenika smirked. *They're so predictable.*

Many of the targets remained the same, so Nash had agreed to the revision of locations and timetable. She'd also been able to convince him to grant her conditional access to the Breacher viewcorder network. She wasn't allowed near the network without supervision. The restriction was galling, but it allowed her to better plan visits like this one.

Tenika knew how to play these games. You had to push for privileges and then prove your trustworthiness. If you waited for rewards, it might take years before someone above you took notice. Tenika didn't have the time nor the patience for waiting. She'd learned how to make herself increasingly invaluable. Experience taught her that people would inevitably drop their responsibilities into her lap to avoid their own work. They never realized what they were giving up until it was too late.

Tenika had an ulterior motive for their current target. The Servators had confiscated most of her assets, but some of them had no ties to official Callan business. The Servators missed those, having no way to learn of their existence. It was time for her to redirect those assets to a new purpose. Money was no longer a priority, self-preservation was. She knew better than to trust Isau Jax. He would use her until she had fulfilled her purpose. She planned to use him and his Breacher assets in much the same way.

Isau was far more dangerous than anyone she had worked for previously. When she looked into his eyes, she saw herself staring back. She found herself as attracted to him as she was wary. Tenika brushed the thought away. She didn't want to consider what it said about her that the first man she felt drawn to reminded her of herself. She would have to be very careful around him. He wouldn't be easily caught off guard like others she'd dealt with. Tenika was confident she could rise in his organization, but Isau would never trust her.

Callan Biologics had developed what they called an energy scythe. It took the power from a portable Exotic Particle Reactor and converted it into a stream of pulses with a thirty-cubit range. Retrofitted to a harvester, it was more than powerful enough to cut through standing grain. It was a potential game changer for the agricultural industry. It meant no more down time — no replacing broken blades from an encounter with the inevitable rock. Safety was an issue since the technology was capable of damaging flesh, but engineers quickly addressed the concerns with sensors and emergency shut-offs. Tenika, however, was interested in other uses for the technology. She had shared her ideas with the former owner of Callan International, but Nes Callan refused to consider the military applications. It was one of many areas where they'd disagreed over the decades. *Well, you're gone now, Nes, and you can't stop me from seeing your research achieve its full potential.*

Tenika had planted a man within Callan Biologics years ago. He had been pilfering schematic diagrams and components ever since. She needed to catch up on his progress while she was here. He was an executive assistant to the manager, so crossing this building off her Breacher list of targets was going to be a simple matter.

Tenika turned her attention to the task at hand. The manager had entered an eating establishment further down the street. She checked her bag to ensure she had enough micro-corders and exited her transport.

As Tenika entered through the glass doors of the building, she noticed the decor had changed since her last visit. The furnishing had been replaced with fashionable upgrades and the lighting fixtures were new. The company was clearly doing well and wanted to convey that success to potential customers. There was, however, still a familiar face from the past. The small woman sitting behind the reception desk hadn't changed at all. Perhaps they should have considered a newer model of receptionist, she mused. Or maybe not, since the woman recognized her immediately, saving valuable time.

"Ms. Sheridan, welcome! It's been a while. How may I help you?"

Tenika waved a dismissive hand as she passed the desk on her way to the stairwell. "No need to get up, I know the way. Please let Wes know that I'm here."

"Oh, but Mr. Kurd isn't here right now."

Tenika pretended she didn't hear and continued up the stairs. She had no doubt Mr. Kurd's *assistant* would receive a warning of her imminent arrival, just as she intended.

Tully Denivar was waiting for her when she entered the outer office. "Ms. Sheridan. What a pleasant surprise! It's good to see you!" He had a knowing smile on his face.

Tenika had found Tully living on the streets when she'd first moved to Denmount. He was alert and intelligent. She'd known immediately that he would shine, given the opportunity. Tully had been one of her first recruits and unquestioningly loyal. She'd rewarded that loyalty many times.

"It's good to see you too, Tully."

Tully gave her a head-to-toe once-over. "It appears you've landed on your feet. That's good to know."

"So you're aware of my current status?"

Tully nodded. "The guys were worried when you went silent and so we did a little digging."

"So, our team knows, but are managers at other locations aware?"

Tully shook his head. "I guess the head office didn't think it necessary to spread that news. As far as we can tell, most people are unaware. It's been business as usual. When we didn't hear from you, we just assumed you were putting out fires somewhere."

"Good! That will make things easier. What do you have to report?"

"We've scavenged enough equipment to build a few prototypes. No one has noticed the missing parts. We've had limited success developing weapons. Accuracy and range are disappointing. The technology seems better suited to close combat. A small handheld device can inflict wounds through personal armour."

"What about the other uses I had you explore?"

"Those are far more promising. The pulsed output is very effective at disrupting delicate circuitry. We've successfully used it to disable vehicles, building security systems, and communication networks. We've even effected localized damage to the power grid."

Tenika smiled. "Excellent! We'll be moving forward with a new agenda and that will prove useful. Can you develop a small baton, primarily for disrupting technology, but also as a defensive weapon?"

"We already have the circuitry — it's just a matter of packaging. How many would you need and how soon?"

"I'd like each member of our team equipped with one in the next few weeks, so thirteen total?"

Tully frowned. "Jules and Oki have gone silent."

"Let's not jump to any conclusions. Put out a call to meet and let the group know I'll be contacting each of them individually. If Jules and Oki don't show, try to find out why."

"I'll take care of it."

"Thank you, Tully. Do we need anything else from Callan Biologics?"

"The development team has nothing new planned, if that's what you're asking. We have everything else we need for our purposes."

"Then it's time for you to resign. I'm going to need you by my side."

"I was gaining too much weight sitting behind this desk anyway. I'm ready for a change."

Tenika grinned. When she'd found Tully, he was as thin as a walking stick. Now after years of good food, someone might mistake him for a fence post. She didn't think he could bulk up if he tried. "Yes, I can see that we'll need to lower your caloric intake before I send you skulking down narrow alleys."

Tully chuckled. "Do you need anything else from me?"

"Here's where I'll be staying for the next few days." Tenika handed him a slip of parchment with an address. "Meet me when you've settled your affairs with Callan Biologics. I'll be needing the team's help distributing some surveillance devices." She showed him the micro-corders and explained how to affix them before giving him a handful. "I'll cover Wes's office, but take the rest of these and hide them in high traffic or high security areas inside the building before you give your notice of resignation."

"Got it."

"How much time do I have left before Wes returns?"

Tully glanced at the wall chrono. "You have at least ten minutes."

"That will do."

Chapter 32

Kade followed Selica up the stairs to the third floor and down the hall to the closet at the end. He cringed with every creak of a floorboard, but none of the children stirred. Soon enough they were up the ladder and through the hatch to the roof. Kade immediately made his way to the parapet so he could look down the rear wall of the building next door. It felt surreal to see it from this perspective. Mere minutes before, he was terrified that he would be spotted exiting the building. It looked like he had managed to slip away unseen. All was silent in the paddock attached to the kitchen. He could hardly believe it.

The escape from his duties had been a close thing. After he'd completed his presentation to the anarchs, he made a beeline for the kitchen. His intent had been to head straight to the paddock, but he was spotted and drafted to the task of ladling pudding into little bowls. The head chef had decided it was time to serve dessert. The frenzied activity was what he needed and possibly the last time it would occur, but he was stuck in an assembly line with no legitimate reason to step away. The wall chrono showed ten minutes before the hour. He'd begun to worry that Selica might leave without him. His mind dismissed ideas as quickly the bowls that were passed from him to the next person in line. The young man beside him looked as flustered as Kade felt. The boy's task was to dust the pudding with cinnamon. In his haste to keep up, he squeezed the cinnamon container a little too forcefully. A cloud of spice found its way to Kade's nose. Kade fell into a fit of coughing and then sneezed right into the vat of pudding.

That drew a gasp of outrage from the head chef. He'd beaten Kade with a wooden spoon as he chased him to the back of the kitchen. Kade was ordered to scrub pots and remain as far away from the food preparation area as possible. Kade hadn't wasted the opportunity, only taking a moment to thank the Maker. As soon as the chef turned his back, Kade made for the exit. He'd thrown one quick glance over his shoulder before opening the door to the paddock. The chef was looking into the vat and shaking his head. The last thing Kade saw before he slipped out was the chef shrugging his shoulders and ordering someone to continue spooning pudding into bowls.

Selica interrupted his internal replay of the night's events "Kade. We have to go!"

He jogged over to watch her lower a rope ladder over the parapet. Kade looked over the edge and considered the three-story drop. A wave of vertigo hit him. "I don't know if I can do this."

Selica finished lowering the ladder and turned to face him. She placed a hand on each side of his face and looked straight into his eyes. "You can do this, and you must. We don't have time for second-guessing or fear. This is it. If we don't attempt our escape now, we've resigned ourselves to a life of slavery. The Breachers will continue to use you. More blood will be on your hands."

Kade winced at that last remark. He knew it was true, but it hurt coming from Selica. No — *I needed to hear that. This isn't the time to be thinking of self-preservation.*

"You're right, I can risk my life now in an attempt to gain my freedom, or I can risk it later at the hands of a capricious megalomaniac. I have no guarantee that I'll live to see another day. Even so, I can make sure I'm not contributing to mass murder. What do I have to do?"

Selica handed him a cobbled together harness. "Put this on."

Kade watched her slip her feet through two loops that were attached to a leather belt and duplicated her motions. A short piece of rope with a clip at the end dangled from each harness. Selica lifted hers and explained. "We'll descend until our heads are about even with the height of the compound wall. Then we'll clip ourselves to the rope as a safety precaution before we attempt to swing over to the wall."

"Will the ropes support our weight?" Kade shifted nervously from foot to foot.

Selica rolled her eyes. "Do you really think I'd risk our lives on something flimsy? Ground transports use these ropes for towing. I'm confident the rope ladder will hold your weight, and don't you dare ask if it will hold mine."

Kade smiled in spite of his growing fear. She was just lightening the mood for his sake. She knew that his fear of heights stemmed from a childhood trauma. A bully had dangled him by his feet from a second-story window. He'd never felt so helpless and terrified in his life. Even so, they'd both agreed this was the only hope they had of leaving the compound unseen. He needed to get his fears under control.

"I'll go first. If I have trouble, you can join me on the ladder to help."

Kade nodded his agreement and watched Selica swing a leg over the parapet. She felt blindly with her foot for a lower rung before grabbing the top rung with both hands and swinging her second leg over. Kade's stomach did a little flip as her head disappeared behind the parapet. The ropes creaked with the added tension and the steel ladder that held them made a pinging sound. He panicked thinking the rope was about to give way and ran to look over the parapet. Selica was descending steadily, no worse for wear. The noises faded as the ropes became accustomed to the load.

Selica stopped and clipped her harness to the ladder. This was the difficult part. She freed one leg and raised it up to her chest so she could push off the wall. Then she freed one arm, ready to grab the top of the wall at the end of her swing. Pushing off the building with a grunt, she flailed with her free arm, but didn't come close. Kade winced as she swung back toward the wall and hit hard. Her knuckles would hurt from that bruising.

Selica unclipped, moved up one rung, and re-clipped her harness before making a second attempt. This time her fingers reached the top of the compound wall but slipped free. She was prepared and used her free leg to cushion the blow as she returned to the face of the building. On her third attempt, she was successful and used both arms to pull herself to the top of the wall. Kade breathed a sigh of relief as she used the short length of rope from her harness to reclaim the ladder. The rope ladder was long enough to reach the ground, so it took some time to pull it up and throw it over the compound wall. She gave Kade a thumbs up, looked in both directions of the alley, and then descended.

We're really doing this. Time slowed as Kade waited for the signal to pull the ladder back up. He imagined the worst — Selica, hauled away under guard —

Selica, a broken heap at the bottom of the wall, having slipped and fallen — Selica, dangling at the end of a ladder that was shorter than it should have been. Kade shook his head. She wouldn't have made that mistake.

A tug on the rope interrupted his grim train of thought. Kade responded quickly. Grabbing for the ladder felt good after standing motionless in tense anticipation. He gathered arm length after arm length without stopping and before long the end appeared. He let the ladder slide back down to the ground on his side and suddenly it was his turn. He double-checked his harness. It was just a delaying tactic. *Come on, Kade, you can do this. You have to do this.* He swung a leg over the parapet and froze. A full minute passed as he waited for the shaking in his arms to subside. He almost pulled his leg back to the rooftop, but then he imagined Selica alone and in danger while she waited for him. He was putting her at risk and that fear proved stronger than his fear of heights. He steeled himself and pulled himself over.

Once settled on the ladder itself, he realized that the transition was the hardest part. He felt better now that he was descending. *Every step down is closer to safety.* He stopped approximately where he imagined Selica had been on her successful attempt. His harness was quickly attached and he leaned over to test his reach. He made the mistake of looking down and gasped as he clung to the ladder hugging the wall. He was grateful Selica couldn't see him like this. She was correct, though — with his greater reach, he didn't have to swing far to duplicate her success. He took a step down. Hanging by his arms alone, he slowly added his full weight to the harness — testing it. When he was satisfied it would hold, he climbed back up and prepared to push off the wall. In his panic, he pushed harder than he expected. He was also higher than he should have been. Instead of grabbing the wall with his arms, he ended up catching it with his heel. He managed to move his harness clip down a rung and pull himself over until he was straddling the wall. It was clumsy and terrifying, but he ended up in the position he needed to be.

Kade took a moment to search for Selica before pulling up the ladder. He spotted her behind some crates, waving to catch his eye. *Thank the Maker, she's safe.* Balancing himself while pulling up the ladder was more difficult than he thought. How did Selica make it look so easy? After a little experimentation, he found a rhythm and soon had the ladder in the alley. This time he didn't hesitate to swing over the wall and begin his descent. He moved quickly, eager to have the ordeal done. Safely on solid ground, he ran to where Selica was hiding and embraced her.

"I'm proud of you, Kade."

"You wouldn't be if you'd seen the first half of that endeavour."

Selica smiled and he knew he'd do it all over again just to see that look in her eyes.

"Isn't this touching."

The unexpected voice startled them both.

"What exactly do you two think you're doing?"

"Decar!"

"That's not an answer to my question."

Kade stood protectively in front of Selica. "What are *you* doing here?"

"Very well, I'll go first. I was on the roof of the administration building, keeping an eye on things as instructed by the Anarch. I have to admit some confusion by Ms. Lor's repeated visits to the rooftop of the children's quarters. Your arrival, Kade, was equally peculiar. I was willing to write it off as a lover's rendezvous, but you seemed too agitated. When you began pointing over the edge of the building, I decided to come down and see what all the fuss was about. Imagine my surprise when I saw Selica perched on the top of the compound wall pulling up a rope ladder and lowering it into the alley on the other side. I had to ask myself, why would you go through all of that trouble instead of simply walking out the front gates? The only reason I could come up with, is that you didn't want the guards at the main gate to see you. Highly suspicious if you ask me. Since I have no need to avoid the guards, I took the easier route to this alley so I could investigate."

Kade worked his jaw, but no words came out. They were caught.

"So, I repeat my question. What are you up to? Are you providing ingress to the compound for an assassin?"

"Of course not, Decar. You know how I feel about murder."

"Yes, I suppose I do. That must mean you're attempting an escape."

Kade glared at Decar in silence. Decar nodded, satisfied that he'd guessed correctly.

"Turn around and walk away. Pretend you didn't see us, Decar."

"Kade, you know I can't do that. I warned you about this. Why didn't you listen to me?"

"You owe me, Decar. I helped save your skin."

"That's why I risked a meeting to warn you when Trantor took over. You deserved that much, but I told you then, I won't cover for you anymore."

"What are you going to do?"

"*We're* going to walk casually back through the front gate. If you cooperate and no one brings it to the attention of the Anarch, I'll hold my tongue."

"And if someone does mention it?"

"Then I will tell the Anarch everything I know."

Kade looked to Selica for input. She slowly shook her head in refusal. They'd come this far.

"We can't do that, Decar. You have to let us go."

Decar's voice rose in anger. "I'm responsible for overseeing the transition of knowledge from you to the Anarch's engineers. What do you imagine will happen if the Anarch discovers you're missing? Who do you think he'll hold responsible?"

"You can come with us, Decar!"

"Are you mad? No place exists where you could run or hide. Kenric has spies everywhere, you can't escape. I won't be dragged into your plotting and risk the lives of my family. How could you even imagine that I'd leave them behind? You're already caught. Come quietly now and you may have a chance. Anything else will end very badly for you and worse for Selica." Decar turned to her. "If Kenric discovers what you attempted, you can forget about your new career as a house mother."

Selica looked ill, then straightened with indignation. "If that happens, it will be on your head, Decar."

Decar nodded slowly. "Yes, that would weigh heavily on me, but not as heavily as the thought of my wife and daughters suffering that same fate." Decar shrugged. "You see my dilemma."

Kade looked to both ends of the alley. No one had noticed them from the main street. Clearly, Decar hadn't told anyone what he was up to. He wouldn't be here alone otherwise. The gate on the pasture end of the alley was closed as expected. They were closer to it than the street, but it would take precious time to open it. He looked to Selica again. She nodded.

Decar took their silent communication for submission. He extended his arm toward the main street, beckoning them to walk in front of him. Decar turned his head to look toward the street, determining if they were still undetected. Kade took that moment to charge Decar, knocking him to the ground.

"Selica, run!"

He needn't have said anything. She was already at the gate working the latch. In a moment she was through. Kade picked himself up and ran after her. He made it through the gate before Decar got his wind back and began yelling.

"Guards! Guards!"

Kade didn't wait to see who responded.

Chapter 33

Marat had cleared Seri's schedule for the afternoon so she could attend this meeting. As acting head of Callan International in Nico's absence, it felt like Seri never had time alone anymore. Someone was always coming to her with a problem to solve or some paperwork to sign. When she wasn't sitting at her desk, she was attending meetings. No wonder Nico found every opportunity to escape the drudgery and look in on their special projects.

She sat next to Brokar Luge who was discussing some of the finer details of the airport they had finished touring an hour ago. They were en route to the seaport for a tour of that facility as well. Seri's anticipation rose as things were moving to completion. It was her fault that the Servator base in Denmount was abandoned. She'd made it her personal mission to enable a return. It wasn't possible to atone for the loss of life, but she hoped she could at least restore people to their homes.

The Q-tech beacons were now installed, providing guideposts along the route from the airport to the sea. Travel took place at night. It was a necessary inconvenience to keep the Lighter-Than-Air transports hidden from public view. Work continued on the gradual excavation of a channel between the valley that housed the new port and the next valley over. Once completed, it would allow unimpeded travel to the sea so air transports could remain below the ridge line. When that was complete, they would be able to travel by day as well as night.

Construction of the port proceeded swiftly. A large natural cave located under an outcropping had provided a convenient foundation for their work. Additional excavation had been minimal and it didn't take long to outfit the space. For all practical purposes it was ready for service — only lacking sufficient staff for operations. Once the Servators returned with a ready workforce, that problem would resolve itself. Nico had spared no expense while outfitting the project. Seri had told him it was unnecessary — Servators were used to function over form, but Nico had insisted. She knew he intended it as a gift. It was his way of honouring her father's memory.

The facility boasted comfortable private bunks for overnight stays. There were meeting rooms, gathering spaces, and dining facilities. The kitchens were state-of-the-art along with everything else, appearing equally important as the air transport navigation systems or maintenance bays. A modern medical facility stood ready to deal with any emergency and a generous exercise area came complete with sparring mats. Pristine hiking trails provided plenty of opportunity to enjoy a little nature and fresh air. One of those trails led to a natural hot spring.

Seri noticed that Nico spent a lot of time visiting the new airport. He had gained a new appreciation for open spaces, now that he spent a considerable amount of his time in the underground base at Denmount. Having grown up on the base, the enclosed spaces didn't trouble Seri, but she could understand how it might affect someone who grew up on the open sea. Most Servators were equally indifferent to life below ground, but she had no doubt Port Vantos would become a popular place for Servator retreats.

Four LTA transports sat waiting for future passengers. Tunnels connecting both air and sea ports to the Servator base in Denmount were complete. An additional tunnel had been excavated between the two ports as well. It was through this tunnel that Seri and Brokar travelled aboard a high-speed rail transport. It was incredible what they had accomplished in so little time, but Seri knew firsthand the financial resources at Nico's command. A lot could happen quickly when money was no object.

Nico had practical reasons for including sleeping quarters in the two construction projects. With workers contracted from around the globe it was necessary to feed and shelter them. Those workers arrived by sea transport to an offshore facility. From there, they transferred by sub during the day, or LTA at night, to the facilities where they were to work. Project locations were kept strictly confidential. As part of the agreement, workers were not allowed to leave their work sites during the term of their contract.

The transfer point for imported work crews was an island a few leagues off the coast of Denmount. It had been a last-minute decision to develop the island. A local destination was necessary for the short-range sub-aqua transports travelling to the sea port. They needed a way to transfer travellers to and from regular sea transports for longer journeys. Seri and Nico had toyed with the idea of building docks a few leagues south of Denmount on the mainland, but then an opportunity presented itself From Callan International's public facing shipping interests. One of Nico's logistics staff had noticed that a number of their vessels were leaving the shipping lanes to travel to Denmount for the sole purpose of transferring cargo to other vessels. The congestion at Denmount's port was becoming an issue. One solution was to expand Denmount's port, but another possibility was to build an offshore transfer point that would both alleviate congestion and save travel time. In the end, the decision was an obvious one for Nico. The transfer point solved problems for both the Servators and Callan International.

Seri and Nico had decided to name the two ports in memory of their murdered parents. Port Vantos lay behind them in the mountains as they travelled toward Port Callan by the sea. It was a fitting tribute to the Callans who began as humble fishermen. As for Port Vantos — Seri had always looked up to her father so it suited her that the port carrying their family name was high in the mountains. It was silly, she knew, but it pleased her nonetheless. She also hoped it reminded people of all that the Vantos family had done for the Servators rather than the mistakes she herself had made.

The progress at Port Vantos was exciting — arriving at Port Callan was equally exhilarating. Workers milled about, adding finishing touches. The crews were strictly Servator associates now that the main structural work was complete. Nico's penchant for technology was evident wherever you looked. He had spared no expense at Port Vantos, but he'd gone overboard at Port Callan. Seri grinned as she took it all in. She understood. It was his first major project for the Servators. He wanted to excel if for no other reason than to prove something to himself. The same comforts and living areas found at Port Vantos were available here. Natural tunnels replaced hiking trails for those wanting to stretch their legs. Floor-to-ceiling aquariums and underwater view ports replaced mountain vistas.

Swimming pools replaced hot springs.

That was where the similarities ended. Nico employed Servator technology in novel ways at Port Callan. Leviticus's involvement had left its mark here. Servator tokens attracted fish that were harvested with stun technology to provide food for the kitchens. Seri noticed that Nico had turned it into a bit of a targeting game in the common area for those who wanted to try their hand at catching their own dinner. The fisherman inside him couldn't resist, she supposed. Loading platforms for the subs alternately materialized or disappeared, relying on QPN templates to create them as necessary. It reduced the clutter of cranes and bridges in the confined space. Seri watched as the workers materialized a steel wall that encompassed the entire sea facing portion of the facility. It was a test of emergency measures in case of a collapse.

A natural beach abutted a raised staging area where people could gather before embarking on a journey or upon arrival. In the centre of it all stood something Seri could only describe as a reverse fountain. Spheres of water materialized near the top of the cavern and then fell into a pool, forming patterns in the air on their way down. It was mesmerizing and Seri stood enthralled for several minutes until the droplets formed the shape of a heart in the air. She looked around to see if anyone else had noticed and found Nico standing behind her with his fingers resting on a wrist Q-view and a grin plastered on his face. She leaned back into him and whispered, "It's beautiful, Nico."

"It was Lev's idea. I think it adds a nice touch."

"I didn't mean the fountain, I meant... everything."

"Hey! Don't cry — what's wrong?"

"Nothing's wrong. Everything's perfect. My dreams of bringing the Servators back to Denmount were never so grand. You've brought that vision to life in a way I never could have managed on my own." Seri turned into Nico's arms and hugged him ferociously. "I'll never be able to find the right words to express my gratitude for all you've done."

"Don't forget whose vision this was. Without you, it never would have happened at all. As for the rest — it was so much fun! I understand my father now, in ways I never would have before. I have you and the Servators to thank for that. Everybody wins!"

Seri looked into Nico's smiling eyes. "How much longer before we let people know?"

"Repairs on the tunnels surrounding Denmount base are complete. The labyrinth is also ready. The final lengths of track for the rail line between Denmount and Port Callan should be in place within the week. We'll need to start opening the labyrinth tunnels before the tourist season ends if we want to go ahead with that part of the plan. I don't want to do that before we have approval from your mother. She may need some convincing. Either way, I think we could give her a tour at any time."

Seri's eyes lit up. "Really?"

"I don't see a reason to delay. The ports are functional. Sooner or later we need to discuss the logistics of staffing."

"That shouldn't be a problem. When the Servators left Denmount, a lot of the family members of support staff gave up their local jobs. Other residents of Denmount filled those vacant positions — they're no longer available. Those who choose to return will be looking for work and are already part of the broader Servator family." Seri looked around the sea port. "They won't be able to work here where you have so much technology on display, but they can fill positions at Port Vantos and the tourism venues we hope to develop for the labyrinth. I'm sure enough Servators remain to staff Port Callan. In fact, if we arrange it as a destination for visiting novices, we'd have a ready supply of temporary workers. After my own recent travels, I can tell you this would be a popular destination."

"That's a great idea. Regardless, we can't do any of those things without the help of the Chief Sentry, so it sounds like we need to tell her sooner rather than later."

Seri was vibrating with excitement. "Oh, Nico, this is so exciting! It's been so hard keeping this a secret from my mother. I can't wait to tell her everything."

"It's settled then. Let me know when you can clear your calendar early next week and I'll arrange for the Chief Sentry to inspect the repairs we've made around the tunnels. From there, we can give her the grand tour."

"It's a date!"

"But for now, why don't we take the elevator up to my place and celebrate? I have a ten-year-old bottle of wine that I've been saving for a special occasion. I'll make you dinner."

Seri sighed. "That would be the perfect end to a perfect day."

Chapter 34

Kade slipped through the sheep gate at the end of the alley. It wouldn't take long for Decar to locate some guards. They needed to delay pursuit as long as possible. He frantically looked for something he could use to jam the gate. His eye caught something swinging in his peripheral vision. He was still wearing the makeshift harness. It had a short length of rope used to clip the harness to the ladder. Kade quickly removed the harness and used it to secure the gate with as many knots as he could manage on the short cord.

The Breacher compound stood a short distance from the river separated by a grazing meadow for livestock. Selica was already at the far end and Kade had to sprint hard to catch up. He was breathing heavily when he reached her. Shrubs grew dense and taller than a man along the banks, starting twenty paces from the water's edge. The flock had stripped the lower branches of leaves and meandering trails wove throughout. Selica led the way, hunched over — setting a quick pace. Kade struggled to keep up, his larger frame snagging on branches as he went. They followed the shoreline, grateful for cover provided by the brush. The thicket gave way at the edge of the Breacher property.

From there, a public boardwalk had been erected. It was elevated to remain clear during the spring floods. The river was lower this time of year so they continued out of sight along the water's edge, moving between the boardwalk's support piles. Kade was grateful he no longer had to hunch over. Unfortunately, the ground remained uneven, covered in rocks placed there to prevent erosion.

Twisting an ankle would end any chance of flight, so their progress remained slow.

They began to hear the shouts of someone ordering a search from far behind them. They had a good lead, but it would be a mistake to continue along this path.

"Selica, stop."

"We're not even halfway to the bridge yet."

"I know, but we can't keep to the river's edge. Decar knows that's where we're headed. It's the first place they'll look. You can hear the shouting behind us. People will be sent ahead of us in ground transports. They'll start working backwards along the shoreline hoping to trap us between their search parties. We need to move inland."

"If we move inland while our pursuers string-out along the shore, we'll find ourselves cut off from the pickup point!"

"If we're caught on the shoreline, we won't make it anyway. We'll just have to watch for an opening when the time comes."

Selica stared at him with terror in her eyes. To have made it this far only to see freedom slip away — it wasn't fair. "Selica, if they get too close, I'll provide a distraction so you can escape."

"No, Kade, I can't allow you to do that."

"It's not your choice to make. If we get caught, it'll mean death or worse. This will all be for nothing. I'm already responsible for too many deaths. If I can save one person, my life won't be a total waste."

"Please don't talk like that, Kade."

"I mean it, Selica. You've lived a lifetime in slavery. You deserve so much more. I can't live with the thought of you suffering any longer. When — if the time comes, I'm going to give you a chance to escape. Promise me you'll take it."

Selica rose on her toes to look him in the eyes and gave him a quick kiss, but promised nothing. "Then we'd better get moving so it doesn't come to that."

Circumstances forced them to continue in their current direction until they could find an exit from under the boardwalk. Eventually they came across a drainage ditch and climbed. Vendors had stalls along the boardwalk providing some cover, but they would need to cross a narrow green space to lose themselves among the buildings on the other side. Street lamps along the boardwalk cast light into the green space. Kade looked around nervously. *Does Kenric have informants looking out of their windows in this direction?* This was no time for second guessing. He grabbed Selica's hand and made to whisper in her ear, walking casually and stopping occasionally for a kiss. *Nothing to see here, just a young couple going for a midnight stroll.* The slow walk felt like an eternity. They were fully exposed, but no shouts of alarm rose in response to their passing. They darted into the first alley they saw and pressed their backs against the stonework, listening intently for any sounds of pursuit.

"Well done, but you'll need to do better if you're trying to avoid attention."

Selica gasped and Kade looked around wildly, trying to see where the voice had come from. It was the second time in the last few hours that they'd been startled by an unexpected voice. A dark shape was leaning against the wall opposite them. Kade hadn't noticed anyone when they entered the dark alley. He wasn't sure what he could do, unarmed as he was, but he stood protectively in front of Selica and started backing away.

"People are searching the streets for someone. I'd advise you to return to your homes — unless you're the ones they're looking for?"

Kade and Selica glanced at each other and then up and down the alley looking for an escape route.

"Ah... You must be Kade, but who's your friend? Never mind, you need to come with me."

"Who are you? What do you want?" Kade whispered angrily.

"It's okay, I'm with Leviticus."

Kade nearly crumpled in his relief. "Why didn't you just say that in the first place?"

"Hey, you came into *my* alley. I wasn't expecting to run into you either. Breachers are everywhere and I had to be certain. It's no safer here for me than for you. You were supposed to make your way to the bridge."

"We ran into a little complication."

"I'd say more than a little. The spy tokens I've placed show hundreds of men combing the streets. Someone really doesn't want you to get away. My counterpart on the other side of the river reports the same kind of activity."

Kade watched as the fellow talked into a device on his arm and nodded in response to some instructions only he could hear.

"What's that thing on your arm, and what's a spy token?"

"No time to explain. I was only supposed to be scouting, but we'll have to change the plan a bit. I can get you close to the bridge and coordinate with my fellow scout on the other side of the river. At the first window of opportunity, make a break for the middle of the bridge. You'll need to jump off the bridge into the river at the right moment. You'll know when."

"Wait — jump off the bridge? What kind of escape plan is that? I can't swim very well and how do we know the water is even deep enough? We could break our necks!"

"Quick, follow me. We don't have much time." Without another word, the scout headed down the alley in a jog.

Kade lifted his arms and let them drop in silent exasperation. Selica shrugged and started after the scout.

"Where are you going?" Kade hissed.

Selica turned, long enough to whisper a reply. "They came, Kade. Now we need to trust them to do what they do."

In two quick strides, Kade was at her side, doing his best to keep up with the swift scout.

The next twenty minutes became a treacherous routine. They would dart from shadow to shadow or run quickly down a darkened alley. Whenever they encountered someone, they would drop into a crouch and wait silently until the way ahead was clear. On three occasions they encountered what were obviously Breacher search parties. Anxious minutes passed as they waited for Breachers to move on. At least they didn't need to worry about missing their ride. Leviticus knew they were coming, he would wait for as long as it was safe to do so. Unfortunately, it was becoming less safe by the moment.

The scout had clearly travelled the route before. He confidently moved from one hiding place to the next, zigzagging to some internal map. Kade was hopelessly lost until they stopped at the edge of a building facing the Aiguptos Bridge.

"Okay. My partner has taken up a position on the other side of the bridge. The Breachers have placed two men to guard each side. They've made it a staging area. Search teams arrive every five minutes to report their progress before continuing their search. We'll wait for the moment when teams from both sides of the river have already reported. It will give us a few minutes while their numbers are few."

"How are we going to get past the two guards on this side?" Selica wondered aloud.

"I'm going to leave you here and provide a distraction from a building down the street. Hopefully at least one of them will come to investigate. Either way, when you hear the distraction and see that the guards are looking in my direction, run as fast as you can to the middle of the bridge and don't stop — no matter what."

"They'll see us coming!"

"We intentionally stopped here, one alley before the bridge. They'll be looking in the other direction and you'll be coming at the bridge from slightly behind the guards. They're practically right across the street. You can run there in less than thirty seconds. All you need to do is get past them before they can react. They won't chase you, because they can easily warn the guards on the other side. No one will be expecting you to stop in the middle of the bridge. Regardless, they'll think they have you trapped."

"They have weapons!" Kade protested. "They'll shoot us."

"If they're putting this much effort into capturing you, then they want you alive. They won't shoot at you unless they think you're getting away. You'll be trapped between four men. They'll feel confident and that's what we want. It will make them methodical instead of foolhardy. That will buy us some time."

"So, we run to the middle of the bridge as fast as we can." Selica summarized. "Then we just jump over the side into the river?"

"Exactly, but don't jump too soon, Wait for the right moment. You need to know what's below you before you jump. You'll know it when you see it."

"This is insane." Kade interjected. "Why can't you just tell us what we're looking for?" Kade glanced over his shoulder when he didn't get a response. "Great, he disappeared."

Selica shifted her weight preparing for a sprint. Kade did the same. "I just got over dangling from a building with a safety harness and now I'm going to throw myself from a bridge without any protection at all. Oh, and let's not forget that men will be pointing weapons at us. Weapons that will begin firing the moment we prepare to jump. If Radix doesn't come through and we die, I'm going to kill him."

Selica turned to him for a quick embrace. "I love you, Kade. No matter what happens, I'm glad we're making the attempt together."

Kade kissed her gently before responding. "I love you too."

As their eyes swept back to the bridge, the guards were pointing in the direction of the scout. Both of them walked a few paces in that direction before one of them stopped and waved for the other to check it out.

The moment had come to run. Kade's heart was pounding as adrenaline coursed through him. He felt like he was running faster than he ever had, but he felt no exertion, just the focus of his objective. Selica was directly in front of him and first to pass the single remaining guard. He spun at the sound of her footsteps as she passed.

"Hey! Stop!" As the guard watched her receding figure, he spoke excitedly into his tote-comm.

Then Kade was on him, barrelling the guard over in his rage at seeing the man lift a weapon in her direction. Somehow the weapon found its way into his hands. He rose and continued running as he tossed the weapon into the river. Belatedly he realized he should have hung onto it, but he didn't know how to use it anyway. At least he'd reduced the number of weapons pointed in their direction.

Selica was waiting for him in the middle of the bridge, looking over the side. The guard Kade had knocked over was dusting himself off as his partner joined him. He was talking into his tote-comm again. Guards from both sides began cautiously converging on their position. *They must think I still have the guard's weapon.* Kade pretended to point from one side of the bridge to the other. The guards on both sides hesitated. Soon they'd be close enough to see he wasn't a threat, and then they'd quickly be overwhelmed.

"Selica? What do you see?"

"Nothing yet. No wait, something's happening."

"Could you be a little more specific?"

"The water is churning. I don't understand — Kade, look!"

Kade looked over the edge. It was a sub-aqua transport! He'd heard of them, but never seen one. "I don't believe it!"

Selica was grinning at him as she swung a leg over the bridge railing. "We're getting out of here, Kade. Come on, jump!" With that, she was over the edge.

Her actions drew the attention of the guards who ran to the railing and began pointing at the sub. More Breachers were running down the street toward the bridge. Some headed straight for the river's edge, weapons drawn. There were too many of them, they weren't going to make it. He turned his attention back to the water in time to see one of their rescuers lift Selica out of the water. Correction, he wasn't going to make it. Selica would be fine. He'd known it might be necessary to give his life for her. He glanced around for an opportunity to do just that when he heard a familiar voice.

"Kade! Jump!"

The hatch of the sub was open and there stood the sage's pet, beckoning him. *Radix, you came through for me.* Kade was overcome with emotion as he watched Selica enter the safety of the sub. He waved Leviticus away. "It's too late. Go! Go!"

But he didn't leave. "Kade, it's not too late, trust me. Jump!"

The Breachers began firing at the sub. Radix just stood there unperturbed. How were they missing such an easy target? Kade rubbed his eyes in confusion. He blinked twice. Some of the Breachers had refocused their attention on him and were heading his way — weapons raised. Then he heard Selica's voice.

"Kade Brixton! I'm not leaving without you. If you don't jump, I'm swimming for the shore."

Selica began climbing out of the hatch.

"No! Selica, don't." She wasn't listening. Fear for her drove him up and over the railing even as Breachers opened fire on him. He felt nothing at first, but knew the Breachers were too close to have missed from that range. Then he felt a curious sensation — a rapid buffeting while he was falling. He felt no pain. Then he noticed that he wasn't falling straight down. He was falling toward the sub. A new panic formed as he realized he was going to miss the water and hit the sub. Just before impact, his body slowed and landed softly in a heap on the deck of the vessel. Kade looked around, bewildered. He could hear the weapons fire and saw the air around them shimmering with hundreds of little disturbances, but Radix seemed unconcerned. *I must be dying and I'm hallucinating.*

"Could you get up please, Brixton? This is taxing and we need to get going."

Strong arms picked Kade up off the deck and helped him through the hatch. As he descended, he saw Breachers swimming toward them. He didn't know how to describe what he saw next, but waves began to hammer the Breachers, sending them back to shore. Then, Radix calmly followed him through the hatch and secured it.

A minute later he could hear Breachers pounding on the outside of the sub.

They must have jumped from the bridge. A familiar voice spoke from inside the sub. He knew it wasn't Radix, but he couldn't place it. "Hang on everyone. I'm going to perform an emergency dive."

Everyone clung to handholds as the craft lurched. The banging on the outside stopped. The next ten minutes passed in silence — then a cheer erupted. They were at the mouth of the river, heading out to sea. Selica clung to Kade, sobbing in relief. They'd made it.

Chapter 35

Kenric wanted to break something. Was everyone incompetent? How could he only be learning about this now? His spies had heard rumours of a Servator Levigator and now they had a confirmed sighting. The wastrel overlords were bad enough under normal circumstances, but they'd been screeching in outrage ever since confirmation had been made. Their caterwauling was adding to his stress. If he didn't deal with the Levigator threat quickly, they might summon him. It was rare for such a summons to occur, but no anarch wanted to be the one called to task. Kenric shuddered at the thought. He'd made it his life's ambition to avoid interacting with the overlords.

He looked at his feet where Decar cowered before him.

Kenric turned his lip in disgust. "First you allow my prized computational engineer to escape and now this!"

"Please, Second Anarch, I've been scouring the network for signs of Kade as you requested, but it's as if he's vanished!"

"I'm not talking about that, I'm referring to this!" Kenric waved toward the viewscreen at his desk.

Decar had a mystified look on his face.

Kenric growled in exasperation as he stormed over to the desk and spun the screen around. "Get up from your grovelling and tell me what you see."

Kenric replayed the viewcording for Decar, watching his face for signs of recognition.

Decar's eyes flicked from the screen to Kenric and then to the floor.

"So, you do recognize this viewcording. Why is it only now coming to my attention?"

Decar appeared confused. "I'm sorry, Anarch, I don't understand. This took place when the Third Anarch was still in charge. He had arranged for the kidnapping of a young man named Leviticus Radix. Villecrest wanted him for work on the algorithm. When the abduction failed, Kade took over the project. Over the course of Kade's network implementation, Radix was flagged in one of the searches."

"And you did nothing about it?"

"Oh, but I did, Anarch! He was in the company of known Servator agents approaching a Breacher depot. I immediately contacted the person in charge at that location to warn them."

"What happened to the young man?"

"I told them to focus their efforts on bringing him in alive — that he was of interest to the Third Anarch. They failed."

"Why am I only hearing of this now?" Kenric repeated.

Decar held his hands up defensively. "We already had a working network. You seemed pleased with Kade's performance and you were dismissive of anything else the Third Anarch had worked on. If I recall, you referred to him as an incompetent fool unworthy of your time."

Kenric sneered. "It appears those below him were equally incompetent. Do you have any idea who it is that you let slip through your fingers?"

Decar looked like he was both prepared to run and frozen on the spot. When he answered, it was in a subdued voice. "Leviticus Radix, a young computational engineer familiar with the facial recognition algorithm." Decar's voice rose at the end making it sound like a question.

Kenric's eyes bored into him. "My agents tell me that he's a Levigator!"

"A Levigator, sir?"

"Do you people not read the histories? A Levigator! A superhuman of some sort — if you're to believe the Servators. They claim that the Maker sends a Levigator to help in times of great need."

"Do you adhere to the Maker's Way, sir?"

"Of course not, you fool. But if the Servators believe this man is a Levigator, then they believe a need exists. It puts them on alert while I'm trying to lull them into complacency. There hasn't been mention of a Levigator in centuries. Only the naive believe they have supernatural abilities, but they definitely have influence — the timing couldn't be worse. I need to know what kind of hazard he poses to my plans."

It was a lie. If Leviticus Radix was truly a Levigator, he represented a supernatural threat at least as great as the overlords themselves. The overlords were not of this world, yet they were very real and very upset. What he didn't mention to Decar was that the Levigator had already made an appearance and was instrumental in Kade's escape. Kenric's agents reported some mysterious phenomenon that seemed to protect the escape effort and hamper their own. They were at a loss to explain those effects. Kenric made a point of expecting surprises, but Decar didn't need to know that.

Kenric couldn't guess at what a Levigator might or could do, but he needed to find out — fast.

"I apologize, Anarch. If I had known, I would have sent the entire horde of Breachers in pursuit — had it been in my power to do so."

It was a pathetic attempt to redirect blame. They both knew that Decar had only been an assistant with no authority to command any more than the few below him in rank. He was lucky to get any response at all when he contacted that Breacher facility. Even so, he wasn't about to let Decar off so easily.

Kenric rubbed his eyes. "I'm going to give you one more chance, Decar. If you fail me again, I'm going to find another use for members of your family."

Decar stiffened at the threat. Kenric preferred to offer a carrot over a stick, but he didn't have time for that. He needed to motivate Decar. A gleam of defiance lit the man's eyes replacing the fear of a moment before. It would do. Unfortunately, it meant he could no longer rely on Decar for the long term. The man was enterprising and Kenric wouldn't waste a resource before it became necessary. Still, precautions were prudent.

"I'm going to assign a few Sicari to assist you. They'll remain at your side to help apprehend this Levigator."

Decar was visibly uncomfortable with the suggestion — as well he should be. The Sicari were beholden to no one. Working with them was a dangerous dance. One misstep and Decar would be courting death. He would have to be nimble on his feet to survive. It provided a little extra incentive to perform well. If he stepped on his partner's toes and suffered the consequence — well, that was the price you paid for failing your Anarch.

"I still expect you to find Mr. Brixton, Decar. He needs to be taught a lesson, but Leviticus Radix is your priority. Bring them both to me."

Chapter 36

Kade and Selica sat huddled together in the back of the sub. Lev had been avoiding them while trying to set aside his animosity. He couldn't ignore them any longer, though. He needed answers before arriving at their destination. Lev sighed. *He's not the same person you knew in school, Lev. Kade's been through a lot. Give him the benefit of the doubt. You're the Levigator. Start acting like one.*

Lev turned from his conversation with Tark and nodded his intent to go talk with their guests. Kade was watching him as he approached. He'd been staring at Lev with a confused look on his face since the moment Kade boarded the sub. *How do I even begin to explain how much I've changed?* Lev wondered. Then again, Kade had probably changed through his experiences as well. Maybe it wouldn't be so difficult to find common ground.

Lev sat across from Kade, their knees almost touching in the cramped sub.

"Why did you do it, Kade?" Lev closed his eyes and pinched the bridge of his nose. He hadn't wanted to start this conversation with accusations. He shook his head. "I'm sorry, that was unfair."

"No — you're right to be suspicious. I made a terrible mistake and I have much to answer for. I deserve your scorn. I'll answer all of your questions. I want to make things right."

Lev noticed Selica gripping Kade's hand in support. That simple act encouraged Lev as much as Kade's confession. It wasn't the action of someone trying to deceive. Lev fell into pattern sight and used the techniques Akhen taught him. He mapped Kade's facial features, pupil dilation and body language to form a baseline for comparison. Once they began their conversation, Lev would catalogue nuances until he could tell the truth from a lie. Lev said no more, but raised an eyebrow, encouraging Kade to elaborate.

"First of all, Radix, I want to thank you. I know you're not very fond of me, but you didn't just save me — you also saved Selica. I can never repay you for that. I'm willing to suffer the cost for my crimes, but Selica is a victim. She's been a slave almost her entire life. She deserves a chance at freedom."

"That raises several other questions," Lev interrupted. "How is Selica involved in all of this?"

Kade opened his mouth, but Selica answered for him.

"The Breachers sent me to Denmount to convince you to come work for them — by any means necessary."

"Is that why you were flirting with me at the beginning of the term?"

Selica nodded. "You didn't show any interest and then you disappeared. I moved on to Kade as the secondary target."

"If you're a Breacher agent, why would I trust anything you have to say to me? Breachers tried to kidnap me. Having seen their handiwork, I don't believe I would have fared well in their custody."

"You're right about that. They would have used you and then discarded you. I'm glad you escaped."

"I almost didn't."

"It's not what you think, Radix. Selica isn't an agent. She's a slave. The Breachers don't treat their female slaves kindly if they're disobedient. She didn't have a choice."

Lev was uncomfortable with the implication. "How did you become a slave to the Breachers?"

"My father owed a debt to the Breachers. When he couldn't pay, he was killed. My mother and I became Breacher property in lieu of my father's debt. Later on, my mother was killed in front of me. I hate them! They stole my family — my entire life. Kade has been the only true friend I've ever had."

Lev glanced at Kade who appeared genuinely grieved by her pain. That didn't mean he could trust Selica. "So, you turned your efforts toward Kade and pretended to care for him so you could talk him into joining the Breachers?"

"No! I mean, yes — I flirted with Kade and we spent time together, but my feelings for him are genuine. He treated me kindly. I didn't want any harm to come to him. I never talked to Kade about the Breachers while I was in Denmount."

Kade treated her kindly? That doesn't sound like the Kade I know. "So you say, yet he did end up with the Breachers and here you are as well. Your words don't line up with circumstances."

Kade cleared his throat. "It wasn't her, Radix. A Breacher named Decar Tosh approached me. He was posing as a recruiter for a global technology firm looking for new talent. He was asking about you. I was jealous, so I told him I could do anything you could."

"Now, that I believe."

Kade looked chagrined. "I knew it wasn't true, but I was in a bad place. I couldn't make my final tuition payment and was about to lose my place at Denmount. After so many years — to come so close to graduating and have it all taken away — it was too much. You wouldn't understand, Radix. You had a sponsor, you had talent, you had everything I wanted and you were about to be offered a dream job."

"So you did your best to undermine my success just as you always have. This time it backfired."

Kade hung his head. "It wasn't my proudest moment. I know this will sound like an excuse, but my family didn't support me. I worked several jobs to put myself through school. Most of the time I was exhausted in class. It was a struggle to balance my time. Everything seemed to come so easily to you. I wanted to believe I was as gifted as you. I thought that I would be at the top of the class if I had your advantages. I resented you for it."

"I didn't know how bad things were for you, Kade, but you made my life miserable without good reason." Lev willed himself to unclench his fists.

"During my time with the Breachers I suffered a great deal, but I also learned that I'm a talented computational engineer. My mistake was in trying to compete at your level. I now know that's not possible. No one else is quite like you, Radix. That doesn't make me a failure. It makes you an anomaly."

"No one questioned your abilities, Kade. Only the most talented weavers were invited to assist with the facial recognition project. You were among them." Lev sighed. "I'm guessing you meant it as a compliment, but you could have chosen a better word to describe me than *anomaly.*"

Kade quirked one side of his mouth in a deprecating smile as he looked over to Selica. "I still have a lot to learn. The point is, I was desperate and Decar promised a signing fee if I could prove my value. It was enough to pay Denmount and ensure my graduation. I jumped at the opportunity. It was too good to be true, but I wasn't thinking clearly. He said they were working on their own version of facial recognition and were searching for people who were familiar with the concepts. They wanted to see examples of Denmount's writ weaving and have me explain certain parts to one of their experts to show I was fluent."

Lev started to stand, but bumped his head on a bulkhead and quickly sat back down. "You stole the weaves from Denmount and gave them to the Breachers? You signed a confidentiality covenant, Kade!"

"I know! They said they didn't need the code, that they just wanted proof. I was only going to borrow the weave. I had no intention of handing it over to them. I took the code with me when I left, but...."

"They copied it." Lev guessed.

Kade nodded miserably. "I was so blinded by the opportunity — I wasn't considering the potential for duplicity. They had a reasonable cover story. The company was legitimate. It was shortly after my meeting with their *expert* that I discovered the truth. Not only did they copy the weaves, but they took a viewcording of me handing them the files and receiving a payment. They played me for a fool. I wasn't a criminal at heart, but they made me one in deed."

Lev nodded. "The Breachers framed Nico. It's something they're very good at."

"That's whose voice I heard earlier! Callan is here, isn't he? What's going on?"

Lev snapped his fingers to get Kade's attention. "We don't have time for that right now. Continue with your story."

Kade had been craning his neck trying to spot Nico toward the front of the sub, but he settled back into his seat and continued. "Some students saw me talking to Decar and told the Court Master. He knew about my financial problems and became suspicious when I suddenly had the means to make payment. He couldn't prove anything, but I was expelled pending an investigation. Decar threatened to show the viewcording to the school, my family, and the authorities. He gave me the option of joining him in Sumakad or taking my chances as a fugitive in Caralithica. I couldn't bear the shame of anyone learning the truth."

"So, you ran — coward!" Lev grabbed a fistful of Kade's tunic. Selica blurted out a protest, but Kade made no attempt to defend himself. He merely closed his eyes and prepared for a blow. Just at that moment, Tark placed a hand on Lev's shoulder. Lev released Kade and took a deep calming breath.

When the blow didn't come, Kade opened his eyes and continued. "At first it wasn't so bad. They paid well and sent a portion to my family each month. It forestalled any questions about my absence. I received official credentials as a computational engineer and was put in charge of rebuilding the facial recognition algorithm. Eventually they dropped the pretense of being a legitimate technology company.

"When things didn't go their way — let's just say you didn't want to be the one responsible for failure. I considered turning myself in, but my keepers had other incentives to keep me in line. They threatened to kidnap Selica as a replacement if I tried to leave. At the time, I didn't know that it was a hollow threat since they already controlled her. I became little more than highly qualified slave labour."

"You were obviously successful in your work. That was clever of you to jostle the viewcorders when I was around. It alerted the Servators." Lev's voice took on a threatening tone. "Innocent people have died as a result of your efforts."

Kade dropped his face into his hands. "I know! When I discovered they were using the technology to target people for assassination, I began looking for ways to stop them. I delayed progress at every opportunity. Selica and I were working on a writ contagion. We hoped to damage the weaves and escape, leaving no one qualified to fix it. Before we were ready to deploy the contagion, Villecrest started using the algorithm to track our former classmates and things became more complicated."

"Wait — which classmates are you referring to?"

"Everyone who worked on the facial recognition algorithm at Denmount. Villecrest wanted to control the knowledge. We don't know for sure if he was planning to kidnap them or kill them. Villecrest is dead now, but the names are still in the system and I don't trust Trantor to leave them untouched. Radix, you need to warn them!"

Lev stared at Kade with rage for a full minute before he dropped his gaze to rub his temples. This was getting complicated. "Tell me the names of the students listed in the Breacher network." He activated the Q-view on his wrist, prepared to enter the names. Kade stared, dumbfounded at the alien looking device on Lev's arm as he recounted the names.

"What is that? It wasn't on your arm a second ago."

Lev ignored the question and focused on a search for two other names Kade had mentioned. "It says here that Toller Villecrest was Third Anarch in Sumakad. You say he's dead?"

"That's the consensus among the Breachers. He disappeared and Kenric Trantor took his place."

Lev's fingers played over the screen making some updates. "Kenric Trantor is a Second Anarch. He'll have a broader influence. Based on what you've said, I'm assuming the deaths we've seen so far were on Toller Villecrest's orders. If he's now dead, that would explain the brief escalation and sudden cessation of murders. Do you know what Trantor's plans are for the algorithm?"

"Decar told me that Trantor originally funded the algorithm project at Denmount. He was angry with Villecrest for meddling. When the Third Anarch began killing Servators, it upset a long-term plan that Trantor had in the works. I get the feeling that Trantor wasn't ready for the Servators to know about the algorithm yet."

"Why do you think that?"

"Just before we escaped, I was summoned to give a presentation to a gathering of the anarchs. Trantor was showing off the algorithm to Breacher leaders from around the world. After I was dismissed, I heard Trantor say something before the door closed behind me."

"What did he say?"

Kade paled. "He wants to use the algorithm to locate every Servator in the world. He plans to kill them all in a single coordinated attack when they expect it least. I don't think Trantor will have much trouble convincing the other anarchs to take part. They seemed fascinated with the facial recognition algorithm. I could see the wheels turning in their minds as they considered the technology's potential."

Lev's fist was tapping his chin as he considered the implications. It was happening. The records from kin worlds that succumbed to flooding saw the elimination of Servators as a precursor. The common thread tied to Servator extinction was facial recognition. "It will take a while for them to install a global viewcorder network. We have a little time before they begin cataloguing the population."

Kade was vigorously shaking his head. "No, Radix. Those viewcorders you encountered are obsolete. When Trantor took over, he introduced new technology to upgrade the networks. He must have been working on it for some time. They're tiny transparent micro-corders the size of your thumbnail. Unless you know what to look for, they're virtually invisible. They run off the wireless tote-comm network. Installation takes less than a minute. Even as we speak, Breachers are blanketing the city streets. Soon, they'll move indoors placing hidden micro-corders inside every building they can access. Places to hide will be few and far between. Finding every device would be a hopeless endeavour. They can detect when one is missing and quickly replace it.

"You know how efficient the original algorithm was. I'm sorry to say that under duress, I've improved performance substantially since you last saw the weaves. Trantor has ramped up production of his micro-corders. Once he makes the devices available to other anarchs..."

"...It will be too late to stop this." Lev concluded. He passed a worried look to Tark.

"We'll be there within the hour, Levigator."

Chapter 37

"Where is my shipment, Trantor?"

"Samitar, please lower your voice. I can hear you quite clearly, you don't need to yell."

"All of the others have received their first shipments! Why do you withhold mine? What game are you playing?"

"Calm yourself. The micro-corders are en route. We had a temporary malfunction on the assembly line, but we were able to affect repairs quickly. Your shipment will arrive a day late, no more."

"I will not calm myself. I don't trust you, Trantor, and you've left me at a disadvantage while others already reap the benefits of this technology."

Kenric knuckled his forehead. A headache was forming again. This was the third call in as many days. Dealing with his peers was like working with spoiled children.

"The manufacturing facility can only produce so many micro-corders per day and someone had to be the last to receive shipment. In order to make things as fair as possible, the first shipments were sent to those anarchs located further away. It will take longer for those shipments to arrive. You're closest in proximity, so you're last on the list. I assure you, nothing nefarious is happening. It was a simple matter of logistics."

"Lies! Kivar is just as close as I am."

Kenric sighed. "It's true that the distance between borders is similar, but the point of delivery is several leagues further in your case. Seriously, Samitar, we're talking about the difference of a day. You know how inept Kivar is. You'll surpass him quickly, and due to travel times, the rest will receive their shipments within days of each other. Your concern is unwarranted. You're not at a disadvantage. In fact, you benefit from recent improvements in the design for this last batch. You'll be receiving the highest quality micro-corders produced so far."

That seemed to pacify the man.

"Very well, but if I don't receive my shipment by end of day tomorrow, you'll hear from me again!"

"I would expect no less, Samitar...." Kenric was unable to finish his sentence as Samitar had already disconnected. He leaned back in his chair and rubbed the back of his neck. It was difficult to get angry when things were going so well. With the exception of Kivar, all other anarchs had their memory stash archives in place — based on the designs he had provided. He'd sent his engineers to help with installation of the algorithm and final tweaking. Now they were just waiting for the micro-corders and the last of those had been shipped. They would all have the core of a working network established in their most populous cities. After that, he'd ship more as they extended their networks.

Kenric smiled, thinking of the advantage he'd gained. By allowing the other anarchs to implement their own networks, he'd given them a false sense of control. Their greed overcame common sense. His people were the only ones who knew the technology well enough to modify the weaves. None of the other anarchs would have access to each other's networks beyond the data they agreed to share, but he would have full access to all of their networks. It would dramatically enhance his intelligence gathering abilities. Best of all, they were paying him for the privilege. He'd been accused of developing the technology to fill his coffers and he was certainly doing that, but he had grander aspirations.

Kenric spun his chair slowly. This had been Villecrest's office before he took over. Knives hung from the wall along with other sharp implements. He couldn't even guess at the purpose for some of them. Villecrest had an obsession with blades. The man was truly twisted. *I really need to redecorate.* His eyes fell on a pair of wall-mounted swords across from his desk. They were a matched set of warkata scythe blades — very rare and very expensive. *It must have cost Villecrest a fortune. Unless he took it from one of his victims.* Kenric decided he would keep those. They would remind him of his goal to cut away the necrotic tissue that plagued the Breachers. His fellow anarchs only thought of their own little kingdoms instead of working together toward their common Breacher goals. He intended to remedy that shortcoming by uniting all of the Breachers under the leadership of one visionary. *We need someone with intelligence, patience, and foresight to lead. If those are the requirements, it will have to be me.* Kenric grinned at his own arrogance. *It's not arrogant if it's true and if the others are unable to stop me, it will be a fact.*

The first phase of his plan was almost complete. The second phase would begin soon. It required that they identify all Servators and their allies, wherever they may be. This would be the most difficult part. He needed to keep the others from killing Servators just because it was convenient. They needed to destroy their ancient enemy all at once or the Servators would go into hiding and rise again when they'd regained some strength.

When the day came that no new leads were forthcoming, they could move on to the final phase. Kenric had been intentionally vague about how that would come about. He supposed that the other anarchs imagined a day of slaughter, but that was inefficient and wouldn't produce the desired outcome. No, when he said that the Servators must all die at the same time, he meant it literally.

One of his labs had developed a toxin that could lay dormant in a human host until triggered by a secondary agent. His plan was to incrementally infect Servators as they located them. It was why he required access to results from all of the networks. He needed time to start that work without the knowledge of the others. When the day came for the destruction of the Servators, they would already be carrying the means of their execution. Triggering the deadly toxin was a matter of releasing a short-lived but highly contagious virus. Only those who had ingested the toxin would die — it would appear as though a plague was responsible. The ensuing panic would serve to obfuscate Breacher involvement. The Servators would remain unaware until it was too late. Within seventy-two hours, they would all be dead.

The other anarchs would be furious when they learned he would deny them the anticipated festival of blood. He'd thought it best not to tell them in advance, but he felt it wrong to deprive his fellow Breachers of the opportunity to witness the imminent victory — or the genius behind it. As a compromise, he decided to share the good news when they, like everyone around them, were feeling unwell from the virus. They would no doubt lay on their sick beds planning some vindictive act of reprisal once they felt sufficiently recovered. He could imagine their outrage. "How dare you release this plague upon your allies! You should have warned us so we could isolate before you began." Indeed, he himself would be safely away in a mountain retreat while the virus did its work.

They could rage and plot all they wished. He felt no need to explain that they themselves had ingested the toxin while they were enjoying some very fine wine at the gathering of the anarchs.

Chapter 38

After the debrief, Lev left abruptly. *Typical*, Kade thought. There was much more they should talk about, but Radix only listened when it suited him.

Kade looked up at Tark who remained behind — whether to guard them or because the front of the sub was too crowded, he could only guess. It's not like he and Selica could go anywhere with who knew how many fathoms of water above their heads. The thought made Kade squirm.

Maybe this Tark fellow will be more informative than Radix. "Do you think I might be able to talk to Nico Callan?"

"He's busy piloting this vessel."

"Why would Nico be piloting a Servator sub?"

Tark shook his head. "You misunderstand. This sub belongs to Nico, not the Servators. He offered his assistance in your rescue."

That was interesting. Kade hadn't known Nico owned a sub. Considering his heritage, it wasn't too surprising. The Callan family owned a ridiculously wealthy international shipping company. They likely had a variety of seagoing vessels. More unexpected was the Servator connection.

"Have you known Nico long?"

"Long enough to know he's a good man."

"How is it that he came to be working with the Servators?" Kade didn't really expect an answer, but Tark spoke freely.

"The Callan family has worked with Servators for decades. Nico only learned this fact recently when he took over the family business."

"So why isn't he running that business instead of risking his life in a rescue attempt?"

"I believe you heard the Levigator mention that Nico was framed by the Breachers."

"What does that have to do with his presence here?"

"He's accused of murdering a high-ranking magistrate."

Kade burst out laughing.

"You find that amusing?"

Kade quickly sobered. "I'm not condoning murder or the injustice done to Nico. It's just that anyone who's met Nico knows that he's not capable of such a thing."

Tark nodded. "Indeed. However, the justice system in Denmount is corrupt. Breachers were hired to assassinate Nico within the prison after he is sentenced. They're not interested in facts, only in receiving payment for completing a contract. Nico is in hiding until his name can be cleared and the corrupt officials rooted out. This sub is safer than the streets of Denmount for the time being."

Kade nodded in understanding before asking his next question. "Why do you mispronounce Radix's name? It's Leviticus, not Levigator."

"Levigator isn't a name, it's a title."

Kade's brows furrowed in confusion. "Like when you call an apprentice a fledgling?"

"More like acknowledging a luminary."

"Oh, please! Radix is a savant, I'll give you that, but he doesn't need his ego fed any more than it already is. He was just a student not that long ago. Are you telling me in that short period of time he's earned the right to be your king or something?"

Tark tilted his head and stared at Kade as though evaluating his intellect. "In a very short time, you shifted the balance of power in favour of the Breachers. Some might grant you the less favourable title of scourge for your *brief*, but disastrous, influence. The extent of damage remains to be seen."

Kade fell silent at the rebuke.

"A Levigator is one who smooths the way and eases a burden. Leviticus is the only one who can address the yoke you've lain upon the Servators. If you're truly repentant for your actions, you'll show respect to the one who agreed to clean up your mess."

Selica broke the uncomfortable silence. "Where are we headed?"

"Our destination is a Servator rehabilitation island."

Kade switched from chagrin to panic in a heartbeat. "Now hold on just a minute. You're imprisoning us? What do you mean by rehabilitation? We *left* the Breachers — we're trying to help. Doesn't that count for something? Don't we get a trial or at least an opportunity to appeal to a higher authority?"

"You've already spoken with the Levigator."

Kade paled as the reality of their situation took hold. "So, we've escaped one prison only to land in another."

"Lev didn't need to risk his life for you." Tark noted. "In fact, we tried to talk him out of coming. You're fortunate that he didn't listen. The outcome would have been less certain if he hadn't been there."

"I do appreciate the rescue. I know that I owe Radix — all of you — my life. It's just that — look, I'm willing to pay for my crimes, but Selica doesn't deserve this. She's a victim who should have the freedom that was denied her as a Breacher slave."

"Where would you go?"

"Excuse me?"

"If you gained your freedom, where would you or Selica go? Would you prefer the corrupt Caralithican justice system responsible for framing Nico?"

"Of course not…"

Tark interrupted before Kade could say more.

"Do you have a way to hide from the Breacher network you helped create? The one you said is expanding to blanket the globe?"

"No." Kade whispered.

"The rehabilitation islands are hidden and far from known shipping lanes. Only the Servators know their locations. The islands are the only places left where we can guarantee your safety."

"Okay, I understand that, but I hoped I could join the fight against the Breachers. I want to contribute in a tangible way. I need to fix this and I can't do that sitting in a cell!"

Selica laid a hand on Kade's arm. "It's okay, Kade. Just knowing I'm no longer Breacher *property* is freedom enough and we'll still be together. We won't have to live in fear." Selica looked up at Tark with questioning eyes.

"We can, right? Be together, I mean? Or will they keep us apart?"

Tark's eyes softened. "It's Servator law that all those who have worked with Breachers to commit a crime must spend a minimum of two years on a rehabilitation island. It's an opportunity to witness a better way — apart from Breacher influence. After those years are complete, you'll have the choice to remain or leave. You'll be granted a second chance."

"With nowhere else to go, those two years will stretch into a life sentence." Kade placed his hand on top of Selica's. "I'm so sorry, Selica."

Tark chuckled. "It's not as bad as all that."

"That's easy for you to say."

"Actually yes, it is. I was a Breacher once."

Kade and Selica swivelled their heads in unison. Kade's mouth hung open as Selica asked, "You were a Breacher?"

"Yes. I spent six years at our destination."

"Six years? You must have done something pretty awful."

"Not really. Petty theft, mostly. I was part of a Breacher street gang in my youth. My life was moving along a dark path. I don't know where I'd be now without Servator intervention. They saved me."

"So, why six years?"

"I could have left after two years, but I was one of those who chose to stay. Chellea is my home. I have many friends I hope to see when we arrive."

"One of those who chose to stay? Why would you choose to prolong your captivity?" Selica wondered aloud.

"Many do. Life is better there than you'd think. The rehabilitation islands are like one big family. Everyone contributes equally to the upkeep of the community. Confinement is unnecessary on an island — the only way to leave is with an escort, but that's not the point. The islands are about living in a community where people care for each other. It's a haven, far from the abusive structure that Breachers try to pass off as family."

"So, it's a work camp?" Kade offered.

"Not at all! More like a tiny country. It has all of the amenities you could find in a small city. Each of the islands — Chellea included — has its own industry, exporting its goods in trade for desired imports. A Servator fleet manages trade logistics. Everyone shares in the profits and many earn a good income. You're expected to contribute, but you're free to choose vocations of interest. You two should have no trouble finding something to do. Technology experts are in short supply."

Kade shook his head. "I find it difficult to believe that a penal colony is as appealing as you make it sound."

"It's not a penal colony, Kade. It's a rehabilitation island. You're imagining something very different. We have such places, but they're reserved for unrepentant repeat offenders. People like that aren't allowed to return to a rehabilitation island for a third chance. In our experience, very few are that recalcitrant. Most are people like you, robbed of their choice. Given a better alternative they make better decisions."

"It sounds too good to be true," Selica mused.

"You'll see." Tark grinned. "Chellea is beautiful. Many Servators spend their vacations there."

"Vacations!" Kade shook his head. "I don't understand you people, but if it's as you say — well, I'm not going to complain."

"I didn't say it would be easy. People will know what you've done. You'll have to prove yourself and gain their trust. You'll also have to answer to your classmates."

"What do you mean?"

"We're tracking down the classmates you told the Levigator about. They'll be warned of their danger and offered refuge on Chellea. They won't be subject to a two-year stay, but it will take time to create new identities for them and they'll need to leave their old lives behind. It will fall on you to explain the reason for their predicament. One of the things we'll be asking of you and your classmates is to find a way to enter false identities into the Breacher network."

"I don't think that's possible."

"Then you'll be denying your classmates a return to a normal life. I suspect they'll be eager to work on that particular project and I suggest you work hard to make it possible."

Selica squeezed Kade's hand. "We'll do our best, right, Kade?"

Kade nodded. His mind was already working on the problem.

Chapter 39

Akhen nodded in approval. "That's good, Leviticus, can you make the material thicker?"

The boy amazed him more each time they met. His level of control was growing daily.

"It's a trade-off. If I make it thicker, I can't move my joints without interference. If I raise it further from the surface of my skin, I regain motion, but the joints become exposed."

Ever since they had learned that Lev was unconsciously mapping the coordinates of his own body, Akhen had been pushing his student to use that ability for defensive purposes. Leviticus was able to sense projectiles and materialize shields to block them, but Akhen was worried about the things he might miss while distracted. To that end, they were experimenting with a type of armour he might materialize over his body.

Creating armour wasn't a problem, but the weight and limited range of motion made traditional solutions impractical. Akhen hoped that Leviticus could materialize and dissipate the elements fast enough that they would never come in contact with his person to become a burden. They'd had limited success so far. Leviticus needed to focus on the material's distance from his skin as well as the constantly changing position created by his motion. It required a great deal of speed and concentration to sustain for a useful length of time. Even so, the armour might save his life if he could call on it, however briefly. *Besides*, Akhen thought, *the boy is increasing his token forming speed exponentially. Sooner or later he won't even realize he's doing it.* In order for that to happen, he needed to push Leviticus to greater heights.

"I see what you mean, but damage to a joint is the lesser evil. If you can't thicken the material at those places, then at least thicken it strategically. Thicken it over your torso where you don't need to map as much movement."

Lev complied.

"Good! Keep practising. I'd like to see you maintain this at a run, not just a walk."

Akhen grinned at the look of exasperation on Leviticus's face. "You'll thank me one day."

Lev tried a cartwheel, only to have pieces of materialized steel spray off his spinning limbs before dissipating a few feet away.

"I'm fairly confident that I never taught you that move in your warkata training. That would be a good way to get yourself killed. A showy flourish doesn't distract trained opponents, it just gives them an opening."

Lev sat on the floor rubbing the bruises from his experiment. "I just wanted to see if I could maintain control while fighting centrifugal forces."

"It was a good thought. Keep experimenting. We're in uncharted territory and you've already shown an amazing ability to master the challenges you've set for yourself."

Lev dusted himself off and rose to try something new.

"Have you considered using something like interlocking scales? Perhaps that would give you some flexibility around your joints."

"Huh." Lev muttered to himself and looked through the template library for something suitable.

Akhen cast a pondering glance over at Lev. "I've been meaning to ask you — how was your meeting with Hemish?"

"It was ... enlightening."

"Was he able to answer your questions?"

"Yes, but those answers raised more questions."

"May I ask what those questions involve? Perhaps I can help."

"Hemish explained about thin spaces and the formation of rifts. I can feel the rifts like my predecessors could. Now that I understand what I was sensing, I can hear the rift of this base from here."

"You can *hear* it?"

"It feels — like how a discordant song would sound. Hemish suspects that each Levigator experiences it in a unique way. He also suggested that I might be the first to sense it this way because of my higher rating."

"That sounds like a reasonable supposition."

"Possibly. Hemish said that Rushoen Nu Lon could sense a thin space from ten leagues away. I took a ground transport twenty leagues from this base and could still hear the rift. It was — unsettling."

"It shouldn't come as a surprise."

"That's not what troubled me. It was something Rushoen wrote in one of his journals. It was one of his final entries on record. He had been reflecting on the theory of parallel worlds and how that relates to the human soul. He wrote, 'If I should pass from here to there, would I be one or come undone?'"

"Yes, I'm familiar with that passage. I've been in many lively discussions on the topic."

"What happened to Rushoen? I haven't been able to find much more written about him beyond the year of that final entry."

"That's because Rushoen disappeared. They never found his body. His last known location was a dangerous district in Ankhor. The officially accepted premise is that he died at the hand of bandits."

"Someone of his abilities?"

Akhen shrugged. "All of us sleep or become distracted. We're all vulnerable in those moments. Now you know why I push you so hard on defensive measures."

"I think he went through."

"Could you repeat that? Akhen asked. "I believe I misheard."

Lev took on a preoccupied expression. "I think Rushoen walked through a rift into a kin world."

Akhen shook his head. "No one has ever passed through a rift. They encounter physical resistance."

Leviticus wasn't satisfied with the answer. "When Hemish first told me that we shared information through the rift, I imagined two people having a conversation, but that's not how it worked. In the beginning it was all sign language or holding up pieces of parchment with words written in large script. It was slow and painful, but eventually we obtained the technology to create tokens and the passing of knowledge occurred at a faster pace. First, scrolls were sent through, and eventually entire memory stash archives. Surely at some point analysts were tempted to send an actual person through to see things firsthand."

"I want to stop you right there, Leviticus. Don't even entertain the thought. Early on, some experimented with the creation of templates for living tissue. Analysts hoped that they could find a way to translate a person from one place to another using the QPN network. It involved a painstaking dissection of some poor creature in an attempt to capture every nuance of life. Every attempt ended in disaster. We can't send living tissue through a rift anymore than we might materialize one from across the room. If Rushoen attempted to use the network in such a way, he would have perished."

"If that's true, then how did we send a flower through the rift on this base?"

"That wasn't a real flower. Haven't you noticed that it's always in bloom? It's an artificial construct for the sole purpose of catching someone's attention."

Akhen didn't like the ironic smile that formed on Leviticus's face. "That flower did a very good job of attracting attention. So good that I reached through and plucked it."

Akhen froze. It was an uncomfortable truth that he had hoped Leviticus would forget in the shock of that day. He and Hemish had gone over it in detail. Somehow Leviticus had done the impossible. It was the undeniable sign that he was a Levigator. Someone always thought their novice might be the next Levigator, but they always failed to prove it. With Lev, no doubt existed. He had proven his credentials without even realizing he was doing it. He'd done something that no one had ever done before.

"Yes, you did." Akhen whispered.

"Do you think I can teleport to chosen coordinates?"

Akhen didn't respond immediately. "No. You can't disassemble yourself and re-form in another place."

"You hesitated. You must at least have some thoughts on what happened."

Akhen sighed. "Not initially, but when we realized that you were your own QPN and that you were constantly mapping your position in space and time, I had a few ideas."

"Go on."

"You've said that you can sense every particle of an item you're materializing, correct?"

"That's right. Usually it's only necessary to recall key points, but at some level I've catalogued every particle. If I concentrate, I can see them like grains of sand."

"Exactly. The QPN network isn't capable of that nuance. The fact that you can pick out key points, facilitating the natural formation of larger template components, suggests that you're intuitively picking up on details that aren't normally available to us. At the same time, you can adapt to accommodate shifts as a pattern is forming. That's a new thing and we've been exploiting it in your recent exercises."

Leviticus waited patiently for more and Akhen shifted uncomfortably. *The boy has been learning his interrogation techniques a little too well.*

"Hemish told me that you said you could sense particles from each side of the rift, matching pairs with slightly different frequencies. Is that correct?"

Lev nodded. "That's right. They're the same, but slightly offset from each other. They fight to share the same space, but are unable because they can't harmonize. I'm not sure if I can adequately explain the feeling."

"That actually meshes with what I was picturing. I think you're so attuned to the particles that make up your being that you can adjust to accommodate the frequency change of a kin world. If what you've described is accurate, then the reason most of us feel resistance from the rift is because the difference in frequency between our two worlds acts like the repelling effects of same polarized ends on a magnet."

"That doesn't make sense. Particles are bleeding in both directions of the rift. It's how I can hear them."

"Yes, but you said those were paired and so those few particles exist in discord, yet remain because of their association with each other. If it were otherwise, wouldn't we feel a gale as particles rushed from one world to the other in some massive exchange? I suspect that those drifting particles are limited in both range and lifespan."

"I'll have to try and follow a pair and test your theory."

"Please do — I will be eager to hear the results. To answer your question more fully — I know you can't teleport, but I think you can modify your frequency of existence."

"Which means that I should be able to pass through a rift."

"Listen to me, Leviticus. Passing your arm through the rift is one thing.

Your mind is something else entirely. Even if you survived, the experience might drive you insane. It's too big of a risk with nothing to gain. We can already accomplish our goals through conventional means. Promise me you won't attempt such a thing. We need the Levigator here and now."

"Don't worry, Akhen." Lev clapped him on the back. "I'm not in a rush to die — despite the insistence of Chief Sentry Abrax to the contrary."

Regardless of the assurances, Akhen *was* worried. Traversing a rift was a dangerous notion that had reared its ugly head time and again. Only this time it might actually be possible. He prayed the temptation wouldn't be too much for his young protege.

Chapter 40

Kade walked the path from the residence he shared with Selica. Chellea was a beautiful uncharted island. As far as the rest of humanity was concerned, it didn't exist. The village was nestled within the caldera of a long inactive volcano providing shelter from storms and prying eyes. A lake had formed in the centre, surrounded by housing and tiered gardens running up the hillsides.

Kade had trekked to the highest spot he could find to see what lay beyond, but discovered only stretches of water in every direction. They truly were isolated. Those who were here against their will were stuck. He didn't feel like a prisoner, though. He was with Selica and they felt freer than they had for a very long time. The Breacher threat was far away and Selica seemed to delight in the mundane chores of everyday life on the island.

He found her on her knees, harvesting carrots. She smiled up at him as he approached, dirt smudges on her cheeks. It filled his heart with warmth to see her so happy. If this was a prison, he wanted to extend his sentence.

"Have you come to help dig for your dinner?"

"I would love to," Kade began, and meant it, "but I've been summoned to Administrator Na Tuni's office."

Selica frowned. "What did you do, Kade? Have you been in another fight with your former classmates?"

Radix had kept his promise to find and warn their former classmates of the threat to their lives. Most had agreed to come to the island for a time, but they weren't happy about it. *Better unhappy than dead*, Kade thought. Two of their classmates were missing and Kade feared for their lives. The fact that the rest had been spared a similar fate didn't ingratiate them to Kade. On the contrary, they blamed him all the more. He couldn't fault them. When they heard the whole story, they were furious. One of the men had decided to use his fists to vent his frustration. Unfortunately, he was a poor fighter and Kade ended up looking like the aggressor even though he was only defending himself. Things had cooled off a bit in the past two weeks since they arrived, but Kade wasn't sure they would ever forgive him or give him a chance to prove that he'd changed.

"Nothing like that." Kade responded. "Apparently, Radix left a message for me or something."

"Oh?" Selica sat up with interest. "Should I join you?"

"Nah, you look like you're having too much fun."

She swatted his leg, but didn't disagree.

"It's probably nothing. I'll fill you in later."

"Can you pick up some shellfish on your way back?"

"You got it, beautiful." Kade leaned down for a kiss before continuing on his way. What could Radix want? Maybe he would finally get an explanation regarding the equipment recently shipped to the island. Kade had been told that his education would be valued on the island and he was eager to be useful, but they hadn't asked much of him so far. The equipment deliveries suggested that might change, but it was a hodgepodge of materials that didn't make much sense. Kade couldn't guess what it was for. Administrator Na Tuni seemed as baffled as he was. Regardless, he had made himself useful repairing any equipment they gave him access to. The Servator communication centre was off-limits to him. He couldn't understand what the big deal was. He probably understood it better than the technicians who were using it. *No point in speculating.* Kade picked up his pace, hoping that he might actually be getting some answers.

When he arrived at the administrative building, Kade was surprised to find the man rather than his message.

"Radix! What are you doing here?"

"You were told that you would be called on to help find a way to counter the Breacher network."

"Is that what all this equipment is about?"

"It's a start. I've had some space set apart for you to build a lab. I want you and our former classmates to recreate the network you built for the Breachers."

Kade laughed. "I saw some of the equipment you sent. I could use it to make a fancy desk lamp for you."

"More is on the way. Here's an itemized list. I need you to advise Administrator Na Tuni of any other components you might need."

"Umm — You want me to rebuild it from memory? Radix, I had original weaves to work from. I can't possibly remember every quantaxiom set and data directive. I could build something new, but that could take years."

"No, it has to be as close as possible to what you did for the Breachers."

"I could probably reproduce my revisions if I had the original writ weaves, but without that..."

Leviticus interrupted. "I've spent the last two weeks reproducing the weaves."

"Reproducing the... from memory?"

"You've always known I have a very good memory."

"Yes, but *nobody's* memory is that good." Kade's eyebrows furrowed in scrutiny. "I suppose I can't rule anything out where you're concerned. You seem to have become a leader of this mysterious group and I'm still trying to figure out what happened on the night of our rescue. Breachers were firing at us — missing us at that range seems impossible, but none of us were hurt. I don't understand how I ended up on the deck of Nico's sub instead of in the water. Something pushed me."

Leviticus looked like he was struggling with a decision. "Suffice it to say that the Servators have been around for a very long time and have developed technology you could only imagine."

"Is that why I can't go into the communications centre?"

"That and the fact that you were working for the Breachers and have yet to prove yourself."

"Look, Radix, I'm already aware that the Servators have some mysterious technology. When I was with the Breachers, they talked about obtaining Servator devices only to have them dissolve before it was possible to study them. If you want my help, I'm going to need to know what tools I have at my disposal. The Breachers hardened the network to protect against conventional exploits. I can't suggest alternatives without knowing what the Servators bring to the table."

"There may come a time when I need to share that kind of information with you, but right now I don't trust you at all, Brixton."

"I get it — I do. I would feel the same in your shoes, but you saw the Breachers shooting at me. They want me dead. I'm not their ally. They forced me to do their bidding and it makes me sick knowing their plans are for the algorithm. I'm guilty of being selfish, but I'm not a murderer. I've been personally paying the price for my mistakes ever since." Kade paused. "Look me in the eyes, Radix."

When Leviticus's eyes locked onto his own, he continued. "I would rather die than see one more person come to harm because of the algorithm. Give me a chance to fix this. Let me help!"

Something changed in Lev's eyes and Kade knew that he'd made a decision. "People keep telling me you deserve a second chance, so I'm going to give you one, but if you double-cross me, I promise that you'll spend the rest of your days on a different island, and life won't be as pleasant there."

Kade straightened. "All I want is to see the Breachers stopped. I'll do anything that I can to that end. You have my word and I'll prove its worth."

Lev sighed. "I have something in mind to start. Let's see how you do with that and we'll see where things go from there."

"That's all I ask. What do you need me to do?"

"I'm going to show you something that you need to keep to yourself." Lev activated his wrist Q-view and it materialized on his arm as if by magic.

Kade watched, mesmerized. "You did that while we were on the sub. This is the Servator technology you mentioned." Kade looked back to Lev for confirmation, but what he saw there shocked him. He leaped to his feet toppling the chair he'd been sitting on. Radix had disappeared and in his place sat a stranger. The man laughed but his mouth remained motionless and his expression didn't change at all. It was disturbing, but not so much as what happened next. The features began to bubble and crumble away as if the man were decomposing before his eyes. And then Radix was back with a knowing smirk on his face.

"How did you do that?" Kade demanded.

Lev shrugged. "Servator technology."

Kade picked his chair up off the floor, keeping his eyes on Radix the entire time. "That's some trick."

"We used something similar to shield us from Breacher weapons on the sub."

"I felt a pulsing sensation when I jumped from the bridge. I thought I was being hit by weapons fire — it was the shielding."

"Correct."

"That explains the lack of holes in my person."

Kade's eyebrows rose in sudden understanding. "And that shield — it lowered me to the sub. Why couldn't I see it?"

"You might have if you'd known what to look for. It was forming and dissolving in rapid succession. The effect might seem invisible at a quick glance."

"That's incredible! I could think of many practical ways to make use of such technology, but you chose to show me a mask?"

"This is something new I'm playing with, something I'm hoping might fool the algorithm."

Kade immediately saw where he was going. "You want me to reproduce the Breacher network so you can improve these masks."

"Exactly. I need you to rebuild the network as best you can and then I want you to scan the faces of everyone on the island."

"I don't understand. Other than verifying that the network is working, how does that help?"

"Once you've recorded everyone, I want you to send me the data. I have some ... *tools* that can isolate key points on the facial maps. From there I can modify it for use with Servator technology. It will allow us to make templates for forming masks. I could make a guess based on the original algorithm output, but you mentioned that you had made some improvements."

"That's right — I found some common facial markers that helped improve recognition speed."

"That's where I need your help. We need to develop some generic composite faces from your collection of scans based on the facial markers you've incorporated into the Breacher algorithm. After that, we need to find the closest matching points for the Servator templates that I can provide."

Kade was nodding. "The masks might be able to fool the Breacher network into making a false positive. If we can't bring the network down, at least we can make it less effective."

"That's my hope."

"You'll still draw Breacher attention with too many mysterious false positives. The system is designed to track individuals for Breacher agents to investigate. If the algorithm fails to find a match in the database, it will continue flagging that individual. The algorithm needs to see the person identified as being of no interest. It won't stop until someone enters those details into the record."

"I'm hoping you can find a way to provide that information to the network."

Kade was shaking his head. "It's not possible to do that remotely. You'd need direct access to the network. Unless you can make yourself invisible, I don't see how that would be possible. The Breachers are on high alert since my escape."

"Are you sure about that? We were able to communicate remotely." Lev prompted.

"A security expert named Tridor Flint discovered part of our communication. I managed to convince him that it was leftover junk directives from experiments with a writ contagion."

"You wrote a writ contagion?"

"I told you about that. I wasn't joking when I said we were trying to stop the Breachers. Tridor is an expert in developing countermeasures against writ contagions. He'll have deleted our conversation as part of his efforts to harden the network against similar attacks."

Lev stood and paced. "When I received your first message, I set up a search function to notify me when it found future strings containing the opening and closing characters we used for our conversation. I imagine you did something similar. If this Tridor fellow deleted the message itself, would he have thought to look for the directives that you created to watch for my response?"

A slow smile crept over Kade's face. "Possibly not. I told him the countermeasures we deployed compared the original algorithm with any corruptions and converted those aberrations to gibberish to prevent further damage. He was under the impression that we then repaired the weaves. I let him believe that I had just been careless in missing that particular segment. He took over after that, establishing what he called industry standard protocols on an isolated test network running a copy of the live algorithm. I don't know if he moved his edited version to the live network yet, so we may have a window of opportunity. Then again, even if he did, he may have missed my directives as you've suggested. The self-inspection weaves are necessarily complex. It would be easy to miss the tiny addition I made to enable our covert conversation."

Lev clapped his hands together. "Then this could work."

"If that line of communication is still open — maybe. It would take some time because of the character limitations, but the information we'd need to supply isn't that detailed, just name, address, etc. We'd need to stick with content that can't be confused with instruction sets, otherwise it could trigger Tridor's countermeasures and alert the Breachers to what we're doing. Other than that, it could work."

"Then that's your first task. Gather our classmates and put them to work."

"Umm, about that — they're not too happy with me. I don't think they're going to agree to work under my supervision."

"If they want to improve their chances at a safe future, they'll have to. They know the capabilities of the algorithm and they know that it's in the hands of those who wish to cause them harm. Don't tell them anything about the masking technology, but you can let them know that it's in their best interest to work towards changing the status associated with their images on the Breacher network. They may not like you, but they have a vested interest in their own skins."

Kade stood and walked over to the window. He gazed across the verdant valley stretching below as he considered everything they'd discussed. This could work. It was an opportunity for reparations. It wouldn't end the threat, but it might save lives and that was a start. "I'll compile a list of equipment immediately and I'll meet with the others later this afternoon. If they don't agree to help, Selica and I will do it ourselves. We both know the Breacher network best anyway."

Lev stood to leave. "If you find you need more help, let me know. I can arrange to have a few Servator engineers provide support."

"How do I enter the personal details into the Breacher network without access to the Servator communications centre?" Kade asked.

"I'll take care of that." Lev assured him. "All I need to know is the proper opening and closing segments you've developed to direct the information to its appropriate place in the memory stash. We can coordinate once you have everything else set up. We can't introduce that information until we've developed the generic facial templates anyway. Give those to Administrator Na Tuni when they're ready and he'll pass them along to me."

Kade nodded. "We'll begin as soon as the equipment arrives."

"Kade — a lot of people's lives are on the line. Do the right thing."

"Thank you for this opportunity, Levigator. I won't let you down." Lev's eyebrows rose in surprise. Kade knew he wasn't expected to offer that honorific, but he meant it.

Chapter 41

"As you can see, we've widened the tunnel for better traffic flow." Nico spread his arms to emphasize the point. "We found some stress fractures at certain points — those areas have been reinforced."

Cello ran her fingers over the freshly painted tunnel walls, appreciating the clean surfaces. The Servator base at Denmount was very old and she'd never seen the tunnels with anything but an aging patina. Some might miss the loss of character, but Cello liked things clean and orderly. "Widening the tunnel was a good decision. I'd never really thought of it as a problem in the past, but the evacuation drew attention to our lack of foresight. We weren't able to empty the base as quickly as I would have liked."

Nico moved on to the next portion of their tour. Chief Sentry Cello Vantos had made time in her busy schedule to sign off on the maintenance work that she had agreed to in the Servator's absence. She seemed impressed so far. Seri fidgeted nervously knowing what was coming next. She'd kept her mother in the dark about their extra unsanctioned renovations. Initially she felt certain that her mother would approve, but she hadn't factored in the considerations of a Chief Sentry. Sometimes Seri had trouble separating her mother from her leader. Would the Chief Sentry feel they had compromised the base further? Doubts started to creep in. Seri pushed those feelings aside. It was too late to turn back now.

"The service lines were showing some corrosion," Nico continued, "so we've replaced those and upgraded everything. You should have more capacity now if you ever need to expand."

"That's not likely to happen for some time, but thank you."

Nico caught Seri's eye. They both hoped Cello would change her mind and consider a sooner return. They'd know by the end of the tour.

Cello stopped mid-stride. "What's this? I don't remember this side tunnel being here before." She looked to Nico for an answer.

"I think it would be best if Seri explains."

Cello furrowed her brows at the cryptic response and turned to her daughter.

Seri sighed. In a few minutes she'd learn whether her instincts were right or if she'd gambled poorly. She squared her shoulders and began her rehearsed presentation. "When I compromised the base, it was because I disappeared from a room with a single guarded exit. This raised suspicion among the Breachers. They decided that some hidden Servator facilities were in the area. Breacher scrutiny has increased since then. They won't stop looking until we put those suspicions to rest. I've been trying to find a way to do just that.

"Over the past several months, I've been planting a false history in the Denmount archives. They paint a picture of natural tunnels running beneath Denmount. As the narrative goes, criminals have used those tunnels sporadically through the years. More recently, some students at the Court of Learning, used them for secret parties. I didn't want to go any further before sharing my idea with you, but I'd like to start leaking that information to news agencies as public interest stories. If the Breachers think the tunnels are a loosely held secret, they might believe I escaped through one of those rather than imagining a Servator installation."

"It's an interesting idea, but the Breachers would want to see those tunnels for themselves and that would only increase the risk that someone might stumble across the base."

Seri took a deep breath. "That's what I thought too, but what if we could provide public access to such tunnels without risk of anyone finding the base?"

Cello looked around the tunnel they were standing in. "I don't see how letting the public down here is going to lessen the risk to the base, but you obviously have something else in mind."

"Not these tunnels, but what if there were other tunnels?"

Cello looked as though she were losing patience. "You know I don't like wasting time with games. Elaborate please."

"Nico and I have been working with Leviticus to design a tunnel labyrinth that touches the edge of Denmount campus and leads off in the opposite direction from the Servator base. That maze of tunnels is accessed from this side tunnel you're asking about."

"You've created an additional point of ingress to the base? Seri, you know we limit access for security reasons!"

Seri held her hands up to forestall her mother's protests. "Let me explain, please."

Cello didn't look happy, but held her tongue.

"First of all, the maze is complete, but the point at which the public would gain access isn't yet exposed. Right now, this is just a labyrinth of tunnels below ground. This entrance in front of us is the only access. Nothing has changed from a security standpoint. If someone from the public were to gain access to the labyrinth and somehow find their way through it, they would end up here. From this point, an intruder would need to breach all of our existing security measures — the same as always."

Cello didn't look convinced, neither did she protest. Seri took that as a positive sign and continued. "Lev has used his considerable talents to create a labyrinth that's impossible to solve."

Cello interrupted. "Every labyrinth is solvable."

Seri glanced at Nico who was grinning as he said, "Not this one."

Seri went on to explain how the labyrinth was ringed by a secondary tunnel — automatically segmented by QPN barriers. "While the public entrance remains static, the exit is constantly moving and redirects you back to a different point of the labyrinth. A solution doesn't exist, because the labyrinth is constantly changing."

Cello looked intrigued. "How would our people navigate this labyrinth?"

"The only way to do that is with a wrist Q-view. When a coded request is submitted, a map to the nearest exit segment is displayed. Once inside that segment, the QPN closes all access to the labyrinth — leaving the visitor trapped in a closed ring. It serves as a secondary security measure. Our security teams can monitor the entire ring via sight tokens. Once they're satisfied that no threat is present, they can manually open an exit to this tunnel."

Cello looked from Seri to Nico and back again. "That's — quite brilliant. You said the Levigator designed this?"

Nico was smiling proudly. "The QPN infrastructure, yes, but the idea for a labyrinth and the fabricated history was all Seri's idea. I'm prepared to develop the public entrance of the labyrinth as an attraction. I believe it has the potential to turn Denmount into a tourist destination. I plan to build a new hotel on some seaside property owned by Callan International. Apart from the tunnels, we can offer sub-aqua transport rides and fishing tours. I've also decommissioned the oldest vessel in our fleet to be converted into a floating museum. If we can get enough tourists to visit, it will mean a lot of new faces, making it difficult for the Breachers to keep track of who's coming and going."

Cello was nodding slowly, seeing the possibilities. "This is very good, Seri. I'd like to have the security team thoroughly test your work. I want their approval before I agree to anything. I can see them implementing some of your QPN strategies into our existing security features. At the very least, we should share the concepts employed here with other bases."

"Send them along with my next group of instructors." Nico offered. "I can walk them through the system between classes."

"You two have done well. It will take time to build up the tourism necessary to provide proper cover, but it offers hope that we can return to our home one day."

"Maybe sooner than you think."

"What do you mean by that, novice? Just how many secrets have you been keeping from your superiors?"

"In all fairness, this began long before I became a novice."

"You've been a novice for a while now and have chosen to remain silent on matters that involve Servators."

Nico shrugged. "You had already sanctioned work on Servator property. Everything else awaits your approval."

"That's dangerously close to insubordination, young man."

"Mother, please, I don't think you'll be disappointed."

Nico bowed. "Apologies, Chief Sentry. I was in an uncomfortable position between mother and daughter."

Cello snorted. "Cowardice is unbecoming of a Servator." Nico caught a subtle smile the Chief Sentry attempted to cover by turning away.

Cello let out an exaggerated sigh. "Show me what else you've done without my permission."

"Right this way, Chief Sentry." Nico opened a concealed wall in another part of the tunnel and Cello's shock was evident as she gasped at the sight of two high-speed rail transports sitting on separate tracks. She managed a quiet, "How?"

Seri led her mother onto the transport. "Bear with us, Mother, we have a lot to show you."

The Chief Sentry remained silent throughout the rest of the tour. The first stop was Port Vantos. A tear crept from her eye when Seri explained how it was dedicated to the husband and father they both dearly missed. She took it all in like a child filled with wonder and hope. When they arrived at Port Callan, she asked her first question.

"Was this here when you showed me your father's escape sub?"

Nico looked at his feet. "Yes, Ma'am," he admitted sheepishly.

Cello just nodded.

Seri thought her mother seemed impressed by Port Vantos, but her amazement was obvious when she took in the technology employed at Port Callan. Nico ended the tour by ordering a meal sent to one of the meeting rooms. They ate in silence and Seri began to worry. When they finished eating, Seri voiced her concern.

"Mother, are you alright? You haven't said more than a few words since we left Denmount base. Are you upset?"

"What? No — this is incredible. I can't understand how you managed to accomplish all of this in such a short period of time. You've improved covert access to Denmount base a hundredfold. You've addressed issues that have been keeping me awake at night. I need to bring the senior rangers here for the same tour, but I personally can't see anything that would prevent us from reoccupying the base immediately. Besides that, you've employed many innovations that I'm sure the analysts will be talking about for years. Most important of all, you've found a way to end our exile. You can't begin to imagine the positive effect this will have on morale at a time when we've been feeling particularly vulnerable."

"I don't understand — you seem troubled."

Cello looked at her daughter with sad eyes. "I'm so very proud of you. Don't mind me — I'm just feeling my age. I'm supposed to be the leader of my people, but I didn't even realize that this project was happening right under my nose. I've noticed myself slipping lately — Tenika Sheridan escaped on my watch. Something like that would never have happened in the past. I've been unable to see a way forward in our current troubles while you've been solving all of my problems for me. I look around in wonder at all you've accomplished and realize none of this would have even occurred to me. A Levigator is among us and things are changing quickly. How can I hope to keep up?"

"Don't be silly, Mother. You're a highly respected leader among the Servators."

"I fear that may not be enough. I think it's time for a change."

"Chief Sentry, if I may say..."

Cello held up her hand to silence Nico. "Thank you for your concerns, both of you. This isn't about an old woman feeling sorry for herself. These are the reasonable concerns of a Chief Sentry for her people. The truth is, we really only have one true leader at the moment, and that's the Levigator. If we're to survive what's coming, we need to be able to adapt quickly. We can't afford to get bogged down in the old ways of doing things. The Levigator needs people like you — people who can think on their feet and do what needs to be done."

"What do you mean? What's coming?" Seri glanced uneasily at Nico.

Cello shook her head. "I'm letting things slip these days. I don't know what's wrong with me."

That frightened Seri more than her mother's previous comment. She'd noticed some changes, like her mother calling her Kayla instead of using her alias. She never would have slipped up like that in the past. The Chief Sentry was a stickler for protocol. Other things had cropped up. She'd been showing up late for meetings or missing them altogether. It was easy to write that off as an overly busy schedule, but now Seri wondered. She didn't want to think about what that might mean. She'd already lost her father. She didn't know how she'd handle losing her mother as well.

"My house is a short tunnel and an elevator ride away," Nico offered. "Why don't you spend the night, Chief Sentry? Some of the senior rangers involved in my training are already there, as you know. We can discuss plans for a return to the base. It might be nice for all of us to relax and celebrate some good news."

"I think I'd like that." Cello said. "Thank you very much."

Seri wanted to hug Nico. She'd thank him later, but for now she wrapped her arms around her mother and held her tight as she whispered in her ear, "I'm so happy you approve of what we've done."

"Your father would have been very proud. So am I."

As they held each other, Seri realized for the first time that her mother needed support as much as she did.

Chapter 42

Leviticus sat at his favourite bench in the hanging gardens of Ebot. He came here as often as he could. The old quarter was quieter, especially this early in the morning. Yori and Tark stood at either end of the garden. They weren't there for protection. He'd long since proven that he didn't need it. Instead, they were there to protect his privacy. He supposed some might object to his claiming the gardens for himself and that was the other reason for coming at this hour. If past experience were any indicator, no one would be awake to complain for at least another two hours. He had plenty of time to do what he came here for.

Akhen had been pushing him to become faster, and to do that, he needed to become more familiar with his body's place in the pattern. The quiet of the gardens along with the scent of growing things relaxed him and allowed him to focus internally.

He took a deep breath and slowly exhaled as he began the exercise he'd created for himself. This was uncharted territory — he had no one to train him. At least, that's what Akhen kept telling him. Lev started at his feet and tried to imagine each particle of his being — separate grains of sand suspended in space. He moved slowly up his body, working his way through his limbs until he reached his chin. Then he imagined the particles of his being spreading apart as if they were distancing themselves from each other. He felt his mind mapping each particle's location in relation to its neighbour and then catalogued its position as part of the whole. He didn't need to think out each step — it came to him naturally, but it was a laborious process. Each time he held one of these sessions, he would pick up where he had left off. He'd noticed that each time he finished mapping a limb of his body, he was able to work faster with that limb. He'd made impressive strides since he began this practice. All that remained to be processed was his head. After today, his entire body would be mapped.

Lev felt a certain level of excitement about completing the process, but he also felt apprehension. It was a natural thing to examine a limb with normal sight — examining a limb with pattern sight had become an extension of that. It felt familiar, but this was different. Now, he would be focussing on something he could only see with pattern sight. The thought of looking within his head at particles that made up his mind was disconcerting. He'd always imagined his thoughts as being within his mind and he couldn't quite picture himself spreading those particles apart. What would happen to his thoughts? Would they remain coherent? How could anyone guess what to expect? As far as he knew, no one had tried this before.

There was only one way to find out. Lev pushed his concerns aside and began the final phase of his exercise. He identified every particle that he could perceive within the confines of his skull — as he'd done with every other part of his anatomy. So far, so good. Next, he spread them apart so he could begin the process of cataloguing. In that moment, everything shifted. Lev felt a momentary disorientation — suddenly he felt himself floating outside and above his body. He continued mapping each particle from his new vantage point. It was a curious sensation and he wondered what it meant. How could his thoughts be separate from his body? He completed the mapping process, at a loss as to what he should do next. How does one reconnect with their body?

Lev panicked.

Am I dead? As he wondered, something strange happened. His perspective shifted again and this time he saw himself as if he was looking through the eyes of another. He saw a presence that he recognized as himself hovering over his body. Faint tendrils extended from his presence in every direction. He followed one and it led to — himself — or rather, a version of himself. Following other tendrils felt the same. It was as if he was divided and spread thin. In a burst of insight, he realized that he was connected to versions of himself on other worlds. At intervals, a new tendril would form and he would feel — reduced. At other times a tendril would form and join with a single large tether. It grew brighter with each addition. When that occurred, he felt strengthened. Lev felt drawn to that bright tether, but try as he might, he couldn't follow it to see where it led. His efforts created a feeling of despair. He needed to know — He wanted to know. Along with that desire came recognition. In a moment of clarity, he understood. It led to the Maker.

Lev came back with a start, covered in sweat — his limbs weak and shaking. *What just happened? Did I just experience a vision or was that a hallucination?* He'd heard that the Maker occasionally spoke to his servants in visions and dreams, but he retained some doubt. If the Maker chose him as Levigator, shouldn't he have received some direction by now? Is that what this was?

Lev raised his eyes heavenward. "What am I supposed to do with this? I don't understand what it means!"

Even as he made that declaration, he realized he did understand, at least in part. He was somehow tied to both the decisions he made and the Maker. His connection to other worlds seemed to align with the theory Akhen had shared, but he knew that wasn't the whole story. Something was missing from the equation. It was time for him to learn more about the Maker's Way. Maybe he could find something in the histories that would help him to understand.

Chapter 43

Nico jogged the empty corridors of Denmount base. Every muscle ached. He was on an advanced training regimen, so he never really had a chance to recover. He'd learned two important coping mechanisms when it came to the physical aspects of his training. The first was to avoid getting hit while sparring. Bruises forming on top of bruises was a good incentive to improve your reflexes. Seri had helpfully informed him that purple wasn't his best colour. The second was to keep moving or your joints would seize into a stiff mass, hence the jog to his next class.

Nico was due for an Administration and Strategies session. Beyond general training, it was required that novices specialize in two areas suited to their strengths. It was no surprise to anyone that his greatest strength was the same as his father's — administration and strategic thinking. His secondary strength was a complementary skill in analysis. Having already proven himself capable of running a multinational company, his instructors felt it best to groom him for a leadership role. After his trial-by-fire at Callan International, it frightened him less than he would have imagined.

Equally unsurprising was that combat wasn't his strong point. Still, he felt he was comporting himself well. Seri seemed to appreciate the new definition he was forming as his muscle mass increased. She'd been giving him sparring tips which proved immensely helpful. His bruises had mostly shifted from deep purple to shades of green or yellow. Seri had informed him that green and yellow weren't his colours either.

At one point, Yori had popped in for a visit. He claimed, with too much of a smirk for Nico's liking, that he needed to *assess* Nico's warkata progress. Some of his bruises had returned to purple after that match, but he'd been able to land a few blows himself. The nod of respect from Yori after the match had made it almost worthwhile.

Nico was surprised by his rapid advancement until he learned that the Chief Sentry hadn't been sending him traditional instructors. Instead, she was having him trained by experts in each required field of study. Unlike his education at Denmount, he didn't need to share an instructor with the class. Each mentor was focussed on his needs. Instructors adapted the courses to build on his personal strengths and overcome his weaknesses. He didn't have to guess at expectations, they seemed to know what his needs were. He felt like a piece of clay sculpted by master craftsmen. It was both a humbling experience and a confidence booster at the same time.

He had even received a visit from the famous Akhen Hor to test for higher-level analyst abilities. Nico's initial test results were dismal in that regard, but Akhen's perspective on the role of an analyst showed him how valuable he could still be. He learned how to use his strengths in strategy to improve his abilities in analysis. Nico could already picture how he would apply what he'd learned in many areas of study.

One day, Akhen heard of his friendly rivalry with Lev's bodyguards. With a mischievous glint in his eye, he offered to teach Nico about the weaknesses he'd observed in Tark and Yori's sparring techniques.

Training with a World Warkata Champion was an amazing experience. Akhen flowed like water and his ability to mimic other combatants was uncanny. At times, Nico was convinced he stood across from Tark or Yori as Akhen instructed him on the best way to counter one move or another. Nico was confident he would surprise them both the next time they joined him on the mat. Akhen seemed satisfied that he'd accomplished his goal.

Occasionally the Chief Sentry would check on his progress. On one of those visits, Nico asked why he was receiving special consideration. Cello had replied that she wasn't going to make the same mistakes with him that she made with his parents. If he was determined to become a Servator, she was determined to make sure he lacked nothing in his training. Nico was grateful for her commitment to his family and made a personal vow to be worthy of the gift she was giving him.

Nico slowed to a walk as he arrived at the classroom for the Administration and Strategies session. He had planned to arrive early so he could cool off and catch his breath. He found he needed a few moments to shift from a physical mindset to the mental one he required for the next few hours.

"Hello, Nico."

Nico was startled into a warkata stance, but quickly relaxed when he saw Leviticus standing in the classroom doorway.

Lev grinned. "Good reflexes, Callan."

"Lev! What are you doing here? It's so good to see you."

Lev struck a regal pose. "That's Levigator to you, novice."

Nico rolled his eyes. "Is that really what you want?"

"Please, no! I don't think I could stand it if you started with that nonsense."

"Yes sir, Mr. Levigator, sir!"

"Very funny."

"Seriously though, why are you here?"

"I'll be presenting for this Administration and Strategies session."

Nico looked around the room expecting Tark and Yori to jump out as part of a practical joke.

Lev smiled. "It's just me."

"I don't understand — you're an instructor now?"

"No, I'm the Levigator."

Something about the resigned way he said it made Nico look closer. Lev appeared older somehow, like he had the weight of the world on his shoulders.

Nico pulled up a chair and sat down. "Tell me."

Lev closed his eyes and took a deep slow breath. "This is exactly what I need — someone who knows me better than I know myself."

Nico waited patiently. He recognized when Lev was gathering his thoughts.

"Your parents raised you in the Maker's Way. What were you taught about Levigators?"

"Nothing. I never heard the term, growing up. It seems to be a Servator specific designation. From what I can gather, it sounds like a cross between a seer and the judges mentioned in the ancient scrolls."

Lev sighed. "I was hoping you might be able to tell me more."

"Haven't the Servators explained it to you?" Nico wondered.

Lev snorted. "Yeah, in a cryptic way. They don't want to *influence my actions*."

"I don't understand."

"I'm told that a Levigator is the hand of the Maker, sent when the world is in desperate need. Whatever actions the Levigator takes will ease a great burden. The Servators won't offer any advice or suggest a course of action for fear that it may corrupt the path set by the Maker. Basically, they believe that whatever I do is the will of the Maker."

Nico's mouth gaped. "Woah. No wonder they whisper when you're around. That's a lot of pressure."

"Tell me about it!"

"So, if you ordered Seri to bring a plate of meat rolls and hand-feed me, she'd have to do it?"

"This isn't funny, Nico."

"Sorry."

"You've hit on the problem. I'm called to a role only partially understood by the highest levels of Servator leadership. I need help, but it can't be someone from the top. They already have too much on their plates. That means I need to find someone I can trust to fill that role. Unfortunately, every Servator I meet is either in awe or too afraid to tell me what I need to hear. I need someone I can trust. I need a Servator who hasn't spent years immersed in Servator practice.

"I think I can see where this is going, Lev, and I'm flattered, but I haven't even completed novice training. I didn't have an answer for you about what a Levigator is or does. Don't you think you'd be better off with someone who has those answers?"

Lev shook his head. "I've already told you. They won't answer questions about courses of action. The rest is academic."

Lev stood and began pacing. "I've been following the progress of your training."

That was a surprise to Nico, but it shouldn't have been. He knew that Lev had regular contact with the Chief Sentry.

"Your instructors are very impressed. They say you would be top of the class if you'd been with a group. Several say you're one of the best students they've ever had."

Nico was uncomfortable with the praise. "I don't know about that."

"Nico, the people who have been training you are at the top of their respective fields. If they're impressed, you're far above average."

"If you say so."

"I'm told that you surpassed the requirements of a novice some time ago. You're already well into the training for a leadership position."

Nico was shocked. "That can't be right. No one has said anything about me completing my novice training."

"You knew they had you on an accelerated training schedule. Did you really think they'd stop for a ceremony? They've been working to prepare you for your ultimate role. When they think you're ready, they want you to hit the ground running. Surely Cello said as much."

"I hadn't thought about it in those terms, but yes, I suppose that was more or less what the Chief Sentry told me." *That same Chief Sentry you just referred to by her first name.* Nico was beginning to understand just how much Lev had changed. "You believe it."

"I wouldn't say you were qualified unless I believed it."

"No, I mean you believe that you're the hand of the Maker! Leviticus Radix, the stubborn agnostic — believes. I knew it! I knew you would come around to the Maker's Way one day."

Lev refused to meet Nico's eyes.

"Wait a minute. You've never accepted anything on another's say-so unless you proved it for yourself. How do you *know* you're the Levigator?"

Lev looked at the chair he had vacated and sent it flying across the room. While Nico was distracted, he materialized thirty practice tokens into Nico's lap. As an afterthought, he materialized a court buffoon's cap on top of Nico's head.

Nico looked down at the tokens — familiar to every novice. He'd painstakingly worked through each one during his training. It had taken weeks, but Lev had accomplished it in the blink of an eye. Nico was so shocked he didn't even take offence at the cap he now clutched in his hand. As he sat there speechless, the tokens dissolved and reformed into sculptures of various animals as they moved through the air in a lazy circle before vanishing altogether.

Nico found his voice at last. "How did you do that? I didn't even see you lift your arm to use your Q-view!"

"I don't need a Q-view."

"Then how can you access the QPN?"

"I don't need the QPN. I'm my own QPN."

"You don't need the..." Nico stammered. "You're your own..."

"Take it easy, Nico. I'll explain everything. What you've just witnessed is only part of it. Suffice it to say that I came to the point where I could no longer deny that I fill the requirements for the Levigator designation."

Nico stared at Lev with round eyes. "Only part of it? What's the rest of it?"

Lev ignored the question. "Look, Nico, things are going to start happening quickly. The world is about to change and I don't yet understand all of the ramifications. What I do know is that old Servator ways are going to be a hindrance. I need someone with me who can adapt quickly to changing circumstances. I need someone I can trust, someone who knows me well. I've already discussed this with Cello and your instructors. By current standards of training, you already qualify for a mid-level rank in a leadership position. All that's missing is practical experience. Word spread quickly about your work on Port Vantos and Port Callan. Your instructors were suitably impressed. What you've accomplished is far beyond the requirements necessary to prove your qualifications for a posting as an Administrative Strategist. A tactician is exactly what I need. Normally protocols exist for this type of advancement, but..."

"...But you're the Levigator." Nico finished.

Lev shrugged. "The instructors felt you were more than ready. I wouldn't have approached you otherwise." Lev picked up his chair and sat facing Nico. "I don't have a lot of time. I want you by my side, but it will be dangerous and I won't pressure you or think any less of you if you decline. I know you already have a lot on your plate with the family business."

Nico snorted. "It's not like I can go anywhere near Callan International at the moment."

"I heard about that. I'm sorry. You need to know that the Breacher corruption is going to get worse if I fail."

"What do you mean?"

"Unfortunately, I can't say anything more unless you accept. As it is, I'm going to have to ask for your word so that you'll say nothing about what I've already shown you."

"Lev, why do you think I asked for training? Why do you think I was so eager to offer my sub on your mission to free Kade? My parents gave their lives to the Servator cause. I want nothing more than to stop the Breachers. It would be enough just knowing my *friend* needed help. Now you're telling me the *Maker* has sent you to accomplish His will and you're wondering if a follower of the Way will say yes?"

"Ummm — is that a yes?"

Nico burst out laughing. "Unequivocally, yes. Where do we begin?"

"I have so much to tell you, I don't know *where* to begin."

Nico spent the rest of that day listening to an incredible tale of prophecy and past Levigators. His worldview was shaken by the news of thin spaces and rifts between kin worlds. His heart filled with sympathy for Lev, having unwittingly contributed to the development of technology threatening Servator destruction. He felt amazed anew by all that Lev could do with his newfound gifts. By the end of Lev's story, the evidence had Nico utterly convinced that his friend was indeed the Levigator. But beyond that, Nico understood — this was what the Maker had been preparing him for his entire life.

Chapter 44

Tully and the boys had been very effective in their efforts to distribute micro-corders to the Callan buildings on Nash's list. Tenika smiled at the irony — compromising the company she'd once tried to build up. She still had some leftover contract forms from her time at Callan International. It was a simple task to fake a document and add her signature. It had been surprisingly effective at getting her men through the door. Apparently, her name still carried some weight — even in retirement.

The ostensible contract was to assess the lighting needs for each facility for a possible upgrade. That gained them access to every part of the building. Light fixtures provided an excellent location to secure a micro-corder during an inspection.

Unfortunately, that ploy wasn't going to work at Callan headquarters where security would be more formidable. An additional problem remained — her retirement would be public knowledge there.

As far as Tenika could determine, few people knew that her retirement was a forced affair. The corporate heads probably thought the optics would be better if they kept that part quiet. It was a tactical mistake that she was about to exploit. Retired personnel often returned for a visit to regale their former co-workers with stories of the places they'd visited and the things they'd seen since leaving the organization. Tenika was going to take advantage by doing the same.

She obtained a visitor's pass after some pleasantries with Arlan, the doorman, giving him a conversational itinerary of the people she wanted to catch up with. He smiled and waved as she sauntered off chatting amicably with everyone she met.

Tenika didn't have a good reason to enter the offices she would have chosen for micro-corders, but she did manage to find a few empty meeting rooms. Those would serve almost as well, considering how often board members would congregate there.

She visited the toilet facilities and a few other public places, leaving devices in her wake. Eventually she found her way to the staff kitchen where people tended to gather for gossip. It was a logical destination for a visitor wanting to catch up with a lot of people. Staff streamed in and out at random intervals, expressing their surprise and pleasure at seeing her again. They would politely ask her a few questions before heading back to work. Tenika didn't have many friends among the staff, so she knew it was just a facade. She'd held herself above them and never felt a need to intermix. It had earned her some nasty nicknames over the years, but it served her purposes well since she didn't really want to talk to anyone.

Tenika was content to let others whisper about her visit. It justified her presence and made it seem like she had indeed been busy visiting people — even while they avoided her. People stopped coming to the kitchen and she was able to place a few more micro-corders.

She'd done reasonably well, all things considered, but she still needed to secure one of the devices in Seri Quin's office. As current head of Callan International, Seri's workspace was obviously top priority for placement of a micro-corder.

Tenika's typical mode of operation was to wait until a facility leader was away. This was no different. Seri had already left — Marret was going to be a bigger problem. A retired employee visiting a former assistant was normal enough, but Marret certainly wasn't going to allow Tenika into Seri's office. She only needed a few minutes alone and so she had come bearing gifts that would facilitate uninterrupted access — a mug of kofa from the kitchen and some of Marret's favourite custard filled pastries purchased before Tenika's arrival. She'd considered lacing the pastry filling with a sedative, but if someone found Marret sleeping after a visit from Tenika, it would arouse suspicion. She settled for a powerful laxative instead. Marret was always munching on something, so no one would be surprised if she suffered a bout of food poisoning. It wouldn't be the first time.

"Marret! How are you doing?" Tenika breezed into the outer office with a smile pasted on her face, trying to affect the relaxed and rested look she imagined a retired person would sport.

"Tenika? I'm surprised to see you here. I thought you were hiking in Jaihuwan."

Tenika mentally rolled her eyes. *That's what they told people?*

"I was, but I'm back now. The trip was a good time to relax and reflect on my past career."

"Couldn't stand the quiet, huh?" Marret smirked knowingly.

"You got me. It wasn't all lost on me, though. I realized that I hadn't taken time to thank people properly for putting up with me over the years. I know I was a difficult taskmaster at times."

"It wasn't so bad."

"Well, as my assistant, you had to put up with more than most. I wanted you to know how much I appreciated all of the support you provided me. I don't think I could have managed without you."

Marret blushed. "That's sweet of you to say."

Tenika held up a finger as if just remembering something. "Ah! Speaking of sweets, I brought you something." She set the mug of coffee on the desk and handed Marret the bag.

Marret's eyes grew when she looked inside. "Custard pastries? They're my favourite! Thank you."

"I know it's not much, but please enjoy them..." Marret had one in her mouth before Tenika could finish her sentence. Tenika leaned forward conspiratorially. "So, what's the juicy gossip I missed while away?"

"Well! A lot has changed. The assistants aren't happy with the extra paperwork — Dani, you know, the girl who works in archives? Well, she married a childhood friend and..." Tenika's eyes began to glaze over. "...Not only that," Marret continued, "but I heard they're planning to shut down three of the manufacturing facilities..." Marret prattled on for a full ten minutes before the laxative finally took effect. "...and then she said — Oh!"

"She said, oh?"

"I'm sorry, Tenika. I think I need to excuse myself." Marret's stomach made a loud gurgling noise as she shot to her feet and ran out of the room.

"Finally!" Tenika didn't waste the opportunity. Already familiar with the office layout, she was in and out in less than a minute. She debated whether she should leave or wait for Marret's return, but decided not to push her luck.

As it turned out, that was the correct decision. She was halfway down the hall when Jin Bhat caught up with her. It seemed word of her visit had reached the ears of those better informed about her status. The security chief's voice was stern. "What do you think you're doing here, Ms. Sheridan?"

"Can't a retired person visit some old friends?" Her response was delivered with a heavy dose of sarcasm that put a scowl on Jin's face.

"I don't think that's appropriate. I was told you're not to be allowed in the building."

"Don't be so suspicious, Jin. I was merely visiting. Ask anyone. I obtained a visitor pass and everything." Tenika wiggled the pass under his nose. "I was robbed of my position and rushed off before I could say goodbye to anyone. You can at least grant me a little dignity."

Jin narrowed his eyes trying to figure out what she was up to. Tenika sighed theatrically and handed him the pass. "Fine, I'll leave. I've visited everyone I wanted to see anyway." She put on an affronted air and strode out of the building, head held high.

Back in her land transport, she noted the locations of the micro-corders she'd placed. It would have to do — Jin would see to it that she wasn't allowed in the building in the future. It hardly mattered, she hoped never to see the place again. She would rather not have come at all, but the Breacher's goals meshed with her own. She wanted to spy on the current head of Callan International as much as they did.

I have you now, Seri Quin. I know you're not who you say you are. I'm going to find out what you're hiding and destroy you for presuming to be my better.

Chapter 45

Seri shifted nervously from foot to foot. She'd unconsciously slipped behind Nico and her mother. Nico's hand found the small of her back and gently pushed her forward for the fourth time in as many minutes. "It'll be okay." Nico insisted.

"What if they're still angry? How can it be okay, Nico? People died because of me."

"People died because of the Breachers, not you. The time for grieving has passed. People will have a different perspective by now."

"You don't know that."

"I know that this is a homecoming and people are in high spirits. You gave them this gift. They'll forgive you."

Seri squeezed his arm. She was grateful for his encouragement, but her doubts remained. It was because of her that they had to abandon Denmount base in the first place. Even if she could take credit for reopening the base, it wouldn't replace what was lost in the interim. She knew it was true that many would have forgiven her for the relocation, but how could those who lost loved ones forgive her? She couldn't forgive herself.

Her warkata instructor and mentor, Jabin Pelle, had recommended her for that fated mission and she had disappointed him. How could she look him in the eye? She cringed when she remembered how many times he had warned her about impulsive tendencies. And how could First Token Ward Deak Bosto trust her again when she had disobeyed a direct order resulting in the loss of at least two men? She hadn't known one of them, but his name surfaced unbidden — it was permanently branded into her memory. *Marcon Fenris, presumed dead at the hand of Breacher interrogators.* Imagining his suffering under torture only made it worse.

The second name was more painful to recall — Toshi Estivado, part of her inner circle. They grew up together. He was betrothed to her best friend Char, whom she hadn't heard from since. A tear threatened to break loose and she hastily wiped it away. Facing Char was her biggest fear. If Char couldn't forgive her, this would feel like the hollowest of victories. Fear of that encounter made her want to run and hide.

Nico flashed her a smile of encouragement and her mother wrapped an arm around her shoulder for a half hug. The first rail transport from Port Vantos was pulling up.

Seri took a deep breath as the transport doors opened. Time stood still in the momentary silence and then a flood of humanity rushed out onto the platform. Chaos ensued as baggage was unloaded and passengers scrambled, trying to locate their luggage. Seri smiled in spite of herself. The base was alive again.

As the crowds made their way to the tunnel leading back to their homes, she held a brief hope that they would pass without noticing her — that she could remain an invisible part of the past. She watched in horror as they queued up to greet the Chief Sentry. She'd been away for so long that she'd almost forgotten what to expect. Being a daughter of the leader for the Caralithican Host meant she would have to face each and every one of them.

She steeled herself for rebuke, but received only gratitude. "Thank you so much, Kayla... We can't tell you how grateful we are for all you've done... It's so good to see you again, Kayla..." Seri was confused for a moment — she'd fully embraced her alias and it felt strange to hear her real name again. *Right, I'm Kayla to these people. I'll need to start responding to my birth name again.* Taking on an alias was a necessary precaution to avoid Breacher detection, but it had grown into something more. Becoming Seri Quin provided an escape from her former life, but it was only a dressing on a festering wound. Each mention of her real name was like a balm to that wound — a reminder that she had lost a great deal as well. The seemingly endless well wishes lulled her. She was caught off guard when strong arms pulled her into a bear hug. "Kayla! I hardly recognized you. What did you do to your hair?" Her mother swatted the man on the arm. "Deak! That's no way to compliment a woman on her appearance."

First TokenWard Bosto ignored her mother with a big grin on his face. *That's interesting. When did Servator discipline become so relaxed?*

Kayla straightened. "First TokenWard Bosto. It's good to see you again, sir."

Deak glanced at her mother and back. "Cello warned me you might still be struggling."

Kayla squinted in confusion. *Cello?*

"It was your first mission. I failed to assess the Breacher threat adequately. That wasn't your fault. It was mine."

"I didn't follow your orders...."

"We all make that mistake. The excitement of a first mission leads to errors. We expect it. That's why we try to limit the risk on first engagements. You aren't the first to forget your training — you won't be the last. People seldom make that mistake a second time."

"But people died."

"Kayla, look at me." Deak lifted her chin so she couldn't avoid his gaze. "Being a Servator comes with the risk of death. We all accept that. The losses hurt, but we move forward because we must. I know you've seen the hundreds of names carved into the memorial wall. Your father's name is listed there."

Kayla jerked at the mention of her father.

"Do you hold your fellow Servators responsible for failing to prevent your father's death?"

"Of course not. I blame the Breachers who killed him."

"Then why do you think the rest of us would blame you? I shouldn't need to say it, but in case you need to hear it — I forgive you."

All composure left her at those three words. Tears flowed freely and she leaned against his chest, heaving great sobs of relief.

"Never fear, little one." He used the pet name he'd given her when she was a child running between his legs. "The people of this base are your family, and family doesn't abandon its own."

Deak gave her a final squeeze and then moved on to make room for others.

Kayla tried to compose herself, but then Jabin was there and the tears started all over again as he held her and whispered encouragement into her ear.

"I'm so proud of you, Kayla. The courage and perseverance you've shown to accomplish all of this — I've always known it was within you, but this is more than I could have hoped for." After a few more words, Jabin moved on as well. Kayla excused herself and moved away from the line to gather her emotions.

She took several trembling breaths and wiped at her eyes. Someone had seen her step away and stood quietly behind her.

"Kayla?"

Kayla recognized that voice and slowly turned. She was undone at the sight of Char standing there. Kayla dropped to her knees, clasping Char's hands as she looked up at her friend. Her words warbled with emotion. "Char... I'm so sorry. Please... forgive me."

Char let go of Kayla's hands and stood in silence, but only for a second. Then, she was on the floor embracing Kayla and weeping with her.

"Of course I forgive you. You're my best friend."

"How can you even look at me? I thought you hated me."

"I was angry for awhile, but that was grief. No one blames you for what happened. I know you would have risked your life for Toshi if you'd known he was in danger."

Kayla shook her head in dismay. "I can't believe he's gone."

"He was your friend, too. I knew you would blame yourself. I was worried and looked for you, but you'd left. Where have you been all of this time? I've missed you."

"I needed some time alone. I think everyone needed some distance from me."

"You're wrong about that. We were worried sick about you."

"Kayla!"

They both turned their heads to see her mother beckoning.

Char smiled. "Duty calls. Promise me you'll stop by later. The gang will want to see you."

Kayla nodded and gave her a quick hug before standing. Char joined her and brushed a strand of hair out of Kayla's face. "You look good as a blonde, but I think it needs some streaks."

Kayla laughed and Char smiled. "Seriously, Kayla, we're good — okay?"

Kayla nodded. "Thank you."

When she stepped back into line, Nico appraised her with a question in his expression. "Are you okay?"

"Better than okay." She was home, but more importantly, she was forgiven.

Chapter 46

It was a productive day. The distraction of reproducing the Breacher network gave Kade's former classmates a purpose. They had been resentful at first. To them it felt like being forced to relive his crimes. It had taken some time, but they came to understand that if it hadn't been Kade, it might have been one of them. True, they may not have gone as willingly, but Breachers could have abducted any of them — righteousness aside.

They learned just how evil the Breachers were after hearing Selica's stories about her childhood. Most were aghast that Villecrest considered Selica his property. They became less abusive in their attitude toward Kade when Selica told them about the threats against his life and the beatings he'd endured. "He's already faced punishment beyond that of the legal system," she reminded them. "He's endured the same kind of abuse you're heaping on him now, and much worse. He accepted it so you wouldn't have to." That sobered them quickly, especially when she told them how he'd put off trying to escape so the Breachers wouldn't look for a replacement. They all knew the pool of candidates was limited. It was an inconvenience, but they were now safe and alive on the island. Unfortunately, two of their classmates were still missing. It was a constant reminder of the danger they all faced.

If words alone were not enough, watching Kade in action proved that he had changed. Gone was the arrogant self-absorbed youth they had known from their Denmount days. This Kade was a team player. He was patient and quick to acknowledge the skills of others. He knew how to leverage their individual talents and gave credit where credit was due. He was self-deprecating and approachable. He was humble and hard-working — the first to arrive and the last to leave. If the others were to describe him now, they would call him driven. No one doubted his desire to right the wrongs of his past.

Everyone commented in amazement at how much of the original algorithm Lev had been able to provide, but they were more impressed by the breadth of knowledge Kade displayed. His modifications were extensive and the improvements were undeniable. Soon they were deferring to Kade and gelled as a team. Each of them wanted to do their part to retaliate against a common enemy.

Selica was proud of him. It was gratifying to see him recognized by others for the man he truly was.

Most of the equipment they needed had been delivered and assembled. The algorithm had been recreated and Kade's modifications applied. They'd done as much as they could to test in simulations, but the real testing couldn't start until the viewcorders arrived. Administrator Na Tuni assured them that they were on the way. Now all they could do was wait.

Kade had closed the lab early, declaring a holiday of sorts. They'd reached a milestone and deserved a break. A few took it upon themselves to plan a small impromptu celebration later that evening. Selica promised to bring a cake. She'd taken to baking lately. It was a decadent indulgence after a lifetime of deprivation.

For Kade's part, he had begun whittling. Time with the Breachers was a thing marked by endless deadlines. Kade had become brutally efficient in order to survive. Now he found it difficult to stop. In those moments when Selica could get him to sit still, his hands were still moving. It was his way of coping. He needed a way to remember that he was no longer under Breacher control, even though he remained driven by them. That freedom expressed itself in whimsical carvings that either made you laugh out loud, or left you in silent contemplation at the beauty of the Maker's creation — perfectly captured in a few deft strokes of a knife. He had become somewhat of a celebrity on the island for his art and had a long list of requests for handcrafted gifts.

Selica had convinced Kade to join her for a walk along the rim of the caldera before the celebration. During their early days on the island, they had found an outcropping of rock with a beautiful view of the valley on one side and the sea on the other. It was a place they liked to come to spend time alone together.

Kade had been quieter than usual, but he seemed content to let her fill the silence with her plans for the week. He smiled fondly when she told him about her intent to learn how to knit from a group of women in the village. She loved life on the island and jumped at every opportunity to try something new. Kade didn't understand how she found such joy in picking weeds or sorting fish. To him, chores were a necessary evil, but to her it was freedom.

As a child she had watched from afar as others went about their daily lives. At the time, she believed she would never experience such things. It filled her with longing — now, here she was, free to live that life. She refused to take it for granted. She knew, better than most, the value of each moment. If someone were to hand her a pitchfork and point to a pile of manure, she would jump to the task with a huge grin on her face. Kade would look on, shaking his head in amusement. The Maker had finally answered her prayers. It had taken a long time, but looking back, she realized it was better this way. If she'd escaped sooner, she never would have met Kade. She wouldn't have had this same sense of security. She knew it might not last, but it had given her soul time to heal.

Selica closed her eyes and sighed as the sea breeze lifted her hair. Kade took advantage of that moment to steal a kiss and she smiled, her eyes still shut. "I'm so happy here, Kade."

"Do you ever wish you could go back to the mainland and explore more of the world?"

"I have everything I need right here." She opened one eye to see Kade nodding in agreement.

"Why do you ask?"

"I don't know... I guess I was just wondering what you'll say when we've completed our sentence and are free to leave. Would you opt to remain on the island?"

"Would you?"

"I asked you first."

"I feel safe here. I don't think I would ever stop looking over my shoulder if we were back on the mainland. Sometimes I have nightmares that the Breachers track us down and drag us back." Selica shuddered at the recollection. "I wouldn't want to raise a family with that threat hanging over us."

"A family?"

Selica reddened, realizing she'd said more than she intended. They'd never discussed children — it wasn't something to consider while in Breacher captivity. She would never put a child through the experiences she had endured. Selica changed the subject.

"Would you want to leave?"

"My former life is gone. The only thing that matters to me now, is you. Where you go, I go. I just wanted to make sure we were on the same page."

"That's not exactly an answer."

Kade smiled. "I like it here too. Besides, like you said, it would be safer for a family."

Her heart skipped a beat and she captured his eyes with her own to see if he was teasing her. "Are you messing with me right now?"

She saw him swallow hard. He looked nervous and she felt a moment of panic. He'd been holding something back all afternoon. Then she noticed his hand tightly clutching something. He turned his hand palm up and unfurled his fingers. It was a delicate ring, carved from coral. The harsh jagged material polished and shaped into something beautiful. A perfect metaphor for their lives together.

"As I said — I just wanted to make sure we were on the same page before I put you on the spot. I want to make it official. I want to spend the rest of my life with you. Selica, will you marry me?"

"Yes!"

She knocked him back a step in her haste to embrace him. After a moment, she lifted her head so she could see his face. Kade raised a hand to trace a tear on her cheek. "What's wrong?"

"Is this really happening? Do we get our happy ever after?"

"I don't know what the future holds, but you've taught me how important it is to cherish every moment. Let's cherish this one."

Selica laid her head on his chest and nodded.

They stayed like that for a long time, feeling the sea breeze and listening to the sounds of life all around them. It felt like the promise of a hope filled future.

Chapter 47

People filled every corner of the auditorium. High-ranking Servators had travelled from around the globe to be present when the Levigator named his chosen assistant. Nico had already been granted the provisional title of Second Chief Strategist. This ceremony would make it official.

Kayla couldn't remember the last time she'd seen all five Chief Sentries together in one room. It was a testimony to their confidence in the new security measures she and Nico had put in place.

Her mother's assistant, Joff, had rushed Nico from her presence with some last-minute coaching to impart. Kayla searched for Nico on the stage as she found her seat. She gave him a thumbs up when she caught his eye. He was sitting to the right of the podium, next to her mother.

Nico looked smart in his new uniform. She chuckled remembering how he'd presented himself for her inspection with his shirt on backwards. It wasn't his fault. He'd never seen a formal Servator uniform. The shirt was designed to button at the side. It wasn't immediately obvious which way it was supposed to be worn. He'd turned bright red. "Just great. I would have been recorded in the archives as the strategist who couldn't figure out how to dress himself."

The room quieted as Chief Sentry Vantos made her way to the podium. "Today is a special day. It is always cause for celebration when a novice is granted a commission, but today we celebrate the elevation of an exceptional young man. Those of you who have travelled here from afar have witnessed an example of his work firsthand. He played a large role in the development of both Port Vantos and Port Callan. He also designed some of the novel uses for Q-tech employed at Port Callan."

Cheers of appreciation and applause erupted. Cello waited for it to die down and then continued.

"Not only has he made us proud, but he would have made his parents proud as well. Many of you knew Nes and Tawni Callan. They were generous supporters of the Servator cause and they were also valued rangers. Nico has picked up where they left off. Know that this posting is well earned. Nico possesses many of the same qualities that made his parents quite a force in industry and innovation. I am confident he will distinguish himself and serve well. He trained with the best of us from around the globe and his instructors agree. If that weren't proof enough of his qualifications, the Levigator has chosen him to stand at his side. Does anyone object?"

The audience held its breath, not wanting any noise interpreted as disapproval. Nico was popular and many were eager to see what he could do in his new role.

"With no objections voiced, I'd like to invite Nico Callan and Levigator Radix to the stage."

Lev and Nico rose and approached Chief Sentry Vantos.

"Nico Callan, having already declared your vow when you agreed to become a novice, do you now agree to uphold that vow in your new role?"

"I do."

Leviticus pinned the two stars of office on Nico's uniform and stepped back.

"Without further delay, I present Second Chief Strategist Callan of the Caralithican Host."

The audience stood and applauded, none so vigorously as Kayla. When the clapping abated, Cello motioned Nico to his seat.

She and the other Chief Sentries had agreed in advance that a little theatre was in order. Many in attendance were seeing the Levigator for the first time. This was Nico's ceremony, but as the youngest and least tested Chief Strategist ever commissioned, his authority would benefit from association with the Levigator. People would gain confidence in them both if they witnessed the Levigator's abilities.

Chief Sentry Vantos held up her hand, asking for silence. "All of us grew up hearing about the exploits of past Levigators. These were leaders sent in times of great need. Heroes of old, performing amazing feats. I'm sure I'm not the only one who has wondered how much those stories have been embellished over the years."

Heads bobbed throughout the auditorium.

"Centuries have passed since the previous Levigator walked the earth. Our current Levigator has agreed to a demonstration, so that you might know the Maker hasn't forgotten us."

Murmurs of surprise filled the air.

"Each of the Chief Sentries has chosen a champion to test the Levigator."

A flurry of activity took place as stage hands covered the floor in mats. While the sparring area was prepared, each Chief Sentry rose and called their champion to the stage. Excitement mounted as well-known fighters stood before a cheering crowd. Beniti Abrax was the last to rise and name his champion. "The undefeated Warkata Champion of the World has agreed to come out of retirement for this event. Akhen Hor will represent Kemetica."

A moment of shock silenced the audience at that announcement, followed by a roar of approval.

Cello moved to stand beside Leviticus and raised her hand for silence once more. The audience watched as Lev removed his wrist Q-view and handed it to Cello. "As you can see, the Levigator won't be using his Q-view. He doesn't need it."

The audience looked around in confusion.

Cello raised her voice. "Combatants, take your position and commence when ready."

Lev stood in the centre of the mat as his opponents surrounded him. He met each one in turn. None were able to touch him. Only Akhen managed to shift him from his position. Lev nodded to Akhen in acknowledgment. The audience was stunned.

Lev waved for them to come all at once. This time, he moved. His opponents were fast, but their motions appeared slow and clumsy. Always too late to reach their target. Lev anticipated each blow. The dance continued, leaving his opponents panting with exertion. Frustration was clear on their faces, and not a little anger at looking foolish.

The display didn't end there. Lev called to the stage every type of weapon. He ordered the fighters not to hold back as those weapons were handed out. They looked with uncertainty at the Chief Sentries who nodded their approval. One of the warriors hesitantly thrust a spear at Lev, only to have it snap in two as though it had struck a wall. He gazed with confusion at the broken shaft in his hand. The others suddenly seemed to realize what they were up against and attacked with abandon. Akhen stood apart and observed as one weapon after another shattered against an invisible barrier. When all of the broken implements lay discarded at their feet, the champions made one last rush as one. Lev sent them flying in all directions.

The audience turned to Akhen as the lone remaining challenger. Lev waited patiently as Akhen chose weapons for himself. He had a much better understanding of Lev's abilities and gathered projectile weapons for his attempt. He set them in a pile — throwing knives, a sling and a crossbow. Then he walked over to Lev and handed him a blindfold. Lev smiled and tied it around his head. The audience gasped as Akhen proceeded to circle Lev at a run, throwing knives and slinging stones with deadly accuracy. None reached their target. Akhen nodded, satisfied. Then he picked up the crossbow in one swift blur of motion and fired. Blindfold still in place, Lev held the arrow in his hand and offered it back to Akhen for a second attempt. Akhen laughed and bowed to his opponent.

The response of the audience was deafening. Lev's opponents no longer felt shame, only awe, as he removed his blindfold and thanked each of them.

Lev turned to the crowd and spoke. "I don't know what the future holds, but I do know that difficult times are coming. Now, more than ever, we need to stand together and support each other. For my part, I promise that I will do my best to serve as the hand of the Maker. I'd like to leave you all with a token of my commitment. It will require your participation. Please raise a hand, palm up, and hold very still."

Lev waited while each member of the audience lifted a palm. He carefully memorized the scene before him. Startled voices filled the room as each and every person found a gold coin in their hand, stamped with the symbol of the Servators. "This is my gift to you. Look at it from time to time — show it to your friends and family — remember who you are."

The audience began chanting. "Levigator, Levigator, Levigator." He bowed and returned to his seat. The chanting continued for several minutes before

Chief Sentry Vantos returned to the podium. Kayla took the opportunity to look for the quickest route to the exit. She wanted to be the first to congratulate Nico when the inevitable receiving line formed.

"Kayla Vantos, please make your way to the stage." Kayla was several steps closer to the exit before the words sunk in and she froze. The crowd cleared a path to the stage. What was her mother up to now? She sighed as she made her way to the stage, having little choice but to comply. Her mother motioned Kayla to her side.

"You all know my daughter. Port Vantos and Port Callan sprang from her vision. She has served Caralithica well, overcoming tragedy to bring our people home. Her efforts made this gathering possible. The world is about to change and we need to adapt quickly to those changes. We'll need innovators like Kayla, Nico, and many others to meet the new challenges we will face. To that end we will be initiating a special training program to find suitable candidates to address that need."

Cello paused to clear her throat. Her voice wavered for a moment. "It has been my great honour to serve as the Chief Sentry of Caralithica, but that time has come to an end."

"Mother!" Kayla hissed. "What are you doing?"

"Replacing a Chief Sentry requires the unanimous vote of the presiding Chiefs."

"Mother!" Kayla whispered. "You can't do this, we need you."

"Kayla Vantos has been recommended as my replacement. She has my full endorsement."

Kayla's eyes darted around the room — this had to be some kind of joke. *Why is no one laughing?*

Cello presided over the traditional rite of transfer. The words came muffled to Kayla's ears, as though she were under water.

"Beniti Abrax, Chief Sentry of Kemetica, how say you?"

"Aye."

"Talia Suul, Chief Sentry of Jaihuwan, how say you?"

"Aye."

"Jokan Pizzar, Chief Sentry of Arapanus, how say you?"

"Aye."

"Desi Yoruba, Chief Sentry of Sumakad, how say you?"

"Aye."

"By consensus of the Chief Sentries, Kayla Vantos is hereby declared Chief Sentry of Caralithica to stand in my stead."

Kayla stood like a statue, mouth hanging open as her mother removed the band of her office from her upper arm and placed it on Kayla's. Her jaw moved up and down, but no words came out.

"Close your mouth dear, you look like a fish out of water."

The comment was just absurd enough to snap Kayla out of her stupor. "You ambushed me!" She whispered.

"Oh, I wasn't alone in this." Several other familiar faces grinned and waved.

Kayla's protest died on her lips as the crowd rushed the stage and hoisted her to their shoulders. It was the start of a new era, one Kayla felt unprepared to face.

To be continued in **Leavening** – Dictates of the Servators Book: 3

I hope you enjoyed reading Levigator

Visit my website https://www.kallensamuels.com and subscribe to the mailing list for information about new releases and exclusive content.

Don't miss the series finale:

Leavening - Dictates of the Servators: Book 3

Chaos threatens the world as the Breachers gain ascendancy. Extermination of the Servators is well under way and the remnant gathers at their final refuge, prepared to make a last stand.

A small hope remains as Leviticus searches the journals of the Levigators. If he can reclaim the knowledge of his predecessors he might prevent disaster — his power means nothing if he can't find the answers he seeks.

A storm is brewing and Leviticus must decide if he should take a desperate gamble.

Read on for a preview of the first chapter in the final book.

Leavening

Dictates of the Servators: Book 3

Chapter 1

The discordant harmony of particles set Leviticus Radix's nerves on edge, even as it called to him. It was a sound that wasn't a *sound*, but the pull was real. It beckoned him like a promise — *a promise of discovery or regret?* He wondered.

The last few years had been a whirlwind of revelation. He was no longer an aspiring computational engineer, recently graduated from the Court of Learning in his home town of Denmount. Any thought of a career or a future along those lines had been irrevocably crushed. Instead, he was drafted into an ancient secret organization in a race against time to prevent the end of the world. More than that, he wasn't merely a Servator contributing to the cause. Somehow, he had become the Levigator. The last person who held that role died over seventeen hundred years ago. All eyes turned to the Levigator as the one who would save them. It seemed ludicrous. He felt a maniacal laugh threatening to break loose at the very idea. *Hold yourself together, Lev. Nothing shatters confidence so much as a Levigator cackling like a madman.* The Maker knew they needed hope and he would play along. It might be all he had to offer.

Levigator. Title aside, the word itself meant *one who eases a burden*. There was no denying the Servators had a heavy burden at the moment, but he had no idea what he was supposed to do about it. For now, he was following the path of his predecessors in the hope that an answer would present itself. He was looking for thin spaces where a rift might be formed.

Lev took a few tentative steps, first in one direction then another. The pull would be stronger in one direction, inexorably leading him to the source.

He had stopped denying that he was the Levigator. No one else possessed these impossible to believe abilities. He could sense the patterns of particles that permeated the world around him. He continually memorized those changing patterns and his place within them. He could call on those memories to form templates and materialize objects at will. To the average person it might seem like magic, but Servators had been doing something similar with their quantum technology for years. Remotely materializing tokens using the Quantum Positioning Network, or QPN was something they took for granted. What made Lev special was that he didn't need the vast computational power of the QPN network. He didn't need the library of entangled templates stored in the memory stash. He was his own QPN and archive. It wasn't possible to hold that much information in a human brain, and yet he wielded that ability as easily as he wiggled his fingers. It was empowering and humbling at the same time.

Tark and Yori had taken up defensive positions and were scanning the horizon with their scopes, looking for some imagined adversary to test their skills. They went where he went. Not that he needed bodyguards, but they were also his friends. *They protect me from myself — they keep me sane.* Nico was among them, a lifelong friend from his childhood. By some strange turn of events, or perhaps by the Maker's will, his best friend had also been dragged into this world-spanning drama underpinning their reality. Like his own, Nico's choices had been ripped away. He was denied access to his family's business, framed for a murder, and on the run until he could prove his innocence. *None of that matters if I fail and the world comes to an end.* Lev shook the dark thoughts from his mind and looked at his friend standing a few cubits away. He was grateful Nico had agreed to accompany him. It didn't hurt that he was now a fully trained Servator. Even Tark and Yori acknowledged Nico's new skills. He'd thought they would object when he named Nico as his assistant, but they assured him they had tested Nico themselves. Lev smiled, imagining what that testing involved. No doubt Nico managed to land a few blows to win their respect.

"The percentage of discordant particles is increasing." Lev noted.

Nico called up the map that Analyst Hemish had given them and stared at the coordinates on his wrist Q-view. "According to Hemish's calculations, the thin space should be within a league's radius of this position. Do you have any idea what it looks like, Lev?"

Lev had studied several of the original rifts formed by his predecessors, but this was his first attempt to find a thin space to create a new rift. They hoped to discover a more advanced kin world and gain a new technological advantage against the Breacher threat. "A thin space? No. The journals of Rushoen Nu Lon didn't describe thin spaces, only the rifts that were formed from them. Hemish thinks I may be the first who can sense a thin space in a way that is more than a vague feeling of discomfort."

Nico grinned. "From the expression on your face, it looks like you may be feeling some discomfort yourself. Unless that's from the porridge Tark served this morning." Nico made a pained expression of his own.

"I heard that!" Tark yelled from a distance. "Oats with mead is a beloved family recipe. It's wasted on your spoiled palate, Callan!"

Nico turned to Lev with a bewildered look and whispered, "How could he have heard that?"

"I hear everything!"

Lev shook his head and shrugged, chuckling at Nico's incredulous countenance. Tark liked to tease and was very good at guessing how people might react to his comments. It was unlikely Tark had actually heard the whisper, but tormenting Nico was one of Tark's favourite pastimes.

"The particles seem to be coming from that direction." Lev pointed vaguely to the east and began walking.

After twenty minutes of walking, Lev was certain they were on the right track. The air held a constant flow of the twinned particles that formed when a kin world was bleeding into their own. From his experiments with the known rifts, he had learned that this concentration only occurred within one hundred cubits of a rift. The thin space had to be very close.

"It's here. Yori, can you head back and bring the ground transport?"

"On it."

Lev continued walking. The sound grew in intensity until he thought he'd go deaf from the roar. Nico and Tark seemed oblivious as they trudged a step behind him. "Can't you hear that?" Lev wondered aloud.

"Hear what? Why are you yelling?"

Right. Lev reminded himself it wasn't actually a sound. It was the closest thing his brain could offer to interpret what he was sensing. He decided to immerse himself fully into pattern sight. Perhaps it would diminish the auditory illusion.

The world snapped into sharp focus and the sound disappeared, replaced by a visual representation of a breeze as particles flowed from a specific point. He could see it off in the distance and started to jog toward it. Within three strides, he found himself moving in the same direction as the flow of particles, *away* from the point of origin. He had passed it. Lev stumbled as he jerked to a halt. He spun around and found the thin space once more. Carefully backtracking, he stopped at the point where particles seemed to be streaming away from him in every direction. He took one large step backward and then traversed a slow circle around the spot where he had been standing. His eyes grew wide in realization. He hadn't been sure what to expect, but it wasn't this. The rifts on Servator bases were large enough for a man to walk through, if such a thing were possible. What he was looking at now appeared no larger than his fingertip. No wonder thin spaces were so difficult to find. "This is it."

Nico walked to where Lev was standing, hoping to see for himself.

"You're looking at it now? I don't see anything."

"You're standing in the middle of it. I can see particles flowing from the top of your head."

Nico yelped as he jumped to the side, furiously brushing off his arms and legs as if he were covered in ants. "Why didn't you warn me?"

"I think there's more on your back." Tark offered helpfully."

"Get it off!"

Tark grinned as he vigorously thumped every spot on Nico's back.

Lev rolled his eyes. "There's nothing on you, Nico. The particles are out of sync with our world, flowing through you as if you weren't even there. They can't do you any harm."

Nico glared at Tark who was laughing hysterically. "I wish you could have seen the expression on your face."

Yori arrived with the ground transport and hopped out. "What's going on? What did I miss?"

"Nico... was attacked... by ghost ants." Tark managed between guffaws.

Lev sighed. "I bet this is why Rushoen Nu Lon travelled alone. This is supposed to be an historic moment."

Yori nodded at Tark who quickly sobered. "What's next?"

"Now I form an arch and hope someone or something on the other side is watching."

The way Lev understood the science, a rift would only form if both sides of a thin space were observed at the same time. Creating an arch would provide a mechanical means to continuously observe the thin space on their side. It increased the odds that a rift would form from a random observation on the kin world side.

Lev noted the position of the fingertip sized hole between worlds. He had memorized the pattern for creating an arch and set it to materialize with those coordinates at the centre. The arch quickly formed, marking the thin space location for his travelling companions. They all stared at the spot, willing something to happen, but the arch remained inert. After half an hour, Yori broke the silence. "Well that was anticlimactic. I guess we set up the marker beacon for the analysts back home and move on?"

"Hang on a moment." Lev was staring intently at the spot that made up the thin space in the centre of the arch. He could see the particles flowing from the gap clearly. According to Hemish, no one had been able to do that before. He knew the exact dimensions of that tiny gap between worlds. His mind had already mapped the coordinates. Once a rift was formed, analysts routinely materialized tokens through the rift to transfer information. He was the first to witness a thin space as a hole. *Does that mean I could pass a token through that gap?*

"Nico, can you find a pattern for a micro sight token that would fit through a hole the diameter of a crossbow shaft?"

"Let me check." Nico's fingers danced over the screen on his wrist Q-view. "I think I found something. Yes, this seems to meet the requirements." Nico initiated the template with coordinates to materialize on the ground before them. A tiny viewcorder appeared.

"That should work. Disassemble and re-materialize it a few more times so I can memorize the pattern."

Nico did as he was asked.

"Okay, I have it. Yori, do we have any stiff, thin wire in the transport?"

"Yes, we always carry a roll of wire in the toolbox. I'll get it."

"Thank you."

There was one other thing he had accomplished which had never been done before. He had passed his arm through a rift and retrieved a token that had been placed on the other side. That was theoretically impossible. Tokens could be formed on the other side of a rift because they materialized using particles from that side. Direct passage of an object or transmission from one side to the other was a different matter altogether. The particle frequencies didn't match and the two were repelled. It was the reason why sharing data between worlds was so painstakingly slow. A form of written material needed to be transferred as a token, whether parchment or writ weave in nature.

Yet he had done it. Lev's mentor, Akhen, had surmised that he was so familiar with the way his body moved through the pattern that he had somehow been able to match the frequency of the particles that made up his flesh with those of the other world. If he could do that for the view token — if he could enable it to exist on the other side of the thin space for just a moment, maybe they could be the observers for both sides and trigger a rift formation. He had memorized every particle of the sight token's template. He'd need that knowledge to shift the frequency of each particle as it passed the threshold between worlds.

Yori returned with the wire and some cutters. Lev wrapped the wire around the sight token to secure it. He played out a foot of wire to use as a grip and cut the wire. After a minute of bending and shaping, he had a suitable handle.

"Nico, can you establish a connection with the viewcorder?"

"Got it. Point it at me, will you, Lev? Yes, I can see myself. it seems to be working properly."

"Okay, I'm going to try to pass it through this hole in thin space."

"There's already a hole? I thought rifts couldn't form on their own."

"They can't. I'll explain later. Right now, just keep your eyes on the screen."

Lev knelt before the arch and began feeding the micro sight token through the spot that only he could see. He immediately met resistance. *What exactly did I do that first time when I passed my arm through the rift?* He couldn't recall since he hadn't been paying attention. Lev set the viewcorder aside and pressed the tip of his pinky finger through the gap. There was a moment of resistance and then his finger slipped through. He pulled it out and repeated the experience using pattern sight to bring the finer details into focus. *There!* He could see the particles shifting frequency to adapt to their new surroundings. Lev grabbed the viewcorder and placed the handle end of the wire against his finger to pass it through at the same time. His finger passed through, but the wire stayed behind. He tried to imagine the wire as part of his body, or rather, he imagined his finger was thicker than it was. This time the wire passed through as well. *Yes!* He needed to visualize the coordinates of the wire in relation to his body.

Lev turned the wire around and tried feeding the camera end through. The lens was facing him to match the perspective of someone viewing the thin space from the other side. It was working. The sight token was completely on the other side. "Nico, what do you see?"

"Nothing. I could see you for a moment and then I lost the signal."

"Of course, the signal."

"Uh, yeah, that's what I said."

"Never mind, keep watching. Let me know when you have a signal and when you don't." Lev pulled the token back.

"I have a signal" Nico reported.

Lev pulled deeper into pattern sight until he could see an oscillation representing the viewcorder signal moving through the pattern. He memorized the wave form and then pushed the sight token back through.

"Lost signal." Nico responded.

Now Lev could see the signal pattern from the other side. It had shifted and was being repelled. He concentrated on the plane of transition. He needed to switch the wave pattern frequency at the moment of translation. He only needed to maintain it long enough for Nico's wrist Q-view to pick it up.

"Signal is back."

In the time it took for Nico to report, the arch began to shimmer as the thin space enlarged. "It worked! We have a rift." Lev's excitement evaporated as the implications of what they were seeing dawned on him. The other side of the rift was a wall of water. It was a flood world.

The four of them stared in silence. They all knew the prophecy. This was what they were trying to prevent on their own world.

Yori spoke first. "I'll grab the transmitter to mark the rift."

"Don't bother." Lev disassembled the arch. We can't afford the resources to monitor a dead end. Mark the coordinates and record the location as a flood world." Lev did his best to mask his disappointment.

At least they knew that Hemish's map held promise, and now he understood how to speed up the process of forming a rift. He had to believe that sooner or later they'd find what they were looking for.

"Nico, plot our next destination. We have a lot of ground to cover."

The story continues in **Leavening** - Dictates of the Servators: Book 3

9 781777 990114